CRO

About
Me

Sunday Times bestselling author Mhairi McFarlane was
born in Scotland in 1976 and her unnecessarily
confusing name is pronounced Vah-Ree. After some
efforts at journalism, she started writing novels and her
first book, *You Had Me At Hello*, was an instant success.
Don't You Forget About Me is her fifth book. She lives
in Nottingham with a man and a cat.

Also by Mhairi McFarlane

You Had Me At Hello
Here's Looking At You
It's Not Me, It's You
Who's That Girl?

Mhairi McFarlane

Don't You Forget About Me

HarperCollins*Publishers*

HarperCollins*Publishers* Ltd
1 London Bridge Street
London SE1 9GF

www.harpercollins.co.uk

Published by HarperCollins*Publishers* 2019
6

Extract from 'Don't You (Forget About Me)'
written by Keith Forsey and Steve Schiff

A catalogue record for this book
is available from the British Library

ISBN: 978-0-00-816933-6
ISBN (Export): 978-0-00-833399-7

Set in Bembo by Palimpsest Book Production Limited,
Falkirk, Stirlingshire

Printed and bound in Great Britain by
CPI Group (UK) Ltd, Croydon CR0 4YY

MIX
Paper from
responsible sources
FSC
www.fsc.org
FSC™ C007454

This book is produced from independently certified FSC™ paper
to ensure responsible forest management.

For more information visit: www.harpercollins.co.uk/green

For my niece, Sylvie
A small superhero

Love's strange so real in the dark
Think of the tender things that we were working on

Simple Minds

Then

Tapton School, Sheffield, 2007

*'You loved me – then what right had you to leave me? Because . . .
nothing God or Satan could inflict would have parted us, you, of
your own will, did it. I have not broken your heart – you have
broken it; and in breaking it, you have broken mine.'*

My most truculent fellow pupil, David Marsden, looked up
and wiped his chin on his sleeve. He had given Emily Brontë's
Gothic novel the emotion of reading from the menu at Pizza
Hut. As a teenage male, it was important you kept it monoton-
ous to avoid allegations from other teenage males of being a
massive bender.

The room was muggy with that syrupy heat you get as
you near high summer, the sort where your clothes feel
grubby by midday. In our squat box of a Sixties building, the
windows heaved halfway up as poor man's air con, we could
hear the liveliness of the school field in the distance.

'Thank you, David,' said Mrs Pemberton, as he closed his

paperback. 'What do we think Heathcliff means in this passage?'

'He's nowty again because he's not getting any,' said Richard Hardy, and we guffawed, not just as it delayed proper academic discussion, but because the person making the joke was Richard Hardy.

There was some muttering but no proper answers. It was six weeks to the final exams and the mood was a febrile stew of excitement at imminent freedom and a bottleneck of panic about the reckoning that awaited. The tortured inhabitants of these pages were starting to get on our nerves. Try getting some real problems, like ours.

'"Then what right had you to leave me" is a bit creepy, isn't it,' I said, if no one else was going to break the lengthening silence. Mrs Pemberton could get testy if they ran on, and make the homework bigger. 'I mean, the idea Cathy had to stay with him or she *deserves* to be unhappy is a bit . . . ugh.'

'Interesting. So you don't think Heathcliff is justified in saying that by denying her feelings, she ruined both their lives?'

'Well,' I took a breath, 'it's the thing about how her love for Heathcliff is like the rocks underneath, constant, but gives her no pleasure,' I say this in a rush due to the inevitable mirth at the word 'pleasure'. 'It doesn't sound like it was going to be much fun? It's all about her obligation to him.'

'Perhaps then the love they share isn't conventionally romantic but deep and elemental?'

'It's mental, alright,' said a male voice. I glanced over and Richard Hardy winked at me. My heart rate bumped.

My teacher had an annoying way of taking me seriously and making me do actual thinking. She once kept me back and told me: 'You play down your intelligence to enhance your standing with your peers. There's a big wide world outside these walls, Georgina Horspool, and exam grades will get you further than their laughter. Pretty faces grow old too, you know.'

I was *furious* afterwards, the kind of fury you reserve for people who accuse you of something that's absolutely true. (I was quite pleased at the 'pretty face' bit though. I didn't think I was pretty, and I wouldn't be old for ages.)

A murmur of chatter spread around the class, and the air was thick with no one caring about *Wuthering Heights.*

Mrs Pemberton, sensing this fatal straying of attention from the text, dropped her bombshell.

'I've decided you're going to change places. I don't think sitting with friends is doing concentration in this room many favours.'

She started going from desk to desk, swapping one in for one out, amid much grumbling. I was convinced I could smart mouth my way out of this.

'Joanna, you can stay put, and Georgina, you're at the front.'

'What?! Why?'

Obviously the front row was reserved for the problematic, lazy, or outcasts – this was deeply unjust.

The seating layout respected invisible but rigid castes: swots and oddities at the front. Averagely well likeds, who worked for good approval ratings, like myself and Jo, in the middle. At the back, the super cool girls and boys, like Richard Hardy,

Alexandra Caister, Daniel Horton and Katy Reed. Rumour had it that Richard and Alexandra were kind of seeing each other but also kind of not, because they were cool.

'Come on. Shift.'

'Aw, *miss*!'

I got up with a sigh and slung my pens in my bag at a speed that emphasised my reluctance.

'Here you are. I'm sure Lucas will be glad to have you,' Mrs Pemberton said, pointing. There was no need for that phrasing, which caused a ripple of sniggers.

Lucas McCarthy. An unknown, who kept himself to himself, like all future murderers. Not social contagion, but not who I would've chosen.

He was lean, with a pointed chin; it gave him a slightly underfed look. He was Irish, signalled by the scruffy-short tar-black hair and pale skin. Some wags called him Gerry Adams, but not to his face because apparently his older brother was nails.

Lucas was looking up at me, warily, with dark, serious eyes. I was taken aback by how easily I could read his startled apprehension. Would I make any disgust towards him humiliatingly public? Was this going to be harrowing? Did he need to brace?

In seeing his concern, I suddenly saw myself. I felt bad that I was the kind of person he'd fear that from.

'Sorry to foist on you,' I said, as I dropped down into my chair, and felt the tension ease by a millimetre. (I liked to use elevated vocabulary but in an ironic, throwaway manner, in case everyone thought I was trying to show off. Mrs Pemberton so had my number.)

'Here's your question to work on together until the end of the lesson, and we'll discuss your joint findings on Friday: is *Wuthering Heights* about love? And if so, what kind? Nominate a note taker,' Mrs Pemberton said.

Lucas and I gave each other uneasy smiles.

'You're the thinker so I best be the writer,' Lucas said, scrawling the topic across a sheet of lined A4.

'Am I? Thanks.'

I smiled again, encouragingly. I saw Lucas brighten. I rifled my memory bank for any stray useful fact about him. He'd only turned up in sixth form, partly why he was someone out on the periphery of things.

He always wore the same dark t-shirts with half faded-out pictures on them, transfers that had fragmented and splintered in the wash, and three red and blue pieces of string as bracelets. I recall some of the boys calling him 'the gypsy' for that. (But not to his face, because his older brother was nails.) In the common room, he often sat by himself, reading music magazines, Dr Marten boot-clad foot balanced on knee.

'I agree with you about Heathcliff. He's a werewolf more than a person, isn't he?' he said.

I realised I'd spent two years in the same building as Lucas, the same rooms as him, and we'd had never had a conversation before. He spoke softly, with a slight Irish lilt. I vaguely expected a local accent. I'd paid him no attention whatsoever.

'Yeah! Like a big angry dog.'

Lucas smiled at me and wrote.

'I don't know, it annoys me Cathy has to take the blame for the whole story,' I said. 'She makes one wrong decision and everything goes to shit for generations.'

'I suppose if she makes the right decision there isn't much of a plot?'

I laughed. 'True. Then it'd just be *Meet The Heathcliffs*. Wait, if Heathcliff is his surname, what's his first name?'

'I think he has one name. Like Morrissey.'

'Or he could be Heathcliff Heathcliff.'

'No wonder he's pissed off.'

I laughed. I realised: Lucas wasn't quiet because he was dull. He watched and listened instead. He was like opening a plain wooden box and finding a stash of valuables inside. Was he plain? I reconsidered.

'It's not her decision though . . .' Lucas said, haltingly, still testing out the ground between us. 'I mean, isn't it the fault of money and class and that, not her? She thinks she's too good for him but she's been made to think that by the Lintons. They grow up differently, after that accident with the dog. Maybe it's all the *dog's* fault.'

He chewed his biro and gave me a guarded smile. Something and everything had changed. I didn't know yet that small moments can be incredibly large.

'Yes. So it's about how love is destroyed by . . .' – I wanted to impress – '. . . an unhospitable environment.'

'Is it destroyed though? She's still haunting him as a ghost years later. I'd say it carried on, in a different form.'

'But a twisted, bitter, no hope form, full of anger and blame, where he can't touch her any more?' I said.

'Yes.'

'Sounds like my parents.'

I'd told jokes with some success in the past, but I don't think I'd ever been so elated to see someone crack up. I remember noticing how white Lucas's teeth were, and that I'd never seen his mouth open wide enough to see them before.

That was how it began, but it *began*-began with four words, three lessons later.

They were printed on lined A4, at the end of shared essays on 'the role of the supernatural'. We had to swap the folder back and forth, annotating it, straining with the effort of impressing each other.

I had a second's confusion as my sight settled on the rogue sentence, then a warmth swept up my neck and down my arms.

I love your laugh. X

It was there, in Bic blue, an unexpected page footer. It was so casual, I'd almost missed it. Why didn't he text me? (We'd exchanged numbers, in case pressing, Brontë-related questions arose.) I knew why. A direct message was unequivocal. This could be denied if necessary.

So it was mutual, this newfound obsession with the company of Lucas McCarthy. I'd never had a spark like this before, and certainly not with a male, whose skin, I'd noticed, was like the inside of a seashell.

I'd gone from not noticing Lucas ever to being consumed

by noticing him constantly. I developed the sensory awareness of an apex predator: at any time I could tell you where Lucas was in the common room, without you ever seeing my eyes flicker toward him.

Eventually, I had printed shakily underneath:

I love yours too. X

I handed the folder back to Lucas at the end of the next lesson, our eyes darting guiltily towards each other and away again. When it was once more in my possession, that page had gone missing.

I didn't know what falling love felt like, I'd never done it before. I discovered you recognise it easily when it arrives.

We found every excuse to revise, out of hours, and the weather meant we could use the excuse of meeting outdoors, in the Botanical Gardens.

We were going on dates, but the revision aids strewn around the grass provided a fig leaf. Truly, I could've hugged Mrs Pemberton.

At first, we talked incessantly, devouring information. His life in Dublin, our families, our plans for the future, favourite music, films, books. This dark, serious, laconic Irish boy was an ongoing surprise. He put nothing on show, you had to find it out for yourself: not the deadpan quick humour, not the good looks he could've worn conspicuously simply by walking tall, not the sharp intelligence. He was self-contained. By contrast, I felt uncontained.

When I spoke, he concentrated on me intently. Through Lucas's fascination, I saw myself differently. I was worthy. I didn't have to try so hard.

The third time we met, in about five days, Lucas leaned over to whisper something in my ear about a group nearby, and I shivered. It was a ruse, he didn't need to get so close, and I felt us move up a gear.

Lucas said, as he tentatively smoothed the wisps from my ponytail back into place: 'Is your hair real?'

We collapsed in hysterics.

'Is that the real *colour!* Colour! That's what I meant. Ah, God . . .'

I wiped tears away. 'Yes this wig is my real colour. I get my wiggist to match them up.'

Lucas said, unguarded and weak from the mirth: 'It's beautiful.'

We both gulped and looked at each other heavily and that was it, we were kissing.

After that, we started revising every day. Barrier broken with that kiss, our feelings spilled out more each time we met. Secrets were whispered between us, fears and desires, the risky intimacies piled up. He had a pet name for me. I had never been seen like this before. I had never dared to be seen like this before.

Before I met Lucas, my body had been something to angst over and regret: not thin enough, chest too big, thighs too much in contact. When grappling with him, I learned to love it. Despite being fully clothed, I couldn't miss the dramatic effect it had on him: the heat between us, his heart rate, our rapid breathing. I pushed myself against him so I could feel the lump in his jeans and think: I caused that. The thought of being some place private where we could properly clash pelvises was almost too thrilling for me to contemplate.

We kept it all a secret. I don't quite know why, there was no moment we agreed to it. It was simply an understanding.

There was still this giant ridiculous stigma at school about anybody getting together with anyone. I couldn't face the whooping and applause in the corridors, the nudging, the smirking, the questions about what we'd done that would make both our faces burn. And I knew I'd get teased, more so than him. For lads, a notch was a notch, and, brutally, I was well liked and Lucas wasn't. The boys would caw and mock and the girls would say 'ewwww?'

It was much easier to wait, because soon the captivity, school and its cruel rules, would be over.

It's factually accurate to say the first male to see my outfit for the leavers' party was stunned, and his jaw dropped. Sadly, he was eight years old, and a right little toerag.

As I stepped out into the balmy early evening, dolled not up to the nines but the tens, the next-door neighbour's son was flipping the door knocker to be let in, using the tattered stick of the ice pop he'd been gnawing on. His mouth was dyed alien-raspberry.

'Why is your face so bright?' he said, which could sound like he'd correctly assessed my mood, but he meant the sixty-eight cosmetics I'd plastered myself with.

'Piss off, Willard,' I said, jovially. 'Look at the state of yours.'

'I can see your boobies!' he added, and darted indoors before I could cuff him.

I adjusted my dress and fretted that Willard – despite being no *Vogue* intern himself, in his Elmo sweatshirt – was right, it was too much. It was deep scarlet with a sweetheart neckline that was quite low cut, and I had the kind of bosoms that tended to assert themselves. I'd been distracted getting ready because it was the first time in my life I'd put on underwear knowing I wouldn't be the person taking it off. The thought gave me vertigo.

Lucas and I were on a promise. As clothed make-out sessions became almost as frustrating as they were exciting, I had suggested to him that we could stay over together 'in town' after the sixth form prom. I acted casual, as if this was an obvious thing to do. Even tried to play it off as something I might've done before. I didn't know if he had.

'Sure,' he'd said, with a look and a smile that got me right in the heart and groin.

I was so excited I was almost floating: I know the exact day I'm going to lose my virginity, and it's going to be with *him*.

I'd gone to the Holiday Inn earlier that day, checked in, left some things, gazed at the double bed in wonder, come back and reminded my indifferent parents I was staying at Jo's. Luckily my sister was away, as Esther could smell a fib of mine a mile off.

The party was in a plastic shamrock Irish pub in the city centre, a function room with a trestle table full of beige food and troughs of cheap booze in plastic bins, filled to the brim with ice that would soon melt into a swamp.

It was strange, both Lucas and I being there, knowing the intimacy that was planned afterwards, but pretending to be distant to each other. I caught sight of him across the room, in a black corduroy shirt, sipping from a can of lager. We shared an imperceptible nod.

Up until now, keeping our involvement to ourselves had felt pragmatic. Tonight though, it finally felt off. What was there to hide? Did it imply shame, whether we meant it to or not? Would he rather have been open? Was it an insult he had tacitly accepted?

I was a little anguished, but we'd set a course we had to sail now. I could raise it later. *Later.* I could barely believe it'd arrive. My head swam.

I was drinking cider and black, too fast: I could feel my inhibitions dissolving in its acidic fizzle. Richard – now, Rick, I'd learned – Hardy said: 'You look fit.' I quivered, murmured thanks. 'Like a high class prozzy with a heart of gold. That's your "look", right?'

'Hahaha,' I said, while everyone fell about. This was grown-up banter and I was lucky to be part of it.

As the evening wore on, I felt like I was in a circle of light and laughter, among the halo-ed ones, and I didn't know why I'd underestimated myself until now. I mean, OK I was inebriated, but suddenly, *being liked* seemed a total cinch.

Jo and I shared a wondering look with each other: could school really be over? We'd survived? And we were going out on a high?

'Hey, George.'

Rick Hardy beckoned me over. He was calling me George,

now?! Oh, I had truly cracked this thing. He was leaning against a wall by a bin of tins, with the usual gaggle of sycophants around him. Rumours were he wasn't going to bother with university: his band was getting 'big label interest'.

'I want to show you something,' he said.

'OK.'

'Not here.'

Rick unstuck himself from the wall in one sinuous, nascent rock star move, and handed his drink to an admirer. He outstretched a palm and gestured for mine – I could feel multiple pairs of eyes swivel towards us – and said: 'Come with me.'

In surprise, I put my drink down with a bump, put my hand into his and let him lead me through the throng. My bets were on either a new car or a large spliff. I could style either out.

I glanced over at Lucas to reassure him this wasn't anything, obviously. He gave me the exact same look as when I'd first been sat next to him.

How badly are you going to hurt me?

1
Now

'And the soup today is carrot and tomato,' I conclude, with a perky note of ta-dah! flourish that orange soup doesn't justify.

('Is carrot and tomato soup even a thing?' I said to head chef Tony, as he poked a spoon into a cauldron bubbling with ripe vegetal odours. 'It is now, Tinkerbell tits.' I don't think Tony graduated from the Roux Academy. Or the charm academy.)

In truth, I put a bit of flair into the performance for my own sake, not the customers'. I am not merely a waitress, I'm a spy from the world of words, gathering material. I watch myself from the outside.

The disgruntled middle manager-type man with a depressed-looking wife scans the laminated options at That's Amore! The menu is decorated with clip art of the leaning tower of Pisa, a fork twirling earthworms, and a Pavarotti who looks like the Sasquatch having a stroke.

He booked as Mr Keith, which sounded funny to me although there's an actress called Penelope Keith so it shouldn't really.

'Carrot and tomato? Oh no. No, I don't think so.'

Me either.

'What do you recommend?'

I hate this question. An invitation to perjury. Tony has told me: 'Push spaghetti vongole on the specials, the clams aren't looking too clever.'

What I recommend is the Turkish place, about five minutes away.

'How about the arrabiata?'

'Is that spicy? I don't like heat.'

'Slightly spicy but quite mild, really.'

'What's mild to you might not be mild to me, young lady!'

'Why ask for my recommendations then?' I mutter, under my breath.

'What?'

I grit-simper. An important skill to master, the grit-simper. I bend down slightly, hands on knees, supplicant.

'. . . Tell me what you like.'

'I like risotto.'

Maybe you could just choose the risotto then, am I over thinking this?

'. . . But it's seafood,' he grimaces. 'Which seafood is it?'

It's in Tupperware with SEA FOOD marker penned on it and looks like stuff you get as bait in angling shops.

'A mixture. Clams . . . prawns . . . mussels . . .'

I take the order for carbonara with a sinking heart. This

man has Strident Feedback written all over him and this place gives both the discerning and the undiscerning diner plenty to go at.

Here's what some of TripAdvisor's current top-rated comments say about That's Amore!

This place redefines dismal. The garlic bread was like someone found a way to put bad breath on toast, though they're right, it did complement the pâté perfectly, which tasted like it had been made from a seafront donkey. The house white is Satan's sweat. I saw a chef who looked like a dead Bee Gee scratching his crown jewels when the door to the kitchen was ajar, so I left before they could inflict the main course on me. Sadly, I will never know if the Veal Scallopini would've turned it all around. But the waiter promised me everything was 'locally sourced and free range' so there's probably a Missing Cat poster somewhere nearby if you follow my drift

Admittedly I was stoned out of my gourd on my first and last visit to this hell hole, but what the f**k is 'Neepsend Prawn'? This city is not known for its coastline. I would have the Pollo alla Cacciatora at this restaurant as my Death Row meal, in the sense it would really take the sting out of what was to come

I told the owner of That's Amore! that it was the worst Bolognese I'd ever tasted, like mince with ketchup. He said it was the way his Nonna made it in her special recipe, I said in that case his 'Nonna' couldn't cook & he accused me of insulting his family! I'm not being funny but he looked about as Italian as Boris Becker

That's Shit more like

2

'When did you know you wanted to be a waitress?' Callum, my only colleague front-of-house says, trying to swill an Orangina in a cowboy manner, re-screwing the cap with a sense of manly purpose.

He has a shadowy moustache, armpit sweat rings and his only hobby and/or interest is the gym, doing classes called things like Leg Death. I often fear he's trying to flirt. I pitch my tone with him as very 'older sister' to discourage it.

'Uhm . . . I wouldn't say I wanted to do this. Or want to do this.'

'Oh. Right. How old are you, again?' Callum says.

Callum, being a not-that-sharp twenty-two-year-old, doesn't realise when his thought processes are fully evident. He once mentioned to me that the step machine was great 'even for people a stone, or a stone and a half over their ideal weight'.

'Thirty,' I say, as he double-takes.

'Woah!'

'*Thanks.*'

'No I mean you don't look that old. You look, like . . . twenty-eight.'

Lately, I am feeling the fact that I used to be 'of ages' with people I worked with in the service industry, but increasingly I am a grande dame. The thought makes my stomach pucker like an old football. The future is a place I try not to think about.

When I took the job at That's Amore! I was a month behind with my rent and told myself that it was retro, with dripping candles in Chianti bottles in wicker baskets, red-and-white-check wipe-down tablecloths, plastic grape vine across the bar, and *Italian Classic Love Songs: Vol 1* on the stereo.

'Why don't you get a proper job?' Mum said. I explained for the millionth time I am a writer in waiting who needs to earn money, and if I get a proper job then that's it, proper job forever. Somewhere in the back of a wardrobe, I have my old sixth form yearbook. I was voted Most Likely To Go Far and Most Likely To Get A First. I have made it as far as the shittest trattoria in Sheffield, and I quit my degree after one term. But apart from that, spot on.

'You're going to be a very old waitress without a pension,' Mum replied.

My sister, Esther, said supportively: 'Thank God no one I know goes there.'

Joanna said: 'Isn't That's Amore! the one that had the norovirus outbreak a year back?'

Having sampled the 'rustic homely fare', I'm not sure that norovirus wasn't unfairly scapegoated.

Now, I could take a lump hammer to the looping CD. I want the moon to hit Dean Martin in the eye like Mike Tyson.

It turns out my role is less a waitress, more an apologist for gastronomic terrorism. I'm a mule, shuttling the criminal goods from kitchen to table and acting innocent when questioned.

They told me that a free lunch was a perk of my meagre wage, and I soon discovered that's an up-side like getting a ride on an inflatable slide if your plane crashes.

What really sticks in the craw is that, due to a combination of confused pensioners, masochists, students attracted by the early bird 'toofer' deal, and out of towners, That's Amore! turns a profit.

The owner, a really grouchy man known only as 'Beaky', claims Mediterranean heritage 'on my mama's side' but looks and sounds totally Sheffield. He comes in every so often to swill the grappa and empty the till, and is happy to let it lurch onward with Tony as de facto boss.

Tony, a wiry chain smoker with a wispy mullet, is tolerable if you handle him right, meaning, accept his word is God, ignore the lechery and remind yourself it's getting paid that matters.

Tonight isn't too busy, and after bussing the mains to the lucky recipients, I sip a glass of water and check my frazzled reflection in the stainless steel of the Gaggia machine.

A call from across the room.

'Excuse me? Excuse me . . . !'

I assemble my features into a neutral-interested expression as Mr Keith beckons me over, even though I know exactly what's coming. He picks up his fork and drops it back down into the congealed, grout-coloured sludge of the carbonara.

'This is inedible.'

'I am sorry. What's wrong with it?'

'What's right with it? It tastes like feet. It's lukewarm.'

'Would you like something else?'

'Well, no. I chose carbonara as that was the dish I wanted to eat. I'd like this, please, but edible.'

I open and close my mouth as I don't know what the fix for that is other than firing Tony, changing every supplier and razing That's Amore! to the ground.

'It's obviously been sat around while you made my wife's risotto.'

I'd make no such wild guesses, as the truth is bound to be worse.

'Shall I get the kitchen to make you another?'

'Yes, please,' the man says, handing it up to me.

I explain the situation to Tony, who never seems to mind customers saying his cooking is rank. I wish he would take it personally, standards might improve.

He takes a catering bag of parmesan shavings out, flings some more on to the dish, stirs it around and puts it in the microwave for two minutes. It pings, and he pulls it out.

'Count to fifty and give him this. The mouth will taste what the mind is told to,' he taps his forehead. I can't help think if it was that easy, That's Amore! would have a Michelin star instead of a single star rating average on TripAdvisor.

Thing is, I'd argue with Tony he should whip up a replacement, but it'll be just as bad as this one.

I sag with embarrassment. My life so far feels like one long exercise in blunting my nerve endings.

★   ★   ★

Having waited a short while to reinforce the illusion, I march the offending pasta through the swing doors.

'Here you are, sir,' I say, doing the Basil Fawlty-ish grit-simper again as I set it down, 'I do apologise.'

The man stares at the plate and I'm very grateful for the distraction of an elderly couple in the doorway who need greeting and seating.

With crushing inevitability, as soon as I've done this, Mr Keith beckons me back. *I have to leave. I have to leave.* Just get past this month's rent first. And booking that week in Crete with Robin, if I can persuade him to it.

'This is the same dish. As in the one I sent back.'

'Oh, no?' I pantomime surprise, shaking my head emphatically, 'I asked the chef to replace it.'

'It's the same plate.' The man points to a nick in the patterned china. 'That was there before.'

'Uhm . . . he maybe did a new carbonara and used the same plate?'

'He made another lot of food, scraped the old pasta into the bin, washed the plate, dried it, and re-used it? Why wouldn't you use a different plate? Are you short on plates?'

The whole restaurant is listening. I have nothing to say.

'Let's be hard-nosed realists. This is the last one, reheated.'

'I'm sure the chef cooked another one.'

'Are you? Did you see him do it?'

The customer might be right, but right now I still hate him.

'I didn't, but . . . I'm sure he did.'

'Get him out here.'

'What?'

'Get the chef out here to explain himself.'

'Oh . . . he's very busy at the stove at the moment.'

'No doubt, given his odd propensity for doing the washing up at the same time.'

My grit-simper has gone full Joker rictus.

'I will wait here until he has a few minutes free to talk me through why I have been served the same sub-par sloppy glooch and lied to about it.'

Glooch. Good word. Just my luck to get the articulate kind of hostile patron.

I head back into the kitchen and say to Tony: 'He wants to speak to you. The man with the carbonara. He says he can see it's the same one as it's on the same plate.'

Tony is in the middle of frying a duck breast, turning it with tongs. I say duck. If any pet shops have been burgled recently, it could be parrot.

'What? Tell him to piss off, who is he, Detective . . .' he pauses, '. . . Plate?'

In a battle of wits between Detective Plate and Tony, my money is on the former.

'You're the serving staff, deal with it. Not my area.'

'You gave me the same dish! What am I supposed to do when he can tell?!'

'*Charm him.* That's what you're meant to be, isn't it? Charming,' he looks me up and down, in challenge.

Classic Tony: packing passive aggression, workplace bullying and leering sexism into one instruction.

'I can't tell him his own eyes aren't working! We should've switched the plates.'

'Fuck a duck,' Tony says, taking a tea towel over his shoulder and throwing it down. 'Fuck *this* duck, it'll be carbon.'

Complaining about the effect on the quality of the cuisine is a size of hypocrisy that can only be seen from space.

He snaps the light off under the pan and smashes dramatically through the doors, saying, 'Which one?' I don't think this pugilistic attitude bodes well.

I Gollum my way past Tony and lead him to the relevant table, while making diplomatic, soothing noises.

'What seems to be the problem?' Tony booms, hands on hips in his not-that-white chef's whites.

'This is the problem,' Mr Keith says, picking up his fork and dropping it again in disgust. 'How can you think this is acceptable?'

Tony boggles at him. 'Do you know what goes into a carbonara? This is a traditional Italian recipe.'

'Eggs and parmesan, is it not? This tastes like Dairylea that's been sieved through a wrestler's jockstrap.'

'Oh sorry, I didn't realise you were a restaurant critic.'

Tony must be wildly high on his last Embassy Regal to be this rude to a customer.

'You don't need to be A.A. Gill to know this is atrocious. However, since you've raised it, I am reviewing you tonight for *The Star*, yes.'

Tony, already pale thanks to a diet of fags and Greggs bacon breakfast rolls, becomes perceptibly paler.

If this wasn't a crisis and wildly unprofessional, I'd laugh. I pretend to rub my face thoughtfully to staunch the impulse.

'Would you prefer something else, then?' Tony says.

Tony folds his arms and jerks his head towards me as he says this, and I know in the kitchen I'm going to get a bollocking along the lines of COULD YOU NOT HAVE HANDLED THAT YOURSELF.

'Not really, last time I asked for you to replace my meal you reheated it. Am I going to be seeing this excrescence a third time?'

I notice Mrs Keith looks oddly calm, possibly grateful someone else is catching it from him instead. Unless she's a fake wife, a critic's stooge.

'I thought you wanted it warmer?'

'Yes, a warmer replacement meal, not this gunk again.'

Tony turns to me: 'Why didn't you tell me he wanted a new dish?'

I frown: 'Er, I did . . . ?'

'No, you said to warm it up.'

I'm so startled by this bare-faced untruth I have no comeback.

'No, I didn't, I said . . . ?' I trail off, as repeating our whole conversation seems too much treachery, but am I supposed to stand here and say this is all my fault?

A pause. Yes. Yes, I am.

'Are you calling me a liar?' Tony continues, entire dining room riveted by this spectacle.

I open my mouth to reply and no words come out.

'Oh right, you are! Tell you what. You're fired!'

'What?!'

I think he must be joking, but Tony points at the door. Across the room, Callum is shocked, mouth hanging open and hands frozen round a giant pepper pot.

'Oh, hang on, this seems excessive . . .' says Mr Keith, looking suddenly chastened. This is why Tony's done it. It's the only way to get the upper hand again, and hope his write-up doesn't focus solely on the gusset-flavoured carbonara.

You could hear a pin drop – apart from Dean Martin crooning about Old Napoli.

I untie my apron, chuck it on the floor, find my handbag behind the bar with clumsy hands.

I dart out, without looking back. Incipient tears are stinging my eyeballs, but *no way* are they seeing me weep.

When I'm round the corner, fumbling for a tissue as my non-waterproof mascara makes a steady descent, I get a text from Tony.

Sorry, sexy. Sometimes you need to give them a scalp. We'll have you back in a fortnight and if critic fuck finds out, tell him your mum died or something so we took pity. Call it a holiday! Unpaid though.

That's Amore.

Then another realisation.

For fuck's sake, I forgot my coat!

3

First thought: it's a prisoner of war. They can't torture it, so leave it behind. Second: damn it, it's the bubblegum-pink faux fur. It's armour, it's my personality in textile form. It's up there in sentimental value after my ancient tortoise, Jammy. Also, I'm shivering already.

Wait, wait – I have a man on the inside: Callum. I message him to ask, thinking he'll surely feel sorry enough for me to do it.

Insta-ping.

I will give you your coat if you will go on a date with me 😊

I blink, twice. You've just seen me get sacked in the most public, humiliating way and now you're holding me to sexual ransom? I consider a blunt response saying, 'I'm washing my nipple hair that night.' Or pointing out it was only £50 in the Miss Selfridge sale three years ago so definitely isn't worth that, concluding with the insult of a cry-with-laughter emoji.

But the objective is to get my coat back, not a load of middle fingers and a photo of it in the scraps bin.

Hahaha if I'm not too unemployed and skint to stand my round ☺
See you at the front door in 1 min?

I would pay. Is that a yes lol? 😖

Is there anything less charming than someone trying to push you into something unwillingly and acknowledging they are pushing you into it, and carrying on anyway?

OK, lying it is.

Sure 😊

. . . LY NOT. And he knows I've got a boyfriend. We had a conversation where he said '*Lol his name is Robin do you ever call him Cock Robin*' and I said no and he said *hahaha, wicked bants.*

Outside the door, there's no sign of Callum. I wait for five minutes which feels like five hours and then text him a question mark. Another three minutes and he appears round the door.

'It's busy with only me on.'

I wonder if I am supposed to apologise for this.

I look down at the material he's holding. A beige trench coat.

'That's not mine.'

'Oh.'

'It's pink and fluffy.'

Callum disappears back inside. Minutes pass and I think: there's no way more than one piece of outerwear the colour of taramosalata in the cloakroom to justify this length of hold up. I bob down and peer under the tea-coloured nets in the window. Callum is taking an order for a table of eight people. He is chatting and joking and obviously in no rush.

Frustration wins out over shame and I wrench the door open and march back in. I feel multiple pairs of eyes on me as I rifle among the row of pegs on the back of the door behind the bar and claim my property.

'Young lady – young lady?'

I turn and see Mr Keith is beckoning me over. I glance warily in the direction of the kitchen, but what's Tony going to do, sack me again?

I approach. He's dabbing his mouth with a napkin.

'I'm sorry about what happened just now. If I'd known the consequences . . .'

'Oh, it's fine,' I say. 'It's not your fault.'

'In the future, remember honesty is always the best policy.'

I stare at him. He's telling me off again? For fu—

'I was honest. The chef was lying,' I snap.

'You're saying he did cook me another meal?'

Ah.

'No he didn't but he told me he wouldn't so I . . .'

'Lied?'

'To keep my job! He told me to lie!'

'And how's that working out for you?'

32

I open and close my mouth and dumbly repeat: 'He was the one lying.'

'Anyway. I've decided not to write it up, so as not to embarrass you.'

My jaw drops.

'That's what he wanted! That's why he sacked me! So you'd feel bad about saying how shit the food is!'

I've become shrill and everyone's looking round now.

'Write it up! Tell everyone what it's like, say I was sacked, I don't care!'

'That's not a very collegiate attitude, is it?'

'Or . . .' I say, I feel the room hold its breath, *'I'll* write it up for you. I could write you a great piece about this place. No conflict of interest anymore.'

Mr Keith clears his throat.

'Well. Employee of the Month.'

I'm about to mention the time the kitchen's tub of Stork margarine had what looked like rodent footprints in it, and Tony used an ice cream scoop to take off the top layer and carried on using it. Or, I could get my phone out and show Mr Keith the text I just received. Yes, that'd do it.

Callum is looking over with an aghast expression. When his line of sight moves to the kitchen door I know what's coming.

Tony swaggers out holding another plate of pasta, affecting a casual air of bonhomie. When he spots me, his eyes are pinwheels.

'Can't stay away when you're not being paid? Go on, Georgina, on your way. This customer doesn't want more hassle from you.'

Tony sets the plate down. It actually looks half decent – he might've Googled 'carbonara' and cracked an egg.

'I'm not hassling him, he spoke to me. I came back for my coat.'

Any noises of scraping cutlery in the dining room are yet to resume, so it's us and *volare, woooooaaah oh*.

At that moment, my eyes settle on someone beyond Mr Keith. A little girl with pageboy hair and a disproportionately large forehead, wearing a large paper crown with BIRTHDAY on it, tomato sauce splattered across her cheeks. She's paused in the middle of eating penne marinara and along with her awestruck family, is listening to every single word in this unseemly stand-off. We're ruining a kid's fifth birthday. Given everyone's poised to see what I'll do next, *I'm* ruining it.

Some of my few good childhood memories are of the excitement of being taken out for dinner, eating chicken nuggets in baskets and hustling for a second Coca Cola.

'Forget it. I only wanted my coat. I'm done,' I say.

'Don't let the door hit you etc. etc.,' Tony mutters. Then louder, to Mr Keith: 'I hope her drama doesn't keep you from enjoying your meal.'

'I hope your meal doesn't keep you from enjoying your meal,' I say, and Mr Keith shakes his head in dismay.

I turn and walk out, conscious of the many pairs of eyes on me. I keep my focus at the level of the SPECIALS chalkboard, acknowledging no one. I never thought this job would go especially well, I didn't think it would end with a dignity ransacking. The door falls shut behind me and I exhale.

I stride and stride some more and I'm still too het up to fumble for my fags. I don't want this to turn into a panic attack. I remember what the counsellor said about concentrating on my breathing when I felt anxiety rising like a sea level inside me.

My phone pings.

Keep our date a secret yeah, Tony will go well ape if he finds out and sack me too lol 😄

Tony's already 'well ape,' it seems: another ping.

DICK MOVE, princess. No job for you here now and anywhere else either once I put the word round. BLACK LISTED enjoy your next job on the pole

I stab out a reply:

LOL. Tony, your surname isn't Soprano. You might know more about Italian food if it was 😄

I'm not really that flippant about his threat. Sheffield's mid-priced bistros are quite a small world and I can't pay next month's rent now. I'm not used to making enemies, I'm usually a champion smoother-over. Appeasement is my middle name.

Although maybe I'm kidding myself: a third text arrives from my sister, Esther, who I've never really succeeded in smoothing over:

Are you bringing Robin on Sunday? Sending Mark to Sainsbury's in morning so would be good to get numbers, swift response appreciated. Rib of beef. Let me know if any allergies to Yorkshire pudding or whatever too.

That's how Esther always communicates with me on text, like I am a lazy temp at her accountancy firm. Although the near-sarcastic last line is a particular tilt at Robin.

No he's out of town! Thanks though x

I'm also a world-class white liar. Robin and my relatives are a bad combination. I tried two family events with my boyfriend and decided to rest the integration project indefinitely.

I turn the corner and psychologically, being out of sight of That's Amore! helps slightly. This is fine, this is nothing. It'll be a tapas bar in two years' time, the sort where they microwave gambas pil pil so the frozen prawns are the same texture as contraceptive sponges.

Plus, Robin's going to *love* the material from my firing this evening.

I can hear myself drafting and redrafting the key passages already, anticipating the points where I expect to get a laugh. At school, everyone used to clamour for my stories, I was good at them. If I went on a terrible summer holiday, I spun it into gold in term time. *George, tell the one about . . .*

Jo once said, admiringly: 'Mad things always happen to you, how are you a magnet for mad!' (that could sound like she was doubting me, but Jo is never ever snide. She only ever says exactly what she means) and I explained: I notice things. Appreciating the absurd was a useful skill in my childhood.

A *snap snap snap* with my pleasingly heavy silver lighter, in trembling hands, and the tip of my Marlboro Light glows. I suck in a big whoosh of nicotine and I feel better already. It's not tenable to give up in current circumstances.

It's an early winter evening, the sort of cold where the air in the middle distance looks smoky, and you can sense a weekend evening getting going. The swell of people in Broomhill, the scent of aftershave mingling with perfume and burble of chatter that comes with being two drinks to the good.

I can see my reflection in the window of Betfred and shift from foot to foot. As much as I argue back with Mum when she says things to me like: 'scruffy is charming in youth but doesn't age well, Georgina,' I am starting to wonder if my playful taste in short dresses and liquid eyeliner is going a bit *Last Exit to Brooklyn.*

'*Be careful with that heavy make-up as a blonde. One minute you're punk like Daryl Hannah in* Blade Runner*, the next you're Julie Goodyear.*'

Boy, how I'll miss Tony's beauty tips.

I open a message to Robin, then think again and press backspace to swallow the you'll-never-guess-what-these-twats-have-done-now rant about the termination of my employment. I have a Friday evening free all of a sudden – this shouldn't be thrown away on a prosaic text.

I want to be stylish about it.

On one of our first dates – I say dates, actually it was being invited round to Robin's flat to drink red wine, until he eventually flapped a takeaway leaflet at me around 9 p.m. and said: 'Have you eaten?' – Robin said: *live your life like this song*.

The song playing was Elvis' 'Suspicious Minds' so I asked: what, suspiciously?

He has a stack Hi Fi with a turntable at the top, which is now old enough to be a fashion statement, with volume lights that ripple.

'The way it fades back in at the end. It's already brilliant, but that is genius because it's unexpected. That's the moment that turns good into true greatness.'

Robin hunched over, rolling his joint.

'. . . Everyone thinks you have to do everything a certain way. Monogamy, marriage, mortgage. Two point four kids, because what will you do with the second half of your life otherwise. Washing the car and the roast chicken in the oven every Sunday. William Blake called them "mind forg'd manacles". People don't want to get rid of the rule book, it scares them. We're all living in captivity.'

I thought I could really fancy some roast chicken. I knew this was an implicit warning to me, as much as Robin sharing his world view.

('*If he was going to settle down, he'd have done it by now, Georgina.*' Ta, Mum.) I was determined to appear unfazed.

'Constructed reality. Like *The Matrix*,' I say, picking up a menu for Shanghai Garden.

'Yeah! So much of "can't" and "not allowed" is an illusion.'

'Tell that to my probation officer,' I said.

Robin laughed, pushing the window open on its latch, before he lit his spliff. 'Good one.'

I felt the satisfaction of being a Cool Girl.

'. . . Would you share the illusion of a Kung Po rice with me?'

4

I toy with the prospect of a taxi to Kelham Island, then consider that now I'm on the dole again, the bus is more appropriate. These sort of internal negotiations are alien to Robin.

It's weird to say, but Robin is sort-of famous. 'Famous' is overselling it really, but 'well known' is positively misleading. He's a face and a name you might know if you're in a very specific age demographic in Britain, watch the obscurer TV channels, follow fringe comedy and are probably a stoner.

When I saw his modern penthouse flat with its lipstick-red leather sofas, white rugs and mezzanine bedroom in a converted factory, I thought *wow, challenging offbeat authored comedy pays well*.

In the six months we've been seeing each other, I've witnessed Robin turn down various offers he thought 'weren't simpatico with what I'm trying to build' and toss bills into the bin unopened, yet the lights stayed on and the hot water flowed. Eventually I twigged that income was coming from elsewhere.

Apparently Robin's dad was some major wheel in the civil service, his parents now retired to the Cornish coast. Robin owned his property outright and 'I get the rental income from the last place.' I didn't inquire any more in case I looked like I was gold digging, eyeing up the portfolio.

'Are they fans of what you do?' I asked, tentatively, as code for *woah they set you up nicely.*

Robin ran a hand through his wild hair. 'I think "fans" might be overstating it. They want me to fulfil my potential, in whatever I see as my potential.'

Our disparity is never an issue except on the occasions I arrive exhausted from a shift. He'll shrug and say: *ah, sod it off then*, as someone who has never understood how it feels to be dangling off the monkey bars with no financial crash mat. His whole inspirational 'life is what you make it' schtick grates a bit, as a result.

Though it has to be said, he's never complained about our differences as a couple, monetarily or otherwise: as the most sinewy, wiry man I've ever slept with, he's very keen on my waterbed belly and marshmallowy arse, and he positively enthuses about staying in my attic room in my terraced house in Crookes.

'Look at it this way, if you ever want to be a writer, you've already got the garret.'

'Glad you're enjoying your poverty safari,' I said, and he said *ah poverty safari I like that I'll use that.* He says that quite a lot.

I stub out my fag as the bus arrives and push a Mentos into my mouth. Instead of serving dog food ragu to dismayed punters I have a night off, and the night is young. Chin up.

When I get off at the destination and walk the two minutes to Robin's, in the dark and cold, I start to question the wisdom of the fabulous surprise concept. I probably should've told him . . . ? This is the trouble with being unconventional. You never know when you're simply being annoying.

As I approach his building, I see Robin near the door: he has a cheap thin blue plastic bag, handles lengthened with the weight of what must be purchases from the corner shop.

This is my moment! I'll call him and say something like: *I hope you have some wine for me in there.* I'll be like Jason Bourne! 'Get some rest, Pam,' while Robin jerks his head to see where I'm standing.

I scroll down, hit Robin's number in my contacts and press the handset to my ear.

Ahead of me, I see Robin pull his iPhone out of his jacket pocket. A moment where he stares at the caller ID, then my line goes blip-blip-blip = call ended. Has he turned it off by mistake? His phone is back in his pocket and he continues towards the flat.

Baffled, and stung, I hit redial. Same process: momentary check, and again, declines it. He's pressing it fast enough that even if I couldn't see him, I think I'd know from the desultory length of time it rang that I'd been drop called.

Stubbornly, knowing I'm being uncool, I try for a third time. He's almost at the door now. If his phone is buzzing, he doesn't react.

I hear: *The phone you have called may be switched off.*

What on earth? He's turned it *off*? I'm his girlfriend and I got the treatment of an unknown Manchester landline phishing for PPI. Is he angry with me about something? I search my recent memory and nothing occurs. Also, despite his hatred of stand-up comedy critics, Robin doesn't do fits of temper: either due to his disposition or the quantity of marijuana he inhales, or both.

I'm hurt. As I watch Robin let himself into his block of flats I try to calibrate: how much, and whether I should be.

I anticipate what his excuse will be. *Wasn't in the right frame of mind, didn't want to inflict myself on you.* I called three times though, in quick succession, during what was supposed to be my shift. It could've been an emergency? I mean, it's sufficiently out of the ordinary. Robin calls me a catastrophist but you can be *too* laid-back.

And I tend to call rather than message as Robin likes to declare himself above 'the myriad ways of being pestered these days'. Maybe he's waiting for an important person to get in touch? He was told the BBC's Head of Light Entertainment might need a chat about now and to keep the line free.

I'm grasping at straws, obviously. My mum used to say that eavesdroppers hear no good of themselves and I feel the truth of that. My temporarily lifted spirits are now in tatters around my feet – I got an insight into how my boyfriend sometimes feels about me, and it's not done anything for my self-esteem.

I think back to other times I might've called and not got an answer: is it often like this? *FFS, what does she want now.*

I light a cigarette and weigh up my options. If I go back to mine, I might see Karen on her way to her shift and that has to be avoided at all costs. My soul concaves at the thought.

I know what I'm feeling and my counsellor told me to name it, when it surfaced: loneliness.

A minute or two later, I'm no closer to a decision, when my phone pings. Esther.

Can you bring red not white? We're running short on it and I can't raise Mum. Ta. (Do NOT get some Turning Leaf bin juice from the cash and carry! Spend a tenner min)

Not an ideal audience, but this gives me a chance to rehearse my story, get the lines right to make Robin laugh when I tell him, and I'm still buzzing with the adrenaline of outrage. I call her.

'Hi, Esther, yes fine about the wine, but I can't spend a tenner – I've just been sacked.'

'WHAT?'

Maybe this wasn't the greatest idea.

'What for?'

'A customer complained about his food being awful, the customer turned out to be a critic for *The Star*. Tony fired me in front of him, as if the problem was the service not the kitchen.'

'Oh dear. This is like that hipster place on Green Lane with the drinks in jam jars where you lost a month's pay after a row about a bowl of sick and gherkins.'

You know how your family can wind you up in a way no one else can quite hear? Like a dog whistle? To anyone else, Esther sounds sympathetic. To me, instantly bringing up another time I lost my job sounds anything but.

'They were "kimchi loaded cheesy tater tots" and not really, the manager kept groping my arse so I had to leave.'

'Well . . . spend a tenner on the wine and I'll refund you when you get back.' I make noises of objection, 'George, Mark is a member of the Wine Society, he's not going to drink something from Spar.'

Offstage, my brother-in-law Mark makes tutting noises and then something that sounded like a question.

'Mark wants to talk to you,' Esther says.

There's a rustling as she hands the phone over to Mark.

'Hi, George,' Mark says. 'Sorry to hear about the Italian. This might be a bit soon but striking while the iron is hot and all that, I know a landlord who needs someone to work an event tomorrow night, a pub in town? Under new management. Only one night but it's cash in hand and a decent amount, if I remember right. Shall I give him your details?'

'Definitely, thanks,' I say. Good old Mark.

'Great, I'm sure he'll be in touch soon. Best of luck and all that.'

More rustling while Esther wrestles the phone back.

'Thanks, darling. Can you go check on the dinner please?' A pause, while Mark is dismissed. 'Mark's involved himself by recommending you for that job, the man's a client.'

Here we go.

'And?'

'And please, don't fuck it up.'

'Thanks!' I say, stung. 'What with me being a known fucker upper.'

'You know what I mean. *Please* don't come back with one of your amusing stories where everything is a huge mess but it isn't your fault. No incidents. I don't want there to be incidents and excuses.'

'Jesus Christ, thank you!'

That's what Esther really thinks – this is what they all think. *Oh how, er, 'unlucky'. Trouble seems to follow her around doesn't it? How many times is that now? Mmmm.* It enrages me and at the same time worries me. I fear they're right. Whenever anyone criticises me, I always worry they're right. I overcompensate with extra outrage.

'You know what I mean,' Esther says.

'In that you mean I'm an incompetent liar? Noted.'

'Oh, don't be a diva, Gog. All I'm asking is that you're considerate towards Mark being connected to this.'

The Gog is definitely manipulative. Makes me and my objections to this characterisation sound small and silly.

'Got it,' I say tightly. 'Thanks, Esther. Oh, my bus is here.' I hang up before she can reply.

I stub out the tail end of my fag. What to do? I know hanging around at night time on my own is a bad idea. I square my shoulders: he's had time to settle himself now, if he says, 'why not warn me?' I called, right? Not my fault.

I rifle in my handbag and find the key. It didn't come threaded with ribbon, in a box – it has a West Ham fob as it used to be his brother Felix's. He crashed with Robin when he was benched with an injury from the Cirque Du Soleil. (Seriously. I wonder if the McNee parents thought they were raising lawyers and doctors.)

Robin handed it over after a row where I'd rung the doorbell endlessly after work, and the Rolling Stones was on too loud for him to hear. He eventually answered to find not only a pissed off, knackered girlfriend but also a very angry, severely jet-lagged next-door neighbour wearing an eye mask round his neck who had heard my endless attempts to raise him. ('Did he not know you were coming round?' I was embarrassed to admit – especially to someone who'd been awake for thirty-two hours – that he did know.)

'Sorry you couldn't get no satisfaction, you can't always get what you want. Did you want to paint my red door black?' Robin said when he finally appeared, not reading the room.

'Pure twat,' said the neighbour.

When Robin gave the key to me I asked, what occasions is it for? Robin said: 'Any time you want to open the door. That's how they work, isn't it?'

So, he said it.

5

After knocking with no answer, I turn the key with a snap, the door opens and the vista of the glamorous bachelor pad is in front of me, music set to deafening as it always is. (Robin was playing it earlier in the week. 'The new St Vincent, it's good. Also not that it should matter but she's got a bum like two Crème Eggs in a satin glove.')

Robin is nowhere immediately in sight. I call: 'Robin? Robin . . .'

Nothing. The stereo drowned me out, I think. He'll be unpacking the Birds Eye waffles and Rustler burgers in the kitchen, no doubt.

Further into the room and still no sight of Robin, though the blue bag is abandoned on the sofa, its contents spilling on to the cushions, multiple tubs of Ben & Jerry's Vermonster. They're going to melt over the leather. I twitch to put them in the freezer but it seems officious before 'hello'.

I peer round into the kitchen, not there.

I lean back and crane my neck to look up, towards the bed on the platform above. I'm about to call 'Robin' again and

then I hear weird strangled sounds, distinct from the official
soundtrack.

Uggggh fuuuu

Nuf-nuf-nuf mmmpppppf

Don't . . . don't . . . oh my God, yes

I freeze to the spot. My skin goes cold and yet hot, prick-
ling with shock. *Did I hear what I think I heard. Is this possible.
Is this happening.* No. No? It can't be. This happens to other
people, not me, not right now. This is a hilarious mistake and
it's going to end up in Robin's act, *that time his girlfriend walked
in on him doing yoga* or whatever.

St Vincent reaches another sonic lull and this time it's:

Uh uh UGH

You like this don't you, say you like it.

The second line is familiar to me and I feel a lurch, a
sudden acrid wash of vomit pending at the back of my throat.
I stand motionless as the rhythmic heaving in the background
continues. I can pick out an intermittent pressure on a bed
frame that's unmistakable now.

I can't look. But I definitely can't not look. Having to focus
to steady my hands, and tiptoe towards the metal ladder, I
mechanically and carefully climb the rungs to the mezzanine
level, planting my heeled boots with precision. I never liked
this thing at the best times, made going for a drunk nocturnal
wee feel like the *Crystal Maze*.

I poke my head up above floor level, sweaty hands fastened
to the aluminium.

In the large low bed beneath the skylight, I see Robin's
bare arse pistoning up and down, a pair of skinny white

female legs splayed either side. Disbelief. Revelation. Revulsion. And the thought: God, do we look like that when do we do it?

It strikes me how weird it is to see two people having sex, up close, in real life. You've *been* one of the people, you've seen it happen on a screen enough, but an on-premises spectator to the act? Totally surreal. I'm still not quite believing what I'm seeing, as if Robin might've tripped and fallen and be having trouble getting back up again.

I can't help comparing. It's a lot more frenzied and noisy than we are. We were.

Do it Robin do it I love you aaaaaahhh

Lou. Talk. Dirty.

This is said while punctuated with a thrust each time, and suddenly, without making a conscious decision to announce my presence, I snap and yell: 'WHAT THE FUCK?!'

Both bodies jerk and spasm with the shock of my joining the conversation and Robin falls sideways from the bed with the effort of getting off the woman, and turning round to look at the same time.

The woman wriggles to sit up and I see that a) she is tied to the bed posts by her wrists with scarves, one of which is a striped football scarf I recently ran through a hot wash for him b) she has small breasts, with nipple rings like barbells, a flower tattoo curling round her ribcage and c) she is coated in some sort of pale, lumpy substance, which after a second's disorientated fright I realise comes from squashed tubs nearby, the emptied-out contents of a Vermonster.

As she boggles at me through a cloud of mussed spirally

brown hair and I boggle back at her I realise I know who she is – she's Robin's PA, Lou.

Robin stands naked, hair like a fright wig, erection now at half mast, as if it's been lowered out of respect for a visit by the Queen. He's as pale as the Vermonster.

'Oh God fucking hell Georgina what are you doing here?!'

'I got sacked from work. What are you doing?'

'What . . . well . . . how did you get in?!'

Robin seems angry with The Fates rather than himself, as if this is one terrible admin cock-up, as opposed to his cock half up.

'You gave me a key?'

'Oh, God . . .' the truth dawns on Robin: the architect of all of his pain was himself. He was going to try some very thin defence that I'd somehow broken in. As the realisation settles, he splutters: 'You don't think you should've knocked first?'

That he thinks he can do self-righteousness at this moment absolutely astounds me.

It also makes anger overtake my shock. I'm back in some control of myself.

I purposely let him watch my line of sight go slowly back to Lou in the bed, who looks like she'd really like to be untied now; squirming against her bonds, red in the face, then back to him, and lastly down to his wilting member. I give it a good withering stare.

'I did. I wasn't heard over the music. You pathetic, treacherous piece of shit.'

I descend the ladder fast, jumping the last part so that my

knees and ankles jar as I hit the ground. Robin gives chase, which means he has no time to dress himself, so as I near the door I'm confronted again by a stark bollock man.

I hate him even more for it – not enough shame to scramble to cover up. He's to some extent performing, even now. *Look at my vulnerability. Look at my unconventional lack of artifice.* I'd like his unconventional artifice to be behind a towel, thanks.

'George, George, wait, I'm sorry,' he says.

'Yeah so am I. It's not every break-up that comes with a therapy bill. I feel sick.'

'Break up . . . ?'

I turn to look him in the eyes.

'You don't seriously think I'm staying with you?'

'No, not tonight, obviously.'

I blink, taken aback. 'Are you clinically insane? It's over, Robin, we're done. I don't know how you can think we could have a relationship after this.'

Robin pauses and says: 'Relationship? I . . . I didn't think we were going out?'

I'm so stunned by this it takes a moment to assemble my expression, and form a response.

I only manage:

'. . . *What?*'

'I thought we were "seeing each other".' Robin makes air quote marks. 'I didn't think we were exclusive . . . as in, forbidden from seeing other people? That whole scene is not my . . . scene.'

My blood feels like it's caught fire. It's one thing to do this to me, it's another to *blame* me for it – to pretend this is a product of my unreasonable expectations.

'Are you fucking serious?! You're going to handle this by pretending our relationship didn't *exist?* That's like a CHILD'S level of lying. Will you put your hands over your eyes next, so I can't see you?'

Robin pantomimes more exhaling, shaking his head in incredulity, rubbing at his hair as he thinks what to say next, a tic he uses on stage. God, the insolence of still having his gingery cock and balls on show.

'I've never seen you like this before,' he mutters.

My jaw, once again, drops. 'Do I need to point out what I've never seen before, either? *Are you for real?*'

He puts his hands on his hips, Mr Reasonable But Aggrieved now, as if we're discussing an inflated quote for lagging the loft.

'What was it I've ever said or done that's made you think I believed in monogamy? I'm pretty sure I said I didn't?'

I splutter, momentarily stalled. It's as if someone's been caught with their hand in the till and their defence is nothing is as it seems and theft can't exist because we're living in a false consciousness created by the CIA. It's not a comeback you've planned for. Fuck me, I'm *raging.*

'This is it, this is your excuse? You thought we were both free to have sex with other people?'

'Uh, yes I did, Georgina. The terms and conditions of our liaison were never discussed. I'm not sure how you'd expect me to know otherwise.'

'*Then why hide it from me by switching your phone off and doing it behind my back?*'

'It's poor manners to shove it in your face, isn't it? I didn't expect you to put up with a running commentary of who else and when.'

'OH HOW EXCEPTIONALLY FUCKING CONSIDERATE OF YOU!'

I have to get out of here, mentally process it, escape this toxic weirdness.

I throw the door open to the hallway. A thirty-something couple and sixty-something parents are passing outside, their attentions already focused in our direction due to the cacophony.

True to his self-described not-sensitive, not-bashful nature, my ex not-boyfriend stands staring back at them, full frontal in their faces.

The dad says, 'Excuse me! Do you mind covering your private area? There are ladies present.'

'I'm in my private area. This is my flat. That makes you Peeping Toms.'

'Peeping Vom more like,' says the son, aka Jet Lag Man, who's suddenly my new hero.

'Having your toilet part on show really is unnecessary,' says Jet Lag Man's dad.

'My toilet part! You want to get less uptight about the human anatomy, mate,' Robin says. 'It's a beautiful thing.'

'I can assure you, not from here it's not,' says Jet Lag Man.

'Give my best to Lou,' I say to Robin, stepping in to the hallway. To the disturbed-looking group, I add helpfully: 'That's the woman I just caught him having sex with.'

'Oh, he finally got you a key cut?' says Jet Lag Man.

'Yeah but apparently we were never in a relationship,' I throw my hands up in 'silly me' way.

'It's never his rubbish in my bin either,' says Jet Lag Man. 'He's full of shit. Much like my bin.'

I vigorously shake Jet Lag Man's hand.

'It's been a pleasure.'

6

'Am I going to have to say it? Oh you pair of . . .' Clem shakes her head in dismay at Rav and Jo, who are both mute and awkward.

Rav tweaks at his expensively pre-frayed navy cuff and Jo has an expression like a sad farm animal in a cartoon.

'What?' I say. I know they all think I'm gutted-but-fronting, but actually, I'm oddly calm. Shiraz is helping. I've found my safe harbour in rough waters. It's a scarlet leather booth in a pub called The Lescar off Hunter's Bar.

It turns out that you can get your friends out for a drink at no notice of a weekend if two of them had got out of the cinema with a thirst, one of them was having a night in due to saving Weight Watchers points and blew it on a whole plank of M&S cheesy garlic bread anyway, and you whet their appetites with a lurid story of bondage infidelity.

I didn't dare hope a spectacularly grotesque Friday night was going to end in my favourite place with my best people, but it does, and I give a silent prayer of thanks over the pork scratchings.

I'm single again and have no job or money and live in a rented house next door to a maggot farm with the region's worst personality, but I have mates and a large red wine.

'Go on, Rav, go ahead,' Clem says and Rav coughs into his fist and glares.

'*What?*'

'Pussy! OK if neither of you are going to tell her, I will. Georgina—'

'Oh God you KNEW he was seeing other people?!' I cry.

The thought is a stab wound, not because Robin was flaunting it, but if they kept this secret from me, this grisly episode has damaged much more than it deserves to.

'No of course we didn't know, you moo!' Clem says. 'Why would we know and not tell you?'

'Oh. I don't know,' I mumble.

'Georgina,' Clem portentously draws breath, 'We all thought Robin was a massive, tremendous, *glaringly obvious arsehole*. What on EARTH have you been thinking?'

'Oh?' I say, dumbly. 'You didn't like him?'

Rav coughs again and Jo stares down into her cider.

'"Didn't like" doesn't quite cover it. *Actively abhorred* is closer to the mark.'

'Clem!' Rav says. 'Fuck's sake, she's just caught him in bed with someone else.'

'Relevant to the abhorring.'

After a very tense few seconds of silence, I start laughing. They look shocked for a second and then start laughing too.

'I thought you were going to burst into tears and slap me,' Clem says, clutching her chest.

'No, I only want to slap myself,' I say.

Jo puts a hand on my arm. 'Not that this isn't awful for you. I'm so sorry for what's happened.'

I pat back. 'I'm well rid.'

'Did he really claim you were in an open relationship?' Clem says, her immaculate vermillion MAC lip curling in disgust. Clem dresses like a member of Pulp, only better: dyed red hair in flapper bob, head to toe vintage, pointed retro nails. She's very pointy, in looks and nature.

'He said he thought we were free to sleep with other people. Which begs the question why he didn't mention doing it, ever.'

'He was sneaking around like your bog-standard shitbag and now he's gaslighting you.'

'What does that mean?'

'Making you think you're going mad, making you think it was your problem.'

'It's true we never said "What are the rules on sleeping with other people". He had said he didn't believe in monogamy as the only way to live, but you know . . . I didn't think it directly applied. He'd met my friends, my family. God's sake, how are you meant to be totally go with the flow, ultra modern, no pressure and find this basic stuff out at the same time?'

'This is the gaslighting. You're questioning yourself. It's him who's put the goalposts on wheels.' Clem sucks on the straw in her gin and tonic, then grimaces. 'He called you "the Waitress". He never missed a chance to act like he was better than you.'

'I thought he was being . . . I don't know, light-hearted.'

Clem widens her eyes and Rav and Jo still can't meet mine and I realise this is Robin's legacy – me uncomfortably working out how I accommodated and rationalised a lot of crappy behaviour that wasn't remotely invisible to anyone else. And forever hating Ben & Jerry's.

'And you knew the woman?' Clem says.

'Lou's his PA. They'd had a thing before but I thought it was long over by the time I was around.'

Robin said he and Lou had slept together once, 'in the day', which I took to mean a long while ago rather than the timing, but who knows.

I was taken aback when he mentioned it, as I'd spent a whole evening in her company thinking theirs was a friendly working relationship and it hadn't once crossed my mind. Not that I'm saying attraction is an exact science but Lou is my complete physical opposite: long wild brown curly hair, a nose stud, knobbly knees in laddered patterned tights and a pair of silver glitter-crusted clumpy shoes. I'd taken an instant shine to her.

It always causes some mental realignment when you discover someone has been where you have been.

'She was cool about it, she's really cool,' Robin said, which I translated as: there were no consequences when I made it obvious it meant nothing.

Robin had paused.

'That's not a thing for you, is it? Who's been with who?'

Yes it's a thing for me like it's a thing for pretty much everyone, that's why there's so many pop songs about it.

'No! Just surprised that's all. Wouldn't have put you together.'

'I dunno if you'd call it *together*. We ended up having a shower in an Ibis in Luton after a food fight, it seemed the next obvious step. Certainly not much other entertainment in Luton.'

I flinched. In this moment, I definitely wasn't the cool girl who wanted to hear the details and I didn't like the way I felt Robin was trying to portray me as uptight and conventional. Even then, I could tell he was getting a kick out of it, congratulating himself as an erotic buccaneer, compared to Georgina the square.

So when he added: 'Would you rather I didn't say, in future?' I instantly replied: 'No,' and changed the subject.

I didn't ask if he'd mind if situations were reversed: when I unpick why, it's because it'd mean either he was a hypocrite or he was totally without jealousy, which might be great for him but sort of flat for me.

Why didn't I tell Robin that his free love, free'n'easy approach wasn't for me? I was scared of seeming like the parochial fiancée in *Billy Liar*, a woman stuck in the past who represented the opposite of everything exciting.

And I was scared my expectations were never going to be met. But I've learned it's better to have unrealistic expectations than none at all.

We're two drinks deep and having established I don't mind if they slag him off, the Robin roast is now a marinated deep smoke over a pit of coals. By the end of the night he'll be nothing but pulled brisket in buns.

I feel a peculiar mix of gratitude and shame that I don't feel sad, or any urge to defend him. It should be as if my heart's been torn out and spat on. I only feel baffled, humiliated and empty. The empty was there before Robin, and he was a distraction from it.

'Stand-up comics are often terrible people,' Rav is saying. 'Think about the personality type who decides to stand alone on a stage and say funny things and risk no one laughing. It's for the maladjusted. The sad clown cliché. I'd rather spend time at Hitler's Eagle's Nest than backstage at the Comedy Store.'

'You might've told me this before I dated one,' I say.

'I was going to, but like a scrubber you disappeared off into the night with him before I could give you my professional opinion. Afterwards I judged it unwanted.'

It was actually Rav's fault that I'd met Robin in the first place. Rav had got us tickets for an open mike night. Robin was the last act, and by far the best. He did an excerpt of his show, *I'm Not Being Funny But*. It was much more of a storytelling style than those who'd leaned on the mike stand and chucked out one-liners, which got tiring after a while.

Afterwards we found ourselves in a group in a late-night hotel bar with him and two of the other acts, a turquoise-haired plus-size woman dressed as a fighter plane pin-up, and a depressive man from Solihull who wore a pork-pie hat. I had finally felt part of a Sheffield creative quarter.

Robin was tall, with a mop of telephone cord-like hair and small, shrewd blue eyes that contrasted with his red tartan shirt. He'd paced the stage rubbing his head, radiating a nervy energy. I could still smell the sweat from performance on him.

I had realised I was excited to meet him. He felt like something different from the usual men I encountered. Going places. Things to say. Knew what he was doing. I decided to wait for my moment to get his attention.

Robin held his mobile horizontal at chin level – a sign of a right tit I should have recognised, if ever there was one – and read a review aloud to his agent. They'd started the tour in London two nights previous, and apparently a verdict had just dropped.

'*McNee has an acute ear for the casual linguistic stupidities that infect daily life. He tries on a Stewart Lee-ish irascible rancour towards celebrities, his professional competitors, and even his audience, but it gradually slips over the line from knowingly self-parodic to plain self-indulgent . . . he becomes the very blowhard he seeks to send up. His ego is a drunk driver, but if his better instincts take control of the wheel, he could be something quite dazzling.* You tell me, Al, is that praise or not?'

Pause.

'Yes I know, I'm asking you which of those two ways you take it.'

Pause.

'. . . Fair enough. I want to fold this cutting up and insert it into "Lee Hill" using a litter-picking claw.'

Pause.

'No I know Chortle is a website and there isn't a hard copy, you might be missing the point.'

He hung up. Everyone was quiet. I wasn't nervous, mainly

due to two powerful drinks that tasted like evil jam, with fat Morello cherries on sticks in them.

'A review with the words superb, dazzling, and "acute ear". I'd take it,' I say.

Robin looked at me.

'What about my ego being a pissed driver?'

I shrugged.

'You can't do it without ego. There's no way Richard Pryor or . . . Lenny Bruce didn't have ego. It's right up there with demons. Ego and demons. It's to making art what eggs and bacon are to making breakfast.'

Robin stared.

'Wow. *Yes*. And you are?'

Introductions were made, champagne was ordered on someone's tab and the night was properly underway.

'You're a writer?' Robin said, with one arm slung round the velvet banquette, in a way that meant it was sort of slung round me.

'Hah! No. Who told you that?'

'Your advice to me sounded like one writer to another . . . ?'

I glowed. This was one of the best things I'd ever heard.

'. . . That said, you're a bit too healthy for it. You don't have the black coffee and fags face. You look like you leave the house and get fresh air.'

I knew I was being hit upon, but my blood alcohol level and the bass-line in a Prince song were in harmony, and I was happy to be flattered.

'I'm a waitress.'

'Ah! That's cute.' (There it was, that tone. Clem was right.)

I'd nearly said: *I'd like to be a writer* but I knew the next question would be, what have you written? and the answer is a big old nothing, bar a diary that I was once quite proud of, so I didn't.

'I have a research question, you can help me with my act,' Robin said. 'What's it like being beautiful?'

Over his shoulder, I could see Rav making a 'gun to temple and firing' gesture.

Maybe in other circumstances I'd have groaned, but it felt like Robin was being refreshing and surprising. And you know, it's never the worst thing to hear.

'I'm not beautiful.'

I resisted the urge to fuss at my hair, but held my stomach in.

'You clearly are.'

'Well, thank you.'

'So what it's like being beautiful, is thinking you're not beautiful?'

I laughed. 'Erm. If you insist.'

'That's a let-down. I'd thought it'd be like being a Disney heroine where you can make the pots and pans clean themselves and the broom dance.'

Rav leaned over minutes later and whispered: 'I bet *you* can make his broom dance, if you follow.'

I laughed and realised I was interested in someone for the first time in ages.

I did something that night I never do: as Robin reappeared and slid back in next to me, refilling my glass: I thought, I'm having you. I'm taking you home.

After whispered *I like you / I like you toos* and kissing by the taxi rank we ended up having very mediocre intercourse in a room at The Mercure, as Robin couldn't even be bothered to travel back to his flat. My big first-night-sex adventure ended with me bouncing around on top of a very drunk, semi-comatose comedian who kept groaning: 'Talk dirty to me, Georgina the waitress, talk dirty! Be filthy and nasty!'

Nasty?

I shouted: 'Shag me, you curly-haired blowhard!'

Rav is still musing Robin's shortcomings.

'You know, I didn't spend enough time around Robin to diagnose the Dark Triad, but I wouldn't be surprised.'

'That sounds like a hip-hop group.'

'Narcissism, manipulation, lack of empathy,' Rav says, counting them off on his fingers, then grabbing for the open bag of Walkers. 'The people who can reel you in and spit you out, without a second's guilt.'

Rav is a counsellor. You'd never peg the skinny Asian lad with the Morrissey quiff and the discreetly peacocky clothing as such. He is coolly analytical and unsentimental and probably the ideal person to have around if you get yourself involved with a technicolour fountain of dysfunction like Robin. Though there's now been enough alcohol-fuelled deconstruction I think we might've turned your run-of-the-mill selfish arse into a Shakespearean villain.

Jo chews the inside of her lip.

'I thought Robin was very idio . . . idio . . .'

'Idiotic?' Clem says.

'No . . . like, idi . . .'

'Idi Amin?' Rav says.

'No, a word for individual that isn't individual!'

'Idiosyncratic?' I say.

'Yes! I didn't like how rude he was to you though.'

I frown. 'I honestly thought it was teasing.'

I prize my capacity to take a joke. It's painful to think my friends were cringing for me, and that I don't know where the line should be.

Clem purses her mouth.

'And whenever you gave an opinion about anything, Robin was straight in there with "maybe the people who disagree have a point" or "maybe you were too touchy". I spotted it right away as a psycho ex used to do it to me. Constant undermining. They don't want you to trust yourself on anything.'

Oh, God. She's right. At first I was bowled over by Robin's iconoclastic take on my life – yet the solution, now I think about it, was always that I should fix my attitude and stop being such a princess. *Wow, I've chosen a smart cookie and a challenge here*, I congratulated myself, *look at how he'll just come right out and say it*. Not: why is this bloke never on my side?

I gave Robin so much leeway because I thought he was 'Other' – an emissary from a cleverer, more rarefied and liberal world than that of Georgina the Waitress. Anything I disliked was down to having not caught up with the latest trend yet, not being an artist with an artist's temperament. I realise, as per the Lou conversation, he was always subtly reinforcing the idea I was two steps behind.

'He's this loaded posh boy and his idea of showing you a good time was you trekking out to the flat his parents bought him to get high and listen to his drivel,' Clem says. 'Did he ever take you anywhere?'

Ah. No. Again, I told myself that was a sign of how gloriously unmaterialistic he was – not short of funds but uninterested in spendy dinners, showing off, roostering round town, trying to bedazzle me with his wealth. He wanted to talk about cerebral things. (Himself and his work.)

I'm sucking down wine fast and writing myself an internal memo about how an athletic ability to find the positive – the sort that's drilled into girls especially: be grateful, smile! – isn't always a good thing. Sometimes you should ask yourself why you're having to.

And I'm reflecting on other signals I successfully blocked out. The first time I properly introduced Robin to the gang was Clem's thirtieth. I'd thought Clem spent the whole night on the other side of the room to circulate, that Rav got lordly drunk due to the units in a pitcher of Dark and Stormy and that Jo was quiet due to pre-menstrual issues. Meanwhile, a visibly bored Robin said he 'wasn't good in crowds'.

I grimace into my glass:

'I hope you don't think I dated a tosser because he'd been on television once or twice.'

'Oh, no,' Rav says, 'We think you dated a tosser as you thought he was something out of the ordinary, am I right? Which, y'know. He *was* . . .'

Jo adds: 'It's not as if the rest of us are doing any better.'

I wasn't going to say it but it's not usually me who brings a cuckoo into the nest. My few boyfriends in my twenties have been albeit-unthrilling, unsuited-to-me, but nice enough guys.

Meanwhile Rav's carousel of internet dates end up being hard to distinguish from his therapy list – 'Only I can't charge for my time' – Jo is long-term hung up on the charismatic neighbourhood rotter, Shagger Phil, and Clem believes romantic love is a concept designed to subdue and enslave humanity. She's rarely seeing anyone long enough for us to meet him.

Rav goes to give Clem a hand at the bar for round three and Jo, from under her blunt, glossy brown fringe – her current dip-dyed style is two thirds cappuccino shade vs one third cappuccino foam (she's a hairdresser) – says: 'You're coping very well. I hope we've not been too full on.'

'Oh, thanks. Not at all. I'm appalled by myself to be honest. I'm wondering if he'd not done this, how long I'd have gone on telling myself we made a good couple. Only we were never a couple.'

The excitement of the night and the adrenaline of unmasking Robin's audacious act is fading, and I'm left with a hollowed-out feeling inside.

'You were! A couple, I mean.'

'We weren't, Jo. I glommed on to someone I thought was cool.' I rub my temples and resist the urge to bang my head on the table. 'I didn't feel feelings, that's the worrying part. I'm wondering if I'll ever actually fall in love with anyone now. Perhaps this is it. Least worst options and growing the fuck up.'

I've entered the maudlin stage of red wine soakedness.

'You will find someone! You could have your pick, you really could.'

I hesitate, worrying at the beer mat in front of me. You can say more to someone you've known for twenty years, who knows the bones of you. Who knows where you came from.

'I don't know if there's anyone I want to pick. I've never fallen for anyone . . .' I plough on, unable to meet her eye, reckless in drink: 'Well, maybe once. When very young and stupid. But turns out it didn't mean anything.'

'. . . Richard Hardy?' Jo whispers, quizzical, but respectful. Oh God. The *danger* of someone having known me this long.

As soon as I've started this conversation, I realise I don't want to have it, not now, not ever. The name being spoken has caused my insides to seize up. I make an indistinct 'mmmm' noise.

'I see his photos sometimes. Is it Toronto where he lives now?'

'Mmmm. I think he moved to Canada, yeah,' I say, and wish my glass wasn't empty, so I had a way of keeping my mouth busy.

Jo pats my arm. I can feel her working out what to say and I don't know how to stop her.

'I didn't know that you—' she starts, and I cut her off.

'Where has Rav got to? Is he trampling the grapes for this wine?'

She looks round, and I know she senses there's something amiss, but that this moment will have passed before she's even started to wonder what it might be.

7

These first few minutes of consciousness with a hangover are the worst, like waking up in a field after being thrown from a car crash, only you were the car crash.

The end of the night plays in my head: licking salt, biting lemons, throwing back tequilas that tasted like nail varnish remover, laughing like hyenas in the taxi. Urrrrrggggh. Shots. Nothing about the experience can legitimately be called pleasurable and the bell tolls heavily the morning after.

Reality reassembles in a series of bare-skin-filled flashes: Lou topless and strung up, Robin presenting his junk in front of passers-by. It has the quality of a very strange dream, and for a second I think it was one, until my eyes settle on a tattered *I'm Not Being Funny But* tour poster on my floor with NOB BAG written on Robin's forehead in lipstick.

Oh God, did I make much noise? Karen will go spare. She works a week of night shifts alternating with a week of day shifts at a biscuit factory and I regularly forget which is which. When I moved in I said: 'Do we really eat so many biscuits that we need biscuits to be baked at night?' and she said 'Is that a joke or are you really that stupid?' which set the tone for our co-habitation.

I poke a lizardy tongue out of a dry mouth, try stretching limbs, my hinges creak. I'll have a fat Coke, two Nurofen Lemon Meltlets and try for another two hours, I think.

What time is it? I tip my phone towards me to check and see a text message from an unknown number. I prop myself on my elbow – seeing myself in the glass chest of drawers opposite, hair like the late Rick Parfitt on a Quo comeback tour, why does drunk-sleep always give you root lift at the crown? – and swipe to unlock.

Hi Georgina, this is Devlin, Mark gave me your number, said you could give us a hand at the wake this avvo. Can you be here around three? LMK if that works, we're pretty desperate!

Fuuuuuuuuc . . . I've got Mark's client's job! The one thing Esther doesn't want me to fuck up! Must cancel must cancel CAN'T CANCEL. I need to not enrage my sister, not to mention the money – there's a second text offering a pretty healthy chunk of cash in hand (plus 'any tips you can cadge') that'll tide me over until next month at least.

It's half eleven. I'm summoned for three. Much as I could do with another hour, better get a move on – oversleeping would be fatal.

I have a hot shower, spend ages on make-up that's supposed to disguise my condition. I know this is temporary, with pink eyeballs and grey skin. In a steamy mirror, you convince yourself you've done a magical Lazarus by piling on the cosmetics, then as the day wears on, catch your exhausted reflection and see Baby Jane.

I can't face solids yet. I drain a strong black coffee, gritty with white sugar, while Jammy the tortoise gives me a shrewd look that says – rough as arseholes again, are we? My my.

Oh, good. Karen's left one of her love notes on the kitchen table.

Georgina.

It seems we have a TAMPON GOBLIN. This mythical creature sneaks around stealing sanitary items. I had a box of Super Plus, with approx. three left, now none. Had to use your Lil-Lets. If I wanted Lil-Lets I would buy Lil-Lets. Plus I have a heavy flow and they have nothing like the absorbency. Plz replace ASAP.

Karen

PS adding this at 6 a.m. as leaving for work: after crashing around your bedroom (alone? I assume) for an HOUR at 2 A.M. you think you can play your Taylor Swift songs on headphones and I won't hear you SINGING ALONG. THE DISRESPECT IS STAGGERING.

Given I can't remember getting home, this will mean buying apology cava, as well as more Tampax.

I'm absolutely sure I didn't use hers, Karen has a faulty memory and a relish for persecution, just one of the many reasons it's such a privilege to share with her.

She also has no sense of humour so drawing Dobby the House Elf and captioning him 'Blobby' is a definite no.

Mark's client is a robust, friendly-but-gruff sounding man called Devlin with an Irish brogue, who has that male thing of talking on the telephone in the way you give someone directions when leaning down to a car window: staccato bursts of necessary information, delivered at volume.

He calls me straight back after I text to say that 3 p.m. will be fine, as he wants to explain a) it's a wake and the wake is for a friend of his, and b) the reason he needs bar staff urgently is because The Wicker on Ecclesall Road isn't yet open after a refit – am I OK with being the only one on for most of the evening? I am, grand, grand, OK then see you at three. Click.

The Wicker, hmm. I hope they had a few quid to spend as that wasn't a small task.

The Wicker was always attractive from the outside: its Victorian exterior is covered in varying shades of intense green lacquered subway tiles, the door is a giant solid gloss-painted black slab. If you didn't know the city, you could be easily fooled into thinking it was going to be all craft ale and cheese boards with pickles in miniature Kilner jars inside. Instead it used to be gloomy and musty and the drinks were always cloudy. It's one of the places you wouldn't contemplate, a place very much for *regulars* only, regulars who must be suffering from Stockholm Syndrome to keep going back.

'Hello?' I rap my knuckles on the imposing door, which lies ajar. 'Hello?'

I tentatively push it open, step inside. You know when you

step out of the plane door abroad and reflexively flinch for the British cold air to hit you, and instead it's this hairdryer warmth?

Like that, but with beauty.

There's a sweeping curve of mahogany bar that's obviously original, lovingly nursed back to rude health from its knackered one-hundred-years-of-being-leaned-on patina; panels of etched vintage mirrors behind, bottles of spirits stacked against it. Classy ones which promise good drinks, too: a dozen different gins, Aperol, proper whiskies. I'm a sucker for this sort of shabby chic mixture of old and new. It's all the glamour, as far as I'm concerned.

They've gutted the place, without tearing its heart out. Booths in the windows are now oxblood leather, instead of that textured, itchy fabric they make train seat covers from. The lights are low-hanging white china pendants.

The floor, which I recall as having a thick wodge of much-trampled sticky carpet covering it before, is varnished mole-dark parquet. The expensively atmospheric walls are the colour of sky at dusk, which if I recall Esther's endless interior project vacillations correctly, is Farrow & Ball's Hague Blue.

I smell meaty food cooking. Trestle tables line the walls, holding platters of triangles of soft white bread sweating under clingfilm, and starbursts of crudités are arrayed around ramekins of dips.

'Hello! You must be Georgina?'

I turn as a man dumps down a sizeable floral display on the floor, words picked out in orange gerberas and lollipop-headed white chrysanthemums, and bolts across the room to shake my hand.

'Devlin.'

He's nothing like I imagined him when we were on the phone. I thought from the singsong, deep voice he'd be a Hagrid-like beast. Instead he's a livewire, five-foot-something with inky hair, deep grooves in his face and a trendy jacket. He's forty-ish and good-looking, in a lived-in way.

'You've scooped us right out of the shit here, grand of you to step in.'

'No problem . . . cor, it looks great in here.'

'Ah, you think?' Devlin looks gratified. 'Been a back-breaker this one but I'm pleased with it. Did you know it before?'

'Er . . . I knew it but I wasn't a customer.'

'Yes, a bit of a drinkers' pub, as they say? The previous owners had let things get very bleak. Could see it was a diamond in the rough though.'

'So much so! Wow.'

It's now lovely enough it makes me feel happier just being here.

'We're still a week off opening so we've not got the tills up and running, so it's a free bar. Still, less for you to do.'

I smile and nod even though I am experienced enough at bar keeping to know free bars are an absolute bloodbath, and free bars at wakes, doubly so. Once you remove the need to pay, people are animals. As Mark said, the money is great, and it's only now I start to figure why this might be. This is a wild lock in with no clear end.

It's also the first time I'd been near a funeral since my dad's, twelve years ago.

★   ★   ★

When I was fifteen or so, my mum pinned the order of service for her cousin Janet, a physiotherapist in Swansea, to the corkboard in the kitchen. It said *A Celebration of The Life Of* and inside there were photos of Janet in a clown's outfit at a party, in a kayak, raising a watermelon margarita to a camera lens next to her girlfriend. The dress code was 'be a rainbow'. Mum sent flowers.

I recall my dad huffing and saying: 'I don't like this "celebrating" and holiday snaps and jollification of mortality. Let death be death. It's sad. It doesn't need this modernisation where we're in Hawaiian shirts, trilling KUMBAYA MY LORD, KUMBAYA and cheering them on their way.'

'Janet chose her own funeral,' Mum said.

'Then Janet is being selfish – it wasn't for her, was it? It's the very definition of an event where you should only think of other people's feelings.'

Mum gasped and Dad muttered about going to the shops if anyone wanted anything and left the room.

It was only years later I realised Mum probably didn't go the funeral because she knew Dad would react like this. Was he really bothered about happy-clappy send-offs? Or was it a way of providing them both with an excuse for their non-attendance, so they didn't have to spend a weekend in Wales with each other for company? The argument wasn't about what it was about. Maybe none of their arguments were about what they were about.

It didn't make Dad's funeral three years later any easier, knowing that he wouldn't have approved of gaiety, that he wasn't religious and said it was 'the plunge into eternal TV test card nothingness.' In a strange irony, he hadn't thought of our feelings.

For his send-off, we had the standard package of inexpensive coffin, MDF with veneer finish, a service at a church that Dad never visited but Mum wanted as it was posher than a crematorium, then a wake in the adjoining hall where young staff in white shirts and dark trousers served hot drinks from catering-sized canisters and vinegary warm wine from boxes.

I can taste the dislocated, bad-dream-like nauseous quality of it as if it happened yesterday. The feeling the universe had taken a sudden mad swerve, a left turn into some grotesque alt-verse that it should be possible to clamber back out of. Mum and Esther had identified the body; I was in my first year at university. An ordinary morning, when Mum heard him crash to the kitchen floor, rushed down and found him prone, lying in a lake of cafetière coffee.

I wanted to walk up to one of the poker-faced, white-gloved men from the undertakers, schooled not to make eye contact, and grab them by the grey lapels. Say: 'There's been a terrible mistake. That's my *dad* in that coffin. Death happens to other people, I get that, but not to my actual dad, and definitely not yet. I need to discuss something with him urgently, so get him out of there.'

The word loss had a new meaning, or its meaning became clear: a person who loved me, in a completely unique and irreplaceable way, had vanished and took with him our relationship. And it wasn't only Dad that disappeared, but his perspective, his encouragement, his approval, his opinion of me. There was no one else who could be my dad and I still badly needed one. I was never going to see him again? Ever?

We hadn't said goodbye.

I return to these memories reluctantly. Then I push them away again. It's like forcing too many things into a cupboard and using the door to keep them jammed in. Knowing it's a short-term fix, and that the next time you open it – instant cascade.

Another clue that this wake might be more 'Cousin Janet' than 'my dad' are the pictures hung like bunting, across the bar. A lantern-jawed, strawberry-blond man in his thirties, larking it up: walking the Peaks, or dressed as a Roman centurion, the yellowy quality of 1990s pub trips, documented when photographs weren't taken on phones and every man seemed to be in lumberjack shirt and light blue jeans. A sagging banner hangs above them, spelling out: RIP DANNY.

Oh, no. It's a young person. The out-of-the-way, non-fashionable venue had made me assume otherwise. It stings. Someone who'd lived a long life, was in a care home and whose faculties had possibly gone to mush is one thing. I look at the images a second time, feel my throat tighten. However late this ends and thinly it spins my wages out, I won't complain.

'Should I start unboxing the glasses?'

I gesture at the stacks of Paris goblets and a spare wallpaper pasting table, with paper cloth.

'Yeah that'd be great. You can pour out plenty of the red and white too because they'll get drunk, of that I can be sure.'

He checks his watch. 'About half an hour to lift off, they're still chatting outside the church, it only just finished. Catholics, you know.' He does a talking hand puppet mime. 'They like a long ceremony.'

My gaze focuses again on the flowers and I see the words for the first time.

'. . . IRN BRU?' I ask.

Devlin turns to them, turns back. 'Aha yeah, Dan loved Irn Bru. When we were brainstorming his favourite things it was Irn Bru, poker, booze and boobs and I didn't think Co-op Funeral Service would agree to the others.'

I laugh, then check myself. 'Sorry for your loss,' I say, knowing from direct experience how inadequate those words are.

'Ah, thanks Georgina, thanks,' Devlin says, and I notice the charm of working for someone who remembers your name and uses it. It says: *I know you are not merely my lackey and have a lively existence outside of this transaction.*

'No age, no age at all, but Danny was never going to make old bones.'

'Oh . . .' I say. 'I am sorry.'

He shakes his head. 'My best mate from my first job in a warehouse. Absolutely lovely guy, do anything for you, you know. But a thirsty one. Always on the hoy.'

I sense Devlin's not easily offended and risk asking:

'Was it . . . alcoholism he died from?'

'Yeah. Well, yes and no. Got so pished he fell down some stairs, brained himself, massive bleed. Doctors said there was no bringing him back round. Not bringing him back round as Dan, anyway.'

'Oh, God.'

'Thirty-three, no age.'

'Thirty-three!' I put a hand to my face. 'Awful. I'm so sorry. Devlin.'

'My sister-in-law died a year ago at the same age so it's been a grimy old time.'

I have no variant on gasping and mumbling sorry left available to me but we're interrupted by a man with his Wranglers falling down his arse – in the old school, can't be bothered to belt them properly way, not as a 'look' – holding a speaker.

I'm feeling less awkward now about my black t-shirt and jeans. I didn't know if denim was too disrespectful a textile.

'Where do you want this?'

'Ah let's see . . . by that door is fine.'

'There's going to be music?' I say to Devlin.

'Oh yeah. Can't have a tear up without tunes,' he says. On noticing my faintly puzzled expression he adds: 'I should've said really, I mean, this is more of a party than a wake. Danny left strict instructions in the event of a sudden departure and we're following them to the letter.'

Devlin pauses.

'I mean, he was probably pissed when he wrote them, but still.'

8

I'm hugely enjoying something I didn't expect to enjoy whatsoever, so the sense of enjoyment is potent – two and half times the strength of a scheduled pleasure. And I'm being paid.

In my defence, everyone here seems to be having fun. The music is blaring, the conversation is near-deafening but always good spirited, and everyone I encounter is polite, no matter how trolleyed.

Dan's wake would surely have made Cousin Janet's do look like a Quaker meeting, and I wish I'd met him, although I might've felt conflicted serving him drinks.

Devlin gave a short speech, during which tears rolled down his cheeks, about how much Dan hated grim-faced memorials.

'He has absolved you from the guilt of still being here without him, and asks you celebrate the fact instead. Which was Dan in a nutshell. To Dan,' he toasted.

'To Dan,' everyone said, as arms went up, and I felt my eyes well as I raised my glass and wiped my face with my apron.

Devlin said to me in the first hour: 'Have one on the go for yourself throughout, won't you? As long as you can see straight, it's only fair and decent. Help yourself to the buffet too.'

I pour myself a champagne and barely get a chance to sniff it, but it's that satisfying-to-the-soul sort of busy where the clock leaps forward rather than crawls and I get a glow from everyone being properly looked after, as if it's my personal largesse I'm dispensing.

Devlin's wife, Mo – 'You'll know her if you see her. She's short, bleached blonde and will be giving me shit' – keeps me stocked up with fruit and ice and otherwise I run the show single-handed.

I remember something I'd forgotten in the trenches of That's Amore! – I'm a good worker. Having served a hundred of them in two hours, I can now draw you a shamrock in a Guinness foam with a flick of the wrist under the tap, while pushing an optic with the other.

As the crowd thins out, the middle of the space turns into a dancefloor.

I find a crate of fizz that's been lost in the melee and mention it to a flushed and expansive Devlin.

'Call me Dev! I am only ever Devlin to my mother and the police. Thanks for letting me know.'

He taps a flute with a fork.

'If I can have your attention! Our wonderful barmaid has found more of the Moët. I always say, get the decent stuff out once the riff-raff have gone home. Let's all have another glass and toast dear Dan.'

A roar.

'And while we're at it, a round of applause for Georgina and her tireless efforts tonight.'

Devlin points at me, everyone claps and whistles and I blush and think: well, at least Esther's going to have no cause to mither that I've made Mark look bad.

As the night wears on, I'm exhilarated, I feel I'm half Gaelic now, in a superficial and appropriative way – like Rose in that bit in *Titanic* where she can somehow blend seamlessly into the revelry below decks by hitching up her skirts and dancing a jig to a tin whistle.

As I assemble a cluster of goblets and start doling out the second wave of champagne, I become aware of a man who's walked in to the party, with a portly, sandy-coloured dog in tow.

He's tall and dark in a navy jacket with its collar turned up. He has curling, jet black hair, just long enough to scrape behind his ear. I realise what's drawn my gaze is that he's not greeting anyone or joining in, but doing a studied, sulky performance of 'brooding', a modern disco's answer to Mr Darcy at a ball.

These rowdy, twenty-first century commoners are swaying to Tina Turner's 'What's Love Got To Do With It' while he stares into the middle distance.

I get a funny feeling, watching him watch the room through the throng of people who keep blocking my view: should he even be here? Usually if you walk in alone you're trying to get someone's attention to announce your arrival? And why turn up this late to a wake anyway? Is he the wake version of a wedding crasher? But why would you make yourself conspicuous by bringing a dog? No. He must belong. I wonder what his story is, if he was close to Dan and can't quite stomach the disrespectful raucousness.

His eyes move toward me and I quickly busy myself.

Ooh, Blondie's 'Atomic'. I dance a little while I tidy the bar.

'Excuse me, blondie?'

I turn and laugh. Devlin beckons me over at the side of the bar and offers me a wad of notes.

'You've been absolutely solid tonight, can't thank you enough.'

I thank him and say honestly it's been my pleasure and then flinch at the inappropriate phrasing when we're marking a hideously premature death.

'Listen. I've been to-ing and fro-ing over who to hire to run the bar full time because I hate interviews and CVs and that bollocks, I'd far rather meet someone and work with them. Get a sense of what they're about. But holding auditions didn't seem fair. How about if this was one, in retrospect? Would you be interested?'

'Yes!' I say. Then, with less windy desperation, more determination: 'I'd be very very interested, thank you.'

'Great. I've got to sign it off with my brother but it shouldn't be a problem.'

As hope surges, I remind myself that job offers made verbally when three sheets to the wind are not binding.

Devlin turns back to me and I notice Lonely Glowering Man is now stood at his elbow, trying to get Devlin's attention. He's quite the knock-out, now I can see him fully: dark sweeps of eyebrow, sulky mouth, lightly stubbled movie star jawline, the works.

Hang on. I freeze. I realise I know this face. The terrain is altered, and it's a long time since I've traced its lines, but it's not as I'd thought, completely unfamiliar. Far from it.

The split second of recognition is a punch to the heart.

My breath stops in my throat as his gaze meets mine.

Blondie's vocals soar as she sings about beautiful hair.

Devlin says: 'Meet my brother, Lucas.'

9

'Luke,' Lucas says, hand outstretched for a brisk, brief shake as I chew air and murmur a vacant hello and the word *Georgina*.

(I bite back an irrational cry of: 'Luke? Since when?')

My skin is basted in a sudden flop sweat which I hope arrived after we made contact.

Lucas starts speaking closely into Devlin's ear in a confidential way that doesn't invite contribution, and after waiting enough seconds so it doesn't look like I'm fleeing, I escape to the loo.

I'm glad of it being empty, a place where the air is cooler and the music pounds through the wall.

I lock myself in a cubicle, sit fully clothed on the toilet and stare at the partition between myself and the empty stall next door.

Devlin is a Devlin McCarthy? Lucas McCarthy is out there? Jesus Christ. How? What? *Why?*

I recall Lucas having some looming threat older brother who'd left school, but he was that many years ahead I never even knew his name. Our mouths were usually fastened on each other rather than used for swapping family biographies.

Oh God, oh God. I wish I'd had some warning. Someone of his significance shouldn't be able to simply walk back in without fanfare, without a build-up. It reminds me of that line about death just being another room. Lucas was dead to me and yet he's in this room. It's impossible.

I mean, I've always known it *could* happen. But after twelve years, you're convinced it *won't* happen.

After a forced wee – strategy: as now I can't plausibly need a real one in five minutes' time – I rinse my clammy hands in cold water and inspect my reflection, my vanity overclocking. I grit my teeth to check there's nothing in them, furiously rub away some make-up that's drifted from above to below my eye.

I'm shaking slightly. And look at him now?!

In my mind's eye, Lucas McCarthy was still the skinny eighteen-year-old I once knew. The idea he'd blossomed into some sort of stunning leading man in the interim hadn't once occurred to me. He's turned from an underfed, slightly hunted-looking slender indie boy into fully fledged Byronic poetry.

And me? I've certainly not transformed into some femme fatale. I fear I'm the same fruit, gone mouldy in the bowl.

I hear Tony's voice: 'Julie Goodyear.'

I tuck my hair behind my ears and stand up straighter and try to think positive thoughts. I'm fine. It's fine. I feel the waistband on my jeans pressing into soft flesh and wish I was hard-bodied and defiant, polished up like a gemstone, and oh God, do I have jowls?

Thing is, I'm fretting – but Lucas didn't recognise me. Of this I'm virtually certain. I'm good at reading people. I know what it's like to have people looking at you, talking about you. To be covertly observed.

With Lucas there was no microscopic tell – no whisper of awkwardness, or apprehensiveness, no acknowledgement whatsoever. His expression was the fixed absent-polite-neutral of someone going through the motions with a person who has nothing to do with you. His eyes were flat, they said nothing.

Is that possible? Georgina's not a rare name, but it's not one you meet everywhere either. It's been twelve years. Is that long enough to forget someone entirely? A voice whispers: you have your answer. And you don't know how many 'someones' there are, do you. Losing a Georgina in a huge playing field of other Georginas ain't so difficult.

I don't want Lucas to know who I am, yet the idea is also utterly gutting.

I decide to be pragmatic, wailing can wait. At least this earthquake has happened as the wake passes into its final hours.

Back out on the floor, and behind the bar, I get a crick in the neck from studiously not looking at whatever Lucas McCarthy's doing. My customers are a trickle, then they dry up completely.

Devlin's wife Mo says I can 'probably get off' and I crush her into a hug of gratitude, moving fast enough not to be asked how I'm getting home. Over her shoulder, Devlin makes the 'I'll call you' sign with finger and thumb to ear at me and I respond with a thumbs up, and a hard weight inside.

There's the exit, don't look left or right, stay on target, door shut behind you . . . And breathe.

I smoke a much-needed Marlboro Light as I wait for the taxi I ordered to sweep round the corner, stamping my feet in the cold. I don't care about the temperature, just relieved to have escaped. I check the tracking app on my phone: my driver Ali is 4 MINS away.

I pace around, ostensibly to warm my body up, more to cool my brain down. The music throbs through the door and I wonder how late they're going to stay up with the remaining bottles of scotch, reminiscing.

Lucas McCarthy is Devlin's brother. Devlin is Lucas McCarthy's brother. I can't get my head round this.

I clutch my elbow with my free hand and pace and watch figures flitting across the non-misted spaces in the patterns in the windows. If I can see them, they can see me.

What if someone asks why the barmaid is lurking, mentions it? It's daft to think they will, but seeing Lucas has left me edgy as a stray cat. I wander round the side of the pub, out of view.

An open window nearby is letting heat from the kitchen escape. As I draw near it I can hear a conversation. Voices come in and out of range as they move around the room. I idly listen in, fiddle with my phone. Tracking app: your driver Ali is 1 MIN away.

'Pick that up. No, it goes there. Look.'

'Which . . .'

'. . . Luke! No, there, look.'

I straighten. One of these disembodied voices is Lucas? I give their dialogue my full attention. I strain: they're speaking rapidly, with forcefulness, but I can't make out the words.

And suddenly, they must move so they're positioned right by me, as I can follow it perfectly.

'. . . Not a doubt. It was bedlam at times and she handled herself well. She's got no attitude. Exactly what we want.'

'Based on what? You're spannered.'

The sound of a heavy weight being dropped, with control.

'Yeah because she kept my glass full!'

The guffaw that follows is unmistakably Devlin.

'Pouring liquid into glasses isn't astrophysics, is it?'

'Nor is running a pub.'

They're talking about *me?*

Oh, no . . . my taxi is here. I make a silent, frantic, 'yes coming, just finishing my cigarette' mime and the driver looks unimpressed.

'. . . Great, our recruitment policy is whichever blondes happen to catch my brother's eye. It's not Hooters, Dev.'

I can't believe this is about me, and yet it's clearly about me.

'She's obviously a nice, sound lass. There's a way about her that I like a lot. I don't see your problem.'

'We don't know anything about her, we don't know she's nice. You've gone over my head and promised her, is my problem. Where's my tick?'

'Give her a chance, you cynical twat. The lesson of tonight was not to be a cynical twat.'

'I thought the lesson was about not doing stupid things when you're heavily intoxicated. Also, who puts shamrocks in

Guinness? To be sure to be sure. Let her go work in Scruffy Muffy's or whatever it's called these days.'

A howl of laughter. 'Ah God, I wonder how we'd fix a flaw in her like that, Luc, I mean it's IMPOSSIBLE . . .'

The driver shouts: 'I'm starting the meter now, love, come on!' and I startle and rush over, trying to pick my footsteps carefully so the brothers don't twig to me having been nearby.

I just heard Lucas McCarthy equate the wisdom of hiring me with killing yourself.

When we pull up in Crookes, as I get money out to pay, I find Devlin's given me fifty quid more than we agreed. Usually you'd put that down to inebriation but I get the sense that Devlin is always this garrulous and generous.

Damn. For a brief, blissful moment, I thought I'd fallen into a job that I'd like, for a person I like. But he's Lucas McCarthy's brother.

And since when was he 'Luke'? I bridle at this, ludicrously, as if he's committing a fraud. A betrayal. *Betrayal.* I turn the word over. It has pointed edges that cause lacerations. It's like swallowing a Sticklebrick.

I walk, trance-like, from kitchen to bathroom sink to pulling on my pyjamas, not present in any single task, mind floating elsewhere.

We don't know anything about her

Oh, really.

It's not Hooters, Dev

Supercilious arsehole! How sexist is that?! Would any place hire you because of your hair? It may be lustrous but I'm thinking not. OK, he's also possibly referring to the DD cup. Pig. Like I chose this pair in the Grattan catalogue.

So Lucas is now a grown-up who owns and runs places. I'm thirty and begging to work in them. The indignity.

I don't want your job anyway, so the joke's on you.

But oh God. I *do* want the job. Before this encounter, I'd have said that working for Lucas McCarthy would've been what my dad called a cheese-before-bed nightmare.

Now the initial encounter is over with, my feelings are more conflicted. I've heard him saying I'd be trouble – or that they 'don't know I'm nice' – and my pride wants to face that down.

Was Lucas only pretending not to recognise me, then ruling out my working for them as a result? That's the version that suits me, so I'm suspicious of it. It would mean he hasn't forgotten, it did matter. Even if nothing like as much as it does to me, I'm not that deluded.

That beats being Some Blonde.

I scour the memory of our reunion for the smallest twitch of discomfort on his side and conclude: no, there was none. No one's that good at a poker face, outside international poker tournaments.

But I didn't hear who won that debate about me. I may yet not have the job.

I weigh up alternatives.

Devlin calls: *Oh dear, my mistake, the vacancy is filled.* This, when he sobers up, seems a likely outcome of what I over-heard. It was unfair to impose me on Lucas, even without our history.

Or, I still get the job, but with Lucas resenting me, and that'll be nothing compared to how he reacts when the penny drops about who I am? That's a high wire act.

Lastly, best case scenario: I get the job, and it's fine. Lucas grudgingly admits I'm sufficiently efficient, we rub along reasonably well. And he never places my face.

I lie in bed, my breath making ghosts in the damp air, wondering why my best case scenario also somehow sounds like the worst.

10

I didn't know what loss meant until I lost Dad and I didn't know what regret meant until I regretted Lucas McCarthy.

Although, as my counsellor Fay told me, I didn't have complete control over the situation and the nature of my regret suggests I was entirely responsible when I only had power over my part of it. Lucas was an 'independent actor'.

I said, 'Hmm OK I regret my part in it.'

'Accept that much, then. It's yours, take it.' She picked up a mug as a symbolic gesture, placed it on the desk and pushed it towards me. I didn't think it worked that well really as it had a picture of King Kong on it and was obviously a personal artefact I wasn't meant to literally accept.

I pulled it toward me and nodded. 'Am I meant to feel any better?'

'Not better as such, not automatically improved, like the words are a magic spell. But it can spring you out of self-defeating thought patterns where you continually berate and diminish yourself for what cannot be undone. You are not an omnipotent deity, you're a human just going along, learning, making a mess sometimes in the process, as we all are.'

I wept then and she said it's good that you can cry about it. I said: *Seriously? Why?* through whirlpools of my Lancôme liner as I plucked at the box of tissues on her desk. She said because admitting hurt helps you dispel its power and lets you get past it.

To be honest, a lot of counselling appears to be accepting you're up to your tits in shit and finding you're zen about it. Saying: at least my tits are warm.

I was glad I went, though. I liked Fay, with her henna-red wispy copper wire hair, billowing black jersey dresses and spectacles perched right on the end of her nose. The weekly hour spent in the calming room with the bamboo plant and the painting of sailboats in Mousehole harbour didn't untie the knot, but it loosened it.

A note on the wall in the lobby told me I could tackle a number of issues, including:

• Emotional Eating
• Anxiety
• Debt Worries
• Histrionic Personality Disorder
• Internet Addiction
• Managing Chronic Pain

I thought: sounds like an average weekend round mine, har har har. (Fay told me I did this as reflex, mocking myself. I told her I couldn't take my problems seriously, given some people are sleeping rough. 'There are always those worse off than you. Your problems are not invalid as a result, or needing to be measured against an internationally recognised pain scale before we decide if your condition is severe enough to treat.')

I didn't turn up to talk about Lucas, it was to discuss my dad, but the counsellor said most people end up on different ground to the area they expected to cover. In family therapy, Fay said, you'd be amazed how often parents turn up to analyse a peculiarly difficult child and we end up looking at their problems instead.

I said: Do you know, I wouldn't.

I never told Jo or my sister or anyone else about Lucas and it felt strange to turn thoughts I'd churned on into actual consonants and vowels, in a room, with a stranger. It gave it life outside of my head.

I still didn't tell Fay the whole story.

I think the real damage was that Lucas and I never spoke after the leavers' party. It wasn't just that our relationship was unconsummated, there wasn't a conclusion of any sort. No conversation whatsoever. Exams were over, school was out forever, and we didn't have any mutual friends to pull us back into the same orbit, that summer or ever after. When there is so much left unsaid, your mind is free to fill in the words that were never exchanged in a hundred thousand different ways, and believe me, I have. Then my dad died, I quit university shortly after, and really it's been a race to the bottom since. Lucas hasn't been a user of social media as far as I could tell from my searches – unless he blocked me from view – or

I might have weakened and approached him in the years after. But being honest, I have no idea what I'd have said if I had found him. It would've been pretty tragic. Better that the temptation was taken away from me. What I wanted was to hear things from him I was definitely never ever going to hear.

At the end of that session, Fay said, What if it's not what happened with this boy you regret, it's you? It's the *you* who you left behind. It's who you were at eighteen and the things that happened subsequently and you look back on it as a watershed. *You broke up with yourself.*

This hit me as fearsomely true.

I mean, if I was *Doctor Who*'s new companion, and he was agitatedly racing round the Tardis, throwing levers on the control panel, the noise like bellows starting as the time machine mechanism booted up and saying, 'Where to, Georgina Horspool?' I'd waste no time in identifying early evening in a crap pub in northern England in the early twenty-first century.

A blonde girl in a red dress from Dorothy Perkins and uncomfortable shoes is unsteadily making her way there.

For the time being, she has no experience of managing chronic pain.

11

If there's one thing you don't need after a dark night of the soul, reliving your worst moments from the past and facing up to a grim present, it's a Sunday lunch with family. Particularly, my family.

I'd love to give Esther a swerve today but she'll be waiting on a debrief from last night, not to mention I'll get a horrendous guilting about how she's catered for me.

In the competition between How Much Aggro To Not Go vs How Much Aggro To Drag Myself There, Esther's vigour makes the latter choice a clear winner.

I'm summoned for midday, decent booze in hand. Luckily, I rootled out some decent bottles of Beaujolais from the last time Robin was here. Despite his 'fresher week' diet, Robin liked classy booze.

I may be skint but a taxi to Esther's is the only plausible option on a Sunday when she lives on the wrong side of the city and a journey by public transport would take in three buses and half the Peak District. I stare morosely out of the window as the view changes: the boxy post-war houses and takeaways and chippies and bookies of the largely itinerant community of Crookes give way to the city centre, then out into the Peaks until we're in greener and pleasanter spaces.

My sister, her husband and their son live in the village of Dore, in an architect-designed detached house. It's palatial, with a double garage and bi-fold kitchen doors leading on to a properly kept rectangle of garden, with a large patio for barbecues in summer.

Inside, Esther is fond of the sort of uplifting wall art that says things like LIVE LOVE LAUGH. It's weird, because she's the world's least whimsical person. It always has a whiff of *the floggings will continue until morale improves* to me. I might get her one saying LAUGH DAMN YOU.

As much as my still-delicate stomach feels like it's on a catch-up delay, like I've walked too quickly on an airport travelator, the scenery from the cab window soothes me.

Of all the ways I could feel a failure, still being in my home town is something I'm obstinately proud of. I love Sheffield, even if it is often freezing and everything is uphill. If cities have a spirit, then its spirit is mine.

'Here she is, the pink sheep of the family!' says Geoffrey, who answers the door and critically assesses my coat. If I had to find a Geoffrey quote to sum up Essence of Geoffrey, it'd be this greeting; ostensibly merry but delivered with teeth, not his place to say it, too close to the knuckle to be easy to laugh at.

Yet I'm required to, or I'm churlish. Participating in my own ridicule: it's what I do best.

He's always in a size-too-small Pringle V-neck, his hair, teased across his pate, and a curious unnatural colour that Esther and I secretly christened Butternut Squash Shimmer. I give a strained smile, pulling my arms out of my furry outerwear as he takes the wine from me and twists the label round to face him, re-balancing his readers.

'Hmm . . . not heard of this one. Looks like it'll help wash the taste of the broccoli away, at least, har har.'

Boom, a one-two punch. He grins and I grimace and not for the first time, I think: I know it was a tough time, Mum, but really, *him*? Then consider I'm not in the strongest position to be thinking such things.

The kitchen is a blur of activity, doors in the range cooker being opened and banged shut and oven gloves being clapped together. Geoffrey considers himself a Yorkies expert – he's one of those men who turns everything into a contest – so he and Mark and Mum cluster round the pudding mix in a Pyrex jug, debating tactics, though Mum is hanging back so not as to get her wrap dress splattered. My mum is expensively silver-blonded, and always immaculately turned out. Geoffrey once referred to her as 'the gold standard'. Eeesh.

Esther calls to me: 'Sit with Milo and I'll bring you a drink through,' and I very willingly trot back down the hallway and into the front room.

My nephew Milo is six, wearing dungarees, and engrossed in what my untrained eyes assess to be a Lego treehouse.

'Hello, Milo!'

''Lo.'

'What's this? Bears In A Forest . . . World?'

'Ewoks,' he says, with evident frustration at having to break concentration.

'Ah! Yeah I knew that. And this is their home?'

Exasperated: 'Yes.' Even the child's pissed off I'm here.

'That one looks very smart. Who's he? Or she?'

Milo actually screws up his face in the effort of pandering to my inane intrusions.

'PAPLOO!'

'Paploo! I like his scarf.'

Milo mutters: 'Head dress.'

Esther appears with a flute of blush-coloured cava for me. Looking at it, I have a moment's reflexive twinge of 'oh God no', swiftly followed by 'actually go on, oh God yes'.

'So how was last night?' she says, peering closer. 'Did you manage to behave yourself?'

Esther looks like me facially, otherwise she's leaner and smaller chested, with layered, short I-have-a-busy-life hair. She boasts various skills I do not possess. How to audit tax returns. How to make a proper béchamel for a lasagne. How to exercise restraint. I know that any detailed chat about last night will end badly, as I'm still feeling too raw to bat on a proper inquisition, but luckily I have the perfect news to distract her – if she massively disliked Tony, I'm reasonably sure that she positively detested Robin.

'It was fine, thank you. The bigger news, really, is that immediately after my sacking from That's Amore!, Robin and I broke up.'

'Oh,' Esther says, eyes widening, and hesitates, before deciding she's going to sit down with the other glass of cava she's holding. 'What happened?'

'I . . . er . . .' On the one hand, it irks me to confirm her suspicions about him. On the other, if I want to be close with my sister, shutting her out isn't going to achieve it. Plus, I can never resist an anecdote. 'I caught him . . .' I rub the side of my nose and look towards Milo. '. . . With his Double-U Eye Ell Ell Why in a lady.'

Esther gasps and grabs at her Tiffany padlock necklace, running the pendant up and down the chain. 'Caught him? As in you were there?'

'On premises and with a clear view of the stage,' I say, taking a bracing swig of cava. 'I would say dress circle. He gave me a key to his flat and obviously I was unexpectedly not working my shift.'

'Oh my God. I literally don't know what I'd do if I could . . . if I walked *in* on it.'

'Neither did I. I shouted a lot. It was his personal assistant, Louisa.'

'Ugh. And he'd told you he was out of town?'

I open my mouth to say 'No, why do you say that?' then recall my fib about why he wasn't going to be here today and hastily turn it into: '. . . Uh? Yeah.'

'I'd say I'm surprised but he didn't seem the most reliable of people. Something of a loose cannon. Cracking jokes about drug-taking in front of Mum and Geoff, honestly.'

'Mmmm.' That was selfish.

And that's it really: above all, Robin was morbidly selfish.

I stare at the column of bubbles whizzing upwards in my glass, and my half chipped off aqua nail polish.

'I couldn't tell how serious you were about Robin.'

'I don't think I could tell either. I wasn't, I guess. I was happy to see where it went, and here we are.'

Esther checks that Milo's engrossed in his plastic figurines, and says, quietly:

'I know you and your feminist friends would flay me for this, and yes it's old fashioned, but I don't think sleeping with anyone on the first night, before you've got to know them, is setting you up for success.'

I groan. A previous unwise disclosure, made for the same reasons as this one.

'Look at me like that if you want!' Esther says. 'It's a hard fact of life, no one appreciates what comes too easily to them, whether you're male or female. You didn't want him to treat you like another disposable groupie. And yet . . .'

She gazes at me, trying to work me out.

My sister has a completely warped idea of my sex life. She thinks I am at the forefront of liberation, that I have one-night stands as often and as with as little thought as she gets a Caffè Nero. I've never bothered to correct her, to explain I've only been with the boyfriends she knows about. I'm not completely sure why. She thinks I haven't found anyone worthwhile because I'm so unserious. I would rather she thinks of me as unserious, than tragic.

'I don't think holding out was here or there with Robin. He pulled the whole *doesn't believe in being faithful to one person* thing, like he thinks he's in the Sixties. We were merely ships, passing in the shite.'

Our eyes flicker to Milo but Milo is whispering something to Paploo.

'Sorry,' I mouth at Esther.

'Careful. He's like a bloody Mynah bird at the moment,' she hisses. Then more loudly: 'What a timewaster. You're thirty. Of course you want more commitment than that.'

She says this the way Mum does, hoping that by asserting it, it'll make it true. I go into mutinous teenage mode, because they're making me feel like a scutter.

'I don't know if I want a proposal or whatever, but yes, maybe more devotion than having ess-ee-ex with other women would be nice.'

Esther drums her fingertips on the arm of the chair.

'Who *are* you looking for? I struggle to picture him. I know he'll have to be different, somehow.'

She sounds like Rav. Am I being obtuse, trying too hard? *Showing off?* Dad once told me I was a natural show-off who hates being the centre of attention: 'a paradox you will have to resolve one day'. Not a day Dad hung around long enough for.

'I strongly suspect Mr Georgina doesn't exist,' I say, lightly. I take a handful of pistachios from a leaf-shaped china boat on the coffee table, and pick at a shell. 'I think that's why I went for a wild card instead.'

'I am sure he does exist. It's just . . .'

Here it comes. There's no tail without sting, with my sister.

'. . . There's what you think being in love is when you're

nineteen or twenty and then what it actually is when you're a grown-up, and these are two different things. But some of us keep looking for the first version long after we should've let it go,' Esther says. This lands hard, particularly with last night fresh in mind, and I say nothing.

'Well, what I thought love was going to be, perhaps, I know you weren't like that,' Esther adds, completely misreading my silence and everything else too. I know she means well. 'What I'm saying is, lower your expectations. Being "in love" is a contented kind of bored with each other. You're not going to find someone who sets you on fire and is also a good idea and you know why? Because being on fire isn't a good idea. It's destructive. When anyone describes love nowadays they usually mean lust.'

I start laughing weakly and put my hand over my mouth so I don't spray shards of nut.

'What's funny?'

'Lower my expectations. I found Robin up to his plums in someone else. Lower than that? Should I start writing to lifers in prison? Dear Peter Sutcliffe . . .'

Even Esther snorts.

Milo says, while lowering a net trap full of pistachio shells: 'Plum. Pluuuuums.'

'Milo! Remember what we said about repeating things? Auntie Georgina was talking about plum crumble. Weren't you?'

'Entirely. That well known autumnal dessert, plum crumble.'

'Crumble,' Milo says. 'Plum crumble. Plumble.'

'Yes!' Esther says, emphatically. 'Plumble! Awww . . .

Anyway.' She shakes her head, gives a beatific Mum Mode smile. 'What's that Ewok called?'

'Shipshite.'

I did say to Esther, once Milo had been given a thorough debriefing, surely it'd be worse if he was repeating the name of the Yorkshire Ripper. She was not mollified.

After we've sat in and are making monsters of ourselves over the roast potatoes – there's some sort of witchcraft going on involving a semolina crust – a large vehicle pulls into the driveway. I see the man at the wheel get out and start unfolding a wheelchair. Moments later, the bulky, octogenarian form of Nana Hogg is helped into it.

Mark's paternal grandmother is feared and despised in equal measure by Esther, due to her habit of being exorbitantly, lavishly rude. Esther claims she's senile but I'm not sure she isn't just cantankerous and decades into the Do I Look Like I Give A Fuck years. An outing from her care home is a chance of anarchy.

Due to a sense of duty and deference to her age, no one has considered not inviting her to Sunday lunches. Esther loathes her but I enjoy her hugely. Probably because, unlike everyone else, I don't have a respectable façade for her to tear down.

'I didn't realise she was coming today!' I say, brightly.

'Mmmm,' grimaces Esther, looking up at the clock. 'Only an hour and a quarter late, lucky us. She thinks she's Princess Margaret.'

'She's had trouble with a water infection, she's slow to get going,' Mark tuts, as he heads to the door. The only time he's publicly critical of Esther is when she runs Nana Hogg down.

I mean, she's his granny so he's going to be defensive, but Mark is an incredibly nice person anyway. Mild, kind, sees the good in everyone, always interested in others, in a self-effacing rather than nosy way.

When Esther first told me she was seeing someone on her accountancy degree 'and I think he's the one!' I was like: *ruh roh,* he'll be at worst a ruthless bastard and at best a crashing bore. She had a taste for mean jocks at school. Thank God, given he turned into husband and father of her child, that Mark is lovely – witness his job-giving generosity with me. He wears hand-stitched moccasin slippers around the house and yet I would lay down my life for him.

'Don't wait for me then,' is Nana Hogg's version of 'hello' and 'sorry I'm late', when she sees the laden table.

'Glad you could make it,' Mark says, leaning in to give her a peck on the cheek. His modus operandi is to simply ignore her tone. And her words. And her behaviour.

She has her silver hair in tight roller curls and the sort of bust that rolls out like the swelling tide.

'Hello!' I say, with a small wave. 'Nice to see you again.'

She doesn't acknowledge me, though she might not have heard during the manoeuvres to get her seated.

'Oh it's beef? I can't digest beef,' she says, and Esther looks like she's been tasered up the birth canal.

'But we asked if . . .'

Mark puts his hand over Esther's. 'You can have lots of every-thing else. Geoff, if you'll hand me the peas and carrots . . .'

'We've met before, I'm Geoffrey,' he says smarmily to Nana Hogg, getting up to offer his hand to shake across the roast, 'Patsy's husband.'

'Yes I know who you are, I'm old but I'm not crackers,' she says, 'not seeing' his hand, and I have to plug my mouth with a parsnip to stop myself from laughing. Why did I contemplate crying off this lunch? Carbs, more alcohol, hot gravy and Nana Hogg lols. It's the perfect distraction from my distress.

'Gog's been sacked from the restaurant,' Esther says, conversationally, throwing me to the wolves as distraction.

'Oh no, Georgina!' Mum says, putting her cutlery down with a bump, 'What did you do?'

'I didn't *do* anything, the restaurant critic from *The Star* came in and complained and Tony the chef made a show of binning me. A sacrifice to the gods, to stop him from writing about the grim food.'

'The vicissitudes of still being casual hire-and-fire labour,' says Geoffrey, with evident pleasure, lifting a glass to his mouth. 'So few rights, unfortunately.'

I almost pull a face at him. Geoff has been retired from vice presidency of a central heating firm since forever, on a giant pension.

'It's time to buck your ideas up. Go on a shorthand course and get yourself something in an office,' Mum says.

'I don't think anyone cares about shorthand anymore, Mum. There's no typing pool. There's no bosses chasing secretaries around desks.'

'Well you're soon going to be past the age where you're chased around anything anyway.'

Whump. Right in the solar plexus.

'We called you "jail bait" in my day,' Nana Hogg says to me, and Esther gets up abruptly to refill the gravy boat, which I know is an excuse because she's fuming about inappropriate talk in front of her young son. What about the inappropriate talk in front of her younger sister.

'Georgina's not likely to land anyone in jail now,' Geoffrey says, with what he imagines is a twinkly-eyed look. Creep.

'There's still plenty that's illegal, Geoff, what with women no longer being property,' I say, and Mum shushes: 'Careful!' with a sharp look towards Milo.

'Oh yeah it's my fault, I brought this stuff up.'

'What was the restaurant called?' Mark asks.

'That's Amore!. The Italian in Broomhill.'

'I don't like Italian food. I had a mushroom soup at an Italian restaurant once and it tasted like they'd put something in it,' Nana Hogg says.

'What had they put in it?' Mum asks.

'I don't know. It tasted like there was something in it.'

'That wasn't mushrooms?' Mum persists.

'Yes. There was something in it. They'd put something in it.'

They is starting sound like a synonym for 'The Illuminati'.

'What sort of thing?'

Nana Hogg shakes her head.

'Something. To make it taste stronger.'

'And how did the job last night go, George?' I could kiss Mark for trying to rescue me here. 'I put George in touch with a friend who needed a capable pair of hands at short notice.'

'Good, thanks so much for the recommendation,' I say. I could still very likely be blocked by Lucas so I don't want to sound too confident of Devlin's job. 'It'd be great if they're recruiting for permanent positions but if not I was just glad to help out with the wake.'

'It was a wake,' Geoffrey says, stabbing at a miniature carrot with his fork. 'I hope you were appropriately sombre.'

He winks at me. *What a . . .*

'I pitched up in a glittery leotard, tooting a vuvuzela, was that not the right thing to do?'

'Oh the chill wind of such withering sarcasm!' says Geoffrey, whose funeral I could happily go to.

Esther returns with more gravy and there's no way she didn't hover in the kitchen counting backwards from fifty until she could be sure she wouldn't throw it in anyone's face.

'The food is lovely,' I say to her and she gives me a tight smile and says Mark did most of it.

'Ahem, and the Yorkie pudding maestro here,' Geoff says and everyone's nice to him and choruses praise. I can't bring myself to join in. There's about nineteen things on this table, Geoff basically management consulted the oven temperature for one element and thinks he's equally worthy of thanks. Argh.

'How's Robin?' my mum asks, a note of disapproval high in the mix.

'We've split up,' I say, hoofing half of another spectacular roastie into my mouth.

'Oh!'

Just when I think my singlehood is about to be dissected

with the same sensitivity as my unemployment, Nana Hogg interrupts: 'I'll have some of that meat, please. I'll suffer for it but I don't want to go home hungry,' and Esther pushes her chair out with a loud scrape and announces *I'llgetmorewine*.

As I help clear the table after dinner, Esther leads Milo back in by the shoulder, the pout on his face visible from twenty paces.

'Auntie Georgina, Milo has something for you, don't you, Milo,' Esther says.

'Do you, Milo?' I bend down.

He puts a finger in his mouth and hands over a folded piece of paper he had behind his back. I open it – a drawing of a female stick figure in a triangle dress, with thatch of yellow crayoned hair. She's in front of a house with a smoking chimney in the background, and there's a male stick figure in brown, in an outsize hat.

'This is brilliant! So that's me . . . that's . . . my house?'

Milo nods.

'Minus the marauding maggots,' says Geoffrey, back in Geoffrey mode.

'And who's this? In the hat? Mr Hat?'

'Dat's your husband.'

'But I don't have a husband.'

'When you grow up and get married.'

I can't help but laugh, which is fortunate as everyone else is. 'I am very pleased you don't think I'm grown-up as I think it means I look young.'

I lean down and give him a kiss and a squeeze.

'I will put it up in my room to fill me with hope for the future.'

Milo nods emphatically and putters back to the living room to his Ewoks, while Mum mutters to Geoff and Esther.

As I get ready to leave, Esther jerks her head backward as she hands me my coat to indicate I'm to step into The Situation Room, where we can't be heard. I coined the name for the understairs loo when I noticed it was always used for tellings-off. It seems to be some sort of 'Try not to make it obvious how much you hate Geoffrey' caution but I decide to head her off and pursue my own agenda. She's also better forewarned if I do end up at The Wicker.

'Hey I don't know if you heard over lunch, I've had a full-time job offer. Last night, the wake? Mark's client has offered me the chance to run the bar.'

Esther's face drops. 'Well that's good but be careful, Gog. Remember Mark's reputation is on the line if it goes pear shaped.'

'The wake went *well*. Thanks again for the vote of confidence!' I say jokily, but I'm hurt, and make short shrift of leaving, the drawing of Mr Hat in my hand.

I wipe hot tears away on the journey home and wonder how much is my sister's lack of faith, how much is my mum's observation that I'm passing my shelf life, and how much of it is what happened last night.

Five minutes later, my phone pings. She really does think I'm an embarrassment, as much as everyone else.

The pub job. Good luck with it. BUT DO NOT, I REPEAT DO NOT, ACCIDENTALLY SHAG ANYONE.

If Esther's going to make it clear her opinion of me is this low, I don't owe her reassurance.

What if it's my 'Mr Hat' though?!

Milo drew that after seeing a photo of Tommy Cooper so I wouldn't get too excited x

My phone pings again, this time a text from Robin, this'll perk me up. I noticed I had four missed calls from him during lunch. I'm not sure why he's bothering: it's not as if there's a talking cure for having overheard the noises he makes when he's inside someone else. Maybe when you tell stories for a living you think everything's negotiable.

Hello. Ignoring me now, is it. I appreciate Friday's encounter was a sub-par experience but let's meet like civilised adults to discuss where we go from here. Lou & I aren't a 'thing' in any way, it should be possible to get past it. We had something good, shame to throw it away on hurt pride & misunderstandings. R

Sub-par??! I shudder that I ever let him touch me.

Also, quite something to be lectured on civilised adulting by someone last seen with caramelised pecans in their pubes.

12

I have the attic, in this narrow house with its rotted window frames, grease-covered light fittings, squeaky lino and poky spaces piled on top of one another. Karen is on the first floor, opposite the bathroom, where she can better monitor and control that shared territory.

I used to wonder why she signed off my moving in, but strongly suspect she'd either vetoed or scared off so many potentials prior to me that the landlord lost patience.

I like feeling out of the way up here, though it's a mixed blessing that myself and anyone I bring home have to tiptoe past Karen's den and up and down a vertiginous flight of shallow stairs. I've developed the stealth of a jewel thief however as, if I disturb her, the very furies of hell in 'Homer Simpson's head' slippers will be unleashed. If I had a deadly serious temperament and lost my temper a lot, I might not wear novelty banana-coloured footwear, but Karen obviously has no fear of the ironic juxtaposition.

She reminds me of the time I saw a security guard dressed as a toadstool arguing bitterly with a shoplifter in Lidl on Comic Relief day.

Lunch over and nothing but a drear Sunday evening to distract me from my misery, I make the rounds of social media, listlessly scrolling through Facebook on my laptop, mug of builder's tea in hand.

You have 1 Message Request
Louisa Henry

Oh, no. Lou, as in Robin? I click to open it. We're not friends on Facebook and if I want, I can read the mail from Lou without her being alerted I've done so. I dither for a moment about being magnificently icy and doing this and then think: no. I want her to know I've seen it. Let her wonder how it went across.

Hi Georgina. Um so – major awks at this end for what happened and soz if you were upset. Robin told me you & him were easy going about spending time with other people and I've never known R to be straightforward about anything!

Part of his charm I guess 😊

Unsure where you guys stand now but totally happy to schedule around / give you some space to breathe, I'm back to London anyway.

I think you bring some really good vibes into Robin's life and it would be a shame to lose youse twos magic over a misunderstanding. Peace out.

Lulu xxxx

I reread it three times. 'Lulu' is as estranged from reality as Robin is, then. A dose of traditional old shame is too much to ask for. 'Major awks' is as far as it goes.

I also concede she's enough of a space cadet that when she said 'love' in the throes of passion she could've meant love with the force of when the butcher says 'Will that be all, love?'

Good vibes. Youse twos magic. Loon. I thought it was sweet looniness but this is sour. On a fourth read, I notice there's no suggestion she'd stop shagging Robin either, 'schedule around'.

Unless what I consider an ordinary relationship isn't ordinary? It's just boringly outdated conventional, as Robin said? Is this the New Normal, fidelity isn't what it was and this is as if she merely pranged my car, rather than TWOKKED and totalled it.

Oh hi yeah sorry you caught us in the act of frenetic penetration, my bad, here's some Lindor chocolate truffle balls and a fairtrade bottle of rosé.

I know Clem said not to blame myself, but I find it impossible. I mean, how did I miss that this was Robin, and these were his people? I convinced myself something was something it was not. I've been here before . . .

I think of my family's exasperation with me, and think, I am exasperated myself.

I type a sarcastic thanks-but-no-thanks-he's-all-yours reply to Lou, and delete it, because there's nothing left to say that I want sitting there on permanent record. That I want repeated, in incredulous tone, as Lou reads it from her phone screen in her Mockney accent, spidery legs in novelty hosiery sprawled across the crimson couch.

After which, Robin shakes his head, lets out a hiss of feigned embarrassment and says: *'I didn't realise Georgina and I were on such different pages. I told her I didn't believe in the two point four thing but I suppose people hear what they want to hear. Shame; she was a nice girl, a good laugh. Needs to find herself a local lad who wants arguments in IKEA and lights-off missionary.'*

Anyway, anger, even the controlled, wounding sort, would make it sound like I care. The trouble is, I don't. I used to at least briefly convince myself I'd fallen in love with my poor choices of men, now look at me.

Lucas's face swims into my mind's eye. Amid the agonies of thinking about him, there's a strange joy too. I am no one to him now. I was possibly no one to him then, but he made me feel things that no one has, before or since. However futile it turned out to be, I like remembering his touch, the things he said, the way he made me want to be the best version of myself. Unbeknownst to me, I was a treasure trove of interesting things, once someone turned up to be interested in them.

Lucas looked at me with – this is going to sound ridiculous and vain, but it's the only word I can find – wonder. I contrast that with the blank look at the wake, and give a watery sigh.

I decide to wallow in some That's Amore! takedowns and head over to TripAdvisor. A light dings on: I could write one. I'm no longer staff, why not?

I create a profile. I consider the crazy chutzpah of being 'Georgina, Sheffield' and then consider not only is it foolish to shine Tony on like that, it could also mean it's reported as malicious. I decide instead to be Greg Withers from Stockport. I have no idea why.

I need to give it the texture of a genuine complaint. I cast my mind back to some of That's Amore!'s Greatest Hits. How about a compilation? All things I recall actually happening during my shifts, which seems fair cop.

THE WORST RESTAURANT I HAVE EVER BEEN T

I feel like, in heated emotion, Greg neglected to notice the character limit. Damn, I am actually really enjoying this.

One star
Hard to know where to start frankly! It was my wife and I's wedding anniversary and she said she didn't want too much fuss. Well, if nothing else I can say That's Amore! delivered on the lack of fuss front.

We were given plastic menus with globs of food on them. You'd have thought it wasn't beyond the wit of man to give them a wipe down. And a squirt of anti bac, for that matter. The dining room has seen better days and they must've been around 1972.

When I asked precisely which invertebrates were involved in my wife's repulsive fritto misto starter I got the answer 'just the chef, Tony' which I think we can all agree is highly worrying. My minestrone was obviously from a tin and served with 'the house style of garlic bread.' The house really should try a different style, an edible one.

We moved on to a seafood risotto, which had crabsticks in it. When I queried the authenticity of crab sticks I was told by the young gentleman serving that 'Everyone Italian eats crab sticks' and when I asked: 'Where have you seen Italians eating them?' my waiter said, 'Walkley.'

By the time we were offered dessert I'd quite frankly had a gutful of their ridiculous carry on but my wife's heart was set on tiramisu and I didn't get to my thirtieth anniversary without appreciating the maxim 'happy wife, happy life'.

Well. If I had to use one word to describe the concoction that greeted her, that word would be 'monstrosity'. A soggy heap of sponge fingers doused in off brand Captain Morgan and tinned custard, covered in a thick layer of – wait for it – instant coffee granules. INSTANT COFFEE GRANULES. I ask you. My eighty-three-year-old mother-in-law, in her twilight confusion, has served us fizzy prawns and bless her soul I honestly think I'd rather try my luck with her cooking than ever return to this abominable dive.

To: newsdesk@sheffieldstar.com
From: GogPool@gmail.com

Hi,
Just wondered if you'd noticed this place has an 88% 'Terrible' rating on TripAdvisor? Is it the worst restaurant in the city?

*Someone should write it up! I don't know if your critic has
been.*

Best,
Another Unsatisfied Customer

13

I remember once asking: 'Am I in a very very slow motion tailspin?' to Esther, after my quitting the Kilner jar hipster hellmouth, and her saying: *You're more like a Roomba, Gog – bumping into walls, pinging back and carrying on.*

I think she and Mum ceased trying to understand me when I announced that university wasn't for me, and in my vehemence, made it clear this was not for discussion. They suspected Dad's death had caused a confidence prolapse, of course, but I built a wall around that conversation and put armed guards on the perimeter.

We went out for a French meal for my thirtieth birthday and the air of concern and disappointment over the rillettes and boeuf bourguignon was tangible. My rootless, direction-less twenties were up, and none of us could pretend this wasn't me any more.

I'm not the greatest at facing things. I'm certainly not the kind of constructive-minded, pragmatic person to think: *Oh I'm psychically disintegrating like wet bog roll draped round a tree for a student prank, I should see a counsellor. Let's investigate what the accredited options are within a two-mile radius and book an appointment.* And then turn up for it.

That's not how I ended up in Fay's office.

Eight years after what a consultant called my dad's 'sudden and terminal cardiac event causing severe neurological insult' ('His heart went bang and so his brain cut out?' 'Yes, pretty much'), I was telling my then-new friend Rav about him.

The night we met, Rav wore a slim-fit, acid green shirt that looked wonderful against dark espresso brown skin, and had a slender face and beady eyes like a watchful bird. I found Clem's all-back-to-mine soirees a bit too full of poseurs at the time, but I knew fairly quickly that Rav – they met when he was another dandy-ish customer at Clem's boutique – was a keeper. He's flip and humorous and light and then he'll slide in some articulate, devastating insight that you find yourself turning over when you're lying in bed trying to sleep at night.

At the time, I was working at a nightclub called Rogues where I got pawed at by drunks and I had painkiller injections in my feet so I could stand for hours in four-inch heels. That might be my worst job to date, and it's up against stiff competition.

Without intending to, I mentioned in passing how I still dream about my dad every night. (Georgina Horspool in full party mode.)

'Every night?' Rav said, hunched forward on the saffron-velvet sofa at Clem's, effortfully making himself heard over Goldfrapp. '*Every* one?'

I belatedly remembered I was talking to a professional shrink.

'Well, a lot,' I said. 'I don't keep a notepad by the bed and keep a tally. Dad, dad, dad. Naked, late for a bus, my teeth rotted away. Caught stealing a leg of lamb from Morrisons. While naked. Dad again.'

'You could benefit from counselling. However, if I hear "naked *with* my dad" next you move into a much more expensive client category, be warned.'

I laughed. Rav always takes risks like this yet they're finely calculated. I love this about him. You'd think with his expertise he'd be super-cautious and worthy but it's the opposite. He goes there. But he packs the right shoes.

I explained the contradiction that although Dad was always in my thoughts (another posthumous platitude that had come to life for me, if that's not the wrong term), I couldn't bring myself to visit the grave.

As I spoke, Rav's forehead became ever more creased until he said: *OK I'm not treating you because it's not ethical and it'd make you feel awkward, but you're going to see my colleague, Fay, and I'm going to book you in.* Rav was obviously very good at his speciality: he'd sussed otherwise I'd take her details and never do anything about it.

'I'm not sure I want to wank on about myself. What do my problems matter? Plenty of people have lost a parent,' I said, as Rav keyed my number into his phone.

'Don't be so bloody British,' he said. 'This country. We'd rather quietly kill ourselves over something than be any bother. Not that I'm suggesting you're suicidal.'

I went to Fay for a year and she helped a lot. Enough that I lay flowers at Dad's headstone now on his birthday. I have a quiet chat with him – if there's no one around in hearing range – and pat the cold curve of the laser-engraved graphite. I gaze at those implacable start and finish dates, that I wish I'd been warned about.

It'd be very useful if everyone in your life could supply those. You could pace yourself.

Death is on my mind still, a week after Danny's wake. And I have nothing to do until Devlin does or doesn't call me (yes I could be proactive and start putting irons in fires elsewhere, but then I'd not be a Roomba), plus the aftershock slump of seeing Lucas McCarthy, and Lucas McCarthy not seeing me, has plunged me into a mule-ish funk.

So I buy a bunch of £4.99 gaudy lilies the colour of Turkish Delight from the supermarket ('To moulder on a plot of land a mile away? You are odd. That's the price of two pints you're wasting. Just swipe some from an accident blackspot,' – Make Believe Dad) and walk to Tinsley Park cemetery. It's well populated, if that's the word, and I have to wander quite a way to find Dad.

I like moody old headstones covered in emerald lichen, with dates from the 1800s and families taken by the scurvy. Modern, gleaming ones make me nervous.

When I reach JOHN HORSPOOL, the monument to the fact it actually happened, I feel the puckering of stomach.

I ponder the hypocrisy of the words engraved on his stone: Beloved Husband, Father And Brother. Two out of the three aren't true.

After the funeral, Uncle Peter couldn't have returned to Spain any faster if he'd used Floo Powder. I could hear Dad making some sarcastic aside about how he was a man who lit up a room by leaving it.

His put-downs about the dourness of ex-pat Uncle Pete – 'He's as welcome as finding cat shit in your house, when you don't own a cat' – always made me shake with laughter. Then as soon as the thought occurred, it was followed by the realisation that I'd never hear his voice or his opinion on anything ever again. Make believe was all I had left forever. Pastiche, weak riffs based on nostalgia, a pale imitation. I was so bereft, it nearly made my knees buckle.

I said to Clem, two years after he was gone, it didn't feel real. I was constantly waiting for it to fully dawn on me, for the other shoe to drop. She lost her dad when she was fourteen. We'd met in a McDonalds at 1 a.m. when she was being hassled by a dubious man and Jo and I had intervened and invited her back in our taxi. We ended up eating quarter pounders at mine and having more drink we definitely didn't need.

Clem said: 'I don't know what to tell you, George. It never feels real or finally sinks in. That moment never arrives. The world continues, but with a bit always missing. And meanwhile you're getting on with it, until it's found.'

This makes sense. Everything feels temporary now. Because it always was, I just didn't know it.

I clear my throat, glance around: 'Hi, Dad.'

'That's us up to date then,' I mutter, feeling foolish, despite my evident solitude in the flat landscape, headstones like rows of dominoes into the horizon. I look up, as if a drone might be hovering nearby, picking up any of my banalities.

I mentioned, in low tone, meeting Lucas, how he was someone back in the day I'd hoped to introduce to him. And the departure of Robin. I try to picture whether Robin would've been received any better by Dad than he was by Esther and Mum. My gut says: Dad would've tried harder, seeing what I was aiming for, but come to the conclusion that I'd missed.

My fingers have gone numb, still holding the crush of cellophane from the now-unwrapped flowers, and I shove them alternately in my pockets. Make Believe Dad: *Why are you in that thing the colour of dentist's mouthwash? It looks like you murdered a Muppet.*

'See you when you don't turn sixty-five, I guess. I've discussed it with Esther and we're going to bring Milo to that one. So no blue language or downing Rusty Nails.' His Christmas tipple. Another sharp blade in the stomach. I lurch forward to prop the flowers against his stone, wave with one hand and give a weak smile.

Mum won't visit the grave. Esther and I have our theories about her reluctance.

I'm stumping towards the exit when, unbidden, a thought rears up and confronts me.

It's like Oscar the Grouch hidden in the garbage can, flopping two tufted green paws over the edge and shooting up, beetling browed and googly eyed: *It's been a week, you can stop waiting for Devlin to ring you now. You IDIOT.*

I pause, stare across the field of gravestones as if they literally contain this unwelcome truth in their earthy depths, then slam onwards.

Rejection on this occasion was always going to cause existential feelings. Yet something makes me sad, aside from the fact that Lucas McCarthy didn't remember me and/or intervened to block my path, and suggested I was best fitted to serve sticky ribs and wings while wearing a vest and orange shorts.

When I examine my disappointment, I discover it's that I really, genuinely liked Devlin, and hopefully vice versa. It's not often that happens these days, I realise. And not calling someone when you've told them you will call them is shabby. Let me down, but do it in a way that lets me still like you.

He could at least send a cursory text pretending he and his brother had crossed wires; hired two people and the other was a one-legged war hero, or something. You know, spare my blushes. If nothing else, this sort of white lying makes it loads easier if you see each other round town. Take it from someone who's had and left a thousand casual jobs round these parts.

Unless he was so lashed he forgot entirely? No. In the unlikely event of that scenario, Lucas would've raised it.

He didn't know I was from his past, and he didn't want to know me in the present. Or, he did know it was me, and feigned not knowing me, and then got rid.

I turn back onto the road and think about Lucas. A night in the park when dusk had fallen and I was upset for being chewed out about something or other at home. He said, with a hand on my face: 'I love you, you know. You have me.' I think it was easier to say it when I was a vulnerable mess. In a moment, it went from a hideous day, to my best ever.

I remember saying, 'I love you too', for the first time, and: 'You have me.' He truly did. I was consumed by him. He was everything: the greatest secret, lust object, soulmate and ally. That cliché about how there's no potency like the first one, that's true isn't it?

Did I have him, even fleetingly? Only my diary stands as proof, yet I can't bear to look at it. It lives at the bottom of my bra drawer, always close and yet forever untouched.

Then, as the first drops of rain start to mizzle downwards, my phone rings with an unknown number. My heart stutters.

'Hello, is that Georgina? This is Devlin. I'm the short-arsed bog trotter you got legless last week.'

I'm silent for a second in delight and surprise, before recovering:

'Hello, yes it is! You didn't need much help doing that, to be fair. I robbed you, if that's what I was paid for.'

Devlin chortles.

I add: 'And thanks for the extra too, very kind.'

'Not at all, you earned it, it felt like you were one of the guests, which to me is the ultimate in service.'

Devlin can't see it, but I'm beaming.

'I was wondering if you're still available for the full-time job we discussed? Sorry for the delay getting back to you. I had to, uh, bottom some things first.'

I take that to mean wrestling his brother into submission. I'm hugely grateful. And also utterly terrified. Congratulations: your prize is, being a subordinate to a hostile Lucas McCarthy.

I'm delighted he didn't object sufficiently to stop this though. Tiny victories.

'Feel free to say no at this notice, but would you be free to pop in later tonight? Say six-thirty p.m.? I'll show you around the tills and you can get your bearings so it's not brand new to you if you get a rush on the first day.'

I look at my watch. An hour and a half's time. Best make myself halfway presentable.

'No problem.'

'You're a gem. Sorry, you know how it is. My diary's suddenly gone fuckin' attention deficit disorder crazy and there's a million things to do.'

'Honestly, I wasn't busy. See you then.'

'If no one answers when you knock we might be out the back, let yourself in, the door's unlocked.'

We. This is happening. He is back in my life.

As I'm about to leave the house, I pause: should I wear my pink fur? My hackles rise: why not? Because Lucas McCarthy suggested I was a bimbo? My coat, my choice. My bravado is a veneer. I'm as much a combination of outward bolshieness and inward terror of inadequacy as I was when I was an adolescent.

As I skip home, my phone starts buzzing again in my bag and I flip the flap on it and fumble around, pulling out a mascara in the process, which means it peals for ages. I'm frantic by the time I finally unearth it: what if it's Dev calling back to rescind his offer?

I see onscreen: Rav.

'Hi!'

'Ey up. You busy?'

'Not as such.'

'Just wondering, did you contact the paper about the Italian place you worked? The TripAdvisor flamings thing? You said you were going to but you were pished at the time.'

I'd told them that? I didn't know I'd told myself that. My memory blackouts from grog are getting worse. It's like there's a whole deleted scenes reel these days.

'Yeah I did . . . ?'

'Well, they used it.'

'They did? Great!'

'Well, there's good news and there's bad news. Alright, more honestly: it's bad from here on in.'

'They didn't mention me?'

'No? Why would they do that, did you name yourself to them?'

'Oh. No,' I say, feeling daft. 'Only as I sent the tip.'

Someone – not Mr Keith, but Ant Something – at the *Star* replied to my email about That's Amore! with a dashed off, 'typed with one hand while the other was clamped round half a Pret egg and cress baguette' effort: *thanks will look into it.*

I thought it was curt not to address me by my name and then remembered I was only Gogpool. I didn't imagine anything would come of it as there was no further question about who I was, why I was Another Unsatisfied Customer. Ah, well, I'd thought. Worth a punt.

'. . . You know they say that revenge is a dish best served cold? *The Star* has served it like That's Amore! Nothing like what you ordered,' Rav says.

'What do you mean?'

'Where are you now?'

'At the . . . nearly home.' I turn into my road.

'Go buy a copy. It's not online yet. I only saw it because someone at work was talking about it. Guess what, she knew someone who reckoned they'd had salmonella from there.'

'You're freaking me out here with the tension and the mystery.'

'Ah no sorry I don't mean to, it's funny really. Get a cuppa and relax into it, it's proper satire.'

I do as I'm told, buy a copy of *The Star* from the news-agents on the corner then home. I'm at a loss to imagine how they've fumbled the scoop of That's Amore! being the worst dining experience since Sweeney Todd started an artisan pop up to rival Pork Farms.

I lay out the paper and flip through the pages until I find it: they keep sticking together in an agonising way, and now I'm agog. Gog is agog. What on earth did Rav mean?!

Here it is – a double spread. Tony is posing, and beaming, outside the frontage, plates of pasta with puddles of sauce balanced on either hand. He appears to have acquired a puffy white chef's hat from a fancy dress shop, or Dolmio advert.

That's Amore! – Sheffield's worst restaurant according to TripAdvisor – says to the haters . . .

SHADDAP YOU FACE!

Wait, what? They're painting the act of serving seriously below par cuisine as an act of sticking it to The Man?!

I read on, and yes, yes they are. That's Amore! – as the number of obliging portraits of Tony stirring pans while making a finger and thumb pressed together sign, or Callum grinning over his shoulder while writing the specials on the chalkboard, attest – has played PR ball. They've success-fully spun this into a 'plucky little engine that could' type of tale, full of self-deprecating humour.

Fuck's, and also sake.

Down the right-hand side of the page, there's a precis of the TripAdvisor lowlights, but they're heavily edited to take the laughs out. Greg Withers makes an appearance – hurray! – but they've cut it to a couple of sentences that a quick skim could bring you to believe he simply wanted more bells and whistles for a special occasion.

Goddammit.

I grind my teeth as I read:

Once upon a time, restaurant complaints were limited to asking to see the manager. In the online era, you're only a click away from broadcasting your displeasure to the world. TripAdvisor is a well-known forum for diners to rate the good, bad and the ugly in our culinary scene – and the users don't hold back about their experiences in the comments.

That's Amore! knows what it feels like to withstand the punters wrath: the Broomhill bistro has been given a savaging by amateur critics who scorned its 'inauthentic' dishes and 'shoddy' service, leaving it with a 88% 'terrible' rating – the worst in the city.

Nevertheless, business is booming, with the sixty-cover eatery booked out every weekend.

That's Amore! insist despite the poor score, they are fighting fit and more popular than ever – throwing into doubt how much influence sites like TripAdvisor really have on our eating out habits.

'At the end of the day, trolls on the internet will have their opinions,' That's Amore! head chef Tony Staines says. 'Being perfectly honest with you I think if you look at the locations on these moaners having a pop, they are all London types or out of towners who want fine dining, fancy frills and amuse bouches. Locally we're a big hit.'

What total shite!

'What we do here is serve good honest homely fresh-cooked fare from scratch, no fuss or showing off, and our regulars love it. These are old recipes from our owner's mother. So if they don't like our classics or say they're not authentic, argue with his Nonna – she lives in Turin!'

MHAIRI McFARLANE

'She lives in fucking Bridlington!' I snort.

The piece swerves into a generalised discussion of the benefits and drawbacks of TripAdvisor as guidance service, so no one's given the chance to answer Tony back. 'Greg Withers' would've been a very chatty respondent, if he could've used email (or if I'd persuaded Rav to moonlight).

Oh man, this is so unfair. Has it not occurred to the reporter that That's Amore! might have terrible feedback because it's terrible? Has he heard of Occam's Razor? Has he tried any of its food? This is basically a big free advertisement for That's Amore! That I prompted. There's no doubt about this, the byline is an 'Ant Haddon.'

That's Amore!, 1, Georgina, 0.

'Good honest fresh-cooked fare', my arse. I've seen Tony up-end a box of Quality Street, take the wrappers off, have a go at bevelling them with a cheese paring knife, pile them in a pyramid on a saucer, stick a dusting of drinking chocolate powder over the top, and tell me to tell the customer they're our in-house handmade chocolates. *Fawlty Towers* 'Gourmet Night' without the slick presentation.

I ring Rav.

'Why do the bad guys always win, Rav? Always?!'

I'm half joking-exasperated, half genuinely upset. 'I mean, they do, don't they? That's Amore! survive anything! Even the critic visiting, thanks to sacking me. What do they have to do? Put polonium in the Pollo alla Cacciatore?'

'Haaaah. It's a bit much, right?' Rav hoots. 'I liked the part where he says everyone thinks they're shit because they're expecting L'Enclume and sea urchin sashimi. That, without a

135

doubt, is what's going wrong. People mincing up from Mayfair and not understanding what two mains for a tenner and half a carafe of rough red might entail.'

I start laughing. 'A That's Amore! tasting menu. Can't imagine what would be in a Tony foam.'

'I can.'

I wheeze helplessly.

'My efforts have filled That's Amore!'s tables for the next month. I mean, even if anyone goes there because of this and ends up agreeing with me, they've still had their money once. There is no God,' I say.

'Yeah, but we knew that. Listen, that's not actually why I was originally going to call you. We all feel a bit bad for ragging on Robin the other night.'

I cackle. 'Oh, Rav, I love you, but if Clem feels bad about that, I am Mr Greg Withers from Stockport.'

'Alright, admittedly, Jo and I told Clem she should feel bad about ragging on Robin.'

'And did she agree?'

'She said: "Why are you defending that conceited jeb-end court jester who treated George like dirt?" which I think you'll agree has a strong subtext of wishing her repentance to be known.'

I laugh some more.

'Look, either way, Jo and I will be getting her to split the bill three ways with us when we take you out – you free tonight?'

'Ooh, where? I have something to do at six-thirty but I don't think it'll be long.'

'Where do you think?'

'. . . Curry?!'

'Ta dah! . . . Or. That's Amore?'

'Oh, God! I can't imagine what Tony would do to my food.'

'. . . I can.'

'Blee!' I pause. 'There's no such thing as karma, is there, Rav? No one gets what they deserve.'

'There's a long answer to that and a shorter one and given you're not paying me for this in a counselling session, I will give you the short one.'

'Which is?'

'Nope, there's no such thing as karma and people don't get what they deserve. It's a comforting myth to reconcile us to the savage randomness of the universe and wrongs inflicted upon us.'

'Argh! Is the longer answer more uplifting?'

'Yes that's why it costs you.'

I laugh, ring off and inhale tart October air. I don't know why I'd still cling to the notion that karma exists, given I've never seen it in action in my thirty years. I should've let it go at the same time as the Tooth Fairy.

14

As warned, there is no answer at the pub when I arrive on the dot of 6.30 that evening. I breathe out dragon-smoke in the cold. Three hammerings of my fist against the door and no response. I try the handle and step inside, saying, 'Hello?'

The room is in complete darkness.

'Hello?' I call again, tentatively. 'Anyone there?'

It's quite spooky with no illumination at all. The pubs I've worked in have always kept those sconces on, even once the overhead is off. The only reason I'm not tripping over the furniture in the gloaming is the street lamps outside the windows.

A bulb switches on in a space beyond the main bar. A figure is silhouetted in the doorway to the saloon. As he steps forward, he throws more lights on.

He's in a black shirt covered with dust and stands looking at me, a giant hoop of gaoler's keys in one hand. I'm eighteen years old again, and Lucas McCarthy is staring across a room, eyes penetrating, expression unreadable.

For a moment, I can't remember any standard British words of greeting.

'Can I help you?' Lucas says, eventually. 'We're closed.'

Uh yeah I sussed that. I wasn't about to say half of mild, thanks and can I borrow a torch.

'Dev—' I cough, nerves a-jangle, clear my throat again. 'Devlin told me to come in, he wanted to show me around.'

'Ah, right. Dev's gone to the shops, he'll be back in a minute.'

'Ah. OK.'

A strained pause as we each wait for the other to say something.

I feel like Devlin's bottoming, as it were, of my being here, isn't as bottomed as I might've hoped. It might even be entirely unbottomed.

I stand around uselessly, until Lucas says:

'Sit down if you want. Would you like a drink? Nothing's working on tap yet but we have stock. A Coke? It's not chilled I'm afraid.'

Much like me haha.

I nod and mutter thank you and drop heavily into the nearest chair, feel the now-intensified layer of stuffy heat trapped between my skin and clothes, my nerves buzzing like faulty electrics.

Are we going to have to make conversation? For how long? Why did I say yes to this, why didn't I tell Devlin something had come up in the meantime? Why would I want Lucas McCarthy to be my boss, does life not contain enough humili-ation? There's an answer to this question, hovering just outside of my consciousness.

Lucas has temporarily ducked out of sight and I glance around.

I hear funny rapid heavy breathing panting behind me and the clatter of toenails on timber and suddenly, at my table, looking up expectantly, is the world's most appealing, low-bellied dog. I recognise it from the wake. Its hind quarters are so hefty, when it's sat down, it's like it's squatting in a puddle of a russet-coloured fur. It has kind eyes and an eager expression. The sort of dog whose face conveys HELLO I AM DOG WHO ARE YOU I LOVE YOU.

I couldn't be more pleased at the unscheduled canine intrusion. I am a friend to any animal at the best of times, and this isn't the best of times.

The dog slaps its paw into my lap, and I lift and shake it.

'Hello! Very nice to meet you! Who are you?'

It has such a friendly face it honestly looks like it's grinning at me, and I laugh.

Lucas reappears, with the swish and clink of ice in a metal bucket as he sets it on the bar.

'Should've said there's a dog. This is Keith. No allergies or anything?'

'Hello, *Keith!*' I cry. 'Aren't you lovely? Is he yours?'

'Yep.'

Petting Keith is a very welcome displacement activity.

'Keith,' I say, as Lucas puts my Coke in front of me. 'Unusual name for a dog. Funny coincidence, the incognito restaurant critic for *The Star* books tables as Mr Keith.'

I was going to carry on and explain it's a coincidence because I'd recently met him in my last place of work, but it's such a stupid conversational gambit, I pause, midway.

Lucas looks at me as if I might be simple and says: 'Not that funny a coincidence, unless you're implying anything? I'm fairly certain this Keith isn't a secret restaurant critic.'

'Hahah, no, I just meant . . .'

I trail off, as I didn't mean anything.

'Keith's reviews would give top marks for baked bean juice on a J-cloth. He's an eager diner but not too discerning.'

I give a strained laugh, unsure if I'm partly the butt of the joke.

These are as many words in a row as I've heard Lucas speak so far. He sounds more posh-Irish than Devlin, his accent less broad. The thuddingly obvious thought lands – he's a total stranger. Just because you kissed someone twelve years ago, that doesn't mean you know them now. He was a stranger back then, come to think of it.

Lucas leans down and rubs the dog's head. I'm grateful for the loss of eye contact and sip my drink. Lucas isn't going to join me, it seems, still standing.

'Did Dev ask you to come in for any reason in particular?'

Argh. Unbottomed, I sodding knew it.

'He's offered me a job?'

'Oh. Right.'

'I worked the wake, last week. We met?'

'Oh, God, sorry, did we? Very busy evening.'

Great. Having to introduce myself to Lucas for the second time. Well, third, overall.

'I'm Georgina,' I say, pointing back to pink fluff, chafing at the weirdness of him not knowing this. Or claiming not to.

'Luke. Or Lucas. Whichever you prefer.'

'So it's Luc, spelled L-U-C. Like, er, Jean Luc Godard.'

Oh, shut up, Georgina . . .

'. . . I'm not French.'

The front door swings open and Devlin appears, dragging and half-rolling a barrel inside. I could swear both Lucas and I heave near-audible sighs of relief.

'You're here! You two getting to know each other?' Devlin says.

'We've established I'm not a film director and my dog is not a restaurant critic,' Lucas says, mild, but bone dry.

'We're ready to open now, got the tills working. Still a fan of the place?' Devlin says, throwing his arms wide, and causing the barrel to wobble, and he quickly rights it.

'I think, in all sincerity, it's bloody incredible,' I say. 'I remember what it was like before and you've worked wonders.'

'See, Luke!'

Devlin pulls a Bruce Forsyth-style triumphal pose, fist to forehead.

'Do you not like it?' I say to Lucas.

'I like it, I think he overspent,' Lucas says, with his less excitable demeanour.

'Pffft.' Devlin pulls up a chair and says, 'I'll take you through things in a sec, Georgina. It'll be you, me, Luke for the time being. I might have to set more on when the function room gets going.'

'Is there one?'

'Yeah, nice size, actually.' Devlin whisks a piece of paper from the bar and puts it under my nose. 'Trying to make its events quite varied, you know. Emphasise The Wicker isn't your spit and sawdust place anymore. Kicking off with this, look . . . Local paper called, looking for a place to host it for free.'

I read:

SHARE YOUR SHAME
Writing Competition / Open Mike Night
Are you a writer who could use a platform?
Read out a short piece on a weekly topic, loosely
based around the theme of shame, embarrassment
and general cringe. A burden shared is a burden
halved, they say. Judges will choose the best of three
events and winner gets a column in The Star.
First theme announced next Friday!
First show the Saturday after Halloween!

'Open mike,' Lucas shudders. 'It'll be slam poetry and men in black polo necks doing experimental comedy with no jokes. Mental New Agers asking you to try to touch your third eye.'

He's feistier than I remember.

'No one's expecting *you* to get involved. Do you know any writers?' Devlin says to me. 'Are *you* a writer?'

This is a kind thing to say to a woman in garish faux fur who's paid to pull pints of Stella, and I want to honour that.

'Erm not really . . . I mean . . . I'd like to write, actually, but I don't think that makes me one.'

The grin that transforms Devlin's face is one you can't help but smile back at. 'You'd be ideal! It's for new starters! You can have time to do it during work and everything. Can't she, Luke? We'll easily cover for half an hour. Encourage our staff to get their faces known, help us launch ourselves into the community.'

I laugh, nervously. Not only write, but perform it?

And I'd thought Lucas McCarthy would be above the customer facing stuff. He would spend his time striding around in Belstaff coats, with a pack of fox hounds at his heels, carrying an oil lantern.

Devlin turns back to me.

'I'll give people trial shifts but I won't set anyone on permanently unless you feel you work well with them. I think good chemistry is vital. You have power of yay or nay.'

Devlin's head jerks up and his eyes narrow and I know without a doubt, over my shoulder and behind my back, Lucas made an: OH THE IRONY face at him.

'Come on, Keith,' Lucas says. 'You alright to see Georgina out?' to his brother. 'See you Monday,' to me, and I nod.

This is more gracious than I expected. I sense the McCarthy brothers, despite the casual manner and attire, have quite considered manners.

'You'll get used to that surly wretch,' Dev says, after Lucas has rounded the bar and a door has closed.

'Do you both live above the pub?' I say, to distract, as my getting used to the surly wretch is something I need to process when I am alone.

'No that's a one-bed flat, Luc is up there and I've rented round the corner.'

So Lucas is the one who'll be on site, most of the time.

'What sort of things do you think you'll write about?' Devlin says, nodding back up towards the poster. 'Shameful things is the brief? I'd be buggered as I've never done anything shameful in my life.' He grins.

I gulp.

'Yeah, same.'

15

If you grow up with parents who are unhappy with each other, you accept it and work around it. You no more directly address or it or expect it to change than if your family home has low ceilings, or you live in a cul-de-sac. You unquestioningly accept your lot. The only time it spooked me was when I'd visit a friend and their mum and dad could amicably disagree without venom, or decibels. *That's possible*, I thought?

When I was small, I used to accompany Dad on his Saturday outings, no matter how mundane: DIY stores, the tip, over to his friend Graham's, dragging round vinyl shops looking for jazz records, watching the football, to collect the fish supper from the chippy. I was never bored, I actively volunteered for service — Esther was invited at first, but made it clear it held no charm for her, compared to doing her own thing.

I used to love staring out the car window, hopping along holding Dad's hand, legs dangling from chairs I was too short for.

A huge amount of fuss was made of me by cashiers and shop assistants. I was never a girly little girl, I liked trousers and sweatshirts with superheroes on them, and somehow that provoked even more cooing.

I can't remember how the tradition began, but every so often, Dad finished whatever the task in hand was and said: 'Where to, captain?'

This meant a treat. And it could be, within city limits and budget, anything I wanted. It was unspeakably thrilling. Imagine, as a kid, being put in charge for an afternoon.

'Chocolate pudding . . . in a glass?'

We went to a department store café, and I had a tower of aerated mousse pierced with a wafer shaped like a fan, while Dad sipped a cup of tea.

'An adventure, with flying.'

The local multiplex, *Batman*, and a bag of Revels.

'Ice skating.'

I did endless unsteady circuits of the rink, hired boots laced so tight they were cutting welts into my feet, while Dad read his paper.

There was an uncomfortable adjustment period when I became too old for our Saturdays. Dad jangling his keys in the hallway, having to shout over blaring music: 'You coming or what, Georgina?'

Mum snapping: 'Of course she's not bloody going to a farm shop with you, John.'

After the uncertain interlude where I felt too old for it, but too young to abandon it, we adapted: I went into town to shop, and when we were both done with our errands, we met for lattes and macchiatos and wedges of gaudily iced sponge cake.

One wet-to-the-bone winter, when I was fifteen, I had a different idea. Darkness had fallen by 5 p.m., Mum and Esther were still out shopping somewhere.

'Can we go for a curry?'

Mum despised spicy food and I'd never so much as had an Indian takeaway. Dad didn't miss a beat.

'It's Saturday. You're the captain.'

An adult saying yes to spontaneous fun: it felt so freeing. Mum always found five reasons to snap: 'Another time, maybe.' Dad understood me, and I understood him.

We went to a place on Glossop Road that's not there anymore. Dad perched his readers on his nose and authoritatively supervised a representative selection of famous dishes, rice, breads and some yoghurt to 'put out any flames'.

To this day, much as I can appreciate an upmarket Indian restaurant with lassi cocktails, colonial fans and stylish plating, what I really want is a neon sign, sitar music, flock wallpaper, sizzling Balti and hot lemon towels and tongs. It's my Proustian rush.

I knew as soon as I was prodding shards of poppadom into the mini lazy Susan with the sugary mango chutney and tangy lime pickle that I was going to be a fanatic.

'But you hardly ever have this food?' I said to Dad, through forkfuls of chicken tikka masala, after he'd expounded on the joys of moving on to more interesting dishes once I'd served my apprenticeship.

'Your mum doesn't like it.'

'Don't you miss it?'

Dad smiled. 'Marriage is compromise. You'll understand some day.'

'I'm not marrying anyone who doesn't like curry. No way.'

Mum usually tolerated our outings as a positive thing, but I remember that night we got back and she needed scraping off the ceiling.

Dad hadn't warned her, cauliflower cheese had gone to waste, our clothes 'reeked' and would need washing, why wasn't Esther invited, why couldn't we do a family dinner, how much had that cost. At first I tried placating her but when that failed, I slid off upstairs and left them to it.

Esther was back from her first term at York, where from what I could tell she'd spent her time mixing with posher people and feeling ashamed of us. She came flying out of her bedroom and into mine.

'Why do you do this?'

'Do what?'

'Stir things up between Mum and Dad? You knew she'd have a fit if you went out for dinner and you know you have Dad round your little finger and he'll do it. Then you waltz off and leave them to a screaming match.'

'I didn't know Mum didn't know.'

'How was she going to find out if you didn't tell her? Dad never uses that phone he has. He doesn't even switch it on.'

Esther had a point. If I'm honest, I *did* know Mum didn't know. I knew she'd just say no, that's why I didn't tell her. But you don't admit to anyone already that angry with you that you know they have a point, or you might as well lie down, like antelope with lion, and invite them to gnaw your carotid vein.

It was in the unwritten rules of our dysfunctional unit: Dad vs Mum could always go nuclear and it was our role to act as go-betweens, to soothe and smooth.

'Why was it on me to tell Mum, anyway?' I said. Only because it was the only defence left open to me, I'd not really thought about it. Later, with Fay's help, I would think about it.

Esther furiously jabbed a finger downwards, in the direction of the heated voices. 'THAT'S WHY.

'. . . I've had to spend my evening eating minging cold cauliflower cheese with Mum's blood pressure going through the roof while you're off having fun and now the atmosphere in this house is even WORSE. Fuck you, Georgina, you're so fucking selfish.'

She slammed out and I lay on my bed listening to the bickering voices below. Mum's voice carried up through the bedroom floorboards.

'She's not your plaything, to entertain you. She should be out with people her own age.'

'I'm glad Georgina still wants to do things together. She won't be here forever, will she?'

'If you want a curry, you could go with Graham or some other friend?'

'She suggested it!'

'To please *you*. She's only trying to please you and you're selfish enough to let her.'

This was untrue, but years ago I'd learned that when

Mum weaponised me against Dad, it went very badly if I contradicted her. Dad and I, the selfish ones. Mum and Esther had decreed it.

I realise with hindsight that even before Mum weighed in, there was a melancholy to the Glossop Road expedition. We were both nervous, Dad and I, about the day I would leave home, looming on horizon. We were pre-sad.

Not only as we'd miss each other; but because he was going to be alone with Mum. It was mine and my sister's responsibility to act as buffer zones and brake pads, and simply to be someone living in their house that they liked. And we were both abandoning our posts. Both Esther and I had wondered how they'd function. They'd each recruited an ally in their children – without us, it was endless civil war.

Then, as it turned out, in a surprise twist, due to three blocked arteries, it was Dad who left home.

Here's what life has taught me so far: don't worry about that thing you're worrying about. Chances are, it'll be obliterated by something you didn't anticipate that's a million times worse.

Anyway, the point is, I love curry.

Cauliflower cheese, I can take or leave.

I wait until the waiter has delivered four pints of Kingfisher, condensation sliding down the glasses, and we've lifted, clinked cheers and sipped, to say:

'Can I check, is my treat tonight invalid if I've got back with Robin?'

Rav does a comedy choke-spit on his lager, Jo sucks in

a shocked breath and Clem says: 'Your sanity is invalid if you've forgiven that rancid hound!'

I lower my eyes, Princess Diana style, and say: 'He's promised me he can change. He says he only slept with Lou because he was frightened by how much he felt for me. It was like a boobytrap in himself, a tripwire. He denies himself happiness with acts of . . . of . . . desecration.'

'Is this real, because if so I'm going to be sick,' Clem says flatly.

'I want to help him be a better person,' I conclude, looking round a trio of nauseated faces.

'Why would you do that?' Clem says. 'Why not pick an achievable goal?'

'I believe he truly wants to change,' I say. I am enjoying the gag, though I didn't think I could convince them I'd be that stupid. Victory: pyrrhic.

'Yeah well. R Kelly believed he could fly.'

There's a pause, while they all eye me uneasily.

'Nice try, George,' Rav says. 'But you love curry way too much to risk ruining appetites in this way at the start of the meal.'

'Balls, you got me.'

I start gurgling with laughter and everyone tuts and scolds.

We're at Rajput in Crookes, which along with the Lescar, is undoubtedly a soother to my soul.

'Are we having poppadoms?' Rav asks and I say, 'YES definitely it's essential, I want all the bits,' and Clem pouts and says, 'They make you too full,' and we say, 'Er don't eat them then?' and she says, 'Well I'm going to have to if they're there, aren't I?'

Clem, tonight in white go-go boots and a minuscule pinafore dress from her boutique, is rigidly controlling of what she eats, to maintain rationing era measurements. To the point where she saw an advert about the signs of cancer that said 'Unexplained Weight Loss' and she said *Ooh I'd love me some of that* and we shouted at her.

Whenever anyone says to her: But you don't need to be on a diet, she replies, with the steely fanaticism of the truly devout, 'I don't need to be on a diet because I diet.'

I only wish Clem's neuroses weren't played out in front of Jo, who is a buxom 14–16, and loathes her figure. She wages war on her metabolism with awful dieters' dinners that look like something from *Woman's Own* in the Seventies – tinned beetroot with blobs of cottage cheese and pepper matchsticks. She has a body blueprint that will never be redrawn by cottage cheese, and the futile self-torture makes me sad. Needless to say, we all suspect her on-off obsession, Shagger Phil, has contributed to a sense of Not Being Enough. Or, being too much.

During our starters, Rav entertains us all with his latest tales of harrowing online dates.

'She said her tarot reader had told her a dark, stormy spirit would come into her life, then disappear, but soon return.'

'Her *tarot reader*?' I ask.

'Yeah she was a real "Luna Lovegood" type. I said I thought it sounded a lot more like she was going to vomit spiced rum, and made my excuses.'

As the mains arrive, Rav and I update Clem and Jo on That's Amore! and I read Greg Withers' comment in full.

'You're so good at things like this,' Jo says, as the laughter subsides.

I turn my phone off again and throw it into my bag. 'Thanks. Sadly you can't spend "thank you" clicks on TripAdvisor reviews. Greg's scored quite a few.'

'You say that,' Rav says, dipping a piece of roti in his dahl, 'but you're a funny writer, you've got a way with words, you're good at telling stories. And you've got lots of experience in the service industry. Maybe you could put the two together somehow.'

Wait . . . sharing shame?

'I suppose I'm quite good at telling other people's stories,' I rattle on, but my mind is whirring. 'Robin once said I had "comic impulses but lacked the discipline".'

'You see, what the hell does that mean?' Clem says, hoovering her lamb pasanda with impressive efficiency. She will carbon offset it tomorrow by living off Heinz cream of tomato, Diet Coke and menthol cigarettes. 'What discipline does he show?'

'He said I said I wanted to write, and talked like a writer, but never wrote. He had a point,' I said.

Nearby, a young couple beckon the waiter over. I sense the man, who can't be more than twenty-five, is trying to impress the date he's with, who has a huge mane of back-combed hair and a very tiny Lycra dress.

'We didn't ask for this? . . . Why bring it then? Make sure it's not on the bill, please.'

The waiter is being apologetic while the lad bristles with

righteous indignation. Ugh. I know the sort. Talking to you like a sultan with a serf.

'He's failing the Waiter Rule,' I say, under my breath.

'What's that?' says Jo.

'It's the theory that you should never trust anyone who's rude to the waiter,' I say. 'Or waitress.'

'The Waiter Rule,' Rav says. 'That's sound. I could've saved time using that test.'

'Had you not heard of it?' Three shaking heads.

'It's one of the great fundamental underpinning truths of life. It's like never dating anyone who's mean with money and dodges the tip or pulls the "oh no I've forgotten my wallet!" move. It's scientifically impossible for them to be a good person. You know all you need to know.'

'They could have forgotten their wallet?' says Jo, who is fair of mind and kind of heart. 'It happens sometimes.'

'They could. And if you'd forgotten your wallet, you'd make sure you paid the person back once you'd found it again, wouldn't you?' I say.

'Yes, of course.'

'Wallet forgetters, funnily enough, never, ever, do this.'

It occurs to me that despite the initial cringe of: 'But I've led too boring a life,' I really *might* have something here for the Share Your Shame writing competition.

'It's interesting when I'm counselling someone who's a terrible person,' Rav says. 'Or behaves terribly, I should say. Their rationale, when they acknowledge they're terrible, is generally that other people shouldn't let them get away with it. Almost like a child, you know, and other people, morally, are the responsible adults. "If they will leave the cookie jar with the lid off, and they know I'm a cookie liker, what's going to happen? Of course I ate the cookies." Very little ability to take responsibility.'

'What if you eat the cookie, and do take responsibility for it?' I say, tentatively. 'Are you a terrible person then?'

'Noooo . . .' Rav says. 'Though I suppose it depends on the size and nature of the cookie. And whether your cookie eating is habitual. And of course, who you want to absolve you for it.'

'I'm lost,' Clem says and I say, *Tell me about it.*

An hour later, the warming combination of curry-house-induced coma and foamy lager in my veins, gives me the confidence to take a risk when telling them about my new job at The Wicker.

'Hey, Jo. Kind of weird. One of the brothers who own it was someone we went to school with. Lucas McCarthy?'

Even saying the forbidden words gives me a shiver of transgression, makes me feel the very inflections I've used has given it away. It's as if those two words weigh more in the mouth.

Jo screws her face up.

'Lucas McCarthy?'

'Yeah, you know.' I break eye contact to dab at an imaginary spot of jalfrezi sauce in my lap with my napkin. 'In our English A-level classes?'

'Lucas, McCarthy . . .' Jo repeats. 'It's not ringing any bells.'

'Dark hair. Irish. I had to sit with him once. Mrs Pemberton made us swap places for a *Wuthering Heights* project and I was landed with him.' I've pushed every gambling chip I'm prepared to bet into the centre of the table now. Jo's on her own if these clues aren't enough.

'Oh I remember that!' Jo cries. 'I had to have that spoddy Sean sitting next to me.'

'Yeah.' I wait, hopefully.

Jo shakes her head. 'Don't remember a Lucas though. Did he remember you?'

I'm pleased to have an intro now. I don't want to stop talking about him. *Lord help me, I'm back on my bullshit.* 'It's a strange one, actually.'

I explain the ups and downs of Lucas not recognising me from school at the wake, then not recognising me from the wake when I was at the pub.

'. . . I've done *two* introductions now, when I could remember him from back in the day, all along. I must be exceptionally forgettable.'

I gabble and come to a sudden full stop, sure I've given myself away with the girlish tremble to my voice and heat in my face.

'You're not forgettable, you're like a darling cherub,' Jo says, stoutly and affectionately, and with that anachronistic turn of phrase she has. Jo's going to make someone the loveliest mother ever one day, but for now she can be my best friend.

Rav says, draining the last of his second lager: 'That can't be right, can it?'

My head snaps up. 'How do you mean?'

'If he argued against you being hired on the night of the wake, like you say, how did he then not know who you were, days later? That'd definitely land someone in your mind even if he didn't know you from school.'

'Uh. He'd objected . . . then forgot he'd objected?'

'Even if he'd forgotten, the sight of you would trigger the memory. He wasn't pissed at the wake?'

'I don't think so, no. He seemed fine. He accused his brother of being drunk, but he seemed in full possession of his senses.'

'A bit of styling things out and acting cool going on, with this lad, I think.'

Lucas was feigning not to know me? Twice? He's a magnificent actor, if so. I don't think this is right, at all, but it pleases me so much I play along to hear more.

'Why would Lucas pretend not to know me, though?' I ask.

'Duh, to impress you. To maintain the upper hand by acting indifferent. And why didn't he want you hired?'

'He said I was an unknown quantity and it wasn't Hooters and hiring blondes that caught his brother's eye.'

'Haaah, he thinks his brother might bang you,' Clem cackles.

'Oh no, Devlin's married and clearly devoted. I'm not just saying that. Dev's not got a hint of that about him and he was over with his wife every chance he got at the wake.'

'If he's complaining about you as temptation then, he must mean for himself,' Rav says.

My heart beats faster. This is all misbegotten and total fantasy, but so glorious to hear.

'I don't think he was saying I was tempting. More . . . superficial.'

'Well something had fired him up,' Clem says. 'You hardly put people through three interviews and a PowerPoint to get a bar job. His reasons were bull. Is Lucas hot?'

'Mmmhmmm?' I say, noncommittally, nodding and wrinkling my nose to indicate both yes and no and maybe.

'You're a sweet and innocent soul around the opposite sex, really, George. Jo, are you leaving that bit of chicken . . . ? Good-oh, heft it over.' Rav shakes his head at Clem and Jo and adds: 'This is how she ended up dating Robin McNee.'

I guffaw at this. 'Oh, come on. He was a mistake but my judgement about men's wiles is not that bad. Is it?'

'I didn't mean your judgement so much as you're modest. Not to be shallow, George, but it was obvious to bystanders that Robin was punching,' Rav says.

'Really?' I ask.

'Yeah. Together, you looked like Cinderella and an enchanted rat coachman.'

16

In the early hours of Sunday morning, I wake up with a startle from a nightmare. I'm in a brutish medieval village and the members of a baying crowd are taking it in turns to fire arrows at me.

The missiles pepper the board I've been tied to, zooming past my face with a *thwiiiiiiick*, planting their pointed ends perilously close to my flesh. The anticipation of being skewered any second makes me cry out.

As I come round, I realise the arrows were a figment but the noise is not. I raise myself on my elbows, waiting for it again. *DWACK*. It's something hitting my window. I struggle out of the bed covers and vault across the room. Opening the window and leaning out as far as I can go, I see a mop-headed man across the street, shading his eyes as if looking up at the sky in direct sun. Hang on, is that . . . ?

'Robin?' I call.

He looks up at me, his face pale in the darkness.

A female voice:

'What the fuck do you think you're doing, you hooligan shitbag?'

Oh, no. That's Karen. Her bedroom is directly below mine and her window must be open.

'Two Rapunzels for the price of one!' Robin says, grinning, then lets go of a short scream and starts dancing around, pelted repeatedly with small objects which are being launched from Karen.

'What the fuck was that?! Ow! Ow . . . stop . . . what are you doing?!'

'Don't like it when the boot is on the other foot, eh? Piss off before I call the police.'

'I just want to talk to Georgina!'

'Georgina—' Karen's disembodied voice rings out below me, 'You know this fucking joker? He's nearly broken my window.'

'Er yeah. Wish I didn't.'

'Five minutes of your time,' Robin says, hand on chest, 'Five, I promise. Or I'll start singing. What should I serenade you with? The Smiths? *Georgina, it was, really nothing* . . . OW! That seriously fucking hurts you know?' Robin glares up indignantly at Karen, as if he is in a position to complain. Robin and his innate entitlement all over.

'Plenty more where they came from, shit stain. I've got whole tins of Cadbury's Mis Shapes, I don't pay for them. No skin off my nose.'

'It's taking literal skin off my nose, Bewilderingly Angry Lady Who Lives Underneath Georgina.'

'I'll come down, five minutes and that's your lot,' I bellow.

I don't wait for any further Karen contribution, close the window and hammer down two flights of stairs to let Robin in the back door.

He seems to take unnecessary time to appear down the ginnel, making me think he and Karen are still picking over differences of opinion.

Great, it'll be me who gets the Karen blowback from this stunt.

Robin eventually rounds the corner, brushing atomised milk chocolate from his navy Harrington jacket with the tartan lining.

He smells of the wind chill outside, and a pub. I can tell from the swagger as he enters the kitchen that he's very pleased with this performance, and that he's thinking it might even make something for a routine. To think I was hitherto impressed by this am-dram bollocks.

'What do you want?' I say, folding my arms, suddenly conscious I'm braless in my pyjamas and resenting this intrusion.

'I wanted to talk to you and you won't answer the phone to me, which I'm finding quite hurtful, to be honest.'

This man is priceless.

'And you decided the obvious next step was lobbing stones at my window at gone one in the morning, and waking up my housemate too?'

'Oof,' Robin makes a face. 'Jesus wouldn't want her for a sunbeam, eh. Has the look of Angela Merkel.'

I shush him while making a furious scowl.

'I was doing something romantic and unexpected, as a

162

gesture. The kind of thing you want in a man. To show you I'm that man.'

I've never told Robin this, so I assume he's either being sexist or he thinks 'not sleeping with other people' is some near-unattainable Mills & Boon ideal.

'What do you want?' I ask bluntly, to shake us out of this infuriating semi-ironic, artificial tone he's trying to set. I would be amazed if this isn't the first draft of something he's working on.

'I want a second chance.'

'You're not getting one. Why would you even want it? What happened to the whole "monogamy isn't my bag, man" thing?'

'Exactly!' Robin says, eagerly, and I hiss 'SHUT UP!' as we are seconds away from another Karen explosion.

'That's what I mean. That's not been me, it's never been me and I thought you knew it wasn't me . . .' I grimace. 'And then I thought: why *isn't* it me? You're an incredible girl. You're fit, you're smart. You make me laugh. Look at our repartee! And you know. I'm forty soon, for heaven's sake.'

'Wow, how inspiring. You're running out of energy for dirty food play.'

Robin looks at me, with what I think he thinks is an intense, earnest longing.

'Let's try this. Let's do it your way. I'm all yours.'

Jesus. He thinks I'm winning the jackpot – the chance to tame Robin McNee. I'm struggling to disguise how revolting I find it.

'Robin, I found you having sex with someone else. I can't

get past it. I'm sorry if that's brutal finality for you, but there we are. Shagging other people does tend to scare off boring normies like me, in a "forever" sort of way. I'm back off to bed now, so get out of my house.'

Robin shakes his head.

'Do you think I care more about Lou? Is that it? That she's eclipsed you? That's not how men see sex.'

'Oh, God, Robin, you're not listening: *get lost . . .*'

'Men and women, we're totally different about it.'

'Please!' Even though I shouldn't be baited, I let myself be baited.

'We just are! There's these ants that scientists have been studying, right. They get possessed by a fungus. The brain is still the ant's brain, but the fungus is in control of its cells. The brain is in the driving seat but the fungus has the wheel. A man's libido is a lot like that. We may know it's wrong, and have strong feelings for someone else entirely. But when it's offered, we have sex. Nine times out of ten, we take it,' Robin says. '*The fungus has the wheel.*'

'You're seriously saying a takeover by hostile brain fungus made you have sex with someone else? Are you practising material on me?'

'No!' Robin rakes at his hair theatrically and tries to put his hand on the worktop, but the toaster is in the way, 'Having a penis, and a job where you meet willing women, is like being tied to the village idiot during a beer festival. It's relentless.'

'And, what, women don't have the same urges, that they can choose to act on, or not?'

164

'They do, but I think women are less overwhelmed by them. More capable of being sensible. I include Lou in that; she had no idea how you felt. She said she'd never have slept with me if she'd known.'

'Oh God, how convenient. Women should've stopped you. This is Rav's cookie jar.'

'What?'

'Look, as anthropologically fascinating as this *Men Are From Mars* chat is, I don't know why you're telling me this. It's irrelevant. I don't know how many times I can tell you. We're done.'

'Listen. Maybe it didn't come across enough but I am fairly fuckin' crazy about you, Georgina Horspail.'

Robin's genuinely got my name wrong in this declaration. I work hard to keep my face straight, as there's no way he's finding out what he just did, and having it for his act. This priceless jewel is destined for my friends' collection of treasured Robin mementoes.

'I don't care. Now, I need to go to sleep, so if you wouldn't mind,' I hustle Robin out of the door, 'Cheerio and thanks for the nice thoughts.'

As he starts to walk away, Robin turns, stagily, thoughtful finger to lips. Like Columbo trying to wrong-foot a suspect who thought the interrogation was over, and relaxed.

Robin's planned every part of this, I realise – from throwing stones, to the ant fungus speech, to this pretence of an impromptu parting shot. Which means he knew I'd probably turn him down.

'Georgina, I know I was wrong, to do what I did with

Lou, but I can't help feel this has come along at the right time, to give you a reason to go. It's finding an unlocked door when you were rattling the handles, looking for an exit anyway.'

'Given what I walked in on, more like opening an air lock on a plane. So what?'

'My point is. Before this happened. Were you actually in love with me, did you want serious commitment?'

Oh so this was Robin's whole game here. If I don't feel enough to take him back then ergo he didn't do anything wrong.

I'm far too tired and disorientated – not only by being woken, but by everything: having spent six months with someone I can't fathom, don't like, and brutally, I am noticing, don't remotely fancy, plus family, plus Lucas – to know whether concession is a wise idea, if it plays into Robin's hands. I just want him to go away and stay gone away. And my pride won't allow me to play him back and claim I did care. As he knows, that's a green light for him to carry on pestering me.

Ugh, the manipulation.

I shrug.

'No, not really. As it turns out.'

'Then what I did didn't matter, did it?'

'Not now, it doesn't.'

I shut the door and lock it.

17

Your real problems are never the things you fret most about. This has an upside – sometimes you've fretted without cause.

My first shift at the Wicker is uneventful, and almost entirely devoid of Lucas. Not that that stops me from flickering and crackling like a faulty radio signal the whole time I'm there. I'm so desperate to prove him wrong in his initial prejudice that I make myself a model employee: diligent, quiet, hard-working, has to be told to take a break. Devlin is clearly slightly disconcerted that The Game Girl At The Wake has disappeared and tries to jolly me out of it. Eventually I accept that Lucas isn't judging me, he isn't noticing me at all. I am performing for no audience at all, or certainly not the one intended.

In what becomes a pattern during my next few shifts, he stays in the background while Devlin and I handle a steady trickle, soon a flood, of punters. The pub is in that tricky transition of shooing away the old undesirable clientele while letting the new ones know they're not what they were. It's got an Under New Management sign outside.

Yet my good fortune couldn't last forever. As you might

expect from a calendar date celebrating the birth of Satan, I discover at the last minute I'll be working Halloween alone with Lucas McCarthy, as fifty per cent of the management will be in another country. And not just any Halloween: it falls on a Friday night this year.

'I know it's inconvenient as hell but I've got to dash back to the motherland. Sick child,' Devlin explains to me. 'It's not fair to leave my wife on mopping-up duty any longer.'

'Your family isn't in Sheffield with you?'

'Hahaha no, God no. Mo wouldn't wear it. We have a four-year-old lad and a four-month-old. Did I not say? No, Luc and I have several boozers over there, too. The plan eventually is for this to be up and running without us and we'll oversee it from over there. Although I dunno what Lucas wants to do, what with everything that's happened. And he's not got any squeakers, like me.'

I don't ask what he means by 'everything that's happened', though I am violently curious. I don't want to pry. Or more accurately, I don't want the image of someone who'd pry. Lucas can't claim I've been gossiping about him.

I'd feared that Lucas would scrutinise my work in this first shift of just the two of us and hang over me, given he'd never wanted me here in the first place. Again, the opposite turns out to be true.

Lucas has barely laid eyes on me, giving me a wide berth. It's like we have separate dance spaces, he keeps rigid control, never stepping into mine.

It might be a little more difficult to avoid me all evening, though.

'Are we doing anything special for Halloween?' I ask Lucas as we set up the back of the bar.

'No, nothing special, the usual. Cotton wool across the bar taps, spiders in the plant pots, fancy dress, "Thriller" on the speakers. I'm doing a few bowls of punch with gummy worms in, and so on. Keith's going to wear devil horns.'

He gestures at Keith in his basket. (As Official Pub Dog, he is already a colossal hit. 'And getting steadily fatter on contraband peanuts; the vet is going to flay me,' Lucas says.)

My mouth falls open. *Fancy dress?*

'What are you here as?' He looks my black-jeans-black-t-shirt up and down, leaving me feeling seen and yet wanting. 'I've got a *Beetlejuice* suit going spare. You could hairspray your hair up.' Lucas studies it. 'Bit of talc.'

I hate antics. And with *him?* I'm going to feel the very dickhead.

'I do ask you stay in character throughout the evening. Can you do a *Beetlejuice* voice?'

A smile flickers onto his face and I finally twig he's winding me up. I wouldn't have been so slow, but I'm on hyper alert around him. My appalled expression softens.

'Oh, you SWINE.' I get my first ever Lucas grin in return. I didn't know his face could still do that. It radically alters it.

'Heh.'

'I believed you for a moment!'

'Nah, nothing, not even a carved pumpkin. To be honest, theme or no theme, it's early days so it's hard to call if we're going to be rammed or not.'

For the first hour or two, it seems 'not', and then things

gather pace. Lucas has been letting me serve alone and leaving me to myself, but we're sufficiently full by 8 p.m. that this is no longer an option. Apart from the occasional muttered 'Excuse me' 'No after you' when we're reaching for the same bottle, there's not much chat.

There is the excruciating moment when I bend down and my backside collides with something solid, and when I straighten I see it was Lucas. There's more padding on me than when we dated and I feel like a panto dame. He moves away from the scene of the collision with a humiliating speed.

Then there's a lull, and we're forced to find some conversation. This is the real problem with working for the McCarthys – I have no blank slate (or, it might be blank for him, it's full of scrawl for me). It makes moments that should be easy or neutral, a minor agony.

'Lot of effort for Devlin to go back and forward to Ireland,' I say. 'I didn't realise his kids were over there, that must be tough.'

'It's only an easyJet flight away, not too arduous,' Lucas says. 'He lives in central Dublin, so it's not much of a hike on the other side.'

'Still, when your child's sick, you want to be with them as soon as.'

'And he is with them.'

'Ehm, OK. Was only expressing sympathy,' I say, no longer able to hide my irritation.

I see Lucas see this and take a breath and rearrange his attitude a little. 'I don't mean to snipe at you. It's a sibling thing. Dev's the impetuous one who acts on instinct and I'm the one who generally gets invited to clear up afterwards. I didn't think it was the right time to be expanding the mini empire to South Yorkshire, with his family commitments. He convinced me it'd be a breeze, us knowing the city from when we were kids. He said we needed a change of scene. Dublin's great but it's small when you've been there as long as we have.'

This sounds just slightly ominous to me. Angry creditors? Scorned women?

'But Dev's done the "whoops would you mind" dropping a custard pie on my feet a few too many times to me lately. Things are a bit strained.'

He means me! *I* strained things. I am a custard pie. I even have custard-coloured hair.

'Oh, I see. I didn't know.'

'No, well. Why would you.'

I get the impression Lucas meant this to be conciliatory statement of fact, but it doesn't land as completely without rancour.

I shuffle uneasily, arranging and rearranging the paper straws in their holders on the bar. The end of this shift can't come fast enough.

'I don't mean I mind him being with Oscar, I should add. I'm just not the right person to muse on Poor Dev at the moment.'

I nod.

'He has two kids, he said?'

'Oscar and Niamh.'

We're drawn away from a discussion that's bringing pleasure

to neither of us, to witness the sight of a dozen girls pouring through the door. They're in angel wings, football skirts and Aertex t-shirts saying BEC'S HEN, and commandeer a large booth in the window, throwing down their paraphernalia and accessories with the entitlement of a gang walking onto their own yacht.

'What's our policy on stags and hens?' I mutter.

One of the women screeches with delight at the sight of wobbling penis deely boppers hauled out from a bag and handed around like Academy Award statuettes. The phalluses are glittery and protrude from gobbets of cerise fluff. Humans are strange, really.

'We don't have one. I have a feeling we will do, by the end of the night.'

'I'm surprised they'd come to a place like this for a hen?' I say.

Lucas gives me a grim look.

'You know why, don't you?'

'No?'

'Cos they've probably been told no everywhere else?'

It's a rule of restaurants that your spunkiest spenders are the most trouble. I guess there's some justice in that, effort versus reward, only if you're not the proprietor, you're not seeing any of the latter.

And let me tell you this, as immutable law: the bigger the table, the smaller the tip. Something to do with diffusion of responsibility, Rav reckons.

So BEC'S HEN are pouring profits into The Wicker with

their unslakeable prosecco thirst, but from my point of view, there's not much of an upside to catering to their whims and shouting to be heard over their squawking. They end up with table service, as we're quite keen on a herd and trap where they stay in their designated area and cause minimal disruption.

I've got a system going where one of them snaps fingers and points at the upside-down bottle in the ice bucket. I collect it from their table, along with their card for contactless, returning shortly after with a fresh fizz and a receipt to prove I'm not skimming.

'Give it here,' Lucas says on the fifth go-round, 'You've got your hands full.'

I watch him set the drink down on their table and soon several of the women have their hands full of Lucas McCarthy. They snake round his jeans, up and down his legs and – I can't help but notice from my point of view behind the bar – rather fine denim-clad behind, as if he's surrounded by Hindu goddesses, or has fallen into a mosh pit.

Woah. I can't see what's happening at the front but I can't imagine they're showing much restraint there, either.

He detaches them with some difficulty and backs off, to shrill whooping and cat calling. I feel a little discomfited by it: it's not as if groping and harassment gets much better when you swap the sexes. He got molested.

'Let me go deal with them next time,' I say to Lucas.

He replies: 'I can cope, thanks,' in a way that seems terse and defensive rather than grateful.

I can't get the measure of Lucas, at all. He's at turns

standoffish, slyly funny, dour, mischievous, helpful, haughty. It's behaviour borne of beauty privilege, I decide, watching him from the corner of my eye, watching the women, watch him.

You don't get treated in standard fashion when you look like Lucas McCarthy. The rules are different. You've got women falling over themselves to understand your complexities and decode your dark moods. When you have his jaw and brow, hair the colour of petrol, eyes with depths you can swim in, it's not common or garden 'grumpy'. It's a brooding saturnine countenance.

It isn't: *What's got into that mardy arse?*

It's: *Ooh. What's up with HIM?*

However, Lucas McCarthy, as Mrs Pemberton said – pretty faces grow old too.

Maybe the years of being overlooked and marginalised at school curdled into some deep resentment, and now he cuts a swathe through the beauties of the Emerald Isle, letting his contempt show after he's completed his conquest.

I smile to myself, imagining him in one of those romance novel paperback covers – shirt open, manly arms trapping a wayward, headstrong damsel in a crushing embrace. *The Irish Publican's Virgin Bride.*

I keep thinking it's a shame if he's grown hard and cold, but maybe I need to face up to the fact that he probably always was.

As the night enters its final furlong, Lucas breaks it to me that he's leaving me alone for half an hour to take Keith to stay at a friend's. He goes into a degree of detail I wouldn't have deemed necessary about why he has to do it now, given he's the boss, which only leaves me wondering if he's spinning a yarn to avoid me.

'Sorry to leave you on your own, it's not fair. This is why I wasn't down with Devlin's brilliant tactical maverick understaffing.'

I shake my head: 'It's fine, go.'

Though I can't tell how much this is authentic concern for me and how much was a chance to knock his brother. (That said, the very thought of working with Esther . . .)

'Sheila's Wheels, over there,' Lucas nods towards the hen, and I laugh, 'As long as they're not disturbing anyone else, keep serving them, though it's incredible they've not keeled over. How many Nebuchadnezzars of prosecco is it now? Nine? OK.'

After a shaky start, I think I can grow to like him as a boss. He might not be all over me trying to be my best mate, but this starchy professionalism is preferable anyway. Whenever anyone acted like your mate at That's Amore! they were either trying to get into your knickers or swap for a Bank Holiday shift.

At gone ten, shortly after Lucas has left, the door slaps open like a saloon bar in a western, with a gust of icy air, and a man in a high end Halloween costume enters. He's got a blond wig with a ponytail, fake armour, a large red cape spilling down his back. He raises a large foam hammer and says, using a cod-dramatic voice: 'I'm looking for BECKY!'

Oh, God.

The hen do erupts into excited shrieking and the warrior makes his way over to their table.

'Becky?' he booms.

'Yes yes it's me!' A woman with a bridal veil attached to an Alice band half stands, at the back of the semi-circle, and windmills her arms.

'Hello, Becky, I am Thor. Do you like my hammer?'

Becky's near hyperventilating in her desire to let it be known that she likes his hammer.

Thor puts down a Bluetooth portable speaker that he had secreted somewhere about his person, and Sisqo's 'Unleash The Dragon' blares out.

Aw God no! A stripper?!

He starts swinging his hammer from side to side.

'You've heard of RAGNAROK! Well who wants to see RAGNACOCK?!'

18

There's deafening screaming and the rest of the pub is split between those who've abandoned their drinks to watch and those who've simply abandoned their drinks, got up and left. We may well not get these people back again. The Wicker is in the reputation-making phase. This is a disaster.

I have to intervene. For self-interest if nothing else – I can't have Lucas walk in to find me standing watching some bloke with his wang out. I could be sacked. 'Well, Devlin, that girl I said was best suited to Hooters? She had a fella wafting his hot rod round the place within minutes of being left in charge.'

Esther's words ring in my ears. *'Don't come back with one of your amusing stories where everything is a huge mess but it isn't your fault. No incidents. I don't want there to be incidents and excuses.'*

This is exactly that, isn't it?

Thor has unbuttoned his cape and is swinging it around over his head, like a matador facing a bull.

'Excuse me,' I say, ducking round the bar and scuttling out, feeling extremely foolish, as Thor turns towards me, finger

177

framing a crotch thrust by way of 'hello'. I feel like I've wandered in from a National Trust garden to the Magic Mike XXL show in Vegas.

'Excuse me? You can't do this here.'

'GREETINGS, MAIDEN OF EARTH!'

'I'm not joking, you have to stop. I'm going to turn the music off, OK?'

I move past him towards the table and Thor throws his cape over my head, around my front, and uses it to pull me towards him.

'Have you heard of ASGARD?' he bellows, in that daft voice he's putting on.

'Let me go! Look, please, you can't do this here—'

'Well, ladies – I am ASS HARD!!'

With one powerful yank, Thor pulls me towards him using the cape and I'm crushed against his armour, arms trapped by my sides, while he grinds and shimmies against my rear.

'Let me go!'

He won't let me go, the barmaid caught in his cape now being a flamboyant improvisation in his act.

And all of a sudden, this goes from an embarrassing, inconvenient predicament to a frightening one. I know this feeling surging up inside me, I recognise it like an old enemy.

The end of the world panic attack that caused me to run from the exam hall at the end of my first year at university and never go back.

The loss of control, the suffocation . . .

The more I wriggle and thrash, the funnier the stripper thinks it is to keep a hold of me, and it's no use. I'm becoming hysterical in the claustrophobia. He's not going to listen, he's not going to stop . . . I push and push and wail until he loosens his grip, momentarily.

It gives me a second or two where I have some mobility in my right arm and I draw it forward free of the cape, gather my might and elbow him in the face. I have no idea how to do this, I've never hit anyone, so I do a best guess. He drops the cape and I fall forwards to the floor, with a hard, humiliating bang to both wrists.

'What the fuck did you do that for?!' he shouts, in a Sheffield accent now. He has blood trickling from his nose.

He grabs me up by the shoulders, pulling me into a sitting position, and for a moment I think he might be helping me up, until I realise it's a far more aggressive approach than that.

My breathing is shallow and my whole body is shaking, awash with fight or flight adrenaline. His fingers are digging into me and I can tell by the tension rolling off him in waves that he wants to hit me but is also aware lamping a woman might be a bad career move.

'Get off her!' I hear a voice by the door.

Help at last. Thank God. Although, oh no: it's Lucas. He strides across the room, Keith bumbling at his heels, brushes Thor to the side, offers his hand and hauls me up. 'Are you alright?' he says.

I mumble I am. I don't want to need rescuing by him.

'Fuck her, look what she did to me!' Thor says, wig lopsided, proffering a hand that's full of blood. It does look terrible. I had no idea I could hit that hard.

'What are you doing in here?' Lucas says.

'I'm a male entertainer. I didn't know you had psychos working here.'

'Yeah well you don't male entertain on these premises without clearing it with management first, which you definitely didn't, so get out.'

The hen-do women are bug-eyed and uncharacteristically quiet, a low burble of disbelief rolling round the group.

Thor collects his hammer, his Bluetooth player and his cape from the floor, his smeared face looking as if he's a zombie that's been feasting on flesh. It's a strangely apt look for Halloween.

'This is not over!' he spits, as he passes me, pointing at his nose. 'Bobby does NOT forget.' Lucas yanks him away, grabbing his arm and propelling him out of the door.

'Poldark-looking fuck!' Thor says to Lucas, as he's bundled into the street. I'm not yet capable of finding anything funny, but I file it away to find funny later.

The hen do decide to follow suit.

'You've ruined Becky's hen, you bitch,' says one of the women to me as they troop out, and I flinch. I don't know what to say other than whimper: 'He wouldn't get off me.'

Am I sacked? Please don't let me be sacked.

Lucas leans over the bar, pulls the cord to rattle the bell for 'time' and takes my hand, firmly. I have no capacity left to find this awkward, I merely submit. He leads me into the kitchen behind the bar and plonks me on a seat. Keith is here! Keith is happy to see me, at least, and breaks off from lapping water for a stroke. (Wasn't he going to leave him at a friend's? I totally clock that was a fib.)

When Lucas returns, a minute later, with brown liquid in a brandy balloon, I'm on the floor with my arms round Keith's neck. I let go guiltily, as if I've been caught in a clinch. Lucas says nothing apart from:

'Drink this. I'll finish up.'

I've never liked brandy but I let it numb my lips as I listen to the offstage, muffled conversations and clanging of the till drawer as it shoots back into the register.

Eventually, Lucas joins me, closing the door behind him carefully.

'You OK?'

'Yes, thanks. I'm sorry I don't know what happened, I told him he couldn't strip in here. He grabbed me and I had a nervo . . . and twatted him. I'm so sorry, I don't usually belt people.'

'Hey, no,' Lucas's eyes are wide with surprise. 'It isn't for you to apologise. This is for us to grovel about the idiocy of leaving you on your own. I'm interviewing on Monday and we'll get others in, and sod what Dev says.'

'Oh? I . . . thanks.'

'Leave it with us.'

He folds his arms. Conciliatory but not quite friendly.

There's a pause and I say: 'Thor is a Norse God. Felt entitled to any wench he chose. Should've known, really.'

Lucas smiles and shakes his head, in appreciation I'm making light of it but also implying I shouldn't, and says: 'I'm sorry I wasn't there earlier.'

'It's fine.'

'I'll call your taxi, I can imagine you want to go home.'

I open my mouth to say something more, something to lever this moment open between us, and don't quite have the nerve. But if I finish this Rémy Martin, as a chaser to so much adrenaline that I could have lifted a lorry, perhaps I will.

As I'm walking out to my cab, Lucas is mopping blood from the floor.

'Lucas,' I say, the sound of the car's engine ticking over outside, knowing this is wildly reckless. It feels like a moment out of the ordinary, when both our defences are down, and if I don't do it now, I possibly never will. It'll only get harder to ask as time goes on. And I have to know.

'I've been thinking. Didn't we go to school together? Or sixth form?'

I hold my breath and swallow hard. Lucas stares at me for a moment. He half-heartedly plunges the mop in the mop bucket water, while he thinks.

'. . . Oh, God. Yes, I think so? I thought I knew you from somewhere and didn't want to say in case I got it wrong.'

I squirm. I immediately wish I hadn't raised this. Every word out of his mouth for the next thirty seconds will crucify me. I've devoted years of my life to second-guessing what they might be, yet he will toss them away, carelessly.

'Did we . . . ? Were we . . . ?' Lucas hesitates. He clears his throat: 'I'm not sure how to phrase this in an, er, gentlemanly way. My memories from eighteen through to twenty-two or twenty-three are very hazy at best.'

He's asking me if we did it? I can feel my heart plummeting through my gut, through the floor, into the sewers beneath the city. Surely, surely not. He can't even *remember* if we did it? That's some score card. That's some lack of meaning I had. Rav says I'm modest? So I've a lot to be modest about.

I say nothing at first. I can't even force my facial muscles to mime polite reciprocation. I'm wearing the misery like a mask.

'We hardly spoke, I think,' I say eventually, thickly.

'Ah!' Lucas says, with an evident 'phew', his shoulders dropping half an inch. 'I wasn't sure . . . Youth, eh? Hah.'

Lucas looks at me in awkward hopefulness. I turn away.

'Night.'

On the journey to Crookes, silent tears that I'm not even able to staunch until I'm home flood down my cheeks.

No doubt Fay would say it's positive I can cry. Fay didn't find out the love of her life forgot her.

'You don't know he's the love of your life,' she'd said, with a benevolent smile. 'You're how old? Lots of time.'

'Cathy and Heathcliff knew in *Wuthering Heights*, and they were kids. I mean, I know that's slightly dodgy.'

'And look how that ended,' Fay said. 'With them dead.'

'That's the outcome in general,' I said, and Fay noticed our hour was up.

19

Anyway, at least now I know the answer for sure.

I hug my bare knees in a hot bath, a washing line of Karen's stout underwear strung above me like bunting, melancholy coating me like tar. It's the morning after and I still feel like I've been turned inside out.

Not to be crude, but someone who doesn't even remember whether he ever fitted a key part of his anatomy into a vital part of my anatomy in the act of physical intimacy – which by the way, would've been my first time, Lucas McCarthy – very clearly *isn't* the love of my life.

Unless he's feigning forgetfulness of course, and he does know who I am. Which is barcly an improvement – so The One is supposed to be someone who shudders at the thought of discussing the fact we were once close? That guy's no Rudolph Valentino either.

I don't know why I find this so difficult to accept. I've had twelve years to get used to the idea that I'm unimportant to Lucas McCarthy.

No, that's not true, I do know why. It's because he's never been inside my body, but he's been inside my head.

And this pain is not because he's now so obviously want-able. I'm not that shallow. It's not due to the way, when his face breaks into a smile, it can apparently still crack my heart open. No. I fell for him when he was a skinny nerd in a Cure t-shirt, overlooked, wan and shy. *I liked his early work.*

I'm finding my irrelevance hard to accept because there's nothing I've ever trusted more in my life than that first flush of how I felt about him. It was pure heady instinct, I never had to question it for a second.

But if Lucas didn't feel it too, if I could be so utterly wrong about his reciprocation, I can never trust my judge-ment again. If that wasn't two people falling in love, then what the hell is?

I lie back and stare at my red-varnished toenails, protruding in the foam.

This is the final contributing factor to my existential bleak-ness that is my turning thirty. In my twenties, I used to think I was a caterpillar, and I was going to pupate into a butterfly. The girl in the pink coat with the melted make-up, the roots that needed doing, holding a bag of chips and batter bits on the night bus after a brutalising shift, being asked if her boobs were fake in Rogues – she was not who I was going to be. She was an amazing origins story.

Sooner or later, superhero Georgina Horspool was going to burst forth, fulfilling all her glorious potential.

But now I am slowly letting go of that hope. Like that

baleful line in obituaries at the start of the paragraph outlining where it all went wrong. 'Sadly, it was not to be . . .'

Lucas's reappearance makes that brutally clear. He is something else. I am still right here.

I point my toes, hold my leg out of the water and drag a razor up my calves, turning them this way and that to check I haven't left a raccoon-stripe of hair.

As a serial monogamist whose relationships have generally puttered out rather than exploded, I've only ever taken a detached interest in Clem's dating advice. Now, heaving myself out of the water, I remember her inspirational protocol after a blow to the feelings.

'Liking yourself is a radical act,' Clem had instructed Jo and myself. 'Never more so than when you've had a crap time from a man.'

So when you get turned down for a second date, when you find out you were one of seven options, when your texts have the Read receipt, when the WhatsApp shows two blue ticks and your Facebook messages say SEEN – Clem says do the opposite of wallowing.

She prescribes: spend an entire day treating yourself as you'd wish to be treated. Take yourself for margaritas, see a film you fancy, have a long walk. Buy something frivolous which brings you joy, order a takeaway. Get sheets with high thread count and lie like a starfish on them, naked.

'It's like *aggressive hygge*. Celebrate how great you are and what a nice time you have by yourself. Refuse to partake in the self-loathing we're virtually commanded to, in this sick society.'

I don't have tons of funds, but I can put my dumb blonde hair in the big rollers, do a face mask, get a gel manicure at the salon two roads over, walk into town and purchase myself a Magnum Salted Caramel and a beautiful Penguin Classic edition of *Wuthering Heights*, which I'm going to re-read. See if it lands differently, now.

So I do.

I get Jammy some yellow bell pepper that he's mad for, and go for a hot chocolate, sitting in a window so I can see the smoky-darkness of a winter evening fall, the street lamps switch on.

And, I decide, while spooning up the last of the foam, I'm going to revisit Fay. I need to tell her about seeing Lucas again. I want her to tell me that despite the fact it feels like my chest is being crushed in a vice, it is some sort of catharsis. *You want to talk to her because you won't tell anyone else. And why is that, exactly?*

I wonder how counsellors feel when former clients reappear with their lives in as much a mess as ever. Is it like cutting someone's unflattering 'do for years, getting them to grow out layers and stop harsh treatments, and then seeing them strutting round town with a backcombed, white straw pompadour, like a French Regency wig? Dispiriting?

I'll have to ask Rav.

'Can I speak to Fay Wycherley?' I say, mobile to ear in the quiet kitchen when I get in, having ascertained Karen's definitely out. Studying my glossy nails, the colour of blood. Aggressive hygge. Glamorous defiance.

'I'm sorry, she doesn't work here anymore.'

'Oh . . . Do you know where she went?'

'She went on to a practice in Hull, I think.'

'Oh. Right. Thank you. Do you have the name? I'll try her there.'

I won't, because I can't see myself travelling to Hull, but it seems a courteous farewell.

'Hang on, do you mind waiting for a moment?'

The receptionist puts me on hold to Flautist Moods: Vol 7. Then there's the noise of a phone being crashed back out of its cradle.

'Hi. Are you a former client of Fay?'

'Yes.'

'I'm very sorry to tell you this but Fay passed away in 2015.'

I pause. 'She's dead?'

'Yes.'

'. . . How?'

'A traffic accident, I believe.'

'Oh. That's so sad . . . Thank you for letting me know.'

I say bye and sit and stare at the washing up in the plastic rack. Poor Fay. She'd be what – mid-fifties? I call up images of her and try to process the fact she's not here anymore. She was so reassuring. She kept my secrets, and she listened. And she's gone. I wonder if she had children, and if they miss her the way I miss Dad.

I remember a Fay remark that was long lost in memory, until now: 'No one else is going to fix you. The only person who can fix you, is you.'

So Coldplay lied.

Rav the counsellor you sorted me out with, Fay, she died?

Sorry yes did I not say at the time? She was a keen cyclist, came off under a lorry on the A6 in Buxton. Grim. She was from St Ives so they held the funeral there & I couldn't get the time off. How did you find out?

Ah. I'd not thought I would be asked. I'll mask it with a bad taste, black humour joke. It's not like Rav is professionally trained and BACP certificated and will see right through it. I text:

Thought I'd make a 'top-up' sort of appointment with her and the centre told me. Rav I'm in no way making light of this or making it about me but my grief counsellor has died. That doesn't seem like a thing that should be allowed to happen.

This is your tragedy, I see! Tell your next therapist to assess you for Narcissistic Personality Disorder (do you need another recommendation?) x

No, thanks. Wanted to catch up with Fay really x

Fay once caught me fagging it in the car park, after our session, and told me to quit.

'Life is so short anyway, don't make it shorter,' she called, as she got into her racing-green Mini Cooper. 'If I sound like your mother, that's because I'm old enough to be your mother.'

I grinned and waved her off and ground the butt under my heel.

I'll stop now, in her honour. I'm only a social smoker, really, I've stopped before and had no cravings.

And there's something else I should do, too. Regarding another thing Fay said that resonated, long after our sessions had ended.

'Sometimes because the people we wanted to care for us, didn't care for us, we live with a deliberate lack of care for ourselves. A way of getting back at them, through self-neglect.'

I.e. treating yourself in exactly the way Clem says you shouldn't.

'You're doing it as revenge?' I'd asked.

'Revenge, perhaps a buried desire to be rescued. And embracing a failure that you feel you're marked for anyway.'

I'd had a creative idea, after the meal at Rajput, and I'd shelved it because I thought: what do I ever do that ever goes right?

I should stop living with a deliberate lack of care.

I'm going to enter that writing competition at the pub, and share my shame. AND, what's more, I won't go down without a fight with That's Amore!

I'm going to email the event organiser first so I don't have time to chicken out, then it's on to Mr Keith, whose address I guess at from Ant's reply.

Hello! You don't know me, exactly, but I'm the waitress who got fired for doing as she was told during your recent meal at That's

Amore! I see the restaurant was in your paper, fighting back against claims it serves really bad food. But you're the Star's critic and you said your food was really bad. So I wondered why the piece didn't benefit from your input?
Georgina Horspool

Dear Georgina, firstly, I would describe my dining experience at That's Amore! as patchy. Secondly, the article to which you refer was in the news section, I work for the features department. I am sure I will review That's Amore! in due course, at a time when they are not involved in staffing disputes.
Best, Alexander Keith

Well Mr Keith, I have an even better idea – why not get a feel for my former job by working a shift in their kitchen for a feature. I am sure it'd be colourful and illuminating.

I am sensing a vendetta, young lady. Your energies would be better spent looking for gainful employment elsewhere.

I type: *Well as it happens I am entering a writing competition* then remember: a column in the *Star* is the prize. Mr Keith might be one of the judges? And now he knows my name.

Urrgghhh.

I remember Esther's words about messes, and me sitting in the middle of them, saying it's never my fault, railing against it. *Well, beloved: you're the constant here.*

I could wail at my stupidity, but the constructive thing to

do is to be so brilliant he has to give me the column, despite his misgivings. God, it's pretty much stand-up comedy isn't it? No pressure . . .

20

I should've known something was up from the offer on Sunday afternoon of a moussaka that same night from Jo. Various rogue factors: the shortness of notice. The non-partying day. The fact that moussaka is quite calorific and Jo is very much on a healthy eating jag at the moment. After Friday night's clusterfuck of an evening with Ragnacock, then the news about Fay, a night in with friends will always be restorative.

I know something's *definitely* up when she additionally asks me to 'Come alone at half five' and 'Don't mention to Rav and Clem.' I say, *Oh sure, so they're not invited?*

They are invited but I want to talk to you first, she replies.

Oh God, is she pregnant? Am I going to be on 'pretending the lemonade is a G&T' wing woman duty? I don't think Phil is solid father material but a lot's going to have to be forgotten if she's going ahead with it.

Jo answers her front door in a 1950s-ish shirt dress with rocket ships firing all over it, and a thin yellow belt, hair a glossy ombré helmet. I've tried to copy her winsome cutie pie look before and it's not worked. I look like a superannuated

Veruca Salt. I carefully keep my eyes on hers and don't study for any signs of a bump. Her giant tabby cat, Beagle, winds protectively round her ankles, and I duck down to pet him. He was a rat-catching farm moggy before he lived with Jo, and is essentially a stripy thug.

I'm clutching a bottle of Rioja from Tesco Express, wondering if it's now surplus to requirements. Actually no, sod that, if Jo's expecting a tiny Shagger Phil then I'll need a stiffener.

Jo bought her red brick semi in Walkley when her hair salon took off, and it's as welcoming to me as being wrapped in a maternal hug. With a bittersweet edge, as I have no idea when I'm ever going to afford the same.

I too want a row of supermarket basil plants in my window, in varying states of decomposition, a framed kitsch art print saying *I Don't Want To Go To Heaven, None Of My Friends Are There* and the comforting hum and rattle of second-hand kitchen appliances donated by parents.

'If you think a tall, dark and handsome man with millions is going to appear out of nowhere, fall madly in love with you and wave his magic wand, you need to think again,' says my mum, chief financial advisor.

'Mmmm his magic wand,' I said. There are no magic spells, said my counsellor, and no magic wands, said my mum. I increasingly see the appeal of paying online psychics who tell you they see great fortune in your future.

The house is full of the warm waft of meat cooking at a low heat. Jo opens a pantry cupboard, gets out two wine glasses and sets them down on the vinyl tablecloth.

Oh. Hurrah?

'I've ended it with Phil,' Jo says, and I say 'Oh, no,' but I know my face says something different and Jo does too, as she adds 'Honestly, George. It's for good this time. I've passed a point.'

I pull out a chair and we sit down.

'I believe you. Tell me what happened.'

'His sister's getting married in the spring. He wanted me to go with him.'

I pause, waiting for the shitty condition that Phil attached. 'And . . . ?'

'And that was it. At first I got excited, found the Joanie dress I wanted to wear. Then I started thinking . . .'

She's canning the Rioja down so I reach over and splish her wine up two inches, the silent signal of *please do go on* solidarity.

'. . . I know you all thought him still being a lad and seeing other people was awful. He's twenty-eight and women fall at his feet and he needed some time to get his head round the idea of settling down. I was prepared to wait. People say timing is everything. I told myself I'd met Phil a few years before I should have, and I didn't want to lose him to bad timing.'

This description of Phil's allure isn't just the 'smitten' talking. Phil has large, expressive, boy-child eyes, thinning dark hair and a rogue-ish grin. He looks like the personable host of a consumer affairs or DIY television show, and if it existed there would be a Facebook group dedicated to housewives fancying him. He's nice enough looking, but that's not where his power lies. What he's got is the ability to fill a room with his presence, boundless enthusiasm, and a big heart (if you're not the woman wanting answers). As a social presence, he's like putting a Mentos in a bottle of Coke; instant froth-over explosion.

Phil can turn his enemies into friends if you give him half an hour, although the drug wears off once you're not physically near him. Clem would strenuously deny this, but I've even seen her give him grudging smiles.

'. . . Why does Phil want to go to a wedding with me in front of all his family and friends, but not actually have a relationship?'

'He doesn't want to be single on his sister's big day?' I say.

'No, it isn't that. You know Phil. He could talk to anyone, he'd barely be left alone. It's because he does care about me, and he does see me as his "other half" . . . he wants me to share it, be there for the first dance, and give his nan a hug.'

I sense why Jo didn't want Rav and Clem here for this. A mistimed poison dart thrown by either of them – intended target, Phil, but potentially wounding Jo – would make it too hard to be this open.

'And I realised, he doesn't care if it makes everyone think we're serious. Your usual man, dodging settling down, he'd run a mile from the spectacle of people saying "You, next!" to us, right? That's not Phil's problem. A special occasion is fine, he's hardly likely to meet a better offer on a day at Whitley Hall Hotel when he's busy being an usher. The fact is, we work in every way, except for one thing, which is in Phil's head.'

Jo draws a shaky breath.

'He can't do the ordinary day in, day out, because he can't

accept that I'm all there is. Making me his full time, long-term girlfriend, George, he sees it as accepting defeat. He's got all this potential, girls going Beatlemania, and yet he ends up with Jo, a hairdresser in his home town who's two years older than him and goes to Weight Watchers and has a mortgage and a cat on thyroid pills. He loves me, but I represent giving up his dreams. He won't even admit that to himself, which is why he never has an answer for me, when I ask why we're only ever sort-of "seeing how it goes".'

I open my mouth to deny it, say how short-sighted of Phil this is, but stop myself and squeeze Jo's arm instead. I learned after Dad died that rushing in with denials when someone says: 'This is a pile of shit, and it hurts,' however well meant, can be stifling.

'Once I realised that, it was easy to end it, Gee. It killed my feelings, like turning a light out under a pan on the boil. It stopped me lying to myself and romanticising about how he needs time, he'll come round. I don't *want* someone who has to come round. Who has to resign himself to me by age thirty-five, when he's worn himself out looking for better options.'

I slide my glass towards hers, chink it, drink.

'Of course, now he can tell I've lost interest, he's bothering me every hour,' Jo says.

'Of course.'

'It's weird, I lived for his attention and now I'm watching the messages pile up, as if I'm just a bystander, seeing how obvious it is. Pull away, he pulls me back. He has to make me love him as much as I did before and he doesn't question why, or what it does to me.'

'I've had exactly that sensation with Robin. I'm only interesting when I'm a challenge.' I pause. 'Phil is a lot less of a git than Robin though, don't want you to think I'm equating them.'

Jo meets my eyes.

'Phil isn't a shagger, you know. He's worse than that. It's not about sex. He wants to win people's love all the time. But once he has it he doesn't know what to do with it. So he moves on to the next land to conquer.'

She's criticised him before, but this is the most pitilessly incisive I've ever heard Jo be on the Phil topic. It makes me think this truly is the end.

She sighs.

'Trouble is, I have to try to forget how good it felt, when it was good. I might never feel like that with anyone again. But that's the risk I have to take, right? When I know it's over and we shouldn't be together. I think I can manage not being in love with Phil anymore – but not being in love with what it *felt like*, that's the hard bit.'

I agree, and wish I could tell her just how much I understand what she means. My words are never eloquent enough. Sorry for your loss.

Jo didn't need to worry about the remaining pair of our foursome not sensing how raw she's feeling. After they clatter in, they're both a great balm to the soul.

Neither of them are scornful about Shagger Phil. It makes me realise how much they reviled Robin, that Phil gets a considerably more respectful send off. It's practically a Viking funeral, compared to Robin's 'tramp the dirt down' farewell.

'Yearning and pining for more, or what the kids call FOMO, fear of missing out, is the curse of the modern age,' Rav nods, when Jo repeats her diagnosis of why Phil can't reconcile himself to being her partner. 'I tell clients, contentment is a wonderful thing, but a state of discontentment sells more goods and services.'

'Yeah, when you think back when you got married to someone in the next village and had a mangle and rickets and everything, you didn't do any of the "compare and despair" thing. Or if you did, it was with your four toothless neighbours,' Clem says. 'Now Instagram makes me stressed that everyone in the world is doing life better than me. I'm sure everyone never made their own door wreaths or did these painted Easter eggs until they could put the Valencia filter on it and shove it in my face.'

'It's Clem Ted Talk time!' Rav says. 'You just need the Madonna headset and the tumbler of water to sip from.'

'I would watch that,' I say, and Jo agrees.

'I know we took a lot of piss, but I did understand why you liked Phil,' Clem says to Jo. 'The time he told the story about doing a hangover puke in his aunt's house and lighting the pain au raisin flavour Yankee Candle? He was a "God tier" storyteller.'

'Funny is the killer,' I say, supportively. I'm aware we have to walk a line here in sisterly condolence that doesn't tip over into making Jo thinking she should take him back. 'I am powerless in the face of funny.'

'Why did you go out with Robin McNee then!' says Rav, nose to finger and the other hand pointing, and everyone cackles.

'Something I've never said,' Clem says, unwinding canary yellow hosiery-clad legs and rearranging them, 'I don't go around keeping everything to hook-ups because I am, you know "incapable of falling in love",' she does inverted comma finger and grimaces. 'I do it because I am all too capable and I know it'd end me. It's like my mum and cleaning the house . . .'

We look quizzical. Clem's mum is known to be fastidious to the point of us suspecting a disorder.

'Here's a truth that will blow your mind: my mum says she's actually really lazy about cleaning.'

We now look sceptical.

'It's true! You should see her in a hotel room! Total midden in minutes. I don't know how she does it. She cleans loads at home, everything has to be in its place, because if she relaxed and did as much as she felt like doing, she'd destroy worlds. Her kids would've been taken in by social services. She is in mortal unending combat with her own true nature. Well, that's me and men. I'm actually a weak sap who would do anything for the right man. So I am careful not to meet the fucker. Or if I do, I get my defence in first: I've dumped him before he's even thought about it.'

Rav rubs his chin thoughtfully, rearranges his scarf. Rav is the only person I know who wears a scarf indoors, as a decorative item.

'Couldn't that mean you miss out on someone you'd be happy with?' Jo asks.

'Yeah but equally I don't think Mr Right For Me exists. I'll worry about that when it looks like he might have turned up.'

'Hmm not a foolproof plan, but then I can't say I'm doing any better on Bumble,' Rav says. 'Internet dating is a slingshot at the moon.' He sighs. 'All I want is a well-travelled, artistic woman who can confidently wear a red trilby, with a mind like a steel trap and fluency in several languages. That shouldn't be impossible, given the length of my—'

Clem bellows 'Please God, no!'

'. . . Length of my search! My *search*.'

'Your perfect woman, Rav, is Prince,' Clem says. 'If only he weren't dead and male.'

'This is true. They are obstacles. But every romance needs them.'

Even Jo is laughing now.

'And what about you, Gee?' Rav looks at me beadily. 'What's the follow-up to Mr McNee going to be? What have you learnt?'

'Is that burning?' I say.

'Aaaargh the moussaka!' Jo wails and dashes off to the kitchen. Minutes later we're all forking up slabs of – I don't want to be ungrateful – really peculiar tasting Greek food.

'It's a low cal version,' Jo says, 'With yoghurt. And turkey mince.'

This makes Clem dig in with greater enthusiasm, while Rav and I lock widened eyes.

'It's great,' Rav says, and I dishonestly back him up.

'Let's summarise our findings,' Clem says. 'Jo's kicking an

obsession with a commitment-phobe. I am a commitment-phobe, but lacking anyone worth being phobic about. Rav's too picky for his own good. What about you, George? What is your fatal flaw that stands between you and happiness with another person?'

No burning food to save me now. I hem and haw.

'I don't know.'

'More positive way of looking at it,' Rav says, 'What are you looking for?'

'Hmm. I think I'd like someone who cares as much about me as I do about them. That might sound a low bar. But it's pretty much everything, and I've never had that.'

'Amen to that,' Jo says, as Beagle nudges my plate out of the way with his head and clambers onto my lap, and I pretend this is an intrusion, but I'll allow it.

'Oh, by the way, I'm taking part in a writing competition at the pub! Will you come?' I say. 'I'm terrified of being crap and you all bearing witness but on balance I'm even more terrified of there only being a portly dog called Keith for an audience, so you need to come fill some seats.'

'Brilliant!' Jo says. 'What have you written?'

I feel snakes move in my stomach. I loved that half hour spent at the kitchen table, scrawling in my notebook, so much. But I have to read it out? To strangers?

'I've had a go at something about a bad day at work. The format is so loosey goosey I have no idea if it's what they want or not. I'm right at the end of the running order so I'm going to avoid seeing anyone else's piece, and work downstairs until they call me.'

'You're so brave,' Clem says.

'Or mad as a wizard,' I say.

'I remember when you used to read me your diary entries out at school,' Jo says. 'They were so witty. I'm really pleased you're doing this. We've always known what a star you are. Now other people get to find out.'

'Oh . . . thanks! Let's hope that's what they find out.'

'Isn't your challenge in writing about a bad day at work, mostly going to be in whittling the shortlist down? Start with that,' Rav says. 'Like judges do at awards. "In an exceptionally strong field with some stunning candidates, it was hard to choose, but choose I must . . ."'

'Hahaha. Yes, true,' I say. 'I am queen of the shitty McJob.'

'Oh, God, G. Remember when you had to dress up as a giant chicken to advertise that rip-off KFC-type place?' Jo says.

'I'd repressed that!'

'I'm not sure I remember this one?' Rav says. I groan.

'It was a disaster. The kids they'd invited to the opening had mobbed me like I was The Beatles and I got bundled into a store room while they calmed down. They left me alone for ages and eventually I got bored and had a fag and then the door swung open and the kids saw a disembodied chicken with a woman's head, smoking, like some really horrifying creature out of Greek mythology. And the company went apeshit that I'd ruined the image of "Captain Cluckee". They were encouraging the kids to make friends with Captain Cluckee and then eat him, which is quite fucked up. Pointing that out didn't help me.'

I am wheezing with laughter now as I recall this episode and so is everyone else.

'There's your story,' says Rav.

'Oh no! There's been *much* worse,' I say, insouciantly, confidently. And then I think: what a really sad boast to be making, Georgina.

Perhaps my problem is, I keep confusing the difference between making jokes, and being the joke.

21

That thing Clem said about working against your own nature, on purpose: it preyed on my mind. My nature has been a pretty terrible sat nav so far, so with this in mind, I went even further with Share Your Shame, and invited Mark and Esther. You don't mess with people who need babysitters. I'd have to do it then.

'Stay and drink afterwards and you can see my new workplace!' I say, 'And Mark can say hi to Devlin.'

Without having boxed myself in, I might easily have backed out.

'Hey, Georgina. Still doing the writing thing? You're my hero,' Dev says, as I hoik my bag over my head, arriving for my shift. The pub seems to have more of a buzz than usual. Is it because of the event upstairs? My skin prickles with danger. I'd told myself it'd be half a dozen people.

'Uhm, yeah,' I mumble.

'You've really stepped up here, I appreciate it. I see the theme tonight is Your Worst Day At Work. Hope it wasn't here, hahaha.'

'Hah. Yeah, don't thank me when you don't know what I'm talking about yet. Or maybe it's about soiling myself on a rollercoaster . . .'

Devlin guffaws as he departs. I am grateful for how easy Devlin is, compared to his brother.

'*Have* you soiled yourself on a rollercoaster?!' Kitty squeals, as Kitty has never met a figurative type of speech she understood as such.

Kitty is the new hire – twenty-three, slim as a whippet, with extravagant, drawn-on eyebrows and long brown hair, and a sing-songy OH MY GAWD! vocal cadence I could swear comes from watching lots of series about ditzy American girls with inherited fortunes.

'Oh, you don't look scary at all, I was worried you'd be scary,' Kitty said when she met me, leaving me puzzled and possibly offended.

'Were you told I was scary?'

'No but you're, like, thirty?'

'I don't think that makes me Dame Maggie Smith in *Downton Abbey*.' I toyed with definitely being offended.

'Hahaha! Lucas said you've worked at loads of places.'

Great. I sound like a raddled old scrubber.

'And you've got a posh name, hahaha.'

'Oh . . . is it?'

'I thought you might be *stern*.'

I smile, completely confused. Then, after the first hour of knowing her, I gathered that Kitty operates very few security checks on what's coming out of her mouth. She's not unpleasant company, in fact she's very entertaining, but I have to adjust to the scattershot workings of her mind. A chat about politics and her crush on 'the last one, President Barry O'Barner' leaves me reeling.

Rav, Clem and Jo arrive with Esther and Mark, who they ran into outside. Jo is smiling, post Phil, and it's not just brave-soldier-smiling. Last time I checked in with her she said now she's made the decision, she feels better for it. Limbo is always the killer. 'Knowing I had to do it but not facing it,' she messaged. 'THAT was the shittiest part of this. At least I'm not pretending to myself any more.'

'Good luck!' they all chorus, having loaded up with drinks and heading upstairs to bag the best seats. Please, God, let them hog so many that other people can't fit in too. I can tell my sister and brother-in-law are politely perplexed as to exactly why I would do this, yet trying to be encouraging about a new avenue of interest for me. It beats a life of only reciting which flavours of crisp we stock.

Minutes 'til the event starts. I have no idea how long other people's readings will be. I need to keep my mind occupied. Luckily Kitty is exactly the tension valve release I need.

She asks if she can call her car insurer back, I say sure, and flit around cutting limes into wedges, while Kitty at the end of the bar discusses the premium on her Fiat Cinquecento.

Kitty says: 'Oh, what? K for kilo. Oh I see . . .'

I don't normally listen in on phone calls but I catch her expression at this moment and Kitty looks so perturbed, it's impossible not to be intrigued.

'I . . . I mean, Insect. Tits.'

I frown in startled confusion at her.

'Tits again. Yellow. From the start? Kilo, Insect, Tits, Tits, Yellow.'

I stuff my fist in my mouth to stop myself from laughing.

Kitty mutters a few more words, and goodbye, and rings off.

I cry: 'What THE HELL was that about?'

'Oh my God, he said to spell my name with the police alphabet and I didn't know it! Oh my GOD! I said tits!'

I am nearly bent double laughing.

'Tits Tits Yellow?!' I gasp.

'I couldn't think of anything beginning with T! Oh my life.'

'Strangely enough, Tits Tits Yellow is my porn name,' I say, and as the words leave my mouth, realise Lucas is in earshot, approaching.

'What if they cancel my insurance?!' Kitty wails.

'What for?' I say.

'. . . Lewd wordness?'

'I don't think "lewd wordness" is an official cause of invalidating insurance.'

Kitty gets her phone out and starts Googling. 'Oh no, Georgina, it should've been kilo India tango tango Yankee.'

'Yeah that sounds more likely than "tits". Or "insect", to be honest.'

'I can never call Direct Line again!'

'Imagine how boring his day is usually, Kitty, you did him a favour.'

We can't help corpsing again. Ah, the bonding power of shared laughter. I'm safe to tell Devlin I approve of setting Kitty on.

'Georgina,' Lucas interrupts. 'Upstairs? They're asking for you. You're on.'

I startle and look at the time. How has the clock flown forward this fast? Oh, the sudden nausea.

'Oh, oh yeah,' I turn to find my bag under the bar, and pull my crumpled notes out.

'Good luck,' Lucas says, when I straighten back up.

'Is it proof I'm out of my mind, to be doing this?' I say. Stage fright has rushed up on me and my teeth are almost chattering.

'I don't know what you're like when you're in your mind,' Lucas says, with a smile.

Ain't that the truth.

Kitty had disappeared round the corner of the bar, and she reappears, handing me a prosecco, like it's a charmed amulet for a quest. 'Take this with you! Good luck!'

I do like Kitty.

In the long walk up to the function room, holding the prosecco aloft, I think about what my dad said, about me being a show-off who hates attention. As I reach the doorway, I see a painter's easel, set up with the topic – Share Your Shame: MY WORST DAY AT WORK! And a running order. They've spelled my name 'Georgina Hawspool'.

I've been in here when it was empty, full of packing boxes, and now it's rammed with people, mostly sitting, but some clustered around the small bar at the far end, which Devlin is manning. Thank God it wasn't Lucas.

Strings of Edison lightbulbs have been strung up against

the green paint and the place still smells spicily musty, you can tell it's had dust sheets thrown off it mere weeks ago.

A shallow stage at the far side of the room has a microphone on a stand. It's real now. What on earth was I thinking?

The compere is a twenty-something feature writer from *The Star* called Gareth who introduced himself to me earlier. He's clearly been killing dead air, as he sights me with relief and says: 'Georgina? Georgina! A round of applause for Georgina, please, who is doing our last reading.'

I take to the stage, unfold my two sheets of paper and survey the room, people shuffling in their seats, muttering.

Oh, there are the judges, sat like three wise owls, a woman and two men. And yes, Mr Keith IS one of them. Well, that's that then. Less to lose.

I open my mouth, cough and feel the weight of expectation.

'Hello, so. Wow,' the microphone gives out a squawk of feedback and Gareth calls: 'Stand back a little, that's it.'

I already feel like a tit.

'Sorry . . . I don't know if you've ever heard of the Waiter Test. It's the idea that you can assess a person's character through how they treat service staff. If you go on a date with someone, don't just judge them by how they treat you. Having been a waitress, a barmaid, a cocktail waitress, and for a very brief and unhappy time, a nightclub hostess – that isn't quite as dubious as it sounds, though it almost was – I know how true this is.'

I glance up at the room. I can practically feel those people who know me willing me to succeed, and everyone else watching me in detached curiosity.

'A couple of years ago I was working at this charming café with chandeliers, gold wisteria wallpaper and pink Smeg fridges that served Kir Royales, chopped chicken salads and giant lumps of gateau that meant you might as well as not have had the salad. It did a roaring trade in afternoon tea.

'That Christmas, a dozen or so women come in from a nearby office. Everyone is lovely, except for this one character with a sharp bob, very hard eyeliner and the look of an evil weather girl.

'She summons me over and says: "I'm a vegan who can't have wheat or sugar, so what can you do for me?"' Bearing in mind here she's looking at a menu full of sponge, cream, jam and sandwiches. She's not warned us in advance. And she's actually asking me to come up with suggestions. We both agree we have no idea what she might eat. "I'll ask the chef," I say.

'I head to the kitchen with a flutter in my heart rate and lead in my boots. The café is in full whirling festive meltdown mode with 3,847 walk-ins on top of the large group bookings and you know when you appear with a dipshit customer query, they're going to be only too pleased to take the stress out on you. I repeat her request and they laugh and say "She can pick the cucumber out of the cuke and tuna mayo baguette" and I say meekly: Definitely, nothing else? Cos I don't think she will like this.

'And the head chef screams: "EVEN IF I HAD THE TIME TO COOK WHATEVER THE FUCK SHE'S ASKING US TO MAKE I HAVE NO IDEA WHAT SHE'S ASKING US TO MAKE SO THIS FAILS AT BOTH THE LITERAL AND CONCEPTUAL LEVEL, YOU GET ME?"'

I pause reading and I think, through the pounding of blood in my ears, am I dreaming it, or did that get a laugh? I plough on, with a notch more confidence:

'. . . I mean, fair enough and nicely put, but not much help to me. I head back out and explain in my most conciliatory tone that without prior warning, there's not much we can do for her, we're so so *so* sorry. Evil Weathergirl starts spitting blood about how this is unacceptable. "You work in catering and you can't think up a recipe? So I have to go hungry on my work's Christmas do?!" Like I'm Jamie Oliver and she's Oliver Twist. And then, she points to italics on the end of the menu saying: *If you don't see what you like here, please tell us & we'll try our best to accommodate your wishes!*

'At that moment, I could stick corn cob forks in whichever innocent-minded simpleton thought it was a good idea to shove that on a menu because it sounded nice, without realising it's a green light to every crank and moaner, and comes with heavy caveats in these times of clean eating neurotic intolerants.

'I said, "It's a busy time and your options are very restricted", doing the grit-smile because I KNOW this lady's not for turning.

'"Oh so this is MY FAULT," she says, and now the whole room's listening.

'I wait for her to calm down while knowing she's not going to calm down.

'"What am I supposed to eat?" she says.

'"If you haven't given us any warning there's a limit to what we can do."

'"There isn't a 'limit', you can't do anything at all! For a vegan! In this day and age! I want to speak to your manager please."

'There was no manager because she was off sick. I told her this.'

I look up at the room. As luck would have it, my eyes fall on Rav, who is grinning from ear to ear. He gives me the thumbs up.

'At this point the rest of the table is kicking off at me because they can't order until it's resolved and I can't whip up spelt risotto made with coconut milk, seasoned with orphan's tears, out of mid-air.

'In sheer panic, I ask: "What about a cucumber salad?"

'She accepts, with much huffing and tutting and hissing, that she will have a cucumber salad.

'I go back to the kitchen. They are absolutely FURIOUS I allowed someone to order off menu, when they explicitly refused the request. More shouting and bare refusals. But I've told her she can have it. At some point between a rock and a hard place, you have to choose.

'So I end up making it myself, with chefs around me deliberately jostling me because they're so angry I'm even in there. I serve it, and she looks like I shat in my hand and shook hers.'

A laugh. That was a bona fide laugh.

'She doesn't touch the salad. The whole table doesn't tip, and leave giving me dirty looks. I got laid off two weeks later because "We don't need so many people after the rush is over" and it's in no way because this woman emailed to complain about "your waitress's attitude" afterwards and her company regularly spent money at this café and had a tab there. No way. I had to sell some of my Christmas presents to make my rent.

'Anyway, a few weeks later I walk past this woman in town and she's demolishing a mint choc chip Cornetto.' I give a small bow. 'The End.'

The room erupts into applause. I step off the stage and neck my prosecco in one, feeling like a badass. I side-eye the judges' table and even Mr Keith is patting his hands together, albeit in a desultory fashion.

'Was that the right sort of thing to read?' I say, shakily, to a beaming Gareth.

'If you want to win the competition, I'd say yes.'

22

I'd thought doing my stand-up debut during a shift at work would be unnecessarily pressuring but in fact, coming back to the bar and saying assertively: 'Who's next, please!' is a good way of dealing with the post-performance ebbs and jitters.

'Hey, come here, you!' Devlin says, following the punters as they trickle back out. He grabs me into an awkward embrace over the bar. 'No one's had this good a laugh in one of my pubs since my nude photos leaked. Luc – this girl was fantastic.'

Lucas is by us, holding a box of Britvic bitter lemons, and merely jerks his head in acknowledgement. Hmm. Appropriate beverage.

'Did you win?' he asks.

'Don't find out until the last one, it's a best of three,' Devlin says. 'You're going to do them all, right?'

'Yes, that was the plan,' I shrug and smile. 'If I didn't tank on the first.'

'That was very far from a tank.'

Lucas glances at me and looks away.

I have déjà vu, all of a sudden. The guarded expression on his face resembles a look he once gave me, when we had to jointly present an essay on 'Is *Wuthering Heights* a story of redemption or despair?' I quoted him without his permission, veering off script to get a laugh.

His face said, back in that classroom: 'I'm not sure who you are.' Only why feel that now? Of course he doesn't know who I am. Maybe people have the same face all their life, the same tics, and I'm overthinking this.

'Was that story true, or did you make it up?' Dev says, jolting me back into the room.

'All true, unfortunately. I'd have preferred not to have lived it.'

It was a well-worn anecdote, polished up. That's the problem with my life: it produces too many anecdotes and not much else. No one wants to be miserable in order to leave a funny-poignant memoir, like Kenneth Williams.

'It was about this vegan, Luc . . .' Dev says, but Lucas has suffered selective hearing, ignoring Devlin in favour of an incoming customer. Even in my euphoria, I have a little flicker of *Why can't he be pleased for me?*

'Here she is!' Rav leads Clem, Jo, Esther and Mark up to the pumps. 'Really good choice, George, told with perfect timing.'

They collectively burble about how much they enjoyed it and I bask in it. I know I have to subtract percentages from the whole for 1) their knowing me, and 2) their being glad I didn't stuff it up, but some of this is authentic admiration. I glow, an unfamiliar feeling which feels like a shaft of sunshine after weeks of rain. For once, I am not in the middle of the mess, but centre of a tiny triumph. I have done something valuable, using my own initiative. I feel . . . oh this sounds daft, but I feel like an individual for a change. My workplaces only ever usually afford me the identity of 'love' or 'darling' or 'the blonde lass'.

My friends pile off to the snug; even Esther and Mark have decided to stay for one more 'as we paid the babysitter 'til ten'. All is well, and calm, until I'm flipping the tap on the fourth European lager in a round for a man in a FAC 51 t-shirt, when the door opens and a windswept Robin saunters in.

He's in a funnel-necked navy coat I've not seen before and is wearing an air of cocky insouciance I've definitely seen before. He's with a short, balding man in a camel Crombie coat who, to my eyes, whispers quiet wealth, in a 'London' way. Robin surveys the room in that way he has, as if he is both apart from and above the company, and it's the job of the contents of the room to impress him. Natural self-consequence.

He sees me mere seconds after I see him, no time for any ducking or dissembling.

'Oh! Hi,' Robin says, eyes widening. 'Suddenly she is nowhere, and she is everywhere.'

I gather myself, passing the change to Mr FAC 51.

'Hi.'

'I'd heard it was good here,' Robin says, as though I was going to accuse him of stalking.

'You heard right,' I say, in android wench tone, making it

clear I don't want personal interaction. 'What're you having, gentlemen?' I continue, now false-bright.

'Is this how we're doing it, Georgina?' Robin says. 'Strangers. Yet more estranged than strangers, as I don't get to introduce myself again.'

The man he's with looks from Robin to me and back again and I grind my teeth at how inappropriate, and inconsiderate, Robin always is.

I pass an empty pint glass from palm to palm and say: 'Lots of real ales.'

Robin sighs, leans back, arms spread, both palms braced on the bar, as he surveys the pump labels. My back stiffens. Never mind Keith befouling the premises, I feel as if Robin is going to do some territorial crapping of his own. He's an invader.

'Think I will try a pint of First Blonde, thank you. It seems fitting. Al?'

Ah, this must be his agent. I sat at Robin's elbow during enough fraught to and fros over whether his fellow panellists commanded a higher fee, while he held his phone like it was an After Eight mint.

'Same, thank you,' Al says, awkward.

I pull the pumps, wait for it to settle, take the money, pass the change, top them up, with Robin's eyes locked on me the whole time.

They'll have one drink, maybe two, I tell myself, then go. Breathe. I serve them with a broad smile that I'm determined to keep fixed on my face for the duration of Robin's visit.

The table with Rav, Clem, Jo and my sister and brother-in-law is at the far side, and they are yet to notice Robin's presence.

218

I find my phone in my bag, text Jo: '*Robin's here. Tell everyone to act indifferent, like I've barely said a word about him since we broke up xx*'

And to think I thought this shift would be stressful for an entirely different reason.

Yet the speed with which Robin sinks his beer, and is soon up at the bar holding foam-streaked glasses for refills, is not promising. He was always a lightweight who got bladdered easily.

Kitty hisses: 'Georgina, Georgina, that's Robin McNee! He was on that show on Dave last year,' to me, after she serves him, and he sits back down, with more meaningful eyeballing at me. He glowered at me the whole time Kitty got his drinks, while I pretended to concentrate on rinsing the nozzles on the glass cordial bottles.

Yuck, I hate how he's trying to act as if we had this deep connection, now cruelly severed.

'Yeah I know,' I say. 'How do you know who he is?'

'*Idiot Soup*! Ta ta ta tum tum tum, *IDIOT SOUP*,' she trills the theme tune to the dire panel show on Dave, on which Robin is a regular fixture. 'My ex loved it. Six cans, doner kebab from Chubby's, *Idiot Soup*, perfect night in, he said.'

'Not surprised he's your ex,' I say with a smile, and Kitty says: 'How did you recognise him if you don't watch it?'

'Another regretted ex,' I say, which I congratulate myself on being both a niftily misleading and yet entirely accurate answer.

My feeling of self-congratulation is short lived.

★　★　★

Robin's table is littered with empty packets folded into foam-streaked glasses which I'm avoiding collecting, his voice is loud enough to carry in its inebriated ebullience. Robin's always been a half pint warrior in terms of tolerance, the signs here are not good.

By my count, Robin's had three pints now, with two sidecar shots of Spud potato vodka – damn it, The Wicker, do you have to stock interesting spirits with artistic bottles that catch your eye, and provide playful excuses for excessive imbibing? And now he's back up for pint four. It's obvious he's not letting Al get a round so that he doesn't miss a chance to harass me.

'Six pounds forty-two pence, please.' I set what I dearly hope will be his last drinks on the beer towel.

'How are you able to turn your feelings off, and pull the shutters down?' Robin says.

I ignore this and turn back to the till.

The answer of course is that there weren't many feelings to turn off, and what I'm thinking is 'get lost'. But this is a trap – if I say that, Robin will act even more like a wounded animal.

And it is an act, whether he thinks it is or not – he's enjoying trying on the new role of spurned lover.

He told me, when we were together: *I'm not being, like, Justin Bieber, but people tend to fall for me rather than me fall for them, which is useful material, as a writer.* I should've said, *You sound nice*, and got out at my soonest opportunity, but I thought I had things to learn from Robin. As a writer, as a maverick mind. Oh, Horspool, you dick.

I bet because *I* finished with *Robin*, it's a novelty to him, not getting to choose the moment.

I mean, I'd always subconsciously anticipated my own dumping. I wasn't so stupid or deluded that I hadn't gleaned what my treatment would be, from his tales of his exes.

'I'm no use as a man or beast to you during the Edinburgh Fest, it wouldn't be fair on you, the comedians' trade fair takes every drop of vigour in me I have. Let's give each other our freedom for the time being, and see if we reconnect, further down the line.' (Translation, he had his eye on removing the dungarees of some sassy petite American woman, lower down the bill from him at The Pleasance, and three weeks is a long time to go without when you're paying rent on a place in the New Town. However, should he feel randy and at a loose end on return to Sheffield, it will be fine to call me. *She's cool with it, she's really cool.*)

He's mistaken the surprise of this inconvenience for heartbreak.

'I can't stop looking at you, Georgina,' Robin says, under his breath, as I give him his change. I drop character for a second in irritation and snap: 'Yeah, can you not?'

I hadn't noticed Lucas behind us until this moment, and I can sense him listening. I curse Robin.

'Everything alright?' Lucas says to me, and I say 'Yes, fine,' with a speed that's almost a snap.

What makes me mad is that if Robin were a woman, this would be called bunny boiler behaviour. As a man, and an artist no less, it's noble suffering. This is a whole dark third album, about how she done gone ruined you.

Another customer appears and I say 'YES, PLEASE?' pointedly, and step away.

When Robin sits down, I notice the FAC 51 t-shirt man has gone up to him, a friend in tow. Oh, no – selfies? Signing beer mats? Lots of jovial male back and forth and handshaking?

'They recognise Robin McNee too!' Kitty excitedly hiss-whispers. 'Lucas, you know who he is, right?'

'Can't say I do,' Lucas says, and his eyes move to me, revealing he definitely overheard the nature of Robin's remarks.

Fifteen minutes later, and Robin's up and swaying for round five, pumped up with this impromptu demonstration of his celebrity, and hoppy ale. As I pull his pint, he leans dramatically on the bar, head in hand.

'George, George. One drink. Just go for one drink with me, that's all I ask. That's all the time I need. If you decide against after that, then I will never bother you again. You have my word.'

Kitty's Bobbi Brown-lipglossed mouth falls open as she witnesses this exchange. I put the glass down.

'Can you serve him?' I say quietly to Kitty. She frowns as I excuse myself to the ladies.

She pounces on me as soon as I'm back.

'Robin McNee's asked you *out*? And you're saying no?'

'Yup.'

'You're not tempted?'

'Nup.'

'He's not your type?'

On the periphery of my vision, I see Robin moving around, and when I risk a proper look, he's dragged a chair into the middle of the room and is clambering atop it.

I'm going to kill him. God help me, I'm actually going to commit a murder.

'Ladies and gentlemen, if I could have your attention,' Robin says, struggling to balance himself, while waving his arms as if flagging a passing motorist for help. I feel a contained rush, a moment when I should be galvanised to Do Something. But what? I glance at Kitty, who's rapt.

The pub falls instantly silent. 'Thank you. I want your help with something . . .'

Lucas appears out of the kitchen, holding his phone, and stops short at the sight of a man doing stand-up on a chair.

I feel sick. I want to run at Robin, shrieking, and force him down. But I can't afford to become part of the tableau. If I start pushing and shoving with Robin, it's a rerun of Thor the stripper, without the hammer and the thong.

To have one physical fight with a man in your workplace might be unfortunate, two is careless.

'This incredible woman here, is called Georgina,' he points at me, unsteadily. All heads turn. 'Isn't she beautiful?'

'Yes!' Kitty squeaks and I shake my head at her while she mouths 'Sorry.'

'Robin, stop this now,' I say to him, with all the restrained ferocity I can muster without raising my voice too much. 'I'm not joking. Get down.'

I feel helpless in a way you don't often experience beyond childhood, like when I let go of my helium shark balloon in the city centre, circa age seven. As it soared up and up I tried to believe it was going to miraculously snag on something and be returned to me, when in fact I knew, as it bounced on air currents, that I was spectator to it dancing away forever. Robin is that sodding balloon, except right now I'd happily see him electrocuted by a far-away pylon.

He addresses the room: 'I need you kindly patrons of The Wicker to back me up here.'

I don't remember Robin ever talking like he's a character in *Blackadder* this much before. Maybe like so much else, I tuned it out.

'Myself and this' – he gestures towards me – 'incredible woman had a blissful six months together. Then the other week I ruined it by sleeping with my PA. Georgina caught us together. In the act. In flagrante delicto.'

I can't look left or right, I'm so viscerally embarrassed. Utter, utter bastard. He's buzzing from this. Lucas is staring at me, frowning. I read his expression as: *What should I do?*

Oh God, the disgrace of it.

I look over at my friends, and my sister. They are watching, mouths agape. Two shows this evening, for the price of one.

A murmur goes round the pub and I detect the odd stifled laugh. Jesus, is Al filming this? He has his phone out and held aloft, silly grin on his face.

'This sordid act meant nothing to me. It even involved tying each other up and ice cream, like we were the Budgens version of *9½ Weeks*. Let me tell you, I'm more Mr Nine And A Half Minutes really.'

Gasps, laughs. Bastard.

'I'm ashamed of how stupid I was to risk what I had with Georgina. I'm not afraid to admit I was wrong, and beg forgiveness. Georgina,' Robin turns to me, chair legs wobbling,

Al following the action through his phone with shaky pan round, 'I'm in love with you—'

An audible 'awww' echoes at this. What the hell? They're actually buying this as a Richard Curtis scene, rather than a horror movie?

'I've begged her for a second chance, to no avail. Please can I enlist your help to try to convince her? Who here thinks she should give a man prepared to lay himself bare like this a second chance? Put your hands up if so.'

A pause, and every arm appears to be thrust into the air, apart from mine and the table with my friends and family. And Lucas's.

'Thank you, thank you!' Robin bellows. 'You are wonderful! Look Georgina, look.'

Kitty's arm is in the bloody air and she's grinning wildly.

'What do you say? One drink! One small chance.'

I shake my head and a *boooooo* rolls around the room.

'Think about it?' Robin says, palms pressed together in prayer. Will acquiescing end this faster?

'I'll think about it,' I say, with straight face. I recognise this feeling, I know it of old: accepting my fate with a determined indifference, acting as if words thrown at me haven't left an impression, and my God, I hate it.

'Yes!!' Robin pumps his fist. He's only pleased to have some sort of result because he has an audience. If he thinks coercion by humiliation will work, good luck to him. The whole room now knows I caught my ex inside someone else. It was his fault, so why do I feel so exposed? He's trying to drag me down with him. I was someone else here, but now I'm that woman who Robin McNee double-timed. I'm unclean, I've got Robin's words all over me.

'I can't thank you enough,' Robin says to the room. He gives a small bow, chair threatening to give away, and jumps down. There's a smattering of applause. Someone male shouts 'G'wan, Georgina!' and whistles.

A murmur of chatter restarts and Robin walks back up to me, flushed with triumph.

'There you are. It's the will of the people, like Brexit.'

'Get out,' I say, through a ventriloquist dummy's smile, for the benefit of onlookers. 'How *dare* you . . .'

We're interrupted. Lucas has walked over from the kitchen and is stood next to Robin. He taps him on the arm.

'Can I ask you to leave, please?'

'Who are you?' Robin says. 'On what authority?'

'I'm the owner.'

'For what reason?'

'Disturbing other drinkers.'

'They seemed to enjoy it.'

'It's not a democracy, it's my benign dictatorship. Go.'

'A word to the wise,' Robin says to Lucas. 'See the bigger picture. This here is a love story for the ages and you can choose your role in it. Don't be "heartless landlord".'

'I think you've got our pub confused with eHarmony. Here we are,' he escorts Robin towards his coat, lying over a chair. As Al stands up, Lucas says, picking up his phone before he can: 'Can you delete that film you took, please?'

'I'm allowed to film if I want!'

226

'Not on these premises without permission first, unless you want a big fine. What's it to be, big fine or deleting it?'

Al huffs and puffs and swears and holds his hand out for the phone, swiping, prodding a button and when Lucas, squinting at the screen, is satisfied, he ushers them both doorwards.

'Excuse me, excuse me.'

They're stopped in their tracks by Gareth from *The Star*.

'Robin McNee, isn't it? Perhaps you'd like to be involved with this? You could help judge!'

Gareth is waving a Share Your Shame bill under his nose and Robin takes it.

Oh, no.

'Or maybe you'd like to contribute to this next week? You missed the first one but I don't think it'd matter . . . Very informal, few drinks, open mike kind of thing. I'm sure you'd be a huge hit.'

God, Gareth is practically simpering.

'It's here? Is there a fee? You know who this is?' Al the agent says, with a lip curl.

'Excuse me,' Lucas says, 'I just asked these gentlemen to leave,' and Robin and Al are unceremoniously ejected into the night.

'He's been tipped to win the Perrier award, you know!' Gareth says to Lucas, after the door's closed. 'He's going places.'

'He can go any place he likes, as long as it isn't this pub,' Lucas says, and Gareth shakes his head.

I am torn between gratitude at care for me, in Lucas's intervention, and a sense that I'm polluting the pub's reputation, and Lucas had felt nothing for me but a mixture of disdain and pity.

My friends and family, whose vantage point means they've not caught what went on in the doorway, but have definitely caught what went on with Robin's speech, have decided to make a tactful exit to spare my blushes.

'We'd have shouted at him and pushed him off that chair,' Clem says. 'But Jo says you didn't want us to make a fuss?'

I nod, miserably.

Esther and Mark are trying to work out how to arrange their faces. I could scream, cry, pummel Robin into a bloody pulp.

Tonight had been about me trying to do something bold and constructive for a change, and thanks to Robin humiliating me in my workplace, it's all but obliterated.

When everyone has left, and I'm mopping up, I see the topic for the next episode of Share Your Shame has been posted up on the pub noticeboard.

Your Worst Date.

Lucas comes back in from putting the bins out in a sudden downpour, running his hands through the water in his black hair, pulling a sodden t-shirt away from his body and letting it limply snap back. Robin has turned off my pilot light for the time being but I can still appreciate the loveliness dispassionately. Lucas catches me staring and jerks his head towards the poster. 'He's barred, so don't worry about that,'

'Thanks,' I say. 'And thanks for getting him out this evening. I'm still mortified. And furious. But mostly mortified.'

'No thanks needed, I ban tossers who harass my staff as a matter of course.'

I'm going to say 'thanks' again but it's witless, so I say nothing.

'That is who he is, isn't it?' Lucas says, hesitantly, keys in his hand, Keith at his heels. 'I mean, tell me if this is a Taylor / Burton type thing and he'll be your boyfriend again by next week, as then the admissions policy needs to be more flexible.'

'Oh God, no!' I say. 'No. Absolutely not.'

'OK.' He rattles the keys.

I see Lucas trying to fit me together with this man, who he got the measure of in ten seconds flat. No doubt the 'fitting us together' mental process damages his opinion of me. I wilt. It damages *my* opinion of me.

23

A constant low level static crackle of sexual interest and harassment, like next door's humming maggot tanks, is something I am so used to in the hospitality trade, I mostly tune it out.

Until The Wicker, I'd never seen it happen to a man before. It didn't take long for Lucas McCarthy to arouse the interest of the female clientele. Possibly some males too, though they're less conspicuous.

Phone numbers on beer mats get slid across the bar. Outright offers are made at closing time by the sozzled. Whispering, giggling groups heavily laden with floral Jo Malone scents come in, and choose particular tables that offer a good view. Kitty and I get asked 'Who's that?' 'Is he single?' on the regular. 'Is the dark-haired guy working tonight?' is a question which, if answered in the negative, causes faces to fall.

If Lucas notices any of this, he doesn't let on, the attention bouncing off his self-contained, serious demeanour. When directly asked out, he shrugs and smiles, bats it away as a patently non-serious query. *Don't get enough time off. Same again?*

Today he's got the open fire at the far end of the main bar going again, after tearing the old boxy fascia from its charming period features in a soot-caked, bare-forearmed bout of manly practical labour that I didn't notice whatsoever, obviously.

The same can't be said for a couple of thirty-somethings who I could swear were taking covert photos. Imagery of Lucas is now whizzing around on WhatsApp groups, captioned with tongue-lolling emojis, and he is entirely oblivious. I felt protective, which I'm sure is empathy, as someone who's had her fair share of arse pinches from slimy old fellas.

When the mid-week shift enters its last hour, Lucas reappears after a shower upstairs, hair still slightly damp, puts a bottle of beer into the opener, flips the lid, drinks.

He says, nodding his head at the Share Your Shame poster: 'Heard from laughing boy since Saturday?' He pauses. 'Tell me if I'm overstepping.'

I'm immediately embarrassed and mutter *Oh no, thank God*. It reveals Lucas has been thinking about me, however, and I don't know if this is a good thing or not. My friends had been in touch with a deluge of 'FUCK HIM'-style texts and calls the next day, including a rather heartfelt 'And I thought I had issues with Phil' from Jo, and Esther, in typical Esther way had called to say, 'You don't half pick them, Gog.' But then, more gently, 'Let me know if you want to talk about it. No one treats my sister like that.' I appreciate this, even if it is an objectively untrue statement.

Deafening silence from Robin, which I hope rather than believe to be a permanent state of affairs.

'I don't want to speak out of turn, but I got a bad feeling about him,' Lucas says.

'Hah, yep. You've saved time there.'

Lucas pauses, waiting for me to go on. I realise this is a gesture of friendship, and possibly an attempt to get to know me.

'Thank you again for being so quick about kicking him out,' I say. 'He's malicious. He does these vicious things, supposedly light-heartedly. He plays everything for laughs even when the effect on you is far from funny. Comedians, I guess.'

Lucas visibly relaxes and says: '*Yes*. My assessment exactly. I've said to Dev, it was a power play disguised as a declaration of love. He discussed your personal life, in the middle of your workplace. It was an act of aggression.'

I nod vigorously, even as my gut crimps a little at the thought of lovely Dev hearing about this shitshow too. Dev's been back from Ireland since Monday and is currently out back tinkering with the kitchen equipment, so it's just Lucas and me behind the bar for the moment.

'Yep,' I agree. 'This isn't about getting me back. It's about winning.'

Your personal life – my stomach flexes. Robin regaled them about Lou, my walking in on them. Lucas must think my life is a bin fire on a patch of wasteland.

Much as I hate that he bore witness to Robin's speech, I'm also struck by real gratitude for a responsible adult spending the time to form an opinion, and not coming to the popular conclusion that it's my fault.

'I don't want to alarm you but he didn't strike me as

someone who will give up, any time soon either,' Lucas says. 'If he's got anything personal he thinks he can use against you . . . well. Get in first and threaten him with a writ, or a baseball batting.'

I suspect Lucas means naked pictures, and I feel heat rising in my face. Lucas breaks eye contact, on the pretext of fussing over Keith, and as I watch him continue to avoid my gaze, I'm certain he means revenge porn. Thank God, Robin and I were a notch too old and I'm a notch too prudish for that.

And I had always known that Robin was careless – if anyone was going to accidentally send a photo of my lace-clad buttocks to the group LADS WALK PENNINE WAY: SEPTEMBER on WhatsApp, it'd have been him.

'No, nothing of a sensitive or unclothed nature whatsoever. Thank God. I am not a fan of what I believe are called "belfies".'

Lucas grimaces. 'I don't even know the word so I won't ask more.'

I hesitate. 'Is that true about the fine for filming? When you got his agent to delete the video?'

'Oh, no. Private property but open to the public, so he was within his rights. But I thought you'd prefer there not to be a record.'

'Hah! But you seemed so certain?'

'That's how you get anyone to believe anything.'

I say thanks to Lucas, a sincere thank you, tinged with slight awe. And a lingering question about whether I've been similarly made to believe anything.

★   ★   ★

'Enough! I can't do my job in these conditions!' Devlin says, over the strains of Ed Sheeran. The last punter has left, Dev's abandoned the kitchen and the clean-up is underway. He disappears for a fiddle with the music system and Guns 'n' Roses 'Sweet Child O' Mine' peals out at deafening volume.

Dev and I get on, we have good colleague chemistry. Both of us understand you don't whine or sulk. If there's a crap task, get on the other side of it; complaining about it only makes it loom larger.

'Fridge my fancy fruit!' Dev calls to me, as I'm putting the garnishes away, and bowls a Sicilian blood orange at me.

I catch it and put it on the side of the bar. 'That was easy. Over arm next time.'

I am conscious of Lucas watching me. First he was looking at his phone, now me. My skin prickles.

Dev lobs another orange and I lunge and catch it.

'Oh you're good. Let me guess, always centre in netball?'

I laugh. Another volley. Another catch.

'I'll leave you two to it,' Lucas says, with a sigh, unsticking himself from the wall and vanishing upstairs.

I wipe the tables down while Devlin rinses the drip trays and crashes empties into the bottle bin.

As he's cashing up and I'm slotting the wine glasses from the dishwasher into the shelves, I risk an observation about the dispositional difference between the McCarthy brothers.

'Oh yeah. I'm louder, but Luc has a strong sense of humour. He's very dry. Dry and sly, that's him.'

'Oh sure, I didn't mean that. Just the outgoingness, I suppose. He's great to work with,' I add, hurriedly, worried that I might capsize good relations by this being relayed back to Lucas in blunt terms.

'You're not seeing Lucas at his best, either,' Devlin says, swigging from a pint of tap water, under the pumps.

'No . . . ?' I say, gingerly.

'Nah,' he shakes his head. 'Not with what he's been through.'

I get the impression that Devlin, while in no way malicious, is fairly indiscreet, and that this might well be another point of friction between the brothers. Especially given the younger is a Sphinx-like riddle.

I can't resist asking now. I mean, I'm clearly being invited to ask.

'Been through . . . ?'

'With his wife,' Devlin says, and the word *wife* hits me like a sparring jab to the ribs. Lucas. *Wife? He's a lad in a faded t-shirt and Dr Martens who has to share his homework with me, he can't have a wife?!*

It's the strangest thing, especially given Lucas is so easy on the eye, but I never considered until this moment that he had any serious Significant Other. He walked back into my life without anyone at his side, and I assumed . . . Wishful? I don't know.

I mean, in time I was braced for some astonishing creature with hair like molasses to sashay up to the bar, and say in a Celtic brogue: *Is Luc about?* then vanish upstairs, as someone with the sort of rights that meant they didn't need to knock first. And for us not to see Lucas at all for the next forty-eight hours, and for me to spend a lot of time trying not to think about that. But she wasn't going to be a wife. I'd made up the rules.

'He's married?' I say, hoping I sound casual. He doesn't wear a wedding ring? *A wife.*

'Yes, well, he was. She died. He's a widower.'

I open my mouth and close it again. Devlin continues:

'Brain tumour. Very sudden, last year. She had eight weeks from diagnosis,' he shakes his head. 'He doesn't say much so it's hard to know what's going on inside his head. I pushed to buy this place because I thought he needed a distraction, something to focus on, you know? He's always been down on Sheffield, I was surprised he agreed.'

'I'm so sorry, I didn't know.'

'Don't say anything will you?' Devlin says. 'He's not one for opening up and sharing and I probably shouldn't have said.'

'No of course not, don't worry.'

I've tried, very carefully, to hide my special interest in Lucas from Devlin – well, from anyone – but there's something I want to know so much that I can't stop myself.

'Devlin. What was her name? Lucas's wife?'

'Oh, Niamh. We called our daughter after her. You know, you say it *NEVE* but it's got a crackpot Gaelic spelling. N-I-A-M-H.'

'That's beautiful.'

Devlin nods back and gives a sad smile.

I don't concentrate on anything I'm doing, as I head off to my taxi in quiet turmoil.

I feel more foolish than ever about my reaction to Lucas to forgetting me.

Before, it was wounded pride, aching heart, knowing it

236

was so significant to me and not to him. I felt like I deserved my misery. Now, I realise I was other things too. Petty, self-important and ridiculous.

I expected him to care about someone he tapped off with during the last summer of A-levels. While he'd been dealing with the love of *his* life, dying.

As I fully expected, she's beautiful. I mean, was beautiful.

Staring into Niamh's deep-set brown eyes, mine following her as she cavorts through holidays, weddings and mimes fake surprise at office Secret Santas, I think, I didn't know her and yet I can't believe she's gone. It's not as if death was ever easy to accept, but this vibrant and informal digital afterlife we have now makes it even more incomprehensible. Dad would hate it.

I've wasted no time finding Niamh online.

I got in from The Wicker, and scanned my latest Karen love note:

- *SHARWOOD'S GARLIC NAAN (1) – MISSING*
- *AMOY LIGHT SOY SAUCE – ONE QUARTER MISSING AND CAP BROKEN*
- *QUAKER PORRIDGE, SYRUP FLAVOUR – PACKET STRANGELY DAMP: ANY IDEAS??*

So many ideas, Karen, involving you accidentally self-immolating while making your blueberry Pop Tarts.

I went upstairs, hauled my laptop onto my knees in bed, opened Facebook and searched Niamh McCarthy (even the name is gorgeously musical).

Straight away, I found a public memorial page. I could see the posts, read the tributes. I think I'm right that Lucas has no online presence because I see no tagging. And there's no sign of him in the many pictures posted either, which seems slightly odd.

It's the right Niamh though, of that I'm sure – not only do the dates match, but every so often, someone refers to Lucas in passing, saying he's in their prayers and so forth.

Lucas's late wife has high cheekbones and a ribbon of a mouth with a pronounced Cupid's bow, constantly curled in amusement. The profile photo is one with her brown-black hair in tendrils, whipping round her rosy face as she laughs, caught in an unguarded moment while doing something healthy up a hill. There's a vast gallery of photos and I click through them, fascinated and voyeuristic.

When looking at a photo with enough dark space, I see my own face reflected back in the laptop. I look like a looming ghost. *It's me, Cathy* . . .

An eight-week illness. He must still be reeling. I can't imagine.

I found out about Dad in one terrible phone call from Esther, as she stood outside the Royal Hallamshire Hospital and I stood in the university library, saying 'What?' on repeat, because she'd just said something so obscene and absurd it couldn't be true. Esther later told me she was going to say Dad was 'critical' so I wasn't alone when I found out, but she couldn't bear to give me the false hope. I don't really remember my train journey down from Newcastle. But losing your parents is still something you expect to go through, someday. Losing your other half at thirty isn't.

Niamh was a 'podiatrist by day, poet by night' apparently. Born: Galway. Lived: Dublin. Thirty-three. Thirty-bloody-three. There's a photo of her petting Keith. Comments underneath about him being the love of her life.

There's none of her looking sick – I guess she wasn't sick for long enough.

Instead, she's holding a stein of beer in Berlin, one thumb up to the camera. In a flowered, strappy dress, hair swept up, head on one side. Caption: 'Tara and Terry's wedding.' Cuddling someone's baby, her lipsticked lips puckered and pressed against its chubby little jowls. Caption: 'Rupert loves his Aunty Niamh already!' Round for dinner at someone's house, the 'before we tuck in' picture, her superior bone structure peeking out of a row of grinning people, poised around a platter of lamb kofta.

Why no Lucas? Does he hate the camera? I don't think it'd hate him.

Wait, buried in a set of five, captioned: '@ Dun Laoghaire' – here he is. My stomach lurches at the sight of Lucas, personal and off duty, which is ridiculous, given he's no one to me. And vice versa.

He's sat looking up at the lens, arm on the back of a sofa. It has peach, plushy, slightly dated upholstery that says it's a parental or even grandparental house. Niamh is next to him, in a striped top and jeans, legs crossed, beaming. Lucas's expression is polite acquiescence, but there's some sort of resentment behind it. I get a peculiar sensation of the telepathy he and I once shared, age eighteen, when I felt I could read his thoughts. Hah, *but you couldn't*, I remind myself.

God, but he's stunning. I feel almost irritated that I was the first to notice the luminous quality of his skin, the inkiness of his hair, the intensity when he fastens his sight on you. A cult band I once loved is now at Number One and my status as Biggest Fan is now lost in a sea of admiration.

Since he's become suddenly single and wreathed in tragedy, it's possible he had to leave Ireland to stop himself being mobbed.

I completely recalibrate my recent judgements of Lucas's behaviour, in light of this horrible bereavement. To think I've been cheeky about his lack of joie de vivre. I almost physically cringe.

As I read about the vivacious, popular Niamh, the light of his life, the light gone out in his life, there's something unnatural I'm feeling. Something weird and ungenerous and irrational and appalling, and eventually I admit it to myself.

I am jealous of her.

24

Esther you didn't tell Mum & G about the free Robin stand-up show, did you?

No! Why?

I have been summoned for a 'coffee and a cake' by them and Mum won't say why. It reeks of Having A Quiet Word About Something. Gx

Well, not guilty. I told them your writing was really good though so maybe it's to congratulate you 😄

AHAHHAHHAHA. YEAH. X

I pocket my phone and twitch with low level anxiety. Mum gets on at me plenty, but she's never gnomic and mysterious.

Across the street, in khaki Barbour, Geoffrey approaches me. Something in his clenched, determined expression is unpromising. He is not doing a saunter, or a cheery amble.

'Hi! Where's Mum?' I say, warily. Hoping for 'just parking the car' while knowing Geoffrey would never let a woman drive him.

'She's not coming,' he says, awkwardly.

'Oh. Is she not well?'

'Bit under the weather, yes,' Geoffrey says.

Oh God, have they had a fight? Why didn't they cancel? My shoulders hunch at what lies before me – a whole social occasion with only Geoffrey. I'd hoped to end my days never experiencing that. I reluctantly follow him into the café, trying to make sure my thought processes aren't revealed by involuntary grimacing.

He jangles his change in his pocket and makes a show of inspecting the cake display.

'What'll it be? Those little tarts with kiwis look enticing. Or perhaps a French Horn.'

'Uhm . . .' I'm not hungry at all – who is, for afternoon tea? – but I feel I should show willing and ask for a bun with my coffee.

'I'll just have a cuppa I think,' Geoffrey says, after. Great. He can't be arsed with his half of this charade.

He tries to order by rapping knuckles on the glass case of patisserie, until a wrung-out looking waitress looks over and explains it's table service. Geoffrey has that manner with strangers where he's not rude, exactly, but always several shades brisker than he needs to be, giving me the adolescent wince of embarrassment. Without doubt, he would crash and burn on the Waiter Test.

We find seats, winding our way past a sixty-something man

reading the paper and eating an egg custard tart, and it makes me think of outings with Dad. I crush the thought as soon as it's formed because with Geoffrey here instead, the universe is warped and will be forever. It's like ripping the stitches out of a wound that never heals.

I find a table and a waitress follows, setting plates and cups down with our order. I pinch my Elephant's Foot, take a tiny bite, wipe the chocolate from my hands with a paper napkin and wonder how on earth I'll find half an hour's conversation with Geoffrey.

'Has Mum seen a doctor?'

Geoffrey shakes his head while blowing on his tea.

'I might pop round,' I say.

'No no no, no need for that, she's sleeping actually. I'm sure she'll be right as rain by tomorrow.'

I sense from this antsy response that Mum isn't ill at all. This is a set-up, either between the two of them, or Geoffrey's fibbing?

'What are her symptoms?' I say.

'Dicky tummy. Bit personal, I don't think she'd thank me for going into it. Let your mum have a day off being "Mum", eh?'

Yet more distilled essence of Geoffrey. You could dab it behind your ears and repel insects. Natural concern for my mum, reconfigured as me being demanding.

At least he didn't say she's 'walked into a door'. I ponder briefly if he'd be capable and decide he's far more of a mental torturer.

'It gives us a chance for a catch-up,' he adds, greasily, and

I realise I've been tricked. Ugh they've said: *something some-thing two of you bonding.* Resentment and apprehensiveness settles over me.

'How have you been?' he asks.

'Fine, thanks, really good,' I say, emphatically. 'You?'

'Oh you know. Trucking along. Still working at that pub?' He knows I am.

'Yes.'

'Going well, is it?'

'It's good, it's great, actually,' I say. 'It's proper Victoriana but with mod cons, my favourite sort of pub. They've really turned it around. And they seem very responsible owners. A world away from That's Amore! And the food's good too. Soup and sandwiches and so on, but by keeping it basic, they've kept it good. No Thai banquet-meets-Venetian-small-plates-fusion sort of over-reach.'

I stop short of suggesting they pop in and try it. I can see Geoffrey's 'smelling guff' face over his Gala Pie.

'Can working in a pub really be great?' Geoffrey says, and my ire rises. This is the danger of a one-to-one, there are no restraining influences on either of us.

'Yes, when it's a nice place to be, and you like the customers and the bosses.'

Geoffrey stirs his tea and looks round the room in an infuriating silence, designed to express doubt or indifference.

My God, every time I'm in his company, I remember I'm right to dislike him. It's a fact-based position. I vaguely worried I'd chosen a flamboyant aversion because it was loyal to Dad, and made me the smart one – contrasting stylishly with Esther's policy of appeasement. Luxuriating in what Esther calls my Little Sister Freedoms. (I.e. she'll be sensible so I don't have to be.)

But I'm not imagining this: Geoffrey's mixture of pompous disregard and unconcealed contempt is borderline obnoxious. When I say he's not rude, what I really mean is he's male and moneyed and got to that age where we allow him his chosen degree of rude as some sort of social entitlement, along with his bus pass.

'It's not exactly bristling with prospects, though, is it?'

'Well . . . I could end up running it. The owners are from Irela—'

Geoffrey isn't listening.

'I've been thinking. How about I get you a job at my old company? Secretarial stuff. You might have to do a typing speed course first but I feel certain I've got the clout to swing it. Another ex-company partner Kenneth's got two of his daughters in there and one of them is a complete fright. Piercings all over her and hideous tattoos. I can't see how they can say no to you, if you smarten your act up a bit. What do you say?'

I open my mouth but Geoffrey continues:

'Your mother thinks it's a fabulous idea. She says to tell you if you accept, she'll take you shopping. Get you some new threads,' he prods a finger towards my pink fluffy coat, hung over the back of my chair. 'Something more befitting a woman who's chalked up the Big Three Oh.'

And . . . here it is. Geoffrey's been sent on a mission to sort me out. What part of this plan didn't strike Mum as utterly abysmal?

'It could be like that bit in *Pretty Woman*,' I say, smiling sweetly, confident now I've got his number. 'I too would be grateful to be rescued from my life as a call girl by a wealthy businessman.'

Geoffrey startles and then manages to return my smile, a twitch of the mouth. I bet he thinks it's possible I'll end up turning tricks.

'And you might want to tone down your, er, anarchic funnies on the shop floor. Not everyone will get it.'

I swallow, and effortfully set aside the usual barrage of insults which Geoffrey wrapped this offer in.

'That's very nice of you and I'll definitely think about it.'

'Ah, the polite brush-off. Come on, Georgina, I may be quite a lot older than you but I'm not some dotty old relic you can condescend towards.'

Wow. I swallow hard. I don't want a fight but Geoffrey's not leaving me much choice. I push my Elephant's Foot away an inch, because clearly the 'faking it' part of this is over.

'What do you expect me to say? "Yes, thanks, can I start Monday and never mind The Wicker, I'll text them my resignation right now"? I have commitments, I *have* a job.'

'Oh for goodness' sake, your indispensability to some grotty boozer! Yes, I am sure they'll be scouring Yorkshire trying to find another person with opposable thumbs, capable of placing a glass on a counter top and counting coins. It'll be like that hunt for a pop star programme. Soda Pop Idol hahaha.'

My blood was warm, and now it's hot. How fucking *dare* he.

'I've got an idea, Geoffrey. Why don't you treat me as an

intelligent adult, with some respect, I'll do the same for you, and we'll see how it goes?'

'The trouble with that is, dear girl, you're not treating *yourself* with any respect. Thirty years of age, no qualifications, not a pot to piss in, roaring around town like a teenager, bringing unsuitable fellas home to meet your parents. You really worry your mother, you know. It's selfish.'

'Do I,' I spit. 'That's a shame. She worries me too.'

'Then there's this bolshie attitude. Why won't you listen to people who want to help you? You're still young enough you could turn things around, but you need to look lively.'

I stand up and begin to gather my things, including the offensively cheap pink coat.

'Geoffrey, thank you for your time, but I'm not listening to you because you're being incredibly presumptuous and unpleasant and acting like you have the right to tell me my life is a disaster.'

'. . . Isn't it?'

'Oh, seriously, up yours.'

Geoffrey changes colour, to a deep magenta.

I detect from the movement of eyes around us that every table in proximity has been listening in.

'Don't you dare walk out on me, or I promise you, you'll regret it,' Geoffrey hisses, with a beetling menace. Not a man used to having women defy him.

'Who the hell do you think you are, my dad?' I say, no longer in full control of myself.

'Good God, no.' Geoffrey does an exaggerated reel back. 'I'm twice the man that useless adulterer was.'

I walk out, which I could promise Geoffrey, whatever he thinks, is preferable to anything I'd have said if I'd stayed.

So Mum knew about the affair, then. What a way to find out. And for all Geoffrey knew or cared, that could've just been the way I found out, too. Virulent dislike is now hatred.

25

As I power home at double the usual speed, clammy with exertion and indignance, I replay the encounter and anticipate the tsunami of familial aggravation this is going to unleash.

Somewhere around Cobden View Road, a long forgotten conversation comes back to me.

It wasn't one of the big days in our romance. It wouldn't make the highlights reel, the supercut. Although for Lucas, as it turns out, none of it qualified. Even to me, it was filler, really, a moment between the moments, when nothing of note happened, which is why I'd not remembered it until now.

It was a scorching day in the Botanical Gardens, a heavy heat, bees sounded drunk on it. Lucas and I were supposed to be contemplating the character of Edgar Linton: is he sympathetic, and is Cathy using him to torture Heathcliff?

'That is such a male question,' I'd said, as a welcome light breeze riffled the ring binder, stuffed with our notes. 'As if everything Cathy does has to be seen through the prism of Heathcliff's feelings for her,' I'd said. 'That's why I can't get on with it. It's as if she's the only one with any respon-sibility for bad decisions. She has to protect their love for both of them.'

'She does go off, fall for someone else and marry him, even though she knows she loves Heathcliff more. Definite spoke in the wheel for soulmates.' Lucas was so articulate and opin-ionated behind the quiet counsel he kept at school, and it was still a lesson to me. I'd always assumed the interesting people were the mouthy ones.

'But Heathcliff becomes a monster. It's as if the monstrousness is her fault.'

'I think he thinks he would never do what she did. His head would never have been turned by someone else like hers was and he can't forgive her that weakness. It sends him mad. He's sent mad by the fact he knows she knew it was the wrong thing to do, and she did it anyway. He can't follow her logic.'

'Sounds like when my dad was teaching my mum to drive.'

I got a laugh, but it was a lazy joke, and quite rightly the laugh was hollow.

After a good fifteen minutes of discussing the set text's subtext, we were soon once again exploring just how much fumbling we could get away with, how near fingertips under outer clothing could slide towards key anatomical areas.

When things became too exciting, one or the other of us would pull away and try to discipline a further period of talking. This time it was Lucas. I remember his faded red Converse with grubby laces, his arm round me as I leaned on his shoulder.

How did he taste so right, smell so alluring? It turned out when they talked about 'chemistry' it wasn't only that 1940s screwball film thing where you riffed off one another, it was something primal.

He murmured something into the top of my head and I said: 'What? I can't hear you.'

Lucas drew back. 'I said: you're so delicate . . .'

'Delicate?'

It seemed an unlikely word for an eighteen-year-old male and when I met his eyes, I could tell Lucas felt self-conscious at having used it.

'It's like your bones are skinny,' he said, circling my wrist with his finger and thumb.

I was delighted, and surprised.

'My mum says I'm tubby,' I said, and Lucas laughed.

'. . . Really? Is she joking?'

'Oh no, she always says stuff like that.'

'Tubby is like a word you'd use for a bear. Paddington Bear.'

'And my nose is too broad at the tip for me to ever be considered a "classical beauty", apparently.'

I would never have told Lucas this, mere weeks previous, in case he started to think of me as Miss Potato Schnozz. But in the runaway train that was falling in love, I was increasingly confident of his admiration of how I looked, and I wanted him to know everything about me. 'Being interesting' won out over the shame of sharing these slights. So I suppose some vanity was still involved.

Lucas frowned and stared at my nose.

'What a weird thing to say. I mean even if you had a nose the size of a shoe, which you don't, what a weird, unkind thing to say to your kid.'

I mimicked my mother's voice.

'*You are pretty, Georgina, but you are not beautiful, so don't expect it to carry you in life. Be nice to people and plan to work for what you have. Men's heads are very easily turned by better options.*'

'Woah what the?! That's horrible,' Lucas said. I could see him really feeling it, on my behalf, and then I wished I hadn't told him. She'd been in an exceptionally bad mood that day. There wasn't much chance of him ever liking her now, I hadn't considered that. I'd made her sound like Joan Crawford in *Mommie Dearest*.

'Why would your mum say stuff like that?'

I could see he was genuinely affected. Ours was a big love, I thought. It reminded me of when we studied *Othello* last year, but with Lucas as Desdemona. 'She loved me for the dangers I had passed / And I loved her that she did pity them.' I'd forgotten at that moment that *Othello* is one of the tragedies.

I drew my knees up to my chest, and said, with slightly affected world weary maturity: 'It's her generation, the whole mindset. She was a real "knockout" in her youth and she's never worked, and got married to my dad at twenty-one. She thinks my prospects in life are based on my appearance, because hers were. It's all about marrying a well-off man and firing out kids.'

I drew breath. I'd barely said this to anyone, only Jo.

'. . . She's not happy with Dad, but she won't leave him because she doesn't want to be a fifty-something divorcee, with a lower standard of lifestyle. She says as much when they fight. It's not her fault – when she lashes out at me, she thinks she's warning me, stopping me from ending up like her.'

Lucas and I sat in silence.

'It is her fault,' he said, eventually.

'She made the wrong choices in life, they made her unhappy. Unhappy people take it out on others.' That I knew all this came as a surprise to me. Lucas had a way of making me surprise myself.

'If I made choices that made me unhappy, I'd un-make those choices,' Lucas said. 'Not take it out on anyone else.'

I agreed, and we beamed at each in other in the certainty and simplicity of this conviction.

After the fourth missed call from Esther, I get a terse 'Why are you avoiding me, I haven't done anything?' text, and I relent, and ring her on the way to work the next morning.

'Hi.'

'At last!'

'I'm walking to the pub so I'll have to go in a minute.'

'That's handy.'

'Esther, if you're going to start on me, seriously, don't bother. I'm never speaking to that arsehole again.'

'By which you mean Geoff?'

'By which I mean Geoff.'

'What's that noise?'

'It's someone's terrier, and a bus.'

I find a quieter route, as Esther says: 'I forget you don't have a car.'

'You sound like Geoff!'

'Look, I don't blame you for being annoyed, I would be too. But however badly done, the intentions were good . . .'

'If we're going to play the intentions-were-good game to let him off the hook, so were mine. I *intended* a choux bun, instead I got told that I'm a clueless tart who's ruined her life.'

'Don't have a go at me, I'm trying to play peacemaker.'

'If you are neutral in situations of injustice, you have chosen the side of the oppressor!'

'Oh my GOD have you been on Twitter too much again?'

Esther laughs and I grudgingly grin into my iPhone handset. I'd thought I was going to be spluttering indignantly at her, but having slept on this helps.

I am bruised and sore but as the fog of battle clears, I don't want to treat Esther as a punch bag and their proxy, I want her on my side. We won't see it exactly the same way, but maybe that's a good thing.

I can't bring myself to speak to my mother though. I don't want her explanations yet. I'm not ready to accept them.

'You know what upset me the most?' I say. 'He had the fucking nerve to tell me that I'm a worry to Mum. In what world does he have the right to say things like that? I didn't say, yes well, it worries us our mum married a controlling old creep.'

'Yeah, I've told Mum it was really stupid to have Geoffrey be the messenger. I get the impression that wasn't the plan at first and then he took over.'

'Hah, well I never!'

'I think his offer of the job gave him the whip hand.'

'Ugh, can you *imagine* how awful it would be if I took that? Lording it over me, telling me off . . . he wants power over me like he has over Mum.'

'Yes. I've told Mum, it'd be a recipe for disaster.'

I know a hefty dollop of me is in Esther's Recipe For Disaster, so say nothing.

'Can I ask you to consider something that you won't have considered?' Esther says. 'Mum needs us.'

'I know that.'

'I mean, she really needs us, Gog. I think it's a potentially abusive if not actually abusive relationship and if she's ever going to find it in her to stand up to him, she can't do that while she's feuding with her daughters over him.'

'You don't think he . . . ?'

'Hits her? God, no. Or I'd be staging an intervention. But there are other types of abuse.'

'What are you saying I should do differently?'

'Keep Geoffrey sweet enough and things creaking along. There are bigger things at stake. He is who he is but he's our stepfather and we can't do anything about that. We *can* support Mum, and help her towards realising he doesn't get to push her around, simply because the credit cards are in his name.'

I've arrived at work now and check my trendily throwback-slash-plastic cheap Casio watch, under the grubby cuff of pink fluff.

'I dunno. I know you're smart about these things, Est, but

I don't think me pretending not to loathe him is going to make much difference.'

'Not true. He's very susceptible to flattery. And you can be very dazzling when you try, even when it's insincere.'

I guffaw. 'Geoff's got a better opinion of me than this! He doesn't think I can fake charm at all.'

'Look, I'm a head person and you're a heart person and I love you for being a heart person a lot of the time, but I'm asking you to be more head on this.'

'You're asking me to give Geoffrey head?'

'GEORGINA! Urrrrgh.'

'Why can't he treat himself to a nice big coronary? We'll just have to serve him lots of extra brandy butter at Christmas and encourage him to buy a midlife crisis Harley.'

'Midlife suggests Geoffrey is going to live to 134.'

'God, please no. Embalmed in his own spite.'

'In the meantime, will you answer your phone to Mum? She's giving me loads of grief.'

This prospect gives me a hard pain in my throat.

'I can't face it for now. Geoffrey was vile about Dad as well,' I gabble. I'm can't get into this with Esther but I need her to understand the depth of my anger.

'Oh, what did he say?'

'. . . That he was useless.' I can't think of a substitute for 'adulterer' off the top of my head, another word which has the same impact without the information. '. . . That he let us down and Geoffrey's better than him.'

'Hmm, well. He shouldn't have, but he'll have heard Mum's—'

'Don't say it. There's no excuse for that man to run our dad down to me.'

'You can't pretend he was Husband and Father of the Year, Gog, and I miss him too.'

'I don't, but that's for us to say, not that crypto-fascist with a comb-over.'

Esther laughs heartily and I feel much better. The conversation ends, and I switch the phone off, haul the door open and meet the dark, perennially accusing eyes of Lucas McCarthy.

'Afternoon,' he says, swigging from a coffee mug. 'Everything alright?'

'Yeah?'

Did I imagine a knowing look, an extra weight in his intonation? Could he hear me talking outside? Does he know Devlin told me about Niamh?

This is the first time I've seen Lucas since that revelation and I was planning on adjusting my attitude around him. Now, I decide if Lucas wanted to be treated like a newly widowed man, he'd have told me he was one, and I should respect that by giving him business as usual.

Dev pops up next to him, in sitcom surprise manner – he must've been doing something under the bar – points at me and says, 'Oh my days, it's shaping up for a turd!'

I startle, until I realise he's pointing at Keith, tucked round the corner.

'That's just the way Keith sits. Unless you mean Georgina,' Lucas says and Devlin laughs.

'Shall I take Keith for a walk round the block?' I say, to

distract from the image of me defecating, putting a hand under his collar.

'No!' Lucas almost shouts, and then says: 'No, no thank you, I'll take him.'

He walks round the bar, clips his lead on and says: 'Come on, boy. Uncle Devlin's making accusations against you, let's get some fresh air.'

As the door shuts behind them in a waft of some citrusy aftershave and slightly damp dog (a heady olfactory combination I never thought I'd appreciate), Dev says: 'Ah, he's very protective of that scragbag, don't take it personally,' which makes me feel worse because I hadn't thought it was that obvious.

The memory of that afternoon in the park still lingering, I hope I never get drunk and bellow at Lucas: *Well you seemed to want me to touch MUCH more than your dog, once upon a time.*

26

'What I am saying, is that she's Monday through to Wednesday'ing me. I am not good enough for a Thursday through to Saturday. I am not priority boarding.'

Clem is trying to explain to Jo and I – while Jo does my hair – why her sort-of-friend Sadie is sort of a friend, and sort of not, based on when she suggests they meet up. The chicanery and machinations in the vintage fashion boutique scene is quite something.

'Maybe those are genuinely the days she's free?' I say.

'Pffft! No. She's always out at weekends. I see the tagged photos. I mean, we all have second tier, third tier friends, but there's no need to make it so explicit. It's not classy.'

Clem often confidently claims *we've all done this* or *we all secretly think that,* and it used to intimidate me, until I learned she enjoys overstatement. As with her clothes. She is sitting, hair bouffed, eyes heavily kohled, legs crossed in gold tap shoes, Afghan coat and vape stick on, enveloping us in billowing clouds of vanilla steam.

'You look superb, by the way, Clem – what is the look?'

'Thank you. My look tonight is Anita Pallenberg arriving at Heathrow from New York in the late 1960s slash early 1970s with Keith Richards, small block of hashish hidden in her bag.'

There's always a narrative. 'Michelle Pfeiffer in *Scarface* after she moves back home to Tulsa to go to rehab' 'Miss Moneypenny at Bond's funeral – but she knows he's not dead' etc.

I'm glad Jo and I met Clem in our early twenties because she'd terrify me now. You get more risk averse as you age.

We're good for Clem I think, and she's good for us. She cuts like lemon juice and salt through the cloying consensus that Jo and I could so easily become, and we stop her hanging around with similarly angular limbed 'influencers,' who seem to be eternally trying to outdo and undermine each other. In looks and attitude, Clem is one of them, in her heart and soul she is not.

Apart from anything else, being a competitive prima donna seems so exhausting to me. One perk of underachievement is you don't meet many of them.

We're at Jo's salon, as every so often, Joanna insists on doing mine and Clem's wash and blow-dries before a big night out. Rav's thirty-first is officially an occasion worth it. Clem waives hers as she's going for the slept-in look. 'Think transatlantic flight then a blizzard of Batiste.'

Jo loves a challenge, so tonight I've brought a diamante and pearl clip in the shape of trailing flowers and ivy that I found in Clem's shop, and asked Jo to give me the 'do to suit it.

'You have some of my favourite hair in the whole world,' Jo says, doing that stylist riffle with her fingers, pulling strands down straight at the front to check the length. 'A starlet kind of shiny buttercup blonde you don't see anymore.'

'Yeah, you make me want to hit the peroxide again,' Clem says, observing the magical effects of Jo's rolling flicks of the wrist, with paddle brush and dryer.

Jo's shop, between Crookes and Broomhill, is called, believe it or not, The Cut And Snark. I remember when she got the bank loan and the lease and I thought she was about to send it all up in flames with poor punning. I mean, chippies like Northern Soul and The Codfather love them, but . . .

'That is a terrible idea and not just because of the Cutty Sark groan,' I said at the time. 'Snark makes it sound like you'll be insulting the customers!'

'It means you can get your hair done and moan about whatever you want. Chatty. Offload!'

'Jo, really, no. It's like a sausage shop calling itself Pork Swords or something.'

'No it isn't because that means penis, doesn't it. This is clean.'

I face-palmed. She was resolute.

Seven years later, and The Cut And Snark is consistently booked to the rafters. Students stop to snap the signage, it gets posted online every time there's a new wave of autumn term arrivals.

I won't concede the name was a smart idea, per se, but the truth is Jo is so welcoming and talented at what she does, no one cares. She does a mix of shampoo and sets and lopping the long locks from undergraduates who've decided to re-invent themselves, shear it off and go unicorn blue and pink.

'It's like the Pet Shop Boys, or corn dogs,' Rav said, when

Jo had bought a house, and it was clear that predictions of commercial suicide had been exaggerated. 'If the product is good you forget the name. It's just a gateway. A portal to pleasure.'

'Corn dogs aren't a portal to pleasure,' Clem said.

'You have lived but half a life,' Rav says.

I tell both Clem and Jo what Geoffrey said to me, doing the same sidestep of the detail about Dad I did with Esther.

'You are kidding?' Jo says, pausing with mouth full of Kirby grips. The way she's winding the hair back in on itself and pinning it is masterful. 'He said your life is a mess?'

'Oh yeah. But if I "look lively" and take a job from him, I might just turn it around. I also "roar" around town like a "teenager" and lack a "pot to piss in". Why do parents think they can attack you for hugely personal things? Imagine if you said to anyone else, who wasn't your offspring: "You are single and poor and have no status. Oh and surely you've put on some timber there?" It's savage.'

'That is a fucking good point,' Clem says, using her vape stick to prod the air for emphasis. 'If you went round saying the stuff parents say to their adult kids, you'd be pegged as a sociopath. Like, just because they had unprotected sex thirty years ago, it doesn't give them the right.'

'And I'm not even Geoffrey's kid! He loves step-parenthood in the most malign way imaginable – getting to order people around he didn't have the bother of raising.'

Ranting when looking at yourself in a reflective surface isn't entirely comfortable. I have the hair of Daisy Buchanan and the face of Ena Sharples.

'I tell you something for free as well, if you took the job, then it'd be "why no partner". If you got a boyfriend it'd be why not married, why haven't you bought a house, then kid, then second kid. They're never satisfied,' Clem says. 'My aunt's like this, with her daughters versus me. She's pitted us in an egg and spoon race ever since it was walking and reading ages, Mum says. Best thing to do is ignore them.'

'What are you going to do?' Jo says to me.

'I don't know. Unless he apologises, which I can't see Geoffrey ever doing, I don't know how I'm meant to stand being around him. Esther thinks I should play nice with him to support Mum.'

'What does your mum see in him?' Jo says.

'One word, his money. OK, that's two words. Ugh. I was about to say – never let me date anyone rich but lol, hardly likely.'

'To be fair, Robin wasn't exactly busking for coins,' Clem says.

'I'm not including Robin as we were never going to be in it for long haul and I'd have been better off putting my money in a Ponzi scheme as expecting any reliability from him.'

'You need to avoid him at all costs. George,' Jo says.

'No, she should meet him for this drink and tell him to leave her alone. And take someone threatening with you,' Clem says.

'Like you?'

'I was thinking someone who looks like they could break his arm off and feed it to him.'

'Still you.'

★   ★   ★

263

'Full-scale crisis, coven!' Rav says, when we pile out of a taxi and through the doorway of our meeting place. Coven is his pet name for us. 'I've seen some bell end dressed like a member of Kasabian buying a round of drinks with his fucking *watch*. We need to find another pub, and fast.'

We've made that error of going to a new bar in town for a special occasion, because new = special, forgetting that new also = untested. And in this case, disappointing. There's an inhospitable lack of seats and the music volume is necessitating shouting.

'Fucking *hipsters*,' Clem says, surveying the diner-style stools and squirrel cage lightbulb candelabra, blowing steam out of the side of her mouth, the tampon-holder of her vape stick caught between two slender fingers with blood-red nails, like a modern day Bette Davis.

To be fair, it's not as if Clem looks unhipsterish herself.

'We need somewhere we can hear ourselves drink, but where we're not going to feel total arseholes for being dressy. Think homely but with some style,' Rav says.

Rav is in his amethyst wool trousers and I agree we can't go to a Bull & Badger type place where they're going to shout PONCE.

'Hang on . . .' Jo says, looking at me, 'What about The Wicker?'

'Oh bloody hell, it's my night off!' I say. As the words leave my mouth, I think: I'd get to see Lucas. When I'm dolled up. Sparks in my stomach. You can tell yourself all kinds of long-form lies, but split second reactions reveal the truth.

'Waaaait, that is actually a very strong notion,' Clem says. 'It's nice there and we'd be treated VIP, because Georgina.'

Rav clasps the lapels of my coat. 'Two rounds, maximum, George. Just to achieve lift-off.'

I roll my eyes, make a performance of conceding, and Clem starts tapping at her phone for a taxi. Ten minutes later, we're at my place of work.

'I'll get the drinks, go sit down,' I say, as they clatter off.

'I thought you weren't working tonight?' Lucas says, frowning, taking in my extravagant hair and make-up.

'My mates wanted to come here,' I say, pulling a 'yuck, sigh' face. I'm rewarded with an actual Lucas laugh. 'It's my friend Rav's birthday, we're going on to the Leadmill.'

'Alright. I'll bring your drinks over. You can have table service, unless we get a rush on.'

'Thank you!'

I smile. Lucas smiles back. And for the merest second, his eyes flicker from my face down to my outfit. It's a claret lace prom shape gown with a deep V at the back, the zip starting so low it almost hits the knicker line and made underwear a headache. I'm wearing a strapless boned corset that's so constrictive it feels like it'll have reshaped me for good.

When I shoehorned myself into this, I didn't for a second think I'd have to parade the results in front of Lucas. It makes me self-conscious in front of him in a new way.

It reminds me of another night, another red dress.

Kitty zooms over, squealing: 'Oh my God, Georgina, you look like a film star! Doesn't she, Lucas?'

I writhe.

'You looked so fit I didn't even think it was you at first,' Kitty concludes.

I burst out laughing. 'Uhhhh . . . thanks.'

'Nice hair,' Lucas says, mildly, as he starts pouring Rav's lager and I mutter that my friend is a hairdresser. *Is your hair real . . . real colour, that's what I meant . . .*

'Where are you going? Leadmill? The men are going to be on you like pigeons on chips,' Kitty says.

Lucas and I automatically meet each other's gaze, and I don't know if we're saying anything to each other with this look.

I pick my way to the table, conscious of the air, and possibly eyes, on my bare skin, sweeping from neckline down my spine, leaving a trail of tingling skin in its wake. Am I imagining it?

Jo's phone is on the table, it goes brrrrrrrrp with WhatsApp messages from Phil.

She flips her phone over and says: 'Don't let me reply.'

Then adds: 'I'm doing the right thing, right? I am ninety-nine per cent sure and then I think, "You chucked him for inviting you to a wedding."'

'No, you chucked him for wanting the rights and time and emotional space of a boyfriend while insisting he wasn't ready to be a boyfriend, wasting your energy and stopping you finding someone who does want to play that role in your life,' I say.

'You are very articulate for one so party ready,' Clem says.

'That's true,' Jo says. 'But . . . do you think someone can change?'

Clem meets my eyes with a 'uh oh' expression.

'Rav, you know the answer to this sort of thing,' Jo says.

'Hmm, well. Professionally my answer is yes, people can address behaviours, and choose not to repeat them, if they're willing. I'd be out of a job if they couldn't. Personally, I'd say no one ever changes in essentials. Your character is your character.'

'So I have to figure out if Phil's problem is behaviour or character.'

'You have to pull someone else and move on,' Clem says.

'Hi. Whose is whose?' Lucas counts out the drinks, as everyone looks up at him with interest.

'Clem,' Clem says, shooting a hand out to shake his, after the last drink is set down. 'I don't think we met at G's stand-up night. What do you think, Lucas? Join our philosophical conversation. Can anyone ever change?'

'Can anyone ever change?'

'Yeah,' Clem says.

I bury my face in my drink.

'My view is no, definitely not. How's that? Too nihilistic?'

'My kind of boy,' Clem says, and I widen my eyes at her.

'And why do you think that?' Rav says.

'In my experience, whatever you call "change" is finding more out about someone's nature. But it was always there.'

My exposed skin prickles.

'Having a real laugh for your birthday, then?' Lucas adds, and Rav guffaws.

'How much is that?' I say hurriedly to Lucas, pointing at the drinks.

'I'll stick it on a tab, make it right tomorrow.'

I have a premonition that this tab won't materialise, and Lucas is looking after me. 'Enjoy. Oh, and happy birthday,' he says to a gratified Rav.

'Good lord,' Clem hisses as he retreats, and Jo says: 'Wow, he is so good looking it's quite nonsensical.'

'Telling me. I think my cervix just dilated,' Clem says, and I hiss: 'SSHHHHHH SHUT UP OH MY GOD.'

Why didn't I consider this could happen? They'd not noticed Lucas on the Share Your Shame night, so I'd forgotten, become complacent.

I have to find a way to say: I am not interested in this man and yet he is completely off limits to you forever, no questions allowed.

'Oh my God, why did you never mention him?' Clem says, as her eyes track him back round the bar.

'Actually, I did,' I say, in a low voice. 'Guy from school?'

'Waaaait. He was in our English class?' Jo says. 'How do I not remember him?'

'This is the one who can't remember you?' Rav asks.

I nod.

'He doesn't strike me as the forgetful type.'

'Well,' I draw breath, gird my loins, and say, in a 'subject closed' sort of airy tone: 'What possible reason could he have for pretending to forget me?'

As I know from the discussion in Rajput's, the view is he could have plenty reason, but I take a leaf from Lucas's playbook and sound decisively certain.

Incredibly, combined with the free shots that Kitty suddenly materialises with, it works.

27

'I don't wish to be melancholy, but at thirty-one, I wonder how many more years I have left until the pursuit becomes undignified,' Rav shouts in my ear, as we suck on our drinks and survey the dancefloor.

'Don't be downhearted. It was always undignified.'

Four has become two: Clem's being chatted up by a Jarvis Cocker lookalike. Jo's gone outside to field a lengthy phone call from Phil. We suspect a reunion pends.

'He's Bobby to her Whitney,' Clem had said, 'Let's hope he doesn't get her into smoking crack.'

We've briefly talked to a friend of a colleague from Rav's work called Julia who I can tell likes Rav, but when I mention this he says:

'Nothing in common.'

'Nothing in common' is Rav's catchphrase dismissal.

'You know you say you want to meet this super bright woman who can wear a red trilby and wants to do the Inca trail and so on?'

'Yes?'

'*You* are super bright. *You* look good in a red trilby, and can go to Peru any time you like. Why not accept a woman who isn't these things, and be these things yourself? Let her bring other things.'

'Are you saying I should be the woman I want to date in the world?'

'Exactly this.'

'Hmm. I mean, I suppose . . . I see your point.'

Fifteen minutes later, Rav is in a circle of acolytes on the dancefloor, Night Fever-ing away, Julia circling him.

'Your hair is priddy,' says a man nearby, in an American accent. 'Kinda like – prom hair?'

I turn to see a heavy-set, bearded, thirty-ish man in a pink shirt, with a friendly, open face.

'Ed,' he says, proffering his hand.

'Hi, Ed. Georgina.'

Ed has moved from Minnesota to lecture on American literature at the university. We talk animatedly about writing, about Sheffield, I tell him about Share Your Shame, half-shouting behind cupped hand.

For the next twenty minutes, he tells me about Minnesota. Aaaaand for the next twenty minutes after that, too. My part is over.

All of a sudden, in American Ed, I see the ghosts of relationships past. It's not often, in your life, you step outside a pattern you create, and see the pattern.

It's not Ed's fault, but this is how every fling in my twenties began: with some nice enough lad liking me, and me feeling duty bound to reward that. *Give him a chance.*

I already know how the first date for pizza goes, and the second in a wine bar, and the sex after that. Me astride his sturdy form, like I'm in a canoe, doing fake moans to hurry it along while he mashes my breasts together as if he's building sandcastles.

Trying desperately to convince myself we complement each other and I'm falling in love and maybe This Is It and you know, as Mum says, *if you want kids*. By month four, when he's discussing what package holiday we should book next summer and it sounds as appealing being held on remand in HMP Barlinnie, accepting it's time to pull the plug before I really hurt him. Realising that you don't become a writer by dating one. Or a comedian, or anything else for that matter.

Ed's holding his phone in his palm, expectantly. It's in no way his fault that I've lived our whole affair in my head, in the time it takes to get my mobile out of my beaded clutch bag.

'You're welcome to have my number,' I say, 'but I'm not dating much or interested in dating at the moment. If you ever want a waitress-eye view of life in the city, or a quote about something, or a pint with a friendly face, you're very welcome.'

'I have enough friends,' he says, but after keying in my digits.

'Lucky you, then,' I reply.

Robyn's 'Dancing On My Own' starts.

'I love this, excuse me!' I say.

It might a bit on the nose to dance on my own to this song, but it feels great all the same. I'm not going to do this any more – feel I'm validated by male interest, or get involved with whoever turns up. It's OK to turn nice guys down. I'm fine as I am.

As it reaches the second chorus, and I'm having a rapturous moment, I feel a bump on my arse and turn round to see Ed, singing along, getting the words wrong, trying to hold onto my waist as he grinds his hips against me.

Sigh.

28

I know the Battle of Elephant's Foot with Geoffrey was bad when I get an email from Mark. It pings on my phone at an ungodly, efficient person's hour on Monday and I traipse downstairs to answer it on my computer because it's larger than my phone, with a strong coffee.

My film star dress is crumpled on its hanger and reality has returned, after an interlude of major hangover. Here was a frisson, though: while in jogging bottoms watching episodes of *Dawson's Creek* through the holes in a fabric face mask, I texted Lucas. I've read the exchange six times.

Do I thank you or sue you for how I feel today? I need a Keith Richards style whole body blood transfusion #freeSambuca

Hah! Bad head? 😖 *Hope you had a nice time (and didn't fall out of any coconut trees)*

Great, thank you very much for the special service 😊 *(Coconut trees?)*

(It was a joke about Keith Richards) (Google it if you have the energy) And my pleasure x

It's not exactly the letters between F. Scott Fitzgerald and Zelda but the unexpected appearance of a sign-off kiss is a warmth I shall cling to.

Karen's left a note for me too. Good-oh.

MORNING.

Your turtle is weirding me out. It was staring at me while I ate dinner last night and smells like cabbage. Please can we move it from that position by the telly, it's not necessary to let it dominate the room.

PS also are its toenails normal they look like a dinosaur's

Poor Jammy. I go to check on him, stroke his rough scaly head with my index finger and feed him some gem lettuce. I knew Karen would agree to me having Jammy and then kick off. It took a lot of wheedling and sweetener gifts and promises to bung in more for the bills, as obviously a tortoise is a heat sponge and water user. And he has to go in the living room: there's no way I could get Jammy's hutch up two flights of narrow stairs.

I flip open my old Dell laptop, and re-read Mark's missive. He's Esther's nuclear option to talk me round. Given his reluctance to scrap, she deploys this weapon sparingly, knowing overuse will diminish its efficacy. The last time I remember Mark trying to broker a settlement was when I refused to wear the real fur stole – with a little petrified rodent face with yellowed teeth like pins, no less – Mum had chosen when I was bridesmaid to her.

Hi G! Hope you're well. Look I will get straight to it, you know I don't usually get involved in this sort of thing but apparently your mum is having conniptions about you avoiding her since you and Geoff had words, and Esther is getting it in the ear. E doesn't want to push you in case you think she's on your mum's side yadda yadda. Do you want to at least tell your mum you're taking some time out? I'm not telling you what to do. I'm just a brother-in-law, stood in front of a girl, asking her to love him enough to stop him having to listen to your sister wittering on.

Which one was that? Four Weddings? Love, Mark xx

Hi Mark. OK. Given it's YOU. 😊
Xx
PS Notting Hill, I believe

Mark is clearly at his desk and in need of distraction because before my toast has popped he replies:

Ahhhh the one with the actress?
M

. . . They all have actresses in?
G

No I meant ABOUT an actress. Oh and I meant to ask, how are you finding it at The Wicker? Mainly dealt with Devlin, seemed a very decent sort of chap. Got to know a fella here when he needed someone in the city to do the accounts.

He's great and the pub is great! Thanks again x

It did make me laugh when he and his brother came in, I think we were expecting some magnates in pinstripes and the look was very off-duty rock star. But that's the difference when you've made your money in the pubs and clubs trade I guess. Most of our clients are a lot greyer. Ooops, shouldn't be typing this on company email. Deleted in 3, 2, 1 . . .

Magnates? They just own a couple of pubs in Dublin, don't they?

I chew my slice of granary with Marmite contemplatively and hope Mark enlightens me, and doesn't mean by deleting he'll be deleting any replies.

Oh my dear sweet unmaterialistic sister-in-law! They 'just' own three places in central Dublin, outright, not leased – do you know how much property is worth there? – and a place a few miles outside, in an area called Dun Laoghaire. Which to give you an idea, is the kind of postcode where Bono has a pad. Portfolio of millions. Took over the family business from the dad I think, a little dynasty. Right, annual review meeting beckons – SUCH JOY. Thanks for being a mensch as always. Mx

I close the laptop and turn this over, adjusting my view of the McCarthys. I knew they were men of decent means, but seriously rich? That had flown over my head. As he said, they don't dress like it.

It's a bit ungenerous of me, but I wonder if their unusual easy-going fairness is borne of always setting the pace themselves, not being in any stress over cash flow or under the cosh from someone further up the chain of command. That could as easily make you a tinpot Hitler, if you were that way inclined, I remonstrate with myself.

Through my morning shower, getting dressed and made up, I can't stop thinking about this latest twist. Had the cool cabal at sixth form known this, I have a feeling Lucas would've been reassessed and promoted. It's to his credit that he never dropped a word of this, not even to me.

To think I was supposedly the greater catch at school. Ha. Supposed by who, though.

With a deep breath, wishing I still smoked, I call Mum on my way into work. Like Esther, I think a conversation with a neutrally imposed time limit is a good thing. Unlike with Esther, I quickly glean it's not going to be very amicable.

'At last! I wondered if we were ever to speak again,' Mum says.

'Oh, as if,' I say, immediately returned to being fourteen years old by the parental dynamic. A worn groove.

'You could've handled this with a little more grace, Georgina, than to simply start stonewalling me.'

'I was busy and I didn't want to get into an argument.'

'There will be no need for that if you simply apologise to Geoffrey. He's being very level headed about it, now he's simmered down. We're very fortunate to have him.'

I stop dead in the middle of Northfield Road, mouth agape.

'*What?* He should be saying sorry to me!'

'What on earth for?'

'Uhm . . . let's see, saying my life was a mess, calling me selfish, implying I'm a bit of a slapper, laughing at my job. Calling my life a disaster. Saying Dad was an arsehole.'

Mum's quiet for a few seconds and I know full well that Geoffrey has not provided these details.

'Funnily enough, he said you were the one who was aggressive. You threw his very generous offer of a job back in his face, made jokes about how you'd rather go into prostitution instead and got very rude and sarcastic at the notion you'd even consider working for a central heating firm. I'm not sure where you get the superiority from, young lady, as from where I'm standing you have nothing to lose from accepting.'

How do I say: your husband is a malicious liar?

Mum isn't only sticking up for him as he's her pay cheque and Lord Protector, I sense. The overselling of Geoffrey's tale clearly shows that she's decided she desperately wants me to take a nice safe position in an office, overseen by him, beholden to him. She wants me to be like her. How long before some twitchy chinless son of an MD would be pointed in my direction, too. ('*He's flying up the corporate ladder and a very smartly turned out young man. At your age, you could do a lot worse.*')

'I already have a job I like a lot and after the way I was

treated by Geoffrey I wouldn't want to owe him anything, thanks.'

A pause where I gather Mum is tutting.

'It's a mystery to myself and Geoff why you are so unwilling to let us help you.'

'If you want to help me then I wouldn't mind a bit of faith and emotional support, thanks.'

'Georgina, you're still working in bars at thirty. You have no savings, no pension, no home. No relationship. What am I supposed to emotionally support, exactly?'

'Me, as a person? Aren't I enough?' I say, pretending to be coolly in control and not on the verge of tears. 'I'm happy.'

'*Are* you?'

'Yes,' I say, in a clipped voice.

'And you should give some thought to giving Robin a second chance.'

'You . . . what? Robin? Why? You couldn't stand him.'

'We ran into him in Waitrose, last week, week before last. We both reached for the same jar of peanut butter, hahaha! Didn't he tell you?'

This causes my stomach to plummet. What the . . . my hands are immediately sweating on my phone and I grip it so tightly I think it might shatter. I can't let her know what a nasty shock this is.

'No, he didn't.'

'Oh, I thought he would have done. He explained how things had been quite casual between you and he'd upset you by saying so, you'd split up and now he really wants to commit. I think he means it, Georgina. Sometimes it takes the right woman to make a man grow up and settle down.'

The thought of this spectacle by the Condiments and Spreads aisle turns my stomach.

'Why did he feel the need to tell you this?'

'He felt we'd misunderstood his intentions towards you. He might not want you to know this but he's really rather *gooey* about you. I didn't realise what a solid family he's from himself.'

'How long were you talking for?'

'Only five minutes. He seemed very pleased to see us.'

I bet.

'Solid family', HAH. He's hinted he's from a minted background and now Mum's opinion of him has shot up. With Geoffrey, Robin's appealed to his ego, shown due deference to their status as elders of this village. Now Robin has bent and scraped and begged for their approval, shared sensitive intel to sweeten the deal, they're prepared to back his cause. The whole thing makes me want a scalding shower.

'Mum,' I say, forcing myself to concentrate, 'Did you tell Robin where I was working at the moment? At The Wicker?'

'Oh . . . I think it came up? Yes, yes it did, as we were discussing Geoff's idea of making his offer to you. And you *might* be interested to hear that Robin think it's fantastic too.'

Mum says this with a 'ta–dah!' rabbit out of the hat flourish. How could she not see they were being played? Whose personality turns 180 degrees like that? I could be sick. I make hasty excuses about being at work, when there's five minutes left to the route, to churn on everything she's said.

Oh, Lucas. You're wise. Robin is malign. And, unless I make him, I don't think he's going to stop.

I'm in dire need of comic relief and The Wicker considerately supplies.

'Steady as she blows!' Devlin says as I dump my stuff behind the bar, as two men, knees bent, huffing and wheezing, drop a multicoloured Wurlitzer jukebox by the fireplace.

'Where's that on its way to?' Lucas says, staring.

Dev slaps its flank and beams like a new father. 'Isn't she special?'

'It is not gendered and no, it's fucking hideous. What's it for?'

Kitty and I exchange a 'here we go' delighted glance. McCarthy brother bickering is a constant.

'Music!'

'What next, a Sky Sports big screen?' Lucas said. 'Ugh. It means an endless soundtrack of Metallica and Girls Aloud.'

'You say that like it's a bad thing.'

'Absolutely no way, Dev. Call them back to take it away. God almighty we've got "traditional" and "craft ale" everywhere. Why not run a place with a plastic leprechaun outside and have done? Serve cocktails the colour of Care Bears?'

'Do you ever think hospitality was the wrong fit for you?'

'It's called taste, Dev, get some.' Lucas seems rattier than usual.

He exits with Keith in tow and Devlin huffs and Kitty and I laugh.

'You wouldn't think someone as lush as Lucas would be single, would you?' Kitty says, once Dev's upstairs clattering about in the event room and it's the two of us.

'Perhaps he's not,' I say, mildly, sipping my water.

'He is, his wife died and he doesn't have a girlfriend.'

Jeez, Devlin. 'His brother said that?'

'No, Lucas did. I asked him if he has anyone back in Dublin and he said no and I said oh you're not married then or anything I thought you would be and he said well I was but she died. I said what of and he said of cancer. I said are you seeing anyone now and he said no.'

'Maybe he's not ready yet, after losing his wife like that.'

'No he said it wasn't that at all, he's well ready but he'd not met anyone he was into and that he had a jawbone view of human nature and that most people only let you down.'

'A jawbone view?'

'A long word like that. Def began with J.'

'Ja . . . jaundiced?'

'Yeah! I thought that was when you turn yellow.'

'It is.'

'He thinks most people turn yellow?'

'No.' Running at two speeds, with one of those speeds being 'Kitty,' is hard work. I isolate what's bothering me:

'I never thought Lucas was that chatty.' I feel slightly put out that he's opening up to Kitty and not to me.

'He isn't 'cos after that I asked him what his type was and he said he'd rather not talk about his personal life thank you and did I think the barrel of Pale Rider was on the tilt.'

'Ah.'

'Don't you think the tragic wife thing makes him even fitter though?' Kitty says, nipping her straw between rabbity front teeth.

'Hahaha, what?'

'You know, knowing he's sad. You want to perk him up with a bit of sex, don't you.'

I almost spit my water.

'What's wrong with that?' Kitty says. 'To be nice!'

'Yeah but you don't . . . people don't say things like that,' I say.

I wish I could simply find that funny.

What if she offers? What if he says yes? What if that happens with the next girl they hire? For the first time I contemplate Lucas sleeping with another member of staff and me having to hear lurid accounts of the boss from the night before and pretend to snigger along with it. I could tolerate the phone numbers on beer mats because they reliably hit a brick wall. But sooner or later, law of averages, when there's women flying at him from all sides? Argh.

'Here, Georgina,' Devlin appears, lightly coated in dust from renovations, 'Can you nip up to the flat and ask Lucas if the plumber's coming at four? Just shout him as you go up the stairs.'

I nod and feel a small-child thrill at being allowed into

Lucas's lair, a new, private part of the building. The flat upstairs is a door on the left behind the bar, as opposed to the right hand one that takes you up to the function room.

I pad up the stairs and call, hesitantly:

'Lucas? Lucas . . . ?'

I can't hear anything beyond so I rap on the open door at the top with my knuckles. Still nothing. I peer round.

I hear his voice before he walks out of a bedroom, mobile pressed to ear. I jolt: he's only wearing a small towel across his mid-section, grasped at the hip with one hand. In all the weeks rummaging in each other's clothes we never actually *saw* anything. At first, I actually turn and cover my eyes like someone in a *Carry On* movie.

'. . . Don't care what you say Niamh would've wanted and don't care what she did want when she was here, either, so invoking the wishes of my late wife is lost on me. Yeah well she's not around to insist so it's up to me. Deal with it.'

My face is hot oh no no no, stop this, I can't blush, it'll make it clear I was excited by sight of his chest and maybe some upper groin and perhaps I will glance again, wave at him to make my presence clear . . .

I look back. Phew. Yes, he has definitely filled out . . . Then his blazingly furious eyes meet mine, and widen, and I blunder backwards and out of the room, muttering 'didn't realise you were busy' apologies.

I'm dying of embarrassment, but also, what the hell was that conversation about . . . ? I hover for a second, trying to make sense of it, put it in a context that makes it innocuous, or at least reasonable. Of all the jarring things I could've overheard, Lucas sounding savage about Niamh is the last thing I expected. It wouldn't have been anywhere near a list.

It would've helped to separate out the issues if he hadn't been half naked at the time. I belt back down the stairs in a slight daze.

I contemplate the possibility that for all his solidity as a boss, Lucas McCarthy isn't very nice to those in his personal life. Yes, he was magnificent about Robin, but I am old enough to know that people are complicated. You can be saviour in one situation, diabolical in another. I don't know him – I must keep reminding myself of this fact. I pull myself up for thinking the way I did, for imagining we were slipping into any sort of relaxed closeness.

I walk back down and Dev says: 'Plumber definitely on his way at four, then?'

'Oh, I don't know!' I feel guilty, even though I've done nothing wrong. 'He was on his phone.'

'Right. I'll catch him in a bit, don't worry. Kitty and I were talking about diaries, did you ever keep one?

'I did, actually!' I'm effusive, in my need to channel my thoughts in another direction: 'That was the last bit of writing I'd done, before this open mike competition. Back at school.' Imagine if you knew the juicy sections are about your younger brother. Imagine if he knew, come to that.

Dev nudges Kitty. 'You should start one. I wish I'd done one now.'

'Oh my God, no one does that, what am I, some sort of Victorian person!' Kitty says. 'Yeah, like, I wrote my diary in my big death nightie and, like, ate mutton pie and that. Wrote it with one of those pens that are feathers.'

'What the hell is a big death nightie?!' I say, putting aside the fact Kitty called me ancient.

'Those nighties that ghosts wear and they put old people in. You know. Like in a Muppet's Christmas Carol.'

'Hahahhaa. The *Muppets'* Christmas Carol. RIP Charles Dickens.' Devlin says.

'I know who Charles Dickens is!'

'Do you? My bad,' Devlin says.

'He's the bear, he tells the story.'

Devlin and I look at each other and hoot and Kitty says, 'Oh piss off!'

Lucas reappears in the bar, fully clad, and the hilarity for me evaporates. I promptly find cleaning to do, keeping my head down and keeping busy. I sense Lucas wanting to meet my eye as some sort of safety check or reassurance, and I manage to swerve any interaction. Eventually, he corners me by the ice bucket.

'Georgina. Would you have the time for a quick chat tonight? After we've closed up? Come find me in the flat at half eleven?'

'Uh . . .' I hadn't anticipated this and feel uncomfortable. I'm not sure I want to hear his excuses. On the fly, I can't think of where I can claim to need to be at nearly midnight on a Thursday, though.

286

Mere hours earlier, I'd have jumped at the chance to have a beak at his belongings, enter his lair.

But I am back to not knowing who Lucas McCarthy is, and I don't want to be drawn in and spat out a second time.

29

At the end of my shift and for a second time today, I head up the stairs to the flat, with considerably less lightheartedness than I did before.

The door's closed this time, and Lucas answers as soon as I knock. 'Drink?' he says.

'Just a cup of tea, thanks.'

'Aw man, making me drink alone? Can't tempt you to a whisky?'

I shrug. 'Sure.'

I don't like this creaky, ingratiating imposter. Say what you want about your late wife, just don't involve me. Lucas heads to a kitchen, off the sitting room we're in, and I survey the small spartan flat, TV in one corner, potted fern in another.

I drop down into the sofa in front of a coffee table that's piled with pub admin flotsam and jetsam, spreadsheets, bank statements. For the first time I realise it's probably quite lonely, being away from your home city, living above your time-sucking place of work.

Keith clatters in, feet loud on the wooden floor, and as

ever, he's gratefully seized upon by me. He settles at my feet while I pat the scruff of his neck.

Lucas hands me a glass and sits down opposite in a wicker (ha) chair, placing his whisky on the table between us.

'I wanted to explain about earlier. The phone call I was having when you came in.' He pauses. 'Saying you don't care about your late wife is quite unusual. Dev says he told you about her?' Lucas rolls his eyes, but smiles, and I nod, self-conscious.

'Lucas,' I say, raising my voice slightly to 'prim', 'you honestly don't have to. It's none of my business. I'd rather not pry.'

'I want to explain,' he says.

He swigs from his drink and I do alike, rather than offer any reply. On the one hand, what I heard was ugly; on the other, why explain himself, if he is a wrong un?

Maybe part of the brooding bad boy psyche. He needs to control his image.

'I was talking to a friend of mine in Dublin . . . A former friend of mine. Owen. He was having an affair with Niamh right before she died.'

I open my mouth and close it again, and gulp. 'Oh.'

I'd made the rules: Niamh was tragic, and devoted. Not unfaithful. *Oh.*

'I found out a few weeks before Niamh got her diagnosis, but it had been going on months before that. She was having loads of nights out with girlfriends and I got suspicious and turned up at the bar she was out at, and caught her with her face locked onto Owen.'

'Oh, God.'

He leans back.

'We were in trouble anyway. We got married too young, for the wrong reasons – her family wouldn't have us living in sin. It was never right. There wasn't a friendship there, which is what it always has to be underneath, right?'

I clear my throat and nod.

'. . . I could say more, but don't speak ill and all that. The point is, I knew we were over, before Owen. It was confirmation. Could've done without knowing the other man quite so well, but there we go.'

I nod as if I understand, except I don't really understand. I feel glad of the heat and tingle of alcohol in my stomach.

'And then she found out she was ill?'

'Yeah. We'd agreed she was moving out. Then she went for a routine check-up after having these headaches and was told there was no hope. It was an aggressive cancer, and it was inoperable.'

Lucas's voice has grown thick and I merely take in this information, knowing I will lie awake for an hour when I go to bed tonight, trying to figure out how it must've felt. She left you and now she's leaving you.

'They gave her six weeks. She made eight. I told her, just go and be with Owen and we'll work out the rest.'

'That's incredibly heroic,' I say to Lucas, then in case he thinks I'm being flip: 'I mean that. Incredible of you.'

'It sounds like that, doesn't it?' Lucas says. 'Funnily enough, it wasn't heroic of me, at all. When she told me she was terminal, she said it didn't change anything between us and I was relieved, because it didn't. I was devastated for her but

290

it's not as if a tumour could make us love each other again, or undo the hurt. I would've been in a far bigger mess if she'd said: sorry we're estranged and I was shagging one of your best mates but can we be husband and wife again for as long as I've got? I wouldn't have known how to do that.'

I nod, as if I understand.

'But, she also wanted it kept secret. She knew a lot of family and friends would judge her for the affair with Owen. We had to go through it all presenting a united front.'

'Literally no one knew you'd separated?'

'No one. I told Devlin after the funeral. He and Mo had already announced they were calling their daughter after Niamh and he was committed. And you know,' Lucas rubs his eyes and smiles. 'It's still a nice name, and they liked her.'

He sounds more Irish than he usually does, in tiredness.

'As to why I'm having frank exchanges of opinion. Niamh took Keith to Owen's when she was sick. I could hardly say no. When Niamh died, Owen refused to give him back. Said it had been her dying wish that Owen keep him and I said, well, he wasn't hers to gift. You can imagine Owen's in a lot of pain and not seeing things straight, at the moment.'

'Oh? Wow that's . . . but Keith's yours?'

'Oh yeah. He was never Niamh's dog, I got him as a puppy. So. Here's where it turns into a Shane Meadows film plot. Devlin and I had to jail break Keith from Owen's, and kidnap him. Dev tricked some guy we knew who was doing work on his flat to give us a spare key, and we staked it out, and burst in when he'd gone out, took Keith.'

'No!'

'Yes. Not long after, I've come to do this work in Sheffield so Keith and I are safely at a distance from Owen's wrath. And he's . . . vociferous, I think is the word.'

'Doesn't he feel any shame for having slept with your wife and borrowed your dog and tried to keep him?'

Lucas takes a large slug of whisky. 'Quite the opposite. He has decided he at last freed Niamh from a tormented marriage, only to lose her, and he's the victim in this. And I know where he's coming from because he did love her so he must be hurting too. But he said . . .'

Lucas pauses. I can see him bracing himself: 'He said that maybe our fighting gave her stress that caused the cancer. I don't believe for a single moment that Niamh and I screaming the odds, killed her. But what a thing to hear. I bullied her into an early grave.'

'Lucas, that is . . .' I swallow. I've gone from wanting to hard swerve all this, to wanting very much to be the friend he needs: 'Unhappy couples fight, and say things they might regret later all the time. You no more knew what was round the corner than Niamh or Owen did. The lack of compassion in saying that . . . what a bastard.'

'Thank you.' He finishes the whisky. 'Mind if I have more? Another for you?'

I nod and hand my glass up. There's only the sound of Keith's light snoring until he returns.

'Waaaait. That's why you didn't want me walking Keith?' I say.

'Oh? Yeah. I think Owen's an unpredictable mess and I don't let Keith out of my sight in case he decides to repatriate him to Ireland. I thought I was subtle in turning you down?'

MHAIRI McFARLANE

'You weren't subtle,' I laugh and Lucas says: 'Sorry.'

A brief silence.

'I don't know how to grieve Niamh. There's not many handbooks out there for how to be sad at the death of someone who, at the time, you wanted to kill.'

'Try a counsellor. They honestly help.'

'Really?'

'I went to one too,' I say. 'When the relationship with the person who's gone is complicated, my counsellor used the analogy of a clean wound versus a dirty wound. The clean one is still a wound, but the healing is more straightforward. When it's like an explosion of shrapnel, there's infections, there's secondary cuts. That takes longer to heal, and it heals differently. You have to accept the damage is different.'

I didn't, for a moment, ever forecast I'd one day be sitting with Lucas McCarthy, repeating this. Fay and I were talking about two men I knew, and one of them is in front of me.

Lucas sits forward. 'Do you mind me asking who you lost?'

'My dad.'

'And you went to see a counsellor about it?'

Somehow, although I could tell the edited version of this history, I already know Lucas is going to be the first and only person other than Fay to hear the full.

The emotion is blunted by Lagavulin and yet I still have to pace myself.

'I was very close to my dad . . .' I'll have to deliver a sentence at a time and sort myself out in the pauses.

'You don't have to talk about this, you know,' Lucas says.

'No, no. I want to. I visited from university after a month. You know, huge bag of washing, you feel like a character who's been on some epic journey, forever changed by their travels.'

Lucas laughs, softly.

'Ah yes. You think you're Frodo. Or is it Bilbo.'

'I told my mum I was coming home that weekend, and my dad hadn't been informed. My mum and my dad not communicating was kind of a hallmark of their relationship. If my dad had known, he'd have been fired up to see me, chippy tea, he'd have bought a bottle of wine. Instead I get home, travel weary from the far-off land of Newcastle and expecting this fanfare and no one's home. But that's OK. I threw all my washing in the machine, made myself a five-slices-of-bread-tall sandwich, head upstairs to scarf it.'

Lucas smiles and I think I see genuine affection towards me.

'Then, thanks to being an underslept fresher, I fall asleep. When I woke up, I could hear my dad's voice. I sneak down-stairs quietly, all ready to shout "SURPRISE, it's me!" and I twig that he's not talking to someone in the house, he's on the landline in the hallway.'

Time hasn't dulled this impact. Even now, twelve years later, I feel almost as shocked as I did when it happened. I also feel like I'm betraying Dad by recounting it. I'd never known until now that's why I've kept it to myself. To protect him.

'And . . . he's saying things, obviously to a woman. Not things you ever, ever want to hear your dad say. Things he's going to do to her. Things he'd like her to do to him. Oh God, Lucas, porny stuff. I've actually managed to block a lot of it out. The C word featured.'

'Ah, no,' Lucas puts a hand to his forehead. 'That's . . . that's so rough.'

'Yeah. So I'm halfway down the stairs, I can't move without him hearing or seeing me and I'm coming to terms with the fact I now know he's having an affair.'

I catch my breath. 'He hangs up. He sees me. He absolutely loses his shit about me earwigging on him, as a way of dealing with what he knows I heard. I'm scared, I lose my shit at him. I say how awful it is to Mum, to me, to my sister. What a terrible dad and husband he is.'

Deep breaths, Georgina, I tell myself. Like Fay said.

'He stood and took it all. He couldn't do anything else. I avoided him for the rest of the weekend, and went back to Newcastle. In pieces.'

Another deep breath.

'He calls me, a day later, conciliatory, and offered to drive up to Newcastle to see me. I told him to piss off.'

Just as I think I've got through this, I break. I break completely on the words *piss off*. I put my face in my hands and my shoulders shake as I weep. This is kept in a safely locked box most of the time, and I try to mislay the key. Sometimes when I open it, the contents feel like they could consume me.

Moments later, I feel Lucas crouching next to me. He puts his arm around me, and without thinking I turn and sob into his shoulder. The fabric smells of him, in a nice way. He is bigger and broader than the boy I was heavy petting with in the park. I wish I could lose myself into this embrace, and not only because of who he is and what he was to me. It feels so good to have someone hold me. It eases this immovable pain in my chest.

'Sorry,' I say, voice gone up three octaves due to crying at same time. 'Sorry. You were talking about your wife and now I'm booing . . .'

'Hey hey hey. It's fine, it's alright to cry,' Lucas shushes me and rubs my back. Keith lets out a confused whimper and it makes us both laugh. Lucas fetches tissues and I accept one. Much as I didn't want to cry in front of Lucas, I feel better for having done it.

Lucas sits down in his seat again. I crumple the tissue in both hands.

'And he—' I breathe, deeply, '—he died, a few weeks later. Giant heart attack. We'd never made up. That was it. "Piss off" was the last time we spoke.'

I sniff and gasp.

Lucas gasps too, in a different way. 'Oh. *No.*'

'I never told Mum or my sister about our fight, how could I? We're burying Dad twenty-five years before we expected to, oh and by the way he was playing away, not sure with who, good luck processing this information.' I shrug: 'And Dad wasn't there to defend himself. So when you couldn't tell everyone you and Niamh weren't together, or you felt let down by her? I get that. I couldn't tell everyone I was the apple of my dad's eye and he mine but my last memory is us at daggers drawn, or me hanging up on him.'

Tears crawl down my face and I wipe them with my sleeve.

'Ah,' Lucas looks down, and brushes a tear away himself.

'There's a post-credits sequence too,' I say, picking up my

whisky. 'I was so traumatised, I had a panic attack in my end of first year exams and never went back to university. It was Dad who really wanted me to get that degree. Even now I flinch when I see photos of people in their mortar boards, Mum and Dad either side. I had been so sure that was something I'd have. Wrong again.'

'This is so brutal. I'm so sorry.'

We sit and listen to Keith snoring.

'You said you and your dad were close, right?' Lucas says.

'Yes.'

'Then your dad knew you loved him. And he loved you. Tell me this, if he were here, if he could have another five minutes, what would he be saying to you? Would he be saying – "I can't believe you were mad at me last time I saw you?"'

I think about it, and shake my head.

'No, exactly. He'd be saying, I'm so sorry I let you down at the end. But you don't need his apology. And he wouldn't need yours.'

This is so insightful and sensitive that I barely have words.

'Thank you,' I say. 'Thank you so much for saying that.'

Lucas looks at me intently.

'This happened when you were eighteen?' he asks.

'Yeah. Eighteen. My first term at university, the winter.'

At first, I could swear that the age lands as significant to him. And just as quickly, the suspicion passes, and I think: wait, was that *not* a flicker of recognition? But someone straining, trying to place you because you've attained a new significance?

'A few months after we finished sixth form,' I say, chancing my arm.

'That's a tough age to have the rug pulled from under you,' Lucas says.

'So much so. You barely know who you are yourself, you need your parents to carry on being themselves.'

'Sure. I don't think I knew who I was or anyone else was until about twenty-five. Kind of nice, that innocence, in retrospect.'

Are we speaking in code?

'Oh, speaking of cheating men,' I say, to move things on more than a desire to discuss it, 'You were right about Robin. He ran into my parents in a supermarket and did a number on them about his devotion to me. It means he already knew I was working here when he came in.'

'Jesus. I can't say I'm surprised though.'

'Do you know, I'd assumed it was chance he met my parents and he'd not be staking Waitrose out, and right as I'm telling you, I'm not so sure.' I pause. 'He thinks he can do things in name of this love for me, which is fictional horseshit.'

Lucas says: 'Georgina. It might not be true, but be careful. Something I've learned is people do much worse things to you in the name of love, than they ever do as your enemy.'

On my journey home, dark streets scrolling past my window, I turn these words over and over until I am not sure if I am imagining a look of total understanding that passed between us as he uttered them. Something shifted between Lucas and me tonight, I'm just not quite sure what.

30

The resolution with Geoffrey is a non-resolution, an impasse, rather than a truce – he won't apologise, I won't apologise.

I'd be quite happy never to see the Tizer-haired old walrus as long as I live, but it's problematic if I want any sort of relationship with my mum. And that weekend, a social occasion comes up where I have to choose if I'm going to boycott: Esther's Sunday lunch.

I wrestled with various evasions or outright refusals and then thought, why should he get to still go to things like that, while I behave like the outcast? Sod him.

Esther suggests I arrive half an hour before official kick-off so that it's my feet under her dining room table when they arrive, as a symbolic gesture, and I gratefully do as I'm told.

Unfortunately, both of us forget Geoffrey is the sort of nightmare guest who thinks turning up forty-five minutes before he's been invited is an act of conspicuous efficiency, as opposed to wildly inconsiderate. His shiny new reg Volvo is squatting on the drive like Mr Toad's chariot when the taxi drops me off.

It irks me so much that Mum is a passenger in this, both

literally and figuratively. I hope I'm never in a marriage where I don't feel I can say: *No we're not setting off an hour early so our hostess has to grit her teeth and miss the shower she'd planned, sit back down.*

'Hi,' I say, in the living room doorway, as Milo singsongs, 'Hiiiiiii, Auntie Georgina,' back.

Geoffrey sullenly throws his cava down his throat without looking at me or speaking, while Mum and Mark say hello.

An unusually antsy Esther bustles off to get me a cava and I sit down. Mark says: 'How're tricks?' and we make small talk. I can see Mum's mind whirring as she tries to find a topic that is both relevant to the company and totally neutral.

I could tell her, from my time with Robin, that if your partner makes your social life much harder for you, you might have picked the wrong partner.

'Here she is, right on time! Look at that, Esther,' Mark says, standing up, as a mobility adapted van sweeps into the drive.

'It's a miracle, the care home must be on fire,' Esther says, as Nana Hogg emerges on to the gravel. With much fanfare and exertion – by others – she's put in a wheelchair and conveyed into the house. She announces her preference to be on the sofa, which displaces a clearly displeased Geoffrey, much to my delight. She gets her knitting out, mauve hedgehogs of soft yarn, and starts clacking away with the needles.

Mark says to me: 'That's a lovely idea about taking flowers to your dad's grave on his birthday with Milo, by the way. I've got time off and I think Esther can take leave too?'

'Yep. The teachers say Milo can have the day off school,' she says.

'Patsy and Geoff, you're very welcome to join. We're thinking of heading there for one, and having a spot of lunch after?'

Mark's guileless decency is actually a fiendish weapon here. If I was saying this, it would have side to it. Mark is genuine. It makes Geoffrey look all the worse.

'Hnph,' Geoffrey says.

'I'm sure we can come along,' Mum says, embarrassed.

'Why?' Geoffrey says, rankled.

I'm bug eyed. Is he really going to be a git about this, with an audience? This is unexpected. He's so furious about me, he's not able to do the greasy backhanded routine. It's war.

'It would've been his sixty-fifth birthday,' Mum says.

'He's not *there* though, is he.'

An awkward, shocked silence, soundtracked only by the clink as an on-edge Esther totters around, refilling glasses.

'In the sense he's not going to rise up out of the ground and start offering us carrot cake?' I say to Geoffrey, the first moment we've spoken. He looks suitably revolted that I've dared. 'This is a blow, I had no idea.'

'There's no need to go,' Geoffrey says, turning back to Mum, ignoring me.

'She can go if she wants,' I say.

'You are nothing but a troublemaker, and should pipe down,' Geoffrey says. Back to Mum: 'You shouldn't go because he was an awful old philanderer and the whole thing's a sham. Just tell them no, Patsy. Enough. They're old enough to hear it.'

Wow. He's doing what he did to me, with an audience. I already know Mum must've known. But did Esther know?

301

I glance at her and she's looking startled, in my direction. I can't tell if she knows and she looks equal parts baffled and concerned.

Milo says: 'What's a Fillunder?'

'YOU'RE AWFUL,' Nana Hogg suddenly says, to Geoffrey, 'An awful man.'

All heads turn. In the excitement, I'd forgotten she was here and I suspect everyone else had too.

'Nan!' Mark says.

'Stop ordering *her* around,' she prods a knitting needle towards me, 'Like you order *her* around,' a second knitting needle prod at Mum.

Bloody hell, Nana Hogg is *phenomenal*.

Geoffrey has gone purple.

'I'm not going to stoop to insulting an elderly lady, *however*—'

'I've seen your like before. My friend Margie's husband Hamish used to make her and the kids eat bread soaked in beetroot juice while he had steak and spent his pay packet down the bookies. You remind me of him. A nasty sort.'

'Nana, you really need to stop . . .' Mark says, desperately.

I start quietly laughing. I'm not trying to be outrageous but I can't help myself. It's bloody brilliant.

'On what possible basis are you calling me a bad husband?' Geoffrey says to Nana Hogg.

'You're a bully. Let her go to her husband's grave.'

'I'm not stopping her.'

'You literally just told her not to go,' I say. 'And slagged my dad off. And called him a philanderer.'

'Yes and I wonder which of his children takes after him.'

My mouth falls open.

'Don't you dare speak to my sister like that,' Esther says, surprising us all. This has turned into a bloodbath, a one-set stage play. Mum is like a statue, eyes wide. Mark's aged a year in minutes.

'Nothing wrong with enjoying a bit of slap and tickle,' Nana Hogg says. 'If I still had her physique I'd be putting myself about a bit too.'

'Right, that's enough,' Geoffrey stands up, makes a fuss of collecting his jacket from the coat stand in the hall. We listen to this, Mum motionless. Her instinct is to side with Geoffrey, yet even she's got qualms.

He lets himself out and sits in his car, fully visible through the bay window, engine running, passenger side door thrown open ready for Mum to obediently scuttle out after him.

'Should I go out and speak to him?' Esther says to Mark, and even Mark shrugs.

Nana Hogg knits serenely through it.

'Mum,' I say, turning to her. 'Don't do as he says. He's been a bad shit. Let him sweat on it for a night and go back tomorrow.'

'She's right,' Esther says.

Mum looks at us, looks out of the window at Geoffrey, chews her lip. He slams the door shut, the tail-lights blaze, and with a squirt of gravel, he goes. Mum says the very last thing I'd expect.

'Georgina, have you got any cigarettes?'

31

We stand quivering with cold in Esther's garden, smoking menthols that Esther managed to unearth from the back of a cupboard. Being unable to provide Mum with Marlboro Lights is not a way I thought I'd fail her.

'I'm so sorry you had to find out about Dad like that, Gog,' Esther says, gripping her elbow.

'Oh, Esther, I knew,' I say. 'I didn't know you two knew. How did you know each other knew?'

'I saw Dad with her when he was supposed to be at Graham's. I was with my friends and he was coming out of Atkinson's, they were holding hands. I came home and told Mum. I was about ten.'

That long.

'I knew anyway,' Mum says. 'From almost the start. He thought he could come home smelling of Yves Saint Laurent Rive Gauche and I wouldn't notice. Silly sod.'

'How did you find out?' Esther says to me.

'I caught Dad . . .' Hmm. Best still be careful, 'making plans to see a woman on the phone, the first weekend I was home from university. We had a huge fight about it, right before he died. I thought I should keep it to myself. Given Dad was gone anyway.'

'Here's us, thinking we had to keep it from you, at any cost. You were always so close, you had Dad on a pedestal. We didn't want to knock him off,' Esther says.

'Thank you,' I say, frowning. This is an adjustment, the idea they protected me.

Mum blows smoke out in a long plume. It's so bizarre seeing her with a fag. I knew she dallied in her twenties, but she gave up when she got pregnant with Esther and never started again.

'Grace, her name was. They were on and off for ten years. Met her at work. Wouldn't give her up,' Mum says. 'She never married so was there at his beck and call.'

'Well. What utter bastardy,' I say. 'To you and her. I don't like what she did but I bet she thought they were in love and Dad might leave.'

'I didn't think you'd think that way,' Mum says. 'I thought you might blame me, for making him unhappy.'

I love my mum, but sometimes it does seem incredible we share DNA.

'Why on earth would I blame you? It's not your fault if he cheated on you.'

Mum nods. 'I'm still glad you didn't know. Caused a lot of tension for you, didn't it?' She nudges Esther.

Esther nods, scuffs her shoe on the ground. 'It was hard to see him in the same way.'

I readjust my perception of Esther's teenage hauteur, her

exasperation with me and my closeness with Dad, and some of the slammed doors.

'Why is Geoffrey spraying the information around all of a sudden?' Esther says. 'What gives him the right? All we said was we were going to the grave, not erecting a statue.'

'He gets jealous, I think,' Mum says.

'Of a dead person,' I scoff, and then consider I might be something of a hypocrite, given the sensations I felt looking at the late Niamh.

'I know he can be difficult, but I have to be careful, girls. He's the one with the finances.'

'Mum, loads of equity in that house is yours,' Esther says. 'You're not powerless. Tell him to sort himself out.'

'It's not that easy.'

'I'm not saying it's easy but you can't let him walk all over you.'

'We'll back you up, Mum,' I add.

'That's very kind but you've both got lives to lead of your own, I can't be a burden.'

'You'd hardly be a burden!' I say, suddenly feeling tearful, like I can't quite swallow around the lump in my throat. I can't remember a time when it's felt so sisterly between the three of us.

'Always a spare room here,' Esther says, clasping Mum's shoulders.

For the first time, I feel the true uselessness of my skintness. I am not the same sort of help myself, whether I like it or not.

'We should go in, the food's ready,' Esther says, with a look at Mark who's waving through the kitchen window.

Mum catches my sleeve, as I stub my fag out under my boot.

'Georgina, about your dad. He never gave up his Saturdays with you, for her. I took some comfort from that.'

This makes me feel gratified and confused and guilty and sad, all at once.

When we've finished the passion fruit mousse, Mum says no thanks to a coffee and I know, I already know what's coming next. She sensibly waits until Nana Hogg is snoring in an armchair and unable to offer input.

'Esther, thanks for the offer of staying but I think I'm going to go home.'

Esther's brow furrows. 'Are you sure?

I want so much to be some assistance, and not always have to defer to my capable sister, who spent so many more years of her childhood shouldering the fact of my father's affair than I did. When I was tripping happily with him from cafés to curry houses.

'Yes, absolutely sure. It'll have blown over and I will tell Geoffrey his response was excessive.'

Good luck there.

'If you're sure,' Esther says.

'I am.'

'How about we share a taxi, Mum?' I say. Mark tactfully gets up to clear the plates and I say, more quietly: 'Why don't you go in, make sure everything's alright and you're not going to have a barney? And text me. If you want to come back out and go home with me, wait for it to cool down, you can.'

Mum nods, embarrassed, and I think that we're doing what is called normalising. We're talking in the language of managing an abuser. I'm not one to pine for a boyfriend to look after me, but right now it'd be so good to have someone to share this with. To have my back, and by extension, hers. To be a team, the way I know Esther and Mark are.

I call a cab and we gather our things. Mark hustled Milo off to bed early and we don't want to wake Nana Hogg. I'd like to give her a medal though.

By the doorway, Esther catches me.

'Thanks for this, Gog. I wish she'd stay, but . . .'

'I read somewhere that leaving someone like that is a "process, not an event". It was never likely she'd have an epiphany. Like you say, we need to stay around her and let her know she's not alone with him.'

Esther gives me a tight hug and I linger in it, feeling small, and made of pink fluff.

When we pull up at the mansion in Fulwood, I remember Geoffrey's principal appeal to my mother – it's a beautiful house, a cavernous Victorian semi made from that burnt toffee-coloured Yorkshire stone. It has deep steps leading up to the stained glass front door that seems designed to lodge in childhood memories.

It is still an ogre's prison, however. I turn to Mum, put my hand over hers. She must find this reversal excruciating. I've never been the greatest at accepting concern myself, after all. Luckily the driver has Magic FM on loud.

'It's no problem to wait. I won't go until you text me.'

She kisses me on the cheek and pats my hand.

The front door closes behind her. The hallway light flicks on beyond.

Seconds later, my phone pings.

Night darling! X

I can tell by the speed of the response, she didn't wait to speak to him before she told me she was alright.

What parts that is made up of pride, recklessness, fatalism or optimism, I can't tell.

32

A bad workman blames his tools, or in my case, her material.

The 'Worst Date' tale instalment of the second Share Your Shame competition is tonight, and I'm angsting over my lack of them. I've had weeks to prepare and yet in the midst of family dramas and trying to work out where my head is with Lucas, I've spectacularly failed to come up with anything. Nothing quite like crashing and burning in front of friends, family and colleagues to keep a girl awake at night.

So much for my grandly telling Jo that good fodder for anecdotes is distributed democratically in life, you only needed the ability to notice them.

'I haven't been on any dates that are truly bad enough to qualify, that "he turned out to be wearing an electronic tagging bracelet under the tuxedo" sort of thing,' I say to Kitty. Lucas hovers nearby, pretending not to listen.

'Closest I can get is that when I was twenty-four, my then-boyfriend Mike took me to New York on a surprise trip. First day we go to the Empire State Building and he proposes. I said no. We still had three days of the holiday left and neither of us could afford to change the flights.'

'Oh my God!' Kitty says.

'Yup. It wasn't even an "I'm not ready" refusal either. I was so horrified, I blurted out that we were best off breaking up. We'd only been seeing each other three months! Then Japanese tourists saw the ring and got the wrong end of the stick and tried to take our picture. But even though Mike's happily married now I don't think he deserves me reliving that with an audience to win a column in *The Star*.'

'This is getting a bit like Laurence Olivier's "have you ever tried acting, dear boy",' Lucas says, as he slots a bottle back on the shelf and tells Kitty to take her break.

Even when he's being mildly combative towards me, I get a kick out of it. I can feel myself falling again. I have to stop myself.

'What do you mean?'

'Well, just make it up? It's a writing competition, not an interesting life competition. I'm sure they're partly looking for that initiative.'

'Guess so.'

'And how are they going to check it's true anyway? Produce receipts from Bella Pasta, circa 2010?'

I laugh and chew my lip. 'Actually, I do have one funny-awful date story. But it's about Robin. Is that morally OK? Or wise?'

Lucas shrugs. 'He talked about your . . .' He stops and restarts, so he doesn't have to say the words 'sex life', and a little voice in my head starts shouting, *Is this significant? You definitely get prudish around your crush, rule of courtship*. Shut up,

DON'T YOU FORGET ABOUT ME

voice. '. . . Talked about personal things in public. I don't see it's that wrong, after that. At worst it's levelling up.'

I nod. 'I suppose. And if he doesn't get to hear of it . . .'

Lucas spots a regular, acknowledges him, swings a pint glass under the relevant pump.

'Just leave his name out of it. If he's not actually in the room, it's quite a stretch it'll ever reach him.'

Lucas is right. And if Robin said 'How dare you!' he wouldn't have a leg to stand on. I mull over the date story, redrafting key passages in my head. Sadly, due to its specific and identifying nature, I'll have to leave out the part where Robin suggested to my parents that if we were a portman-teaued celebrity couple we'd be 'Robgina' or 'Hornee'.

A young man in a Superdry sweatshirt walks in. He looks vaguely familiar.

'Georgina! I heard you were working here!'

It's Callum, erstwhile That's Amore! waiter and its junior sex pest: I didn't recognise him out of the grubby off-white frilled shirt and without his giant pepper pot.

'Hi, Callum,' I say. 'As you can see, you heard right.'

'You said if I did what you wanted, you'd go on a date with me. Then you totally ghosted me! Cold.'

'I didn't say that. If you want to get technical, you were meant to get my coat and you didn't, so no deal done.'

Oh great, out of context this still makes me sound terrible.

'Yeah, well, now we've been shut down. Health and safety. They found a dead rat by the scraps bin. Tony said, "It's dead, we dealt with it" and the man was like, "Nah, mate. Not how it works."'

I try to keep a straight face so I get to hear more.

'Yeah that would be . . . not how it works.'

'I think it made it worse that there was only half a dead rat because they reckoned there was a live one somewhere that had nibbled on it. They couldn't find that one, though, so, no proof.'

He does a shoulder-dropping shrug with hands up, as if the complex, controversial case of That's Amore! vs Hygiene Standards is one for great legal minds to battle out.

'Anyway, Tony's left and we're going to reopen with a new name once Beaky gets the licence going again. I'm going to be manager! Want in?'

I'm about to politely decline when Lucas says:

'Er, mate, she's working here. Maybe recruit on LinkedIn, not in front of me?'

'What's it to you? Free country,' Callum says, fists now thrust in sweatshirt pockets, showing the quick wittedness that made him so skilful in service at That's Amore!

'I'm the boss,' Lucas says.

Callum gives a slack-jawed smile. 'Lol. Yeah well we're going to pay time and a half so maybe you're going to have to work extra shifts, tell *your* boss.'

Lucas blinks.

'I'm not her manager, I'm the boss, it's my name above the door. Piss off, you chippy little herbert.'

I have the decency to wait until the door's swung shut behind Callum to collapse laughing.

'"*I'll date you if you fetch my coat*," alright, Lady Penelope,' Lucas says, with a grin.

'I didn't say that . . . ! Oh my God, I'd been sacked, they threw me off the premises, he tried to hold my coat hostage in return for a date. Oh my God!' I splutter, while Lucas laughs heartily. 'For the record I did not offer to go on a date with him.'

'Given your current predicament with the writing competition, that might've been a mistake. Speaking of which,' he looks up at the clock, 'I think it's about to start.'

'Then she said, "I'm sorry, that's actually my Mooncup." I can't drink ruby port to this day. The End.'

The thin man in the flat cap takes a small bow amid much laughter and applause and I feel a ripple of fear that I'm going to end the night with a damp squib. The date story I've decided on is more of a slowly unfolding disaster than bam-bam-bam jokes.

Once again, I'm last in the running order at Share Your Shame and unlike last time, I've decide to watch the other acts first. My shift downstairs is also over and I arranged to finish early so I could concentrate on my craft and get drunk after.

Kitty is working the function room bar this time and the brothers are downstairs.

I sip a white wine with my friends, sister and brother-in-law and wait to be called up. I was touched when Esther went out of her way to inquire when the next event was.

When I say so, she said: *We honestly loved it! I admit I was doubtful beforehand but I was very proud of my witty little sister. I told Mum and she says you can say anything you like about her as long as you make it clear her house is always clean and tidy.*

That's handy as I did want to direct some satire her way with my date story. Omelettes and eggs.

The other contributors are an uneven bunch, some jittering, some speaking for ages, some barely speaking at all. A couple are really good: a date with a sensitive man on *Guardian* Soulmates, who it turned out was only working with dis-advantaged kids because of his community service, and the girl who ended up going home with the date's divorced dad. The latter was very likely invention, but it was hilarious – you were right again, Lucas McCarthy.

'Georgina, is Georgina here?' Gareth calls from the stage, sheaf of papers in his hand. My eyes involuntarily move to Mr Keith among the judges. I'm feeling more buoyant about his presence though – surely when news reaches his ears that That's Amore! was running a petting zoo, he'll see it my way. (It'd be awful if anyone were to email their news desk.)

I step up to the microphone, noting that having done this before doesn't make it one bit easier.

'My Worst Date,' I clear my throat. 'Wasn't a first date. My parents asked to meet my boyfriend of three months. Let's call him Dave. My mum said she'd throw a "fizz and picky bits evening." Fizz and picky bits is mumspeak for prosecco and olives, dips and so on, with some breaded things from the oven. Shortly after arriving, my mum offered Dave breadsticks and a pot of hummus. Strike one.'

'He said: "I'm afraid I'm both a coeliac and a chickpea refusenik, Mrs Horspool." It would've been helpful if he had told me he was coeliac, and it was news to me too, given he'd seen off several Hawaiian deep-pan pizzas in my company. I wasn't aware Papa John's catered to gluten intolerants. Later he said, "I'm not a *coeliac*-coeliac. I just find wheat doesn't agree with me and people prefer labels don't they? They're easier to grasp." I'd have thought it was easiest to grasp the breadstick.'

Some laughs.

'I could already sense that he was becoming sillier in the face of stern social pressure, imagining it would jolly things up, when actually it was going to go very badly. Like a pilot recklessly grabbing the controls and pitching into the sea when he should ignore the dinging lights and turbulence, and let the aircraft steady itself at that altitude. Then we had the "and what do you do for a living" chat.

'Dave was a comedian, sometimes on the television.

'My stepdad said: "And what might we have seen you on?"

'"Ketamine?" he quipped. I don't know if you're keeping track of the strikes but I count this as strike two.'

I glance up, more laughter. They're a half cut and eager to be pleased group, but I'm still gratified.

'"Does it keep the wolf from the door, as it were?" my stepdad said, offering a sour cream Kettle Chip.

'"More or less," Dave said. "I have other gigs on the side too. Social media stuff. Twitter."

'"That pays?" my stepdad said.

'Dave said, "It can do. I write tweets for humorous accounts."

'My stepdad sniffed. "Other comedians?" he said. "Can't they write their own?"

'"No, corporate ones," Dave said. "The PG Tips monkey, that's me. Sorry to ruin the illusion."

'Dave grinned at their blank faces.

'"The chimps' tea party?" my stepdad said.

'"The knitted one," Dave said. "With Johnny Vegas. You know: MUNKEH!" He bellowed this, spraying shards of soggy crisp.

'"Have I got this right," my stepdad said, reaching sixty-seven-year-old system overload. "People log on to their computers online, to read the remarks of a stuffed toy, which is in fact, *you* pretending to be a stuffed toy?"

'"In one," said Dave.

'"Good grief," said my stepdad. "I'm probably not the right customer for that sort of polytechnic talk."

'Dave was drinking wine, at a clip, and he was on flu meds, which his doctor had warned him not to mix with alcohol. At some point during glass four, he went full-on stoner philosopher.

'My mum asked if he wanted marriage and kids. (Thanks, Mum.) He said "It's a case of whether you choose the red pill or the blue pill isn't it?"

'"Viagra?!" said my stepdad Geoffrey.'

A laugh, a proper laugh.

'Dave went on to explain the plot of popular sci-fi action-adventure *The Matrix* to them, in relation to his hard-left politics. My mum was surprised to discover she was in a simulation created by capitalism, especially as she'd just had the kitchen done.

'"I like Fulwood!" my mum said.

'"It's a constructed reality," he said. Then burped. "You should read Noam Chomsky's *Manufacturing Consent*."

'"Got to grow up some time, sonny Jim," said my stepdad.

'"Have you?" my boyfriend slurred. "Have you? Numbers, man. Who cares. You're seventy," he said to my stepdad, who

317

said, "I'm sixty-seven, thank you very much!" My boyfriend looked at my mum and thankfully decided not to risk it. "She's thirty . . ." he pointed at me. "And this house is what? A hundred years old? Right! Numbers. All meaningless."

'"Not if you want children, they're not," my mum said, and at that point I decided I was trapped in a simulation designed by Satan. She continued, "Georgina's fertility is going to fall off a cliff at thirty-five, I sent her a clipping from the *Telegraph* about it only the other day."

'"Thanks for that, Mum," I said. "I don't really see what Kate Middleton has to do with me, to be honest."

'"Ugh, the Royals?!" Dave's face twisted into a mask of contempt. "In my revolution, Kate Middleton would be in a dungeon."

'"With three beautifully dressed children as a comfort to her though," my mum said to me, as if it was a scold, at which point I collapsed in hysterics at DaveWorld meeting MumWorld and trying in vain to make sense of each other.

'"In those velvet and bibs! Those posh kids are dressed like ghosts that died in a fire!" Dave bellowed.

'Ten minutes later, my boyfriend nodded off during my stepdad discussing his allotment, and did a sleep-fart.'

I look up.

'My boyfriend Dave and I are no longer together.'

I fold my notes and feel it's gone well. Everyone is clapping and whooping and someone's even whistling. I'm awash with pleasure and relief.

Until I see that the person whistling is Robin McNee.

33

Before I have time to react, I'm being herded from the stage by an excitable Gareth.

'I have a treat for you tonight, guys. There's a special guest here who has asked to be added to our line-up, as a one-off guest appearance. We're honoured to have him. Put your hands together for Robin McNee!'

Shaking, I trace my way back to my seat and share 'WTF' looks with my table mates. How the hell did he get up here without one of the McCarthy brothers spotting him and chucking him straight back out?

Robin is raking his hand through his hair, doing his 'aw shucks' sort of moves: little dip of the head, bashful expression. He detaches the microphone from the stand.

'Good evening, drinkers of The Wicker and fans of sharing shame. And congratulations, 'Georgina . . . ?' he feigns uncertainly picking me out, 'I loved that.'

No really, how the *hell* has he got in here? I feel rage well up and even as it does, I know I'm being unfair. Barring someone, unless you have a bouncer, isn't foolproof, and it looks like Robin had help, a man on the inside. What the fuck is he going to do?! After the havoc and misery he wreaked last time, I am vibrating with the potential malignancy.

I catch a movement by the door and, unnoticed by everyone but me, see Lucas, his brow knitted, taking in Robin and scanning for my face. I don't know how long he's been there.

When his eyes meet mine, Lucas makes a neck slashing gesture at me and I do a subtle head shaking, 'leave it,' two handed, palms down wave. Dragging him off stage now would end up being a scene. A bigger scene than the one Robin has in store? I don't know.

'Have you heard the phrase "teachable moment"? It used to be one for education wonks, now it's something that comes up in Ted Talks, and political long reads,' Robin says. 'The idea is that it's a window of opportunity, an unplanned event or experience which provides the chance for growth. But for the moment to teach you, you have to be open to its lesson. You have to recognise that it is one.'

Robin unscrews the cap on a bottle of water, handed to him by Gareth, who thinks he's booked Ricky Gervais here. He isn't using notes.

Why did I talk about Robin, WHY? I've left myself so compromised by it. *In the middle of a mess, saying it's not my fault, making excuses.* This is me. There's no longer any denying it. God, the idea that Robin fucking McNee gets to bring me to this point of utterly deflated self-awareness. Just when I thought I might be turning things around.

'It made me wonder: what have been the teachable moments

in my life, which I missed?' He sets the bottle down. 'I was dating a girl who came up to me after a show, and told me she liked my work. She was smart, interesting. A cynical under-achiever who has seen my act and is still prepared to sleep with me, just my type. Aaaaand she was way out of my league. I hate that phrase, makes you sound like you believe in eugenics, doesn't it? Use your own shorthand here for: "People would think I won her in a competition."'

Everyone laughs, in a gentle, beguiled way. Like they're squirrels and he's feeding them nuts. 'Cynical under-achiever', you shit. Look at how he slipped the knife under the rib cage there, with a flick of the wrist so small and fast that it goes unnoticed by everyone but its intended target.

'We went on an early date to see the new *Blade Runner*. We settle down to watch it and will inevitably discuss how sequels are always inferior, afterwards. Five minutes into the film, we hear a man, somewhere behind us, say "HE'S A ROBOT!" We glance at each other, ignore it. Again, someone is on screen, he trills: "ROOOOOW-BOT!" like it's a spoiler. Followed by giggling. We glance again. Uh oh. Is this a ringtone irritant, a sodcaster, a chattering millennial who thinks he's in front of Netflix at home? Or is he someone with mental impairments? The doubt is landing your woke lefty with a conscience here in a tricky spot. So I do what all middle-aged, middle class men do in such situations, I silently panic and hope a proper adult comes along and deals with it.'

Laughter.

'Unfortunately, the man doesn't let up. Whatever and whoever comes on screen, there's a comment. Now his voice sounds mocking, sarcastic. "SEXY GIRL." "NICE CAR." All I can think of is a joke about how I don't think much to the director's commentary edition.' He twinkles at the admiring crowd. 'Never come to a comedian in a crisis. My girlfriend whispers she needs the loo and stands up. At which point the gentleman disturbing us all says "OOH AND HELLO LADY!"'

'I snap. We've missed the first half hour almost in its entirety to the psychodrama of Mr Robot and now he's harassing my girlfriend? Enough. I tell her to sit down, wait, and I leave my seat. I find a member of staff outside, explain the situation. He enters with a torch, and the man is ejected. Like a handwringing liberal, I say to him as he passes me: "Look I'm sorry but you were ruining it for the rest of us." The man stares at me and pushes past, no reply, and I feel vindicated. No remorse, and how rude. I tut, loudly.'

'I return to my seat to muted cheers from the disgruntled filmgoers around me. I feel manly at having taken action, and protected my partner.

'Afterwards, we go for pizza and I say, over my thin crust American Hot: "I can't believe he ignored me when I apologised. Why should I apologise anyway? Some people." My girlfriend says: "I think he was profoundly deaf. If you've been deaf from birth, you don't use language in the same way. I had a customer where I worked who gave me Christmas cards with THE GIRL written on the envelope."

'I say: "Or he was simple."

'She says: "But he's obviously seen the first *Blade Runner* and understood it." "Why?" I say. "He knew who was a robot and who wasn't straight off, and you wouldn't immediately know that from what was on screen without that context."

'And, people of The Wicker, I was annoyed at her. I said: "What did you want me to do, leave him there to carry on shouting "RAIN!" and "SCARY GUN"?" She said, "No, I'm not getting at you, I'm only thinking about what his perspective on it was." I said: "You'd be having a go at me now if I'd done nothing!"

'She looked baffled. "I didn't expect you to do anything."

'I spent the next half hour sulking, thinking: where's the gratitude? Doesn't she appreciate me? Why doesn't she care about *what I did for her*?

'It took me losing this woman I loved, who I still love . . .' pause for fakey steadying of himself '. . . a while later, going back over my mistakes, for it to click. I put that pressure on myself because I thought it was a test, where I had to be who she wanted. But I had what she wanted, completely wrong. She didn't want The Guy Who Got The Other Guy Thrown Out. She wanted The Guy Who Took The Time To Understand The Other Guy. He was the deaf guy, but I was the one who didn't listen.

'So my worst date is me. I was the worst date. Thank you.'

Robin slots the microphone back on the stand.

As I get up to leave, amid the 'You Are A Genius' level hullabaloo, he's thronged by women.

Game, set, match. This isn't love, it's not even adjacent to love. It's a grotesque imitation of adoration to give Robin an excuse to hound me. He just wants to dominate me and win, and right now, it feels like he has.

34

Robin is ejected, my indignant friends and family are safely gifted drink in the snug, Share Your Shame's Gareth quibbles over the politics of Robin's involvement in the show with an aggrieved Devlin. Wherever I go, I cause trouble.

Lucas steers me into the kitchen, and amid the wiped-down stainless steel surfaces and static of dormant machinery says: 'Georgina, I am so so sorry. This is entirely on us. I forgot to give Dev a visual and he snuck past when I was occupied. There's no excuse not to have kept a close eye out for him.'

'It's OK.'

'I can't apologise enough. Two attacks by that guy in your place of work is two too many, and this one should've been entirely preventable.'

I'd have to be a much better person than I am not to get a frisson from Lucas grovelling.

'Robin has more brass neck than C-3P0, hardly your fault. That wasn't a date I remember having, by the way.'

'Really? I just assumed it was with you.'

'Oh it was, but it was nothing like that. He didn't complain about the man or get him thrown out, he swore loudly and slow-clapped the staff when they finally did something. He's a straight up liar. Sorry, artist, using his artistic licence.'

Lucas folds his arms and hisses and shakes his head.

'You must think less of me for ever entertaining him,' I blurt. I can't help it.

I am gratified that Lucas looks genuinely startled at this.

'Er, no. God, no. I'm not without mistakes myself.'

I swallow. Not a road I want to set off down with him. An awkward silence.

'"Dave" was Robin though, right?' Lucas says.

'Oh, yes.'

'Please don't tell me any of that wasn't true because given how much I enjoyed it, it'd be like hearing Father Christmas isn't real all over again.'

I laugh loudly. 'Swear down, every word.'

Lucas looks at me and I see he was trying to cheer me up, and it worked, and I am so grateful that he even tried.

The morning after Share Your Shame, I think, it's time for me to stop agreeing Robin McNee is a problem, and do something about it.

Here's the thing, I decide, having slept on it. Robin isn't a physical threat, he's a psychological terrorist. Intimidating him with muscle, despite what Clem said – and how much it appeals on a base level – it doesn't make sense to me. To catch a thief and all that.

So what is his vulnerability? On panels, he's very much

the away-with-the-fairies surrealist amid the bloke-ish badin-age. I'm not surprised he's the one that Kitty considers the star turn. He's clearly used to this boyish manner meaning he can easily consort with women ten or fifteen years younger than him too, me being a case in point. A whiff of 'grotty, manipulative old letch' following him around would do him no good.

I have an idea.

Robin was disorganised enough to use my phone from time to time when his was out of juice. I wouldn't have suspected him playing around with other women because his phone was habitually unlocked, or notifications appearing with full text of the message on screen: where technology was concerned, he was an open book. I know now of course it didn't mean he had nothing to hide, he just didn't give much of a shit.

He called Al his agent enough times from my mobile that I was fed up of getting mis-sent messages from a string of unknown numbers, and so Al is there in my phone book.

I might've felt guilty at dragging Al into this, but for the fact he turned up at my workplace and turned amateur docu-mentary maker.

I'm not stupid though. If I've stored Al's number, he might've stored mine. And if CLIENT'S EX WHO YOU MIGHT'VE INFURIATED WHEN DRUNK flashes on his phone, I can very easily see him drop-calling me.

I sit on my laptop, doing my due diligence – Al is on Twitter, and active on Twitter at that, which is useful. I fire off a direct message.

Hi Al – this is Georgina, Robin McNee's girlfriend

Ugh, it says something I find those words hard to type. I've restored myself to full privileges as I'm sure Al will simply assume we've made up in the meanwhile, and 'ex' would signal I might be hostile.

Sorry to bother I'm just a tiny bit concerned about him ATM and wonder if I could run some things past you? Between us? Gx

The main part of getting one over on someone, I have learned down the years, is not rat-like cunning, but the benefit of surprise. Ask any cold call scammer. If Al sat and thought about this, he might shout Robin first and check what was what. More likely, he will simply want to know what's up. Hence this is a carefully gauged approach, me being both non-confrontational and intriguing, which will see Al unthinkingly take the bait. All I need is for him to answer his phone.

It works.

Hi Georgina! Of course. Chat now?

Yes! Thanks. I've got your number, I'll give you a bell in ten minutes x

NP x

I call. He picks up. I'll never know if he'd have picked up without the preamble, but I feel vindicated in my manoeuvrings all the same.

'Hi Al, so. You saw what Robin did in the pub the other day? Getting on the chair?'

'Oh . . . yes . . . ? Hah. I was quite tanked that night, I forget how strong that craft beer is!'

'Right. I've split up with Robin as I found him having sex with Lou, as you know. When you came to where I work, I thought it was a coincidence. I've since found out he's talked to my parents behind my back, told them a pack of lies and extracted that information. Then used it, as you saw.'

'OK . . .' Al says, guardedly, realising he's been tricked. 'I didn't know that.'

'Sure, I'm not suggesting you did. Then yesterday, he did the same thing again. Got into where I worked, made a speech about me to a busy room.'

'Eeesh.'

'The thing is, Al, I have a problem and I want your advice. Since we finished, Robin's come to my house at night, thrown stones at the window and scared my housemate. He's turned up at my workplace and caused a scene, twice. After which, I only kept my job by the skin of my teeth . . .' – might as well make this a three-egg cake – 'I made it abundantly clear, when I caught Robin red-handed, having sex with another woman, that we were over. He hasn't been given the slightest signal that there's any hope I'll take him back and I don't answer his messages. This is a one-sided game. This is what we call harassment.'

I draw breath into silence, hoping Al's still on the line.

'It's starting to worry me, to be honest. If he doesn't back off soon, I'm going to have to explore my options.'

'I hear you, but what do you want me to do? I'm his agent, not his minder. I'm 200 miles away again.'

'Sure. But you've been there merrily filming Robin, cheering him on. I thought we could put our heads together.'

'I didn't know this background – yes, sorry, leave it there, Charlie – or I wouldn't have. The clip got deleted.'

He's speaking from his office and going to pull a Sorry Must Dash any second, I have to make my point quickly.

'Yes. But here's my problem, Al, your client is hounding me and if I can't find anyone to call him off, informally, then I'm going to have to go to the police and get a restraining order. How's that's going to look, if the local paper turn up at the magistrates court?'

I have absolutely no idea how restraining orders, magistrates, or local press coverage on such matters work, but then Al didn't know how filming on private property worked, either. *Just sound certain.*

'Wow! I had no idea things were bad enough to go the police! Don't you think that's a sledgehammer with a nut?'

He's finally snapped to attention, sensed danger. I have him.

'"Nut" being the operative word here, Al. You tell me what I should do. I don't want to. But when "please leave me and mine alone" hasn't worked, many times over, what else do I do?'

'Oh, this is . . . let me shut the door . . .' I hear shuffling and slamming noises. 'Look, this is getting out of hand. I'll speak to Robin and make it clear you're upset and he needs to calm down. I'm speaking in strictest, strictest confidence here you understand, but have you ever thought Robin might be a little . . . bipolar?'

'Er . . . no . . . ?'

'His mood swings are all over the shop. He goes from periods of sitting indoors getting fried to being incredibly hyperactive. It could be flights of the artist's fancy but I do wonder if there's something diagnosable there. I don't know if the whole overdoing it, love bombing you, comes from that.'

'Ah. I don't know either.'

I consider: I could take the high road or the low road here. But I want a fast, no fuss result. Low road it is.

'Would he plead mental instability in court?' I say, sweetly.

'I'll speak to him,' Al says, swiftly. 'He won't turn up at your pub again.'

'Thank you very much, I appreciate your help.'

Hah. *Your move, Robin McNee.* Well, don't make one please, but in rhetorical terms. Your move.

Al clearly was spooked, as fifteen minutes later I get a text from Robin.

Hi! OK you win. Message received. Can I speak to you about something else? Important. No requests for drinks, promise. About work. Rx

Nope, not biting.

35

'You absolutely said no way to getting back with Robin McNee then?' Kitty says, sucking on a thin straw in a bottle of Diet Coke.

'Hell to the yeah,' I say, while I wipe out a drawer underneath the bar, with a vigorous scouring motion. I haven't heard from him since yesterday's message so I'm feeling quite satisfied that my scheming has worked. Also, I don't know if Lucas is round the corner but I can guess which way this line of questioning from Kitty will go, and am planning on answering as if he can hear, for safety. It's coming up to 9 p.m. and the bar is quiet for once.

'Yer not seeing anyone then?' she says.

'Nope.'

'Don't you want to meet someone? Get married, have kids and that?'

'Those are three different questions,' I smile up at her. 'I'd like to meet someone but I'm not in any rush. I don't know if I want the other two until I'm with someone.'

'You should get on Tinder.'

I straighten up, rinse the cloth, wring it out, check the time. A slow shift and not much of it left.

'I'm more looking for love than bunk-ups, to be honest. Proper romance. I'm re-reading *Wuthering Heights* at the moment. It has the best line: "Whatever our souls are made of, his and mine are the same."'

Kitty looks dumbstruck and I briefly flatter myself I might get the queen of social media into classic literature.

'Whatever ARSEHOLES are made of they have the same arsehole??!' she shrieks, and Lucas sticks his head round the corner and says: 'Shhhh!'

'Our souls! Souls!' I say, shaking with laughter.

A woman with a severe ponytail approaches the bar and something in the set of her face, and the speed of her movement, strikes me as off, somehow.

'Yes?' I say, composing myself, which isn't the usual greeting, but somehow I know something's up.

'Are you Georgina?' she says.

'Yeee-es?'

'This is from Bob.'

I open my mouth to say I don't know a Bob when she raises a Tupperware container she's been holding with one hand, behind her back, and throws the contents directly into my face. It's cold and acrid and stings my eyes, making me cry out, temporarily blinding me.

I hear voices shouting, men and women, and feel myself bundled along the bar and into the kitchen.

There's the sound of the door slamming shut behind me and I hear Lucas's voice say: 'This is going to be cold,' before my face is pushed under a tap and water flows over my face. It goes up my nose and I start squeaking in shock and struggling, as if I'm being waterboarded.

'Georgina, you have to do this, stop pushing!'

I go limp, trying to catch a breath through the running water and hear Lucas saying *fuck fuck fuck* rapidly and I wonder why he sounds so scared and why I am being held down in a sink instead of towelled off, and why I can feel him pulling at my clothes, sleeves being yanked over my hands, then I'm pulled upright and my t-shirt goes all the way over my head.

Before I can blink the water away or catch my breath, my head goes back under the tap. This time I can feel it flowing over my neck and spattering my chest, the shiver of bare flesh in direct contact with the air. What on earth, why make me even wetter? It runs down me in rivers and into the top of my jeans and I scream: 'Stop, it's cold!' like a child.

I'm jerked out of the sink and upright again like a rag doll and I feel warm hands on either side of my head and Lucas's voice saying: 'Can you open your eyes?'

I tentatively unstick the lids. The kitchen comes blurrily into view, through a lot of H2O, tinted grey by displaced mascara. I blink. Water trickles warmly out of my nose.

'Blurgh, what happened?'

'Can you . . .' Lucas trails off. 'Can you see me?'

I focus on him and say: 'Yeah, course?'

He pushes gently at my temples, face an inch from mine, as he moves my head left and then right. He holds me at a slight distance, looking down, running the fingertips of one hand along my collarbone, watching me to see my reaction.

I gulp and mentally save the sensation to remember later, and look down too.

Like an anxiety dream made real, I'm only wearing my bra on my upper half. The Fair Isle cardigan I was wearing is lying discarded nearby on the kitchen tiles with my t-shirt dropped soppily on top. Thank God this bra is an opaque black balcony, if there were actual nipples in the room I'd have to kill myself. I didn't dress this morning expecting Lucas McCarthy and I to be jointly inspecting my cleavage today.

'Er. Why am I not wearing my top?' I say. Thinking: this is an enterprising move, Lucas. I got something thrown in my *face*, didn't I?

'Are you alright? You feel alright?'

I blink more water out of my eyes and smile and say: 'Yeah? Apart from being half naked and very damp and completely freaked out.'

I sniff and cough and wonder whether to cross my arms and decide styling it out and not acting embarrassed is better, while discreetly holding my stomach in. I pick up my wet t-shirt from the floor and hold it against myself.

'Oh, God,' Lucas stands back and slumps against the microwave. 'God, that was . . . Let me get my breathing back.'

'What's the matter?' I say.

'I thought it was acid!'

'Oh!' I exhale and Lucas's eyes widen.

'You mean you *didn't* think that?!'

'No. Does that make me stupid?'

Suddenly everything in Lucas's response makes sense and

I feel a heady combination of immense naiveté and wild relief that it didn't occur to me.

'It's a blessing, I guess. Lucky you. I've just had forty or so seconds of my life I never care to relive.'

'Classic man! I'm the drowned rat here, in my bra.'

'Hah! Oh God, sorry. I thought your skin possibly peeling away with a corrosive fluid was more important than modesty.'

Lucas reflexively glances down at my chest, and away again swiftly, and I cross my arms and then both of us want the ground to swallow us.

'Oh I'm so relieved, Georgina, I can't tell you. I thought we were straight to A&E . . .'

'You were quick with the water. Impressive.'

'I've done some health and safety on burns. I can't believe you didn't consider it was acid. I saw it happening in slow motion.'

Lucas shakes his head and I see that he's been genuinely quite traumatised by it. I am touched. I've also been touched. I can feel his fingertips on me . . .

'Why did she do that?' I say. 'Who's "Bob"?' We stare at each other utterly mystified, until the realisation clangs. Who – related to this workplace – might want to throw a noxious substance over me? 'Hang on. Wasn't the Thor stripper called Bob?'

'I'm not sure . . . ?'

'Yeah! When he left he shouted: "Bobby does not forget!" This must be his revenge. Why throw water?'

'Uh, I doubt it was water.'

I pull a strand of my hair round to my nose and inhale.

'You did such a good job of hosing me down there's not much left. So we suspect . . . stripper's piss? That's one for the craft ale names, if you run out.'

I gurgle with laughter.

'You will honestly find the dopey lols in fucking *anything*, won't you?' Lucas says.

Before I can respond, he traps me in a completely unexpected hug. The t-shirt falls from my hands. I surrender to it, caught tightly in the right angles of his elbows, hesitantly wrapping my own arms around his back. I can feel his heart still pounding. Lucas mumbles into my hair: 'Of all the faces to destroy.'

What? *What?*

We pull back and gaze into each other's eyes for a second, mere centimetres apart, and I think, Christ alive: are we going to kiss? In shock and stripping and fear and shared crisis, everything between us is up in the air. What's been revealed, other than a quarter of my breasts, is that Lucas cares about me. Electricity crackles between us.

The door opens, and Devlin peers round. He takes in the embrace, and his eyes travel down to my exposed abdomen. I automatically start to pull away but Lucas's grip tightens fractionally and I stop.

'I'm presuming the lass is alright if my brother's jumping on her. This is a food preparation area, Luc!'

Kitty's voice can be heard squeaking: 'What's going on? Is Georgina OK?'

Lucas gallantly manoeuvres himself without letting go of me, bending down and returning my cardigan, which I accept and hold draped across my front, like a beach towel. The top is going to need a good wring out and to sit on a hot radiator unless they want this to be a wet-t-shirt establishment for the afternoon.

'All sorted; seems Georgina got a dousing from an unknown clear liquid.'

'I'll refrain from any off-colour jokes which aren't occurring to me right now, you know that's not my style.'

'Get LOST, Devlin.'

'Hahaha. The assailant ran off and it took Kitty too long to get round the bar to give chase. What was it about?'

'The prime suspect is the strip-o-gram we ejected, Georgina says.'

'I think it was revenge served cold for me hitting him.'

'Right. Never a dull moment, eh?' Dev says.

He withdraws and I pull my cardigan on and rebutton it, which strangely feels more intimate in front of Lucas than not wearing it. Must be something in the implications of the process of getting dressed around him. There's only one other sort of occasion when it might take place. I think he feels it too because he looks away and blathers vaguely about the necessity of calling the police.

'What do we say though? Someone throwing water is like reporting a toerag for a balloon in the street.'

'I think it might've crossed their minds you'd think it was acid, the sadists,' Lucas says. 'I think it's worth flagging. If it sends someone in uniform round to see him to remind him of the sentence for throwing worse things, it won't be in vain.'

'True. What a shift!' I say, tucking sodden hair behind my ears, aware my make-up must be 'member of Kiss'.

'Yeah, it's been eventful,' Lucas says. 'All things considered, you're allowed to knock off now.'

'I'd like to go home, shower, change, come back and down several large stiff drinks, please.'

Lucas gives me an appraising look. 'For the shock?'

'For the shock.'

'We've established my shock was worse,' Lucas says.

'You best have a stiff drink too then.'

Lucas checks his watch. 'See you in an hour or so.'

A session? The two of us? I'm aquiver with anticipation. I keep thinking of what Lucas said when he held me. He gave himself away.

I have hope.

36

'Yes, madam, what'll it be?' Devlin says.

'Half of Strippers Piss, please,' I say, when I present myself back at the bar half an hour before closing, fluttery with expectation, having spent more care over my freshening up and outfit than was strictly necessary for a lock-in. I'm wearing a tight Cure t-shirt. Sometimes being subtle is overrated.

'I've taken it off, that was coming through cloudy. I think the pipes need cleaning,' Lucas calls over, and we laugh in a goonish way. It's Devlin rolling his eyes for once. Wow, Bobby, you did me a favour. Extraordinary.

I can't believe I only recently thought of Lucas as stand-offish. Seems I had to learn the lesson of the person behind the façade, twice. He just needs to trust you.

Usually when Lucas is working, I'm working too. Parked with a glass of red wine at a table, I get to watch him for once. I have a covert ogling licence and I intend to use it.

I'd not admitted to myself until now what the sight of Lucas does to me. It was too masochistic, with someone who didn't like me, who thought so little of me that he had erased

340

me. Now I'm wondering if this wasn't in fact, ideal – no history to worry about. An untainted second chance.

I prop my chin on my hand. He reaches up to get a bottle from a shelf and his t-shirt rides up, exposing several inches of abdomen. A considerate customer changes their mind about which gin they want, and he has to put it back and get another one down, and this time I see the muscles above his belt flex as he strains to grasp it. My own, less flat gut flexes in response.

Even the way he stands over the till does something to me, the tension in his shoulders, the loose way his body moves. Oh God, and look at the way he's pushing his inky hair out of the light sweat on his brow . . . He glances over at me and I quickly move my eyes back to my phone.

He did suggest he might drink with me, right? My disappointment if he doesn't will be considerable.

I adore Dev and yet I'm effusive with gratitude when he says apologetically that he would have a jar but Mo and the kids are over and he's leaving early. Lucas waves away my offer to help with the clean-up. When the last punters clatter out of the door, it's me, Lucas and Massive Attack on the speakers. *Stand in front of you . . .*

I shiver with anticipation.

'Is that, this?' he holds up a bottle of red, points at the label, points at the glass.

I nod. He walks over holding it, with a glass, and I sit rod-straight with contained tension. He sits opposite on the second shabby-chic easy armchair at my table, unscrews the cap, tops me up, pours his, and says:

'So then, Georgina Horspool. This is highly preferable to us sitting in some hospital's serious burns unit, eh?'

He picks up his glass and clinks it against mine, pulling a grimace.

'Us.' Is that significant? Wouldn't it be more natural to say 'you'?

I remember this precipice of excitement from long ago. Not knowing if he feels the way I feel, knowing I could fall from a huge height, if not. Even though you could be utterly destroyed by hitting the rocks below, there's no feeling like it.

We talk easily, having enough in common now that it's effortless. He tells me how he hated university too, didn't want to do his business degree.

'Dad wanted us to take over the family firm, end of story, no other ideas tolerated or indeed, funded. It was a glove-like fit for Dev, but . . . I don't want to sound ungrateful, but I didn't want to run bars.'

'What would you have liked to do?'

'I quite fancied teaching, actually,' Lucas says, batting his glass from one hand to the other.

'I can see you as a teacher!'

'Is that a jibe?'

'No!' I grin. I am incapable of objective judgement, but it feels like we're flirting to me.

'You could still retrain?' I say.

'Yeah, I could. But I'm quite long in the tooth to begin again now and I'm used to this income, so. Look, I didn't say my problems were worthy of sympathy.'

He gives me a sly grin from under his brow and I think we're definitely flirting, surely.

'Are you loaded then?' I ask, curious as to whether he'll be honest.

'Errrr. What's the tactful response to that?'

'Honesty.'

'Yeah, I am. We are. The Faustian pact with my dad: do as I say, it'll all be yours. He was quite the bully, to the point of not entirely respecting the law in his dealings with the fruitier side of Dublin nightlife. We cleaned all that up. I'm relieved he's retired.'

'How did you and Dev turn out so well?' I say, unguardedly, and Lucas looks genuinely gratified.

'That'd be my mum.'

I know glorying in wealth is unseemly and that Lucas isn't more valuable as he's worth a lot, on paper. I still allow myself a brief flight of fancy, imagining being his. The men I've dated have been fairly inert and hapless, borrowing off me before payday. Ugh, Georgina, no, stop this. You're not an Austen heroine, make your own money. Think of your mum and Geoffrey.

We talk about Robin, and I tell Lucas my side of catching him in bed with Lou, and he boggles and guffaws and gasps in the right places and I see us bonding, from the outside, and quite like who I am, for a change. I might've dated an idiot but I can take it to the metaphorical Cash Converters and turn it into something of entertainment value.

Bottle gone, Lucas asks if I've tried a cherry liqueur they've been sent and we do sticky shots, smacking our lips together

and debating whether it's delicious or saccharine. The illumin-
ated clock over the bar says half one. My mind is fuzzed by
drink but I know a moment of reckoning is drawing near.

'Look at the time! Best call your cab,' Lucas says.

'Luc,' I say. The nickname is deliberate. I take a risk. A
premeditated risk. 'So you know when you hired me? I . . .
overheard you saying to Dev you didn't want the pub to turn
into Hooters.'

Lucas startles.

'Did I say that?'

'Uh . . . I thought you did. I was having a fag outside the
kitchen window, after the wake.'

'Oh, I was probably pissed . . .' He looks awkward and I
worry I shouldn't have pushed my luck.

'I didn't think I had the dumb blonde, big rack look.'

'You don't!'

'Robin called me "Topshop Diana Dors".'

'Wow. He looks like Leo Sayer.' Lucas pauses. 'I was . . .
probably just putting Devlin in his place for jumping in and
hiring when he was half cut.'

'Right.'

'. . . I'm really sorry if it sounded like I was passing judgement on your appearance. It came out flip and rude because
I was jibing at Dev. Oh . . .' he rubs the back of his head, 'I
feel like such a wanker now.'

It was always a risky gambit, confronting Lucas with this, and
right now it's deservedly backfiring. He's uncomfortable
and I've damaged the easy-going mood.

'No, I know you'd never insult me. It's just – sometimes I

worry that I don't attract the right sort of man. Robin was surprised I'd read books. Maybe I should dye my hair dark and ditch the pink coat.'

That's better, Georgina, I think. I mean, creakingly manipulative compliment-fishing, but just about getting away with it.

'Any man who doesn't recognise an intelligent woman because of her hair colour isn't worth knowing.'

'Yeah. True.'

Well that trap failed.

'I'm not tanned enough for Hooters anyway.' Argh, let it go, Georgina. Can you hear yourself.

'I really wouldn't worry about it. You're lovely as you are.'

WOAH. Scored in injury time. *Lovely*. Lucas McCarthy thinks I'm lovely. *Of all the faces to ruin*. That meant something. It had to. My heart is pounding so loud I'm surprised the neighbours haven't knocked on the wall to ask me to turn it down.

'OK.' Lucas glances at the wall clock. 'Taxi.' He gets up to call from the phone behind the bar.

Make a move, make a move.

'One for the road?' I call, as Lucas puts the phone back. I'm not sure why pubs still have landlines, really. I shouldn't have let him call it. I could've pretended I was getting one on my app.

'Ack, go on,' Lucas says.

Gleefully, I pour out more as he comes back to our table. He picks up the glass, clinks with mine, the back of his fingers making the faintest contact against my own. Our eyes meet as we down it. I unconsciously lick a drop from my lips and his eyes flick towards this movement so briefly, I can't tell if I saw it or saw what I wanted to see.

Car lights sweep up to the window and Lucas stands up and says, his tone impossible to read: 'Oh, that was quick.'

I think *no no no no*, getting to my feet. The lights travel onward and Lucas says 'False alarm.'

I'm right by him, and I'm looking up at him as he's looking down at me and the world is holding its breath and I know that it's now or never.

'Lucas?' I say.

'Yeah?' he replies.

'I feel a bit drunk,' I say. 'I should go. But . . .'

'What?'

'I don't want to.'

He reaches out and brushes a stray hair away from my face because touching each other now seems to be a thing we do, and I think: signs won't get stronger than this.

Before I'm even fully sure I'm going to do it, I close the distance between us, put my arms around his neck and kiss him.

37

It's still terrifying, but inebriation makes it slightly less terrifying to tough out the seconds of not being sure if he'll respond. Never mind dancing on your own, kissing on your own's the truly lonely activity.

The moment I worry it won't happen, suddenly Lucas is kissing me back, with equal passion, his hand on the back of my head, fingers wound into my hair.

No one kisses as well as this. I'd thought my teenage memories were rose tinted, but if anything they had faded like an old photograph. Everything he used to do to me is still there. It's like my body remembers him and lights up in response, a ping-ping-ping of recognition and lust travelling the length of my body. I've had dozens of kisses–with–grappling in the years in between, and they were all pale shadows of this: the push of him, the pull of him, the whole effect of him.

I'd told myself: well yeah, but you mythologise your first love, don't you, it's nostalgia playing tricks. It wasn't. My God, it wasn't.

He needs to know how much I want him. Since I've not had the courage to tell him, I throw my efforts into this mode of communication instead.

Not only am I making it a deep and quite filthy kiss, I slide my hands under his t-shirt and on to bare flesh underneath, hopefully making it clear this is not a 'let's have a quick snog at the end of the night', this is a full on, 'take me to bed' bid.

Lucas slides a hand under my top in response – yes! – and I put my hand over his and move it straight up to my breast, my hand over his. I am certainly not playing hard to get. The euphoria of the moment is carrying me. He squeezes me gently and tugs at the lace of my bra cup and his fingertips brush my left nipple. We're miraculously back at that same second base (I never understood the bases) we dexterously managed to achieve undetected in the Botanical Gardens. Only this time, we don't have to go home separately, aching with unfulfillment.

When I fumble around his flies, he grabs my hand and says: 'Stop.'

I step back an inch, getting my breathing back.

'What?'

'We can't.'

I look at the windows. I suppose he's right, the blinds won't be foolproof and there's still enough light in here we could be seen.

'OK. Upstairs?'

My clothing is rumpled and my face is hot.

'No. I mean, best not do this.'

I don't understand. He steps back a little further and it feels like a million miles.

'Wh— what? Did I do something wrong?'

He looks at me from under his brow and says in a thick voice:

'Hardly.'

Nnnggg. I am in a state my mum would deem unladylike. I go to kiss him again and he stops me, hands firm on my upper arms.

'Seriously, Gina. We're both being pissed and silly.'

Gina?

'I know,' I say. 'Is that a problem?'

'Hah,' he shakes his head and says: 'Maybe not for you.'

Eh? A performance issue? 'How do you mean?'

'It might be fun now but we have to get up and work together tomorrow.'

'I don't care,' I say, forcefully.

'Well, I do. Your taxi will be here any second. Got your coat?'

I'd thought he was kidding, maybe making me work harder for it. Now I know this is not a bluff, and I'm bewildered.

'What's the problem?'

'I don't like getting involved with anyone I work with,' he says, voice still low. 'I don't want the complication.'

'Oh, my God!' I say, hurt, offended, a little too loud. There's no job on earth I'd sacrifice a night with Lucas McCarthy for.

'What?' Lucas says, quietly, far more in control. 'There's nothing wrong with that.'

I'm so hurt and raw, the words just spill out of my mouth, unchecked.

'*I don't want to get involved with anyone I work with* is an obvious fob off. Everyone meets people at work. Just say you don't fancy me enough, that's fine.'

It wouldn't be fine of course, it'd be devastating, but I don't believe anyone who could kiss me in a way that made me feel like my bones had melted, felt no connection himself.

'It's not that.'

'. . . Why kiss me?'

'You kissed me.'

My mouth falls open. 'Oh right, sorry, I thought this had involved two people but I accosted you, did I? I just fondled *myself*?'

'Georgina,' Lucas says, and he looks upset now, 'You're gorgeous. You're amazing. No one would easily turn you down. But you work for me. So, no. I can't.'

I know consolation prize compliments when I hear them. He's turning me down with no real trouble at all.

'Honestly, Lucas, spitting me out like you found a lump of cat food in your chilli con carne is one thing, making up reasons for it is another. You can tell the truth. I'm a grown-up. This polite brush-off is the worst.'

Lucas looks stung by this, more agitated than ever. 'That's bollocks though, isn't it? The truth isn't some wholesome thing that sets us free. It's messy and best left alone, and you should know that better than most.'

Does he mean my dad? Or . . . ?

We're breathing heavily, silent as his words land in the space between us.

'So,' I choke. 'So you're admitting that you're not actually bothered we work together, and it is something else?'

'. . . Yeah,' he says, hesitating. I can tell he already wishes he'd not said what he just said, that he was needled by me and didn't think more than one move ahead. Too late.

My bluff has been called. In my confusion and mortification, I've been pretending so much more confidence than I actually have. This is gutting, even frightening. But I've come too far to back down.

'. . . You didn't hear what I was saying to Kitty? About . . . love? I can clarify that if so. I'm not looking for a ring.'

He frowns. 'No.'

'Then what?'

'It doesn't matter.'

'It does.'

If the real reason was bad enough to need a white lie to cover it, it's going to be awful. And he doesn't know I've gossiped with Kitty about him being ready to date again, so if he invokes the spectre of Niamh, it's another white lie. I think I know what might be coming and yet I would rather hear anything – *anything* – other than what I think he might be about to say.

Could it be . . . ? No, surely not . . .

'Really, I'd rather hear it.'

'Why? To what end?'

'It's better than wondering,' I say around the lump in my throat.

Brash claim: I have no idea if it's better than wondering. The pub doesn't feel cosy any more. It feels dark and silent and treacherous. The spark between us has snuffed out, now smoking like a guttering candle. Lucas looks away, then back, right into my eyes.

'I associate you with one of the worst nights of my life.'

We stare at each other.

'What do you mean?'

'You know what I mean, I'm sure.'

'But . . .' I trail off. Not ready. I've had twelve years to prepare and I am not ready.

'Cast your mind back. We were eighteen years old and what I think was once called "going steady".'

He's known who I am all along. *Worst night of his life?* Ha. He has no idea. And I've spent all this time not knowing he felt this way.

My face must be ashen. Lucas says: 'And yes, I did pretend not to remember you, once Dev had given us no choice about working together. I thought it was easier.'

'You're the boss. You could have said you wouldn't work with me.'

This is irrelevant, but I need to say something as a placeholder while I sort my thoughts out. He knew?

A cab beeps and both of us ignore it.

'I didn't want to persecute you for something that happened in another lifetime. It's not as if I could care less now. But yeah, with the choice of any barmaids in Sheffield, for pref-erence I'd have gone with one who hadn't broken my heart.'

He's telling me this now?

'I broke your heart?' I say.

Lucas doesn't reply.

'You broke my heart,' I say, into the silence.

Lucas laughs. He actually laughs at this.

'Nice try. I think that might be false memory syndrome.'

There's so much to say, but I'm completely unprepared for this. I don't know how, in hostility and rejection, to discuss it. While I can still feel the pressure of his lips on mine, where he's touched my skin.

'But . . . you didn't want me?' I say.

Lucas gives me a look. Heavy, sardonic. Full of contempt, and things he won't say and I ought to know.

'Yeah. That is true. Afterwards, I didn't want you.'

Time stands still for a moment. I stand still, I say nothing. I accept my coat from Lucas, pick up my bag from the seat nearby, and walk away.

'Night?' he says, half-sarcastic, half hopeful.

I answer him only with the door, swinging back in his face.

38

I allowed for the possibility I might wake up and feel different. I don't. If anything, I am even more empty. And yet with nothing to lose, I feel myself gaining strength I hadn't known was there.

When I arrive for the lunchtime shift, I catch Devlin on his way out to collect some new furniture. Lucas won't be here 'til mid-afternoon, I'm told, which suits me just fine.

'I'm afraid I've got to give you my notice. Is it a week for the first six months?'

He looks like I goosed him.

'For treasured staff like you, it's as long or short as you like, but never mind that, where are you going? What utterly sneaky bastard has poached you?'

'Nowhere, actually. I've saved up a bit of cash and I'm going to assess my options. Can't pull pints forever, at the big Three Oh,' I say, with a wan smile. The money saving is actually true. The Wicker pay fantastically well, and have thrown bonuses at me, and I've been working too hard to spend anything. I really shouldn't be leaving.

But I can't stay.

Devlin looks baleful. 'Awww no . . . I'm knocked for six. You feel like one of the family. Tell me this, is this a negotiation, is there anything I could offer you to make you stay? Or is your mind made up? I know Mo sometimes wants me to guess the answer.'

I laugh. 'No mind games, I promise. It is what it looks like.'

Not entirely true, but I'm hardly going to enlighten him.

I expect Lucas to hear soon enough, but I don't expect him to know already when he finally arrives after four. Dev must've texted him, because from where I'm standing, they've had no chance to confer in person.

He gives me a straight hard look when he reappears. While Kitty's handling the front of house transactions with relative ease, I hear Lucas shout me from the back.

'Can you point me to where the limes are?' he asks, from inside the kitchen, holding the door open with his foot.

'Aren't they in the top of the fridge like usual?'

He doesn't answer, so, braced for impact, I walk inside and he shuts the door with a sharp click, standing in front of it.

'You're leaving?'

'Yes.'

'Why?'

I can't meet his eye, can't tell if he's trying to meet mine.

'Taking a break. I have some money I've . . .'

'Yeah I know what you told Dev. You're leaving with nothing to go to. Why are you really leaving?'

I shrug, nudging the edge of the lino with my foot.

'As you said. You don't need complications with someone you work with.'

'We don't have any complications. We didn't complicate it.'

Oh, boy. *We didn't sleep together, I knocked you back, so everything's cool.* I am angry enough that I have to fight to control it.

'You think we've got no problem, after what you said to me?' I say, with force.

Lucas looks taken aback; chastened, almost nervous of me. This role reversal where he feels under siege – and wants something from me I won't give – it's cold comfort, but it's some comfort nonetheless.

'I did say raking up the past wasn't a good idea. You wanted to know.'

'I did. Now spoken, it can't be un-known.'

'So I'm being punished for telling you something you wanted to know and I told you, you wouldn't like?'

'You're being punished? Ha. *Of all the barmaids in Sheffield*, I'm sure you can find a replacement. I'm the one foregoing my salary.'

'I don't want you to!'

'I can't stay,' I say, simply.

'I don't . . .' Lucas puts his hand on the back of his head, his body taut with tension. I can see him trying to figure out how much more truth will help, or make things worse.

'. . . Was it honestly that much of a surprise I felt that way? All I said was that what happened, it upset me. At the time, I mean. It's like it happened to someone else now.'

I can feel an urge to pursue this, to point out he can't

simultaneously be indifferent and repulsed by me. But my simple steeliness is the only thing holding me together right now, more from him on this might break me open. I breathe deeply.

'That's not all, though, is it. You branded me a brassy slut.' I say this emphatically, deliberately, and he can't meet my eyes.

'I didn't do that!' Lucas says, flushing. 'Oh my God, we were kids, who cares, honestly.'

'You do, obviously, given what it stopped.'

Lucas swallows. 'I'm sorry if I offended you or misjudged anything I said. I felt we'd been down that path before and it didn't need a revisit.'

Didn't need a revisit. His attempts at minimisation are only going to offend me further.

'. . . I meant to say: I like being friends, let's not spoil that.'

'I'm not happy with the whole "pretending not to remember me" thing either, the game playing. We could've got it out of the way at the start.'

'Well, were we going to chew the fat about it? *Oh hey remember when we . . .*' He trails off, glowering. I ignore his sulky beauty, it can go to hell. 'You baffle me, Gina.'

Is it deliberate, resurrecting his pet name for me? Much as I'd like to hate him for it, call him sassy things like 'a player', I suspect it isn't. This is why he didn't want to discuss the past, it makes him vulnerable. He's forgetting himself.

'I'm sure I do. If you're so arrogant you thought I'd accept your poor opinion of me, and carry on.' My voice nearly breaks on my last words but I'm holding this together while I still can. I will damn well leave with some dignity.

'I don't have a poor opinion of you. You've been great here, and we don't want you to leave. Both of us, me and Dev. And if seeing less of me is what it takes to keep you, I'm going back to Dublin soon. It'll be Dev and Mo running the show until they hand over to a new manager.'

Bloody hell, he doesn't even want me here because he cares about me, it really is about professional competence. What he thinks is his ace card is in fact the worst thing he could've said. I'm not leaving for the reason I told Devlin, and I'm not actually leaving for the reason I'm giving Lucas, either, and this knowledge allows me to pull myself up, raise my chin and meet his eye again.

'Thank you. I'm still going.'

I sidestep him and smash through the kitchen door, back out to the bar and say, loudly: 'Yes, who's waiting, please?'

Screw Lucas McCarthy, and not in that sense.

Funnily enough, telling Kitty is the worst. She cries.

'I feel like you're my sister,' she says, hugging me.

'I'll still come in here, we'll still see each other.'

'Yeah but it won't be the same. I feel like I've learned so much from you.'

'You have?'

'Yeah. You were the one who explained to me that "offal" is what the meat's called, when I thought people were saying eating brains and bumholes was "awful".'

'We will be friends forever. I promise. I make friends for life,' I say. Lucas walks past and I squeeze Kitty again.

'How can you let her go?!' Kitty wails to Lucas, in an excruciating moment I can nevertheless only commend her for.

'Sadly, God gave her free will,' Lucas says to Kitty. 'To use as she pleases,' he says to me.

'Or misuse, apparently.'

This is a glib riposte, not thought through. I see a hurt look on Lucas's face and tell myself I don't care. I do.

39

In the end, I didn't stay a week. That was my last shift as I knew I couldn't bear to spend another second in Lucas's presence. Dev was brilliant about it and after thrusting far more than he should have into my hands, he kissed my cheeks, twice, and gave me a hug that felt like it cracked my ribs.

'Don't be a stranger now, Georgina, d'you hear? There'll always be a job here for you.'

I'd thanked him, gathered up the pink fluffmonster and left, not looking back, no goodbye to Lucas, who'd slammed upstairs, not to reappear. I told myself I was fine with that.

Now, sitting at home on my laptop on my first afternoon of unemployment, listlessly scrolling, I got an alert about Robin's latest triumph. He never bothered with a personal account on Facebook, but I'd forgotten I'd 'Liked' Robin McNee's fan page.

Once upon a time, you broke up with someone, and if they didn't live in your postcode, you never saw them again. You might not have heard of them again either. I'm not a fan of this modern alternative where you can become a spectator of everything they do for the rest of their lives, simply by typing their name into the search bar on Facebook, or vice versa.

I promptly click Unlike. Then my eyes drift down to the item.

Hey everyone! See Chortle's write up below! We've got a few tickets left for a special sneak preview of Robin's new show which he's doing at The Last Laugh tonight. Rolling out to a full tour plus Edinburgh in the new year!! SEE YOU THERE ☺ ☺ ☺ £5 on door / 7 sharp

Despite finding TV fame with Idiot Soup, *Robin McNee's long been a cherished secret of the comedy circuit. With this new self-revelatory work, Sheffield's finest stand-up is unlikely to be secret much longer.*

'My Ex-Girlfriend's Diary' uses fictional excerpts of his lost, much lamented love's journal, which he 'finds' when prowling in her bedroom. It's My Dad Wrote A Porno meets Judy Blume. He recounts how his nosiness rebounds on him, as he's privy to her lustful feelings towards her teenage boyfriend. By contrast, their time between the sheets is somewhat lacklustre.

McNee uses the diary discoveries as a jumping off point to ask – can men ever understand what women want from them, and have a hope of fulfilling it? By snooping on her fevered adolescent fantasies about another man, McNee realises his own inadequacy as a later life successor. Expect to laugh, cry and wince at the use of 'cleft'.

I stop, palms slick with sweat. I read it. I re-read it. I read it four times more and pace the room, saying, 'You utter BASTARD' out loud. I tear up the stairs and check, hands clumsy as I push my clothes aside in the drawer. It's there. It's still there. I yank it out and riffle the pages, heart pounding. It's all here. I hold it to my chest and sob, like a scene in a soap opera. My words, taken from me.

With shaky hands, I flick through the pages. This would be hard to read at any time, but after the showdown with Lucas, it's excruciating. Like peeling back a bandage and plunging your fingertips into the surgical incision underneath.

. . . I lose track of time when we're Doing Stuff, I mean completely, three hours had passed and all I can remember about the entire time is thinking about where his left hand was. Got home and felt like everyone could see on my face what I'd been doing all afternoon. Rubbish tea, I hate lamb stew with the fatty speckly bits. George Best has died and Dad seems sad about it. Mum said, 'He had it coming with his behaviour' and Dad said, 'Mr Best, where did it all go wrong?' and they had one of their moods with each where they've pissed each other off at some special level Esther and I can't understand . . .

. . . Persuaded Mum I needed new bras and pants and so we went to Marks and Sparks and she tried to have THE TALK with me after about being safe with boys after aaaaarggh noooo. I said, 'I don't have a boyfriend' which would've worked like a dream with Dad, probably because he doesn't want to think about it. But Mum just raised an eyebrow and said, 'they're not always your boyfriend.'

I knew what was coming next, some 1950s code for 'don't be a slag' and YES there it was: 'Georgina, remember nice boys want to date nice girls.' . . .

. . . He is the most sexy boy to ever live, I'm sure of it, even though he's my first and I've only been alive for 18 years. He is the person-ification of sexy and I don't think he knows how beautiful he is. He says that to me! I keep trying to imagine what actual sex will be like. How are you supposed to know what to do? You have to patch it together from films, TV, the gross magazines that Gary Tate used to bring in to school and the awful 'How A Baby Is Made' video we were once shown in biology GCSE, when a man and a woman were smiling at each other, went up to a bedroom and then it cut to a ballet dancer leaping around with a ribbon and the whole class started laughing . . .

I slam it shut again and feel a wave of shame and disgrace and fury at this invasion.

How? I remember one time, no, maybe more than that, a few times, when Robin stayed in my room after I went to work. *'Leave by the back door and pull it shut, it's a Yale, then you don't need my keys.'*

Left unattended in here, he went through my things. He read my diary. Did he copy out sections from my diary? I wouldn't put it past him, and from what I can tell he's either got perfect recall (with the amount he smokes? Unlikely) or (so much more likely) took photos of the pages. And he put them into his act.

What did Lucas say? 'If he has anything he can use against

you'? Right now, Lucas doesn't look smart so much as clairvoyant.

It takes a very large wine and five more re-readings of the preview on Chortle to come up with what I should do.

I may have been able to bounce Robin McNee's agent into talking to me, but I'm not so Machiavellian as to work out how to get into Robin's dressing room.

The Last Laugh is at City Hall and I arrive at 6 p.m., an hour before curtain up. From what I knew of Robin's habits, he will be here, swilling a beer, scrolling on his laptop, eating a tub of his lucky guacamole with extra hot Doritos (I'm not kidding, he did this. 'Performers have rituals,' he told me, as if he was Nikki Sixx with a bottle of Wild Turkey).

I could say I'm somebody other than I am, but then that's not going to help me when I don't know who that somebody who'd get access might be. 'I'm a girl who'd like to have sex with the famed wit Robin McNee,' might get Robin to say yes, but the venue wouldn't wear it.

I'll simply have to hope that once again, the unexpected nature of my appearance bears fruit.

'Got a Georgina Horse Poo here for you,' says the pallid girl on the desk, into the phone. I am tense with worry. I have no Plan B if he says no. 'Sure, go on down, it's on the left,' she says to me.

I'm vaguely stunned. Robin's show is called *My Ex's Diary*, and he doesn't think I'm here to tear a strip? Then it dawns:

he doesn't think or care about my motivations all that much. Ironically. *My Ex-Girlfriend Who I Was Never That Bothered About's Diary.*

'It's good to see you,' Robin says, after I knock and push the door open. He's positioned at his laptop, wearing a t-shirt that says You Versus The Guy She Told You Not To Worry About with cartoon characters underneath. A large bottle of chocolate milk is next to his rose gold MacBook. Pretty ironic he's about to spend an hour and a half ripping the stuffing out of my adolescent nonsense. At least when I was behaving like one, I was one.

'You look sensational in this lighting,' he adds, pen in corner of his mouth. Obviously thinking that by being here, I've finally come to my senses, and might be up for some pre-show warm-up.

Ugh.

'You read my diary,' I say, flatly.

'Had a little scan through,' Robin says, with a 'Forgive Me' teeth grit.

'You absolutely despicable, evil, morality free, thought rapist,' I say.

'Thought rapist!' Robin puts his pen down. He is half affronted, half whirring about whether he can use this encounter for his act, too.

'Really. You piece of shit,' I conclude. 'I don't know how you can live with yourself. Reading a woman's diary, a woman you were in a relationship with. Then putting it in your act, and leaving her to find out by accident, hours before you entertain hundreds of strangers with it. Please at least tell me you know who and what you are?'

'You left me alone in your bedroom! The drawer was half open! It was practically an invitation.'

Rav's cookie jar.

'. . . I thought it was very sweet, very innocent, and that wonderful wry Georgina voice coming through so strongly . . . I was so infatuated, I wanted to know how you tick. Then I got jealous. Like, who is this rival who you desired more than life itself? Whose touch you craved like a drug?'

I flinch. Who would want anyone reading their callow erotica, much less hearing it repeated on a stage? If Lucas ever found about this show, he would surely work out it's based on him. The two other performances he's seen by Robin were about me, after all.

He's trying to weaken me, and it won't work.

'It wasn't for you. You didn't ask to read it, you didn't tell me you had. Please explain when you thought it was OK to share it, and humiliate me in public? I mean, walk me through the thought process?'

'Right, a few points. No one's being humiliated. It's a very tender, very life affirming . . .'

'I'd rather affirm your death.'

'Hah! No, it's not in any way vicious and your identity is completely concealed in it. I mean the whole thing even plays on whether you exist! Seriously, watch it. Make a judgement after.' Robin sips more beer and does a palm up *that's that* gesture. 'I did try to meet you and warn you, but you wouldn't consent.'

'Yeah, because your campaign has been about getting me

to date you again. Nothing about "oh hey, George I'm about to use your diary, any views on that?"'

'Er well, sugar pie, last time I saw you, you were telling stories about me making a pissed-up idiot of myself in front of your fam. No application for permission was received by me. So who's using who here, exactly? Looks like we're doing exactly the same thing.'

I knew he'd say this, and it makes my hands curl into fists.

'The diary is completely different. What happened at my mum's house involved both of us, and what happened in my diary happened to *me* and me alone. This is a transgression of totally different magnitude and nature, and you know it.'

He shrugged, completely indifferent.

'Seems like I'm in trouble for simply playing this game better.'

Game.

'Fuck you, Robin. Have you even thought about the context around what you're using? What might have happened with that boyfriend off the page? What else might have gone on in my life at that time?'

'Well if he dumped you, he's the fool, isn't he?'

Imagine. Imagine being a man, and thinking your approval has such value, that this sort of oily fob-off compliment can stitch a wound this big.

'You are a disgusting person. Don't hide behind this light-hearted, carefree bullshit. What you are doing to me is utterly serious and completely unfunny.'

'Oh, look. You knew who you were involved with. How many girlfriends do you think end up in acts? Loads. Lots.

This is what artists do, we cannibalise our lives. We feed on its flesh. You were very into all that until Lou happened. You were quite the fangirl. Look how we met. Tell me this: on the night we met, who was using who? Who dragged who home? You wanted Robin McNee on your score sheet.'

I feel queasy. I've learned a lesson: if someone can justify anything they want to do to themselves, they will do anything. What did Lucas say? People with no boundaries are dangerous people.

Robin's standing up now, brushing the Doritos crumbs off him, preparing to shoo me out.

'. . . And I tell you, I could win the Perrier with this. Imagine. You're too close right now. Years from now, you'll look back and be so glad of it. It's a tribute, it's a love letter. I go on and on about how . . . mesmerising you are in it, Georgina. I mean, the person who looks a chump in it, is me. You're the muse. You think Warren Beatty is still bothered that Carly Simon called him vain?'

I try to contain my rage as I know I won't get him to listen if I go ballistic, but it's taking every last drop of my self-control.

'You have no idea who I am. We spent six months going out and you never bothered to find out. You're using my diary for cheap ridicule, to burnish yourself. You don't know what's happened to me, in the past. Or the present. You don't know the damage or the hurt caused by using what you've stolen.'

'But then do we ever know anyone? I mean the show explores that exact thing. You should come see it! I think once you get past your shyness, you'll be blown away.'

I've been in control up until now, but calling it 'shyness'

tips me into full blown warlord mode. I slam my hand on the desk, leaning forward, forcing him to take a half step back.

'You're not some great, fascinating artist, Robin! You're a passable comedian trying to elevate himself with bogus sensitive "insights", pretending to be New Man Caring Dude, when you're anything but. You're a selfish twat, posturing as something more interesting than that by using a woman's words, against her will.'

Robin's face is all of a sudden, a mask of pained fury.

'Oh really! Great to have your critical verdict, tavern wench. At least I've put myself out there. What have you ever done? Whinged, expected men to help you and coasted on your boobs, that's what.'

'Robin. Here's what you're going to do. You're going to cancel tonight due to a sudden bout of ill health and second thoughts. Then you're going to rewrite the show, before you perform it again, and take out everything from my diary. Do some actual writing. Do what you said, and invent an ex-girlfriend, and her diary entries. Change every last detail from anything that was ever associated with, or adjacent to, Georgina Horspool.'

Robin makes an *As If* smirk.

'If you don't, I will *fuck you up*. I will go on every place I can find you discussed online, and I will post about how you have betrayed me. I will give interviews about how it feels to be turned over by someone you cared about. I feel like this is just begging to be in *Grazia*, or *The Pool*.'

'Mmmm, I mean, that would draw more attention . . . ?'

Robin says, his eyes shifting back and forth, still looking for the win.

'It would, but I wouldn't believe that thing about any publicity is good publicity, if I were you. I wouldn't test it, when it's mistreating a woman. Check out how a few careers are going, since the man in question was outed as a creep. Other women have a way of feeling solidarity with that woman. They might even turn up to heckle. Comedy festivals might think twice, if I'm ringing up saying they'll have blood on their hands if they let you perform it. Sooner or later, the story isn't your life-affirming whimsical diary show, it's the fact your ex is following it around like a curse, calling it the abusive treachery it actually is.'

Robin exhales windily, but I'm not done.

'Thinking about those interviews, and the fact I can say we split because I caught you shagging someone else, something you've publicly confirmed. I mean, it could get really scummy. I wonder how long it would be before *Idiot Soup* decide they needed some fresher, more wholesome faces on the roster. You always said you wanted to be like Bill Hicks, being dropped from Letterman. This could be your chance to find out what being too dangerous a comic to touch is actually like.'

Robin is tapping his fingers on his desk, trying to figure a way out. I play my final card.

'I'm also going to outline this proposition to Al. See if the man who does the sums thinks the risk versus reward makes sense,' I add, turning the screw as tightly as possible.

'You can wind your fucking neck in, with this calling my

agent,' he snaps, all geniality gone. 'That is over the line, he's a business associate, not someone to be used in your spurned woman games.'

I relish the real Robin being revealed now. Despite his begging for me to come back, I'm a *spurned woman*, and despite it being a sole act of retaliation, I'm the one playing games. The same old misogyny, behind modern shop frontage.

'Oh, so different from spurned man games! Like talking shite about me to my parents, behind my back, finding out where I worked—'

'I have no idea what you're talking about. You're becoming slightly mental.'

And there it is: 'that one, she's crazy,' the last refuge of the arsehole with any woman who calls him to account.

Robin has now judged that given he won't ever be meeting up with me again, he can invent as he wants.

'So what's it to be?' I eye him steadily. 'Do we leave here with an understanding that you're doing some rewriting? Or is it a declaration of all-out war? As you said, tavern wenches don't have much to lose, compared to great artists.'

He huffs and he puffs and I can see the very moment he decides it's not worth it.

'Fine,' he says. 'I'll rewrite it. This was only a preview anyway. You really are a small-minded person, with limited horizons.'

The degree of nastiness affirms he is ditching the show, and needs somewhere to dump his needled anger.

All he cares about is his writing, I realise.

'You know. When we first met, I couldn't figure how

someone so bright was a waitress. Now I can see it. You've got the chance to be immortalised in, let's face it, a fairly uneventful life, and you're rather be a bitter shrew. That's incomprehensible to me.'

'Well. I guess you just answered your own question about whether you'll ever understand women then,' I say. 'See you later.'

Seconds later, I put my head round the door, catch him scowling murderously.

'Hey, Robin. I think this is what they call a "teachable moment".'

I don't believe in fate, or karma, or Noel Edmonds' cosmic ordering. Yet the timing still seems pointed, and cruel. As if there is someone up there, trying to tell me something.

After I lurk long enough to see the surly receptionist paste a 'show cancelled' sign on both doors, I leave West Street, high on the feeling of having faced the dragon and won. And then, heading towards my bus stop, I see him, across the street. His pin-thin, drawn wife has dark wavy hair and a hassled air, in a hoodie and tight jeans. He's looking bored, and they're debating where they go next, or how long they have left on the car parking meter.

It's the first time I've seen him, since sixth form. I've jolted at the stray tagged photo, heard rumours of him being back to see his folks for Christmas, yet never seen his face. And now, here he is in the slightly baggier flesh.

I'm hardly unbiased, but it strikes me that he hasn't aged well. Perhaps due to his former standing, I judge him more harshly. The mop of lead singer hair is the same length around his collar, but thinned and greasy looking, the eyes are pouchy, the set of the mouth is mean. The leanness you take for granted in youth has filled out. At school he was a superstar, now he looks like any other bloke.

The time though, something is different, there's someone with them I've not seen before. He turns, stoops and picks her up, throws her over his shoulder with practised ease. She's wailing, wearing stripy woollen tights and a tiny pinafore, maybe three years old. He kisses her cheek.

Richard Hardy is a father. Richard Hardy has a daughter.

What did I just use to vanquish the hold Robin had over me? Words. My words saved me.

I put my mobile to my ear and call Devlin.

'Would you mind if I still do the last Share Your Shame thing, now I've left?'

40

I let Jammy out of his hutch for a roam around while I sit at the table and get my A4 notebook out.

'Imagine if I had my own place,' I say to Jammy, as he makes slow but steady progress in the direction of the sink, 'This could be us every day.'

Karen is away for the weekend, back to see her parents in Aberdeen, and the timing couldn't be better. Not that Karen going away would ever be unwelcome. I print at the top:

My Worst Day At School

It's the final Share Your Shame subject, and although I haven't decided if I can bear to get up and perform it, I know what I want to say.

I write. I write some more. I try to rephrase the first thing I wrote and score it out. It's all so facetious, so striving to amuse, so false. In the peace of the kitchen, with the hum of next door's maggot tanks, I try to banish the thought that keeps bubbling up, every time I look at the block print subject letters.

My chest rises and falls and eventually it heaves. Fat tears roll down my face and spatter the paper, so I move it from under me.

The door behind me bangs and before I have any chance to gather myself, or conceal the fact I've been weeping, Karen is in the kitchen, with sticky-uppy hair, a rugby top and her usual look of flushed belligerence. She drops a Karrimor rucksack down.

A pause.

'What's up with you?'

I try to talk, and I can't, having to cup my hand round my mouth while I make a strange wheezy inhalation noise, the inward drawing of air in a sob.

'Have you had some news or something?' Karen says. Even in my diminished state, I notice how she's sort of angry that I might've had a bereavement and that it's affecting her enjoyment of her own kitchen.

I shake my head and fight to get control of my vocal cords.

'I'm writing about My Worst Day At School for a writing competition at the pub,' I gasp. 'And I know they want something funny and light and easy. But my worst day at school. It was terrible. I think it might've ruined my life.'

I put my hands over my eyes and sob and wipe the tears, and afterwards, when I'm back in control, Karen is still staring at me. I gulp again.

'It's the truth but no one ever wants the truth. I've never told anyone the truth. I'm sick of being the person who tries to fit in and tells people what they want to hear and acts like nothing bothers her, it's not got me *anywhere*.'

'So tell them the truth,' Karen says, shrugging. 'Fuck the fuckers. Worst day at school, right?'

'Yes.'

'Not funny or light or easy or whatever. Worst. They asked for worst, give them worst.'

'Should I? Even if everyone sits there saying oh that's grim, you're grim, thanks for ruining my evening?'

'They've all turned up to hear people talk about their worst days at school. As far as I remember it, school was fucking awful. If you had to live through your worst day and they only have to hear about it, in the name of entertainment, I'd say they got off lightly.'

I nod, slowly.

'I should just hit them with it?'

'Yeah. Pull no punches. Why the fuck should you? Why is it your fault that your worst day was that bad?'

With Karen saying that, something clicks.

'Yes. OK. Thank you. You're right. I'll write it my way.'

'Right. Glad that's sorted. I've had the worst train journey of my life and when I got halfway, my mum calls to say they've been snowed in and to turn back round. Pile of piss.'

No one is as wedded to the using of swear words as Karen, and I include myself here.

'Karen,' I say. 'Thank you. You've really helped.'

'Have I? OK.'

She looks nonplussed and a little self-conscious.

I offer to make some Ovaltine, and a newfound camaraderie

settles between us, until Karen screams: 'WHY IS THAT CREEPY TERRAPIN WANDERING ABOUT, PUT IT BACK IN ITS BOX!'

When she goes up to bed, I spend an hour writing, barely pausing to take my pen from the paper. The words flood out of me.

Mrs Pemberton taught me the word for what I'm feeling. Catharsis.

Now all I have to do is find the courage to read it.

41

A stage. A microphone. A long walk to the stage. A quiet in the room that feels greater and more intimidating than any quiet in any room I've ever known. *I can't do it I can't do it I can't do it.*

I can do it. I have to prove it to myself by starting speaking. Deep breath. Jump.

'When I first tried to prepare something for tonight's show, I knew what my worst day at school was, without a moment's hesitation. But I didn't write about it. Instead I was going to tell you about the time me and my friend Jo drank a bottle of Malibu and pineapple and pierced each other's ears with ice cubes and safety pins. Jo got a staph cocc infection, hers swelled up to the size of *The BFG* and I was grounded for a month. Only one of mine actually worked so I went around wearing a single large hoop, like a pirate.'

A ripple of laughter. *And breathe.*

'I've never told anyone about my worst experience at school. Not my best friend, not my sister, not my mum, not any boyfriend, then or since. Not the counsellor I saw in my twenties. But I'm going to talk about it now.'

I glance up. I shiver when I see Lucas, standing against a wall by the bar, eyes fixed upon me with intensity. I knew he might watch, knowing the subject matter, but the confirmation gives me a thunderclap of the heart. I have no time, no space, to be more terrified.

'It was the night of the sixth form leavers prom. I went to that do on a cloud of excitement and hormones, shoe-horned into a red dress I'd saved up for. It cost £55, which seemed a fortune at the time. I was reeking of vanilla and tonka beans, whatever they are, having snuck three large squirts from a perfume bottle in my older sister Esther's bedroom. And I had Durex in my handbag, hidden in the zipped compartment. I bought them in a pub vending machine, and had never felt so grown up in my life. I hadn't told anyone but I'd started seeing a boy, another pupil. We planned to stay together after the party, for the first time.'

I glance up at riveted faces and gather myself, careful not to look at Lucas this time. I see Jo, her eyes glued to me, frowning. Talking about condoms feels so personal that I question whether I should be doing this. Too late. I turn the page.

'I wasn't popular, exactly, at school. I was popular enough. I didn't get picked last for netball, I wasn't bullied, the cool kids knew my name. I felt as if popularity was something you had to work for, and rigorously maintain, and I spent every day aware of it. I clowned around when I thought it would win me approval, I didn't always admit to knowing the answer in lessons. I made sure if I got A grades, I didn't show off. I knew who not to cross. And I knew who I had to impress.

'At the party, at first, it felt as if those years of striving were paying off. The most popular boy at school told me I was "fit". He was That Boy – I'm guessing every school year has one – who carries himself like he's Jim Morrison. He is revered and desired. His word is God. When it came to girls, he only consorted with queen bees, the handful deemed attractive enough to be worthy of him. I didn't fancy him, and I didn't expect him to fancy me in a million years, but I wanted his approval, above all others. Everyone did. His opinion of you could make you, or break you.

'And he'd complimented me. This was unprecedented. This was a coronation. It was like being in a daytime soap, and being nominated for an Oscar. Then he added: *You look like a high-class prozzy.* "That's your thing, right?" Everyone laughed. I laughed too, to show I wasn't stuck up. If I laughed, I was part of the joke, not the object of it. I wanted to believe he meant I looked seductive, when in fact I knew he wasn't paying me a compliment at all. He was making it clear I was viewed as a girl hopeful for that sort of attention, and that I was actively inviting being treated a certain way. He was saying you're cheap, and I was enthusiastically agreeing.

'He told me he wanted to "show me something". When I think back to that moment, much as I wanted to believe me and this boy were friends, I knew I was being mocked. Remember those times in life, when you sense everyone is on something, and you're not? The holding of breath while they see if you fall for it, the murmuring, the giggling they catch in the throat, so they don't ruin the prank? It was that. Nevertheless, I said "Ooh OK . . ." with a stupid grin on my face, wanting them to accept me, wanting to be game Georgina who was up for anything and so, so likeable. Above all, be likeable. Never stop smiling. Keep smiling, laugh along, and you can't go far wrong.'

The room is so still, I could hear a pin drop. I continue.

'Onlookers outside his gang watched in envy and wonder as he led me away from the party, by the hand. A huge public gesture, being prepared to be seen with me like that. I was being anointed by the king. Georgina Horspool just got a major promotion. If *he* wants her, then she's made it.'

I shuffle and turn my sheets of paper and in the now sepulchral silence, the rustling sounds painfully loud in the microphone.

'The Boy took me into the disabled toilet. He locked us in before I really comprehended where we were, and put himself between me and the door, a smirk on his face. Suddenly, I knew I was out of my depth.

'"What are we doing here?" I said. He pushed me roughly against the wall and tried to kiss me. I pushed him away and tried to laugh it off. I heard the noise as if it had come from someone else, strangled and false-sounding.

'"What's the problem?" he said. "You like me."

'It wasn't a question.

'"I do like you," I said, quickly, because I wanted this boy to think that, and I wanted him to like me.

'"Then what's the problem?" he said.

'He pushed his mouth against mine again. It was sloppy

and aggressive, teeth first, and tasted of Strongbow. But he was That Boy. This was an extraordinary honour, if he wanted to kiss me. So how could I stop him?

'Nothing in my life so far had equipped me for this. School teachers, my parents, getting on and fitting in – my experiences had taught me nice girls say yes please and thank you, we oblige people, we meet their expectations, we don't hurt feelings or offend. We don't say no. This boy wanted something from me, so I should reciprocate.'

I glance up again and see Jo, tears now coursing down her face, her hands gripping Clem and Rav's on either side of her, both of whom look pale and shocked. I look away again before I catch Jo's tears, still not able to look back to where I know a man with dark hair and dark eyes is watching me.

'He went to kiss me again, and tugged at the front of my dress, trying to wrench me out of my bra. Fortunately the fact my dress was a size too small meant it was tight as sausage skin, and he barely moved it a centimetre. "Don't!" I said.' Here, my voice breaks for the first time. I swallow it down and continue.

'But I tried to say it in a light, playful, coy way. A don't that was supposed to translate as: *Don't, but of course DO another time, only maybe not right now, because I am a Good Girl.* An instruction, that was begging.

'"What the fuck is wrong with you?" he said. I hated myself for not succeeding in deflecting him. I was funny, cool Georgina, and I wanted to prove I could cope. I wanted it to turn out well. I didn't want to upset him. That shouldn't be beyond me. Yeah, what the fuck WAS wrong with me?

'He might not have managed to pull my clothing down, but he was exposing a terrible truth. I wasn't what I seemed. I tried to fool everyone I was this bouncy fun girl who nothing fazed. But I was inexperienced, and scared, not at all cool. I still thought that this being found out was the primary threat. I had been plunged into the psychological warfare of trying to work out how to reject him, without him thinking I'd rejected him, because rejecting him would go very badly for me. He wasn't worried about how this story would play, but I was. He would be the storyteller.

'"I've got a boyfriend," I said, gambling that a prior claim wouldn't wound his masculinity.

'He said, "Hah no you haven't! Who's that?"

'I didn't want to drop my boyfriend in it. I didn't want to sell him out, and have outsiders storming in and trashing what we had, which was more precious to me than anything. He was blameless, and he was mine, and he must be protected at all costs.

'I said, "You don't know him."

'"Bollocks, Georgina. Everyone knows you've never been with anyone and you're gagging for it. Going on about romance all the time like an old biddy in English class."

'This was like a series of precise stab wounds to the major organs. The worst thing imaginable – everyone smelling my desperation to be liked. This boy telling me it was common knowledge. I was hideous, gauche, needy, pathetic.'

I'm crying too now, but only tears, my voice is still steady.

'He tried to kiss me again and I pushed him off saying, Let's go back to the party, let's get some of that punch, and he said, to show he wasn't buying my casual deflection routine: "Are you a virgin?"

'I said: "No."

'He said: "Well then."

'He unzipped his jeans and I stood, pinned against the wall, under the medical-bright lights, wondering why I was here, how to escape. How everything had gone so wrong, so fast.

'It was my fault.'

I glance up at the room and see a sea of upturned faces. I can no longer focus on any one individual.

'. . . A cleverer, more charming, *better* girl than I was, would have the right words to extricate herself and please him at the same time. That I couldn't find a route out was yet more proof of my idiocy, my immaturity. Of course boys at parties try to get off with girls in loos, what did I expect? I was lucky enough someone so far out of my league wanted it. Ungrateful AND ridiculous. Maybe the cleverer, more charming girl would simply be complying.

'I had lied. I was a virgin. I'd never seen the male anatomy before, not in real life, not like that. Suddenly there it was, liberated from his Levis, like seeing the alien burst from John Hurt's chest. I panicked. Not only because I knew he'd expect me to do something with it. I knew that he'd gone too far to take this back now. He'd want something in return. There was no way I could leave with the ability to embarrass him, there was no way that was going to happen. There would be no transfer of power.

'He grabbed my hand and I pulled it away, his hand large enough and my fingers small enough I could wrench them through his. He grabbed my hand again, I did the same. On the third try, with a grasp so tight it left bruises, he managed to keep hold of my hand, and put it on him. He let out a huge cackle of triumph, even as I instantly wrenched it away. We both knew he would now tell everyone on the other side of the door that I'd done something with him willingly, something I couldn't take back. This is how it works. You're broken down by stages.

'The hand grabbing and pulling continued, my begging to leave continued, ignored. I felt like I'd been in here for an hour, it was probably minutes. I knew in social terms, in terms of my reputation, it might as well have been overnight.

'"You know how to do this, don't you?" he said. "You're a sexy girl."

'Switching to flattery worked, for a second. He'd cut me down and now he was building me back up again. He was throwing me a lifeline that I could leave here with a good review.'

I look up from my page.

'The moment where you consider giving in, or do give in, that's the moment you torture yourself about for the rest of your life. That's the moment where you think it happened to you because you are a bad and weak person, who wanted it really. When in fact, it's about survival. And whichever choice you make, it wasn't really a choice at all.

'His hand was over my hand in a vice-like grip and he moved it up, then down, up, then down. "Now you do it," he commanded. He let go. I did it, once.

'"Yeah!" he shouted, in triumph. "Like that." I had done it. I couldn't take it back.

'I'd let all this happen for the sake of the thing that mattered above all else, popularity. The great religion. Being liked. But I wasn't liked. I looked into his eyes, the contemptuous expression, and I could see he didn't like me at all. In fact, I could see my capitulation made him despise me even more. *Yeah, I knew it*.

'Realising this stopped me wheedling him with sweetness, thinking I could bargain. I said: "I want to go back to the party now," and moved towards the door. He stopped me, grabbing my wrists and throwing me against the wall. Before, he was forceful, this was violent. I was already scared, now I felt something more like terror. My dad used to say you don't know how impossible it is to move a dead weight until you try to shift one. You don't know how you can be physically dominated, until someone much taller and stronger than you, really tries. Even in films, I used to think, with the trapped damsel beating dainty fists against manly Tarzan chests, you could push him off if you wanted. You can't. It comes as a shock. And with the shock, panic, as I knew at that moment that whatever he wanted to happen – it was going to happen. He was pulling at the hem of my skirt, grabbing at my crotch.'

The room is holding its breath, the tension as taut as a drum, a vibration of anticipation humming through everyone there.

'I thought: *Not like this, not with him*. I'm not a selfless person, but thinking of someone else nearby, someone I wanted to save myself for, it helped. When I say "save myself" I don't mean chastity, in a sexual way, the full meaning – I knew he'd want me to save myself. One last roll of the dice occurred to me, a counter intuitive way of getting this boy to let me go. I said: "What are you, some sort of gross rapist?"

'He dropped me like I was radioactive.

'"Don't flatter yourself," he spat. Someone who had locked me in a room and sexually assaulted me, told me I was over-rating myself as a temptation. Being raped was too good for me. "You think you're all that, Georgina Horspool, but you're bang average."

'But it worked. I'd said the R word out loud, called it by its name, and he didn't want to see himself as that. He zipped himself up and curled his lip at me, muttered his disgust as I unlocked the door and claimed my freedom.

'Except I was walking into a different sort of trap and in some ways, one I've been in ever since. As I rejoined the party, it was as if everyone was waiting for us. Shocked noises, laughter, hands clapped over mouths, a ripple of conversation, as if our joint exit was somehow also an announcement.

'I looked back at That Boy, and he was making a gesture: tongue pushed in the side of his mouth, fist shaking under-neath. Everyone in his clique whooped and wolf-whistled. He gave a bow. I was motionless.

'That Boy put a drink in my hand, saying, "You're quite a girl, mad technique", to more hollering. What should I say? Should I shout that I didn't do it, I hadn't wanted to do it? Everyone saw – I'd gone by choice into a toilet with him. Then I'd let him kiss me. I'd touched it, when his hand wasn't gripping mine. I HAD done it.

'And no one was taking mid-league, not-thin-enough, try-hard Georgina's word over this Rock God, no one. When I'd be lucky to pull him, but he'd chosen me from a pool of eager hopefuls? UGH. Vindictive slag. A slapper, and worse, one with ideas above her station.

'He high five-ed with his mates, who were awed. The queen bees, looking at me, were a mixture of admiration and repulsion. Someone muttered something about my surname should be "Whores-pool".

'He was That Boy and I was no longer Georgina. I was That Girl who waltzed into the toilets at the party, performed a sex act, and reappeared, bold as brass, to claim my free rum cooler as a prize for a blowjob. Ask anyone I went to school with, they probably know this story. It instantly became part of my official biography.

'My best friend approached me, smiling, slightly scared, but thinking I'd taken some decisive leap across the threshold into adulthood, and decided to do it with the highest status boy there. *Go, Georgina. Wow.* How could I tell her that nothing was what it seemed, that I was devastated, that this triumphant night for us was now trauma? I didn't have the vocabulary to repel this boy, and I didn't have the vocabulary to explain what had happened to me.

'I didn't run out. I didn't burst into tears. I didn't behave anything like a victim. The damage was done. And I didn't want to be a victim. That's not how I saw myself, it wasn't part of my identity. It wasn't even part of my story for this very evening. I hadn't been ruined. No. I could choose for this to all be OK. I still had control and choice, the control to make this normal and the choice not to make a fuss.'

Now, a deep breath, for the last part.

'But this denial, it all fell apart when I looked across at the boy I was in love with. He was kissing someone else. Possibly a reaction to what he thought I'd done, but I couldn't be sure. I wanted to howl like an animal in pain, at the injustice. I'd lost him. Georgina the casual favour-giver couldn't also be Georgina the girlfriend. I don't even remember the rest of the party or when he left, I drank like I wanted to black out. Eventually when I looked around for him, he was gone. Forever. Nothing else mattered after that.

'I'd told my parents I was staying at Jo's to cover for my hotel room stay and I couldn't go home instead and face their questions. I went to the Holiday Inn and lay on the double bed in my red dress and cried myself to sleep. I hated myself.

'I have, in some ways, been hating myself ever since that night. I never admitted it, so there couldn't be any forgiveness. And I needed to forgive myself. Not the boy who did it, he can go to hell. But myself. I have been so hard on myself for not being stronger, for not seeing it coming. For being so weak as to want to be liked. For not thinking of the right words to stop it, sooner.

'Tonight's show is called Share Your Shame. But this story doesn't qualify. Because it's his shameful secret, not mine. It wasn't my fault. If any part of this experience is familiar to you, then please let me tell you – it wasn't your fault either. Thank you for listening.'

I close the notebook, in a shocked silence, as a tear rolls down my cheek. One clap, two claps, it builds and bursts into thunderous applause and everyone stands up.

My friends come up to the stage and hug me, in tears too.

Over their shoulders, I see Lucas McCarthy bound to the door to the stairs and wrench it open, without a look back at me, and disappear. I don't care.

I feel a light-headedness, and a newfound lightness. I'm not carrying it anymore. I spoke the words aloud, used my words, and broke the curse.

42

The only downside to discussing what went on with Richard Hardy is that my friends, especially Jo, are stricken that I never felt I could tell them. I've tried to reassure them that I could've been friends with Oprah Winfrey and I still wouldn't have spoken about it. 'Why now?' they asked, not unreasonably.

I told them: the writing contest theme, almost like a challenge from the universe. Robin, and his exploitative invasions, ventriloquising me. Richard Hardy, and him having a little girl I have no doubt he'd never want treated that way. The fact he emerged unscathed to have that happiness. And Lucas McCarthy. Rejecting me a second time. The price of keeping the secret, it was too high to keep paying. I had snapped.

As much as they were appalled at my ordeal, Clem struggled to cope with the raw drama and intrigue of *Oh my God that gorgeous bar bloke is the ex-boyfriend? Oh MY GOD* – before Rav gave her a look that could turn her to stone.

Esther, make-up streaked down her cheeks, came up and clung to me like a koala. 'Why didn't you tell me!' she said, while poor Mark hovered in the background, eyes to the floor and hands folded, as if he was a kindly vicar with his parishioners.

'I've not told anyone, honestly. I wouldn't tell myself. I had to tell myself, first, and that has only just happened. I didn't mean for you to find out like this.'

'Oh don't be a dick.' Esther paused, wiped her eyes again. 'We joke around with you and chivvy you, George, but we all think the absolute world of you. We *want* the world for you. Sorry if that got lost.'

'I know,' I say.

I didn't win the competition. It went to a man called Tom with a man bun who told a story about vomiting Kendal Mint Cake on a geography field trip to Mam Tor.

But I did win. For the first time, I'm not scared of the future. I want to use its potential. Words saved me. My words.

At ten, the following night, the front doorbell goes. Kids running past sometimes ring it, I'll ignore it unless it sounds twice.

A few minutes later, the doorbell rings again.

Either Karen ordered a pizza, or we have a visitor who's never been to the house before and doesn't know to knock at the kitchen at the back. Karen's spark-out, I can hear the snoring from the stairs, so I hope it isn't a twelve-inch thin crust margarita with extra jalapenos, as I'll have to risk waking her to see if she's responsible, or letting her go nuts that I didn't. I also really fancy eating it.

I poke my head warily round the side of the curtain and see a tall, dark-haired man on the other side, his hands thrust deep in his coat pockets, his chin buried in his chest. My stomach does a queasy revolution.

I can feel my heart beat in my neck. I take a very deep breath, and open the door.

'Hi.'

'Hello,' I say.

'Sorry to turn up like this. I wasn't sure how to word it, on a phone. Can I come in?' Lucas says.

I stand back to let him past.

'Let's talk in the kitchen,' I say, pretending to be steady. 'The door closes on that room.'

Lucas nods and follows me. I click the door shut. We position ourselves either side of the dining room table.

'I saw you do your reading, at the pub.'

'I know. I saw you. You left straight after.'

'I . . .' I realise he's momentarily unable to speak, and it shocks me. I stare at him, as a moment stretches between us. Lucas's eyes fill up. He blinks back the tears and clears his throat.

'. . . I had to leave as I needed to think, and I didn't want to speak to you in company. I hope you didn't think I was flouncing or anything.'

'Well. I wasn't sure. I was kind of in my own head space, really.'

Lucas nods. 'Please, please believe me when I say that I had no idea what happened to you, Georgina. Not the slightest clue. I know that's bad in itself.'

'I know you didn't,' I say. 'I'd have had to tell you and I didn't tell you. I didn't tell anyone.'

'I didn't ask though,' Lucas says.

I swallow. I've come too far to say the easy thing, rather than the honest thing.

'No, you didn't.'

Lucas shakes his head as he composes himself and we sit in silence again. I wouldn't call it a comfortable silence, but it's not a blank or an unwelcome silence either. Letting things settle.

'I was . . . hearing you describe what went on. I failed you so badly. I am such an arrogant bastard that I thought the story of my life was people failing me, but that's not true. I failed you in the most awful way.'

I shake my head. 'You made decisions without all the information, which I've discovered is how we make every decision.'

I sound calm. I notice I'm gripping the back of the chair in front me so tightly that my knuckles are white.

'I did, Georgina, I failed you then, and I failed you now. That night . . . I keep thinking about me saying that I didn't want you *afterwards,* how it must have felt. It makes me want to cut my own tongue out.' He rubs his face with his hands, looks back at me. I nod slowly. I can't pull these punches, not now.

'Yeah. It hurt. Like I am damaged goods.'

'And you saying you were worried about us, thinking about us, when you were trapped with him . . .'

Us. After all this time, he is using 'us', and he'll never know what that means to me.

Lucas has his arms folded in front of him, leaning back

394

against the counter, long legs propping himself up. 'Georgina, I saw what person you are – I mean, I already knew, I should've known – and I saw what person I am. Petulant and self-absorbed.'

I give a small laugh. 'Bit harsh.'

Lucas closes his eyes. 'I'm so sorry.'

'Thank you.'

'It wasn't true, either.' He clears his throat. 'I did still want you, afterwards, of course I did. But I was so full of jealousy and outrage, I lashed out, using someone else. Thought I'd show you I didn't want you, if you didn't want me.'

My heart contracts for the people we once were and I have to clear my throat, too, before I can speak. 'I thought that was what it was but I couldn't be sure. It didn't make things much better, so I didn't set too much store by it.'

'It was cruel, immature shit on my part.'

'I think eventually it became easier to believe you'd never cared, rather than it being revenge, as it would've meant Richard Hardy truly ruined everything for me. And when you said you didn't remember me this time round, it confirmed it.'

Lucas shakes his head.

'I didn't know how to deal with it, when you asked me if I recognised you, that night after the stripper fracas. I took the first exit, as fast as possible. I reasoned I'd never mattered to you, so best off acting like it was the same for me. In wounded male ego, I might've overdone it and come off as this arch, "dozens of bed notches" tosser.'

I laugh and he winces. 'I'd thought I might see you in passing in Sheffield, I braced myself for it. Then there you were behind the bar with my brother at the wake and I almost fainted. I had a few minutes to get my face straight, to decide how to play it.'

'Ha, well, I completely believed you.'

'Well, I had a lot staked on you believing me.'

He pauses. I wonder if bracing himself, almost fainting, if these things mean we still have something left here.

'It's not right that I had to find out something so awful had gone on, to have any compassion for you. I saw how you were treated afterwards, I heard what people said. I shouldn't have needed to be told you were assaulted. There's such a thing as peer pressure. There's such a thing as just making a mistake, or being a kid. Given what we had, to ask you, "Tell me what happened" . . . that question should not have been beyond me. Imagine how different things could've been if I'd had that much courage.'

My eyes are smarting now. 'I was never the best at resisting the crowd. I know you didn't like that about me. Playing to the gallery. Wanting to be popular.'

'Getting to know you at this age, I could reassess all that. Yeah, seeing you again, I came in with that prejudice – that you were somehow shallow and meaningless, didn't have any real principles. What do they say, "a feather for any wind"? But now I see that you please other people, you put their feelings first. That generosity of caring what someone else thinks, it's a great quality, it's not weakness. It's not your fault if others have exploited it. Sorry, I'm mansplaining you to yourself.'

I laugh.

'And George, at school, I was just insecure. Frightened those people would be more appealing to you, than me. You did what you had to, to get by. We all did. I had no right to judge you. And if I couldn't manage that at eighteen, I fucking well should've been man enough by thirty.'

Lucas draws breath.

'I shouldn't have needed to hear what you said last night. I wanted to be everything to you, and instead I was another one of the men who was angry with you for not being able to have you, the way I wanted.'

I expected Lucas, if he found out, to feel bad. I hadn't expected this level of self-reflection, or self-excoriation. For all my yearning to hear his side of it, I actually hadn't dwelt on what his reaction to the truth might be, until now.

I, in turn, underestimated him.

Why didn't I message Lucas, in the weeks after, and say: Hey, just so you know, that wasn't what it looked like? Because he was either that easily unfaithful or he'd gone with another girl to rub my face in it, so there was nothing left to fight for.

Because I didn't think he'd believe me. And I thought, in the brutal laws of teenaged courtship, with the naiveté of inexperience, that I had done what they were saying.

But most of all, it was because in my gut I knew that if Lucas had said: *Now I know you're a victim, you can have my heart again*, it wouldn't have been worth anything.

Love isn't meant to work like that.

43

There is a pause while we recalibrate with the new information we both have. It's not uncomfortable, just reflective.

Lucas looks up, smiles a bashful half smile at me.

'I have other thoughts, but apology now made, do you want me to go on, or do you want me to sod off out of your kitchen?' he says.

'I want you to go on. Tell me whatever you want. If I disagree, I have a voice I can use here too.' I smile.

Lucas nods, and swallows.

'I think you might know, maybe you didn't, but I had a weapons-grade crush on you, before we were put together on that English homework.' He smiles at me, this adult version of Lucas, and I can't believe I was ever so lucky. 'I worshipped you.'

Oh. Wow. I definitely didn't fall in love by myself. I can have those memories back, restored, like old prints colourised.

'I knew you'd not be able to pick me out of a line-up, in return. It was a grind of a couple of years, to be honest, coming to Yorkshire, leaving my mates behind in Ireland, being teased for my accent and trying to play it down. Then I saw this vision, with an infectious laugh that I could hear across the common room. You were like the human anti- dote to my misery. A rainbow in the grey. I felt like God sent me the girl with the golden hair, to remind me there were still things worth hanging around for.'

I don't know what to say, other than grin like an idiot.

Lucas shuffles his feet and breaks eye contact.

'You didn't know how well liked you were, how popular you were. Not only with the dickheads, with everyone, because you were kind. You had a lot more status than you thought. You talked on stage about having to work for approval, being some sort of an also-ran, but that's not how it appeared to everyone else. Having got to know you as an adult, I'd say that's still true. People flock to you, they're drawn to you. Not because of the way you look, because you're warm.'

Lucas feels this way about me? I will cherish these words 'til I die.

'Anyway, then we were put together on that project, and I panicked that I'd make a tool of myself, and idolised-from-afar Georgina Horspool might be a let-down. Like, even your name was like reciting a magic spell to me. How could you live up to that? But not only did you live up to it, you were nicer and wittier and more interesting than I could have dreamed, and most incredibly of all, you seemed to like me. I was . . . what's the word . . .'

It's a bittersweet pleasure, hearing you made someone feel like this, but in the past tense, and I don't know whether to laugh or cry.

'. . . I thought you were too good to be true, I couldn't believe it. That idea ended up being a problem. Paranoia crept in, that I was right, that it couldn't be true. Do you remember the evening we had to walk home on opposite sides of the street because you thought you'd seen your mate?'

'No . . . ?' I say, squinting. I had genuinely lost this to mists. Concentrating, I vaguely remember something involving hiding from Jo's brother. I'd thought it was larks.

'I started to worry after that: I was a guilty secret. That you'd never want to be public. That I couldn't ever be your boyfriend. You were using me for practice before university. I mean, even being used by you was not something I could turn down but I'd fallen so hard in love, it was no longer enough.'

'You had?'

'Oh man, Georgina, I wanted it all from you. I would've switched to Newcastle to study, you only had to say the word. But that was it. YOU had to say the word.' Lucas smiles, uneasily. 'I took the page out of the folder where we'd first flirted, in those notes. So that I'd always have some sort of physical proof you'd liked me. Do I sound like a serial killer?'

I laugh, but I'm heartsore.

'And I knew Richard fancied you. He wasn't the only one, much to my chagrin. There was a lot of laddish conversation in PE changing rooms. He always boasted he could have you anytime he liked, that you were "into him". You can imagine that once we were seeing each other, I wanted to decapitate him.'

Lucas raises his eyes to mine.

'So, Georgina, it's even worse than you think, because I knew. I knew when he took you by the hand and walked you out of the party what his intentions probably were, and I did nothing. I could've spared you that whole ordeal, and I didn't. For what? So people didn't laugh at me? So you weren't embarrassed by me making a scene, maybe even chucked me for it? Because I wanted to test you? Because I was worried in that moment, you'd choose him? Yeah, all of those reasons, and particularly the last one. That's my character moment. And you paid for that.'

'It's not your fault,' I say. 'And it's not your character. It's a shitty thing you were caught up in and I know for a fact, your character is the instinct to stand up for people. Look at how you've been since we've worked together.'

'Now it's like I'm pushing you into reassuring me it wasn't my fault,' Lucas says, rubbing his forehead. 'It was, Georgina. It was partly my fault. Let it be.'

'Hah, you sound like my counsellor. I didn't tell her the whole truth either. I told her I'd gone with another boy and hated myself for it. I think I believed it. It's taken me so long, Lucas, to say: it wasn't my fault. When you say it was your fault, I know you mean it, and that means a lot. But I think it's only one person's fault, and he's not here worrying about his blame, whatsoever.'

'I have such an overwhelming urge to pay Hardy a visit in a rusty Bedford van in the middle of the night, with Dev's friend of a friend, "Dean The Cunt", you know.'

I laugh, I actually manage a big hoot.

'You never considered going to the police?' Lucas says, quietly.

'No. His word and my word. Everyone would've backed Richard's version up. And the hotel, that would've come out, and imagine how that would've been used against me.'

We glance away from each other, awkward for the first time.

'I wish I'd gone to you,' Lucas says, haltingly. 'Not for *that*. So I could've been there for you, listened. Everything could've been different.'

Could've been.

I shrug. 'That's nice to hear. For me, not reporting it means I've felt guilty that he might have done it again, and by not speaking up, I dropped those women in it.'

'Once again, that is not your fault. At all.'

'I bet he's not thought about it once since it happened, you know.'

'I think you're right. Scumbag. And his band was shit.'

I smile and Lucas smiles back. I want to hug him but I don't know my rights.

'Do you mind if I ask you something I always wondered?' I say. 'It's a bit personal so no worries if you don't want to say.'

'It's the night for personal, shoot.'

'As I said, it would've been my first time, that night of the party. If we'd stayed over together. Would – would it have been for you too?'

'Oh. Yes. Quite pleased that wasn't already obvious, to be honest.'

He smiles and I smile and blush and I think honestly, Georgina Horspool – you're thirty.

'I'm sorry what we had got destroyed. My memories of you are really great memories,' I say.

'Same here,' Lucas says.

'Whatever you thought,' I say these words rapidly, before I can chicken out, 'I was head over heels in love with you and only you, Lucas.'

'Same here,' Lucas says. 'And what you said about protecting me, when he was attacking you. The shame that I didn't do the same for you will stay with me forever. I wish I could've saved you.'

I smile. I once thought I'd never hear the words I wanted to from Lucas. 'It wasn't for you to save me. It never was. And you coming here tonight, it's enough, Lucas. I'm not just saying that.'

We gaze at each other. There is an obvious question about whether there's anything left, but I don't have the strength or will to ask it. Tonight has restored so much decency and dignity. Putting Lucas in the position of saying: *That doesn't mean I want to resurrect anything now,* would ruin it. Oh God, and imagine if he pretended otherwise out of pity, or guilt. I reason with myself: you threw yourself at him, and he passed. If he's not offering anything now, then assume his views haven't changed since that night.

There's a long pause.

'You're not coming back to The Wicker, are you?' he says, eventually.

'No. I'm not. Sorry. I love it, but I feel like I've drawn a line now. I'll go back, on the other side of the bar, see Dev, see Kitty. And you're going back to Dublin?'

'Yeah. The plan was always I'd help out at the start, to launch it, and then we'd hire a manager locally.'

There's my answer to the previous question. Of course Lucas doesn't want to throw his lot in with me, anyway. Look at who he is now and look at who I am. We made sense in a very different era.

'Right. Devlin said you didn't like Sheffield much,' I say.

'It's got its good points,' he replies, with that smile, that bloody bastard heartbreaking smile.

I put my hand out for Lucas to shake. He gives a small, sad laugh, and accepts it. Even just touching him now feels like a hole opening up in my gut, ready for me to fall down as soon as he's gone.

'I'm glad I've known you,' I say to him.

'The feeling is entirely mutual,' he says.

I open the kitchen door and Lucas walks back into the sitting room.

'Is that a hutch?'

'Yeah it's my tortoise.'

'Oh my word, Jammy's still going?'

'You remember his name!'

'Yeah. Imagine how many times I was trying not to catch myself out by referring to something I knew from when were at school.'

He grins and I marvel at how there is now nothing unspoken between us. It's such a good feeling. I like being able to feel good about him again.

As I open the front door, Lucas turns and takes a deep breath and says: 'Gina.'

'No one calls me Gina!'

'I know,' Lucas says, 'That's why I want to.'

We gaze at each other.

We have word for word recreated a conversation from our time in the Botanical Gardens. I thought I was sole keeper of this flame. He's already made it clear I'm not, but this call-and-response is proof.

'When I saw you again at the wake, you were every bit as luminous as I remembered from school. He didn't take that away. Don't ever let any man take that away from you.'

And before I can react, he pushes his hands deep into his pockets, nods at me, and walks off into the night.

I close the door. A hot flash flood of tears courses down my face. They're sad tears, but other things too.

Lucas McCarthy came back into my life and do you know what, it turns out I'm glad he did. We got a few things ironed out. And he has a fabulous dog.

I exhale. Sometimes the truth is messy and difficult but it isn't always best left. Sometimes it saves you.

Upstairs, a voice roars:

'GEORGINA HAVE YOU QUITE FINISHED TALKING DOWN THERE I AM TRYING TO GET SOME SLEEP GOD ALMIGHTY YACKETY FUCKING YACK.'

'We're done,' I shout back, fingers wiping under my eyes. Wishing that weren't true.

44

You don't appreciate youth when you have it, do you. When
I was age appropriate to be doing a degree, I felt gauche,
conspicuous, like everyone could see through the fact I wasn't
bright enough to be there. Now I'm knocking thirty-one and
I feel completely out of place thanks to my age. What was I
worried about age twenty? With my sheen of cluelessness,
ignorance of the set text, Tippexed Dr Martens and permanent
moderate hangover, I fitted right in.

After the Sunday lunch incident, Esther and I secretly, or
not-so-secretly, hoped Mum might leave Geoffrey. She didn't,
but I get the impression that the balance of power moved a
little more in her favour in the aftermath. Even a protest of
that minimal size, registered.

Maybe Geoffrey realising her family wouldn't stand for it
helped.

Mum asked me if she can buy me a new coat for Christmas.

'The thing about the pink furry thing, darling, is that it

406

doesn't encourage people to take you seriously. It sort of *sends you up*.'

I sighed, and considered that I could be testy, or I could accept the offer and keep the colourful fluffy one for weekends.

We went to John Lewis and I chose a mid-length navy coat with bracelet length balloon sleeves and a belt tie and big collar. I admit, as Mum chorused approval and I turned this way and that in the mirror, it made me feel quite elegant. A bit like a vampish woman in a black and white film who'd say, '*Promise me we'll be together when this horrid war is over*', next to a steam train.

We went for coffee afterwards and Mum asked about my job. I'm waitressing at a cocktail bar on Leopold Square. The fifty-something owner, Rita, wanted somewhere women could have a quiet drink without being hassled and the atmosphere is so civilised. She and I took such a liking to one another, she made me manager on my second day. 'Your manner sets the right tone,' she said.

If you asked me for the best places to drink in the city, I'd happily, with no vested interest, recommend it, along with the revamped Victorian place on Ecclesall Road which I hear they've done great things with. I used to work there, but I've not been back.

Mum asked if I saw it as a long-term thing or if I was going to hunt further. I got the feeling she was not being as combative about this as usual. I explained that I was looking into retraining.

'I say retraining, I mean actually training for something,

given I never did in the first place. I was wondering if I could do an internship on *The Star* or something. So it could involve writing.'

'I was thinking,' she said, stirring her flat white, 'you never finished university. And your father so wanted you to get a degree. I have quite a lot of money sat in ISAs not doing anything, and it was your father's money too. I've been so angry at him for so long that I wasn't very interested in what his wishes might've been, and you've suffered for that. I think you should have it to finish your education. Whatever that might be, you choose.'

'Mum, I couldn't take that,' I said, touched and not a bit stunned. 'Not at age thirty, that would make me a complete moocher.' Also thinking: Mum, you might need a Fleeing Fund.

'Don't be ridiculous. Of course you can,' she replied, brisk now that it was out in the open. 'It's money you'll inherit, further down the line, so why not have it now, if you have need of it? It would make me happy to see you put it to use. I know you won't spend it on cruises. Or let's face it, with your tastes, designer clothes! Hahaha!'

I rolled my eyes.

'Think of it as a challenge. I'm setting you a challenge to spend it wisely. I am actually very excited to see what you do with it. Where you can get to. I think you have a lot going for you, Georgina.'

'Do you?' I said. The narrative has always been mitigating disaster, with Mum and me.

'Yes. I know I've not given you that impression. I think

. . . your father so adored you and monopolised you, it didn't leave much room for us.'

I got it, all of a sudden – I knew where the resentment and hostility I've always felt from Mum, came from. Her problem with me was that Dad fell out of love with her, and stayed in love with me. It made me a rival as well as a daughter. Now we'd discussed the affair, things had moved. She realised I was always on her side, too.

'I miss Dad, Mum,' I said.

'So do I,' she said, 'though Lord knows why.'

'I'm so glad I still have you though.' I squeezed her arm, and her eyes were shiny.

Now, sat in my English Literature tutorials in a modern office block at Sheffield University, I feel like a cat at a Mice Only party, trying to conceal my tail. At first I flattered myself that I look youthful enough they might not notice my incongruity, but I soon gave myself away with my punctuality and cheerful introducing of myself.

Sometimes I think the undergraduates are grateful for my interrogations of the tutor, giving them plenty of time to go blank and sneak a look at their phone screens.

Except when the hour is nearly up and I ask when our essays are due in and the tutor says, 'Oh thank you for reminding me, Georgina, that would be Friday.' I hear the audible groan and irritated exhalation that the keeno mature student has gone and dropped everyone in it, *again*.

I can't help myself though, I'm so excited to be here. I've had four first-class essay marks! I even got to grips with *Beowulf*!

I find the lectures almost luxurious. An hour to tune out of the city outside and live in the world of ideas and study and enjoy a sense my brain is being improved, knowledge increased, critical faculties sharpened, I said. 'Yeah, like when you plug your phone in overnight for an iOS upgrade. Only I'm allowed to sleep through that,' says Jared.

Jared is a very hairy tall boy in a beanie and the only student so far who's spoken to me. He found out my age and told me he would totally take me out if I wanted, and 'age isn't a thing for me, if we vibe'. It made me feel like we'd be recreating *Harold and Maude*. I thanked him and said I was having some time out of the crazy game we call dating.

'Right, are you like, divorced?' he said. 'Any kids? I'm probably not down for that whole scene.'

YOUTH.

I bounce into my classes every day, I walk around the campus with a smile on my face, and I don't care if anyone thinks I'm a divvy. It's such a novelty to me, to feel like I'm fixing things.

I want to get a First, not to be obnoxious, but to prove that there's no shame in travelling the long way round to get where you want to go. It doesn't matter if you take wrong turns. Arriving somewhere you want to be, in the end, is what counts.

So I reach out into the past, take the hand of that vulnerable, hopeful girl I used to be, and pull her forward to join me.

'This is very profound, and moving,' Clem had said, when I finally told them about Lucas coming to see me, after my reading. 'But why aren't you boning each other's brains out?'

'Have you really never considered training as a counsellor?' Rav said to Clem.

'I'm just saying – what's not to bone about this man? He's admitted his mistakes. He has great honour. Handy with some DIY. Stinking rich. And so handsome he could be a vampire.'

'Urgh,' Rav said. 'What does that even mean?'

'Undead high cheekbones. Moonlit skin. Angry dark hair.'

'Cock like an ice-cold Calippo. Oh WHAT, Clem? You're going to start acting like *I'm* too much?' Rav said.

'Well. I'd be on my back faster than an old lady on a frosty walk,' Clem concluded.

Today, it's my thirty-first birthday and I asked my friends if we could go hiking in the Peaks. Oh God, the UPROAR. Clem wasn't going to be able to wear the Mary Quant dress she planned. Rav had some new navy suede shoes that he'd earmarked for an outing and: 'Look, I know you feel like Miss Marple around these freshers but the self-loathing can go too far.'

'You and I can go another time,' Jo soothed, always the peace weaver.

I offered them a compromise – a night in The Lescar. No fuss, no frills. Clem was so disappointed she included a tiara from her shop in her gifts, which she bid me put on straight away. 'Otherwise it's nothing but a night in the pub.'

I felt a bit of a dick at first, but alcohol's helping with that. Rav checks his watch, says: 'My round,' and goes to the bar.

'But to be clear, you do fancy Lucas, right?' Clem says. It's been six months but she is still a dog with a bone.

I adjust my tiara. 'It's not difficult to fancy him, let's be honest.'

'What if he fancied you?' Jo says.

I snort. 'You're kidding right?'

'Why not?' she says.

'I dunno: our grimly tortured history and the fact that when I tried to kiss him once, he pushed me away and told me I repulsed him? I can read those sort of signals you know, I speak fluent "Man".'

'No,' Jo says, swirling her drink in her glass, a double Monkey Shoulder on the rocks. I love her blokish taste in liquor. Jo is on Tinder, and having the time of her life since we got the tech sorted for her (she initially set it to 'Men Within 100 Yards' and Rav had to point out if there *was* a man hiding in her shed, he was unlikely to be Mr Right). Shagger Phil is, as best we know, a pining, celibate mess. The jury is still out on whether they'll end up together, but this way, he'll have waited for her.

'Only because he was mixed up about your history. None of that means he isn't attracted to you, and now you have your history sorted out . . .'

'Exactly,' Clem says.

'Oh, you two! I know it would be a lovely postscript if Lucas and I got together after all this, but life's not like that. And he's going to marry a woman who looks like a member of The Corrs, I'm sure, not an ageing blonde in Yorkshire in fishnets.'

I see both her and Jo looking beadily at me. 'Let me leave the memory of Lucas McCarthy with that handshake, not making a desperate hopeful arse of myself,' I say, toasting them with my glass.

'Yeah, you see,' Clem says to Jo, 'push needed.' I see Jo nodding at her, and suddenly feel something is out of the ordinary.

'You know we haven't given you a birthday present? We sort of took a mad risk that will either see you grateful to us for the rest of your life, or . . .' Clem trails off.

'Or . . . ?' I say, with a hard intonation. Oh. God. If Clem thinks it's 'mad' and a 'risk' . . . ?

'Or it's a friendship-terminating calamity that will haunt us all 'til our end of days.'

'Oh well, this is magnificent! Have you bought me an easyJet flight to Dublin and some Ann Summers crotchless pants? I am willing to waste your £100.'

'No. It's a bit wilder than that.'

'OK, I'm honestly worried now, what have you done? Jo, you're pale!'

Jo shows me gritted teeth and then glances up behind me and I go stiff, turn slowly and see Rav, who has a tray of drinks. And with him, Lucas McCarthy.

45

'Surprise!' Rav says, and I stare, dumbstruck, and wish I didn't have a tiara on my head.

Lucas, his hands in the pockets of a dark jacket, eyes on me, says: 'You know when you said I should definitely turn up for her birthday as a surprise and she'd love it and there was absolutely, without question, no flaw in this plan?'

'Yes!' Clem says.

'Is that Georgina looking pleased to see me?' He pretends to inspect my expression, and smiles. I am too shocked to smile.

'She's speechless with joy!' Rav says, bustling past, setting his tray down. I feel their tense expectation.

I swallow, and try to collect myself. 'Hi. Erm, what's going on?'

'We were trying to think how we could give you the greatest of birthdays, the birthday you deserve after everything you've been through . . .' Jo gabbles, 'And we thought, the best gift would be . . . that you'd like to see Lucas. And Lucas was up for a visit . . .'

414

'They thought we should talk,' Lucas says. 'I was already thinking about getting in touch, then Clem and Jo got in touch with me . . .'

I look at Clem, full of delight at her own connivance, and a still very nervous Jo, back to Lucas, who has no right to look so at ease. He smiles again.

'I wouldn't have come if I didn't have something to say. But I can go home again if this isn't welcome, no hard feelings.'

'No! No. It's OK,' I say. I will kill my friends later, slowly.

'I'm fine to say what I have to say in front of your friends, if it won't embarrass you.'

'We would really like that,' Clem says, before I can reply.

'Oh you fu—' I say. 'How do I know if it'll embarrass me when I don't know what it is?'

'It's only embarrassing to me, really,' Lucas says.

'OK.' I plant my sweaty hands on my knees, to steady myself.

'I was wondering. Now we've sorted out our past. I was wondering if I could be part of your present again.'

My heart stutters and then stops. I am dead. I open my mouth and then close it again. Then open it.

'Are you asking me to come back to The Wicker?'

'No. I'm asking if I could take you out to dinner. Sometime; I can see you're busy tonight. A date.'

I pause, sunshine spreading inside me. Lucas McCarthy is asking me on a date? 'Aren't you living in Dublin?'

'No, not if you're here. I've applied for a transfer. Hopefully the boss will sign it off but he's a right wanker.'

I can't help it. We grin stupidly at each other. He came back for me? He'd do that for me?

'I've practised this with Devlin,' Lucas says, 'And I quote, "Come on you surly bastard you can do better than that, you've said more to me when you've been moping over her for the last few months."'

I laugh. *Moping.* I never imagined, for a second, he could want me again the way I want him. I thought that had flown forever.

'I said, Dev, *I've got to not pressure her and play it cool, just ask her on a date and leave it at that.* He said, Luc, you are so far beyond the point you can play it cool with this broad. You've already been such an almighty butthurt dick around her, you made her quit, and she was a really decent hire so thanks for nothing. Tell her how you honestly feel. From what you say, you owe her that.'

'Yes! This is incredible,' Jo sighs quietly.

'So – when I say I wondered if you'd like to go for *dinner* sometime . . .' Lucas draws breath and continues: 'What I really wonder is, if you, too, hope we have one of those first dates that turns into days and nights, not only due to lust but because we can't stand to be apart.'

A lady-gasp goes up from the table, and I blush.

'What I really mean by dinner is, I wonder if you'd like me to take your top off again in a hurry, and this time not because it's covered in stripper urine.'

I guffaw.

'A lot of history here indeed,' Rav murmurs.

'I wonder if you'd like to end up spending so much time

at each other's places, sooner or later it makes sense to get our own place. With room for Keith, obviously.'

'Who's Keith?' Clem loud-whispers.

'My dog,' Lucas says.

'Oh I'm sorry I thought you had an idiot brother or something. Carry on,' Clem says, while Rav puts his hand over her mouth.

'I have that as well,' Lucas says.

'What about room for Jammy?' I say.

'And Jammy, certainly.'

Lucas draws breath.

'I wondered if you wanted someone to help zip your dress up before a night out. I wondered if you wanted someone to call first in a crisis. I wondered if you wanted someone to text to bring you fish and chips when you can't be arsed with a proper dinner. I wondered if you wanted someone in your corner when you visit your family, someone who will tell them how lucky they are to have you. I wondered if you wanted someone to fetch the Lucozade when you have the flu. I wondered whether, if that comedian shitbag ever comes within ten paces of you, I can hit him in the face. To be honest if I see him, I will probably do that whether I'm your boyfriend or not because he is an utter shitbag and he has it coming. No court in the land would convict.'

My friends applaud and shout 'hear hear'. Lucas reaches out and takes my hand in his, his warm fingers curling around my palm.

'I wondered, Georgina, if you could imagine being in love with me again, the way I'm in love with you. And that given you're the best thing to ever happen to me, if you could give me the chance to try to be the best thing that ever happened to you.'

'Ah my God,' I say, because I'm half-laughing, half-crying, as it seems is everyone else, except Rav, who mutters: 'Well cheers, the bar just went up for the rest of us.'

I stand up, straightening my tiara.

'I want all those things, from you. Thank you. Offer accepted. I'm going to hold you to the chippy run in particular.'

'Did I embarrass you? I think I made good on only embarrassing myself.'

'You . . . I falter, as declaring yourself is difficult enough with this little gallery of eager faces in the Lescar. '. . . It was everything I could ever want, to be honest. You are everything I could ever want.'

It wasn't embarrassing until now, but reaching the And We Kiss moment with onlookers? Yeah, that is.

We look at each other uncertainly and Lucas says: 'Excuse us for a moment, please,' and holds his hand out for mine. I take it and let myself be led out of the pub. We head through the doors and into the arctic cold of the street and Lucas turns, pulls me to him and kisses me with a passion that is still somehow unexpected. It's got a *purpose* to it that's so incredibly hot: something he's waited and planned and wanted to do, and now he's demonstrating just how much he wanted to do it. I can feel our future in this kiss.

I kiss him back just as hard, my fingers in his hair, this time not needing to persuade him of anything, not having to hope. I thought nothing could rival how we felt as teenagers, but I was wrong. This time is better. This time, we're not blank sheets of paper, we're grown-ups who've written who we are, who've decided who we want to be. We're bringing so much more to each other, and saying we want to share it.

When we break free, Lucas says, nodding his head towards the door: 'Sorry, but I have my limits with what I'm prepared to do with an audience. I'm not *that* modern.'

'Neither am I,' I laugh. 'I'm stuck in . . . I think 2005 was the glory year, for me?'

'And for me,' he says, hand on my face. 'God. Georgina. I've missed you. Why didn't you call me?' Lucas moves both his hands to my upper arms. 'All you had to do was say you wanted me around, and I'd have come running.'

'You went back to Ireland!'

'I only said that when you asked me, to make it clear I wasn't – *you know.* Looming over you, and moping. Haunting you, like Heathcliff. I thought it was obvious I'd be back and forth. I thought the speech about how I was dementedly in love with you was enough encouragement, if that's what you needed.'

'In love with me *twelve years ago.*'

'Why would that have changed? Nothing's changed. Actually, that's not true. I feel even more for you now than I did then.'

Lucas and I nearly lean in to kiss again, and Lucas hesitates. 'I have to say I'm only one more kiss away from saying let's sack your birthday plans off and dragging you off to my cave, and that feels rude to your friends. Shall we save it for later?'

I laugh, and agree. Later. I can hardly believe it will arrive, and yet this time, it will.

We turn, go back inside, still holding hands.

'I'm thinking you're stopping then, Lucas,' Rav picks up a pint and places it in front of him.

Lucas shrugs off his coat and takes the spare chair, still holding my hand tightly, and Clem and Jo clasp his arm in the over familiarity of half-cut emotion. A small moment is incredibly large, and everything has changed.

We got here. The long way round.

As the evening rolls forward, Lucas, politely concentrating on the conversation, holds my hand underneath the table, unable to let go. I wind my fingers through his.

I glance at him, and his dark, amused, intelligent eyes meet mine.

I don't know what he's thinking. I look forward to finding out.

Acknowledgements

It takes a village to raise a child and it takes quite a few people to make a book, so, hoping very much I don't forget anyone 😊 here goes. Thank you to my editor, Martha Ashby, for all her hard graft and tireless dedication in making it the very best it can be. Our two-hour phone call discussing storyline deserves a special mention alone. Other editors would've reasonably bailed at least the one hour mark of *but maybe, how about this . . .* thinking-it-through, but you were nails. And I like to think the value of that patience is all on the page. Thanks also to the whole team at HarperCollins for your enthusiasm and support, without going too 'Gwyneth' you always make me feel valued – Lucy Vanderbilt, I now live for your seal of approval. No pressure. Props to Keshini Naidoo, my copy editor, a funny joy and a great respecter of text: thank you once again.

Much gratitude goes as always to my unflappable agent Doug Kean of Gunn Media, to paraphrase Fleetwood Mac, you make working fun.

I'm so lucky to be in an industry where women generously

'signal boost' each other, as they say, so thanks to Lindsey Kelk, Paige Toon and Giovanna Fletcher for being absolutely the best wenches and so nice about the last book. This is the first chance I've had to thank you in print and by God I'm taking it.

Thank you to my first draft readers, you always help more than you realise – Ewan McFarlane, Tara de Cozar, Sean Hewitt, Kristy Berry, Jennifer Whitehead, Katie and Fraser, Jenny Howe and Laura McFarlane (great notes! You gonna go far, girl).

Thanks to Julian Simpson and Stuart Houghton for being my de facto office colleagues in the magical internet space and providing jokes worth nicking.

Thank you to my brilliant readers, because I'm on my fifth outing and still blown away you give me a book's worth of your time! I hope I earn it. (Shout out to superfan Kay Miles, I always love hearing from you.)

Thanks to all friends and family who cheerfully let me use their anecdotes, keep me sane and accept they're not going to see much of me around a deadline, without complaint. (Maybe it's a bonus to be fair.)

And last but never least, thanks to Alex, for his endless belief and support. I'm only mad and sweaty and still in pyjamas at 3pm some of the time during the artistic process, be fair.